THE HUMMINGBIRD KILL

LUC VAN HUISZEN

ISBN 978-1-7377691-2-5 (paperback)
ISBN 978-1-7377691-3-2 (ebook)

CHAPTER 1

BIRDS, BEES AND TROUBLE...

So how did I end up in the trunk of a car? It's a long story, but I can tell you that it's fucking uncomfortable being scrunched up like a pretzel. I guess being six-four doesn't help, but I'm getting ahead of myself here.

Not surprisingly, the trouble started with a dame and some dough, a lot like Eve and the Apple. Mama did warn me about the four Ds – Dames, Dough, Drink and the Devil, but for as far back as I can remember, I was obsessed with the first two, tormented by the third and flirted with by the fourth. Mama was right, well, at least about a certain kind of dame, and certainly about the bloke running things south of the Hades.

She was hot. Way too hot to be bothering with a wiseass, rough-and-tumble guy like me, but there's no accounting for taste. I've seen some drop-dead babes hanging on the arms of dudes who'd scare their own mothers.

Now, I wasn't that bad but I wasn't going to make the cover of GQ or be mistaken for Ryan Gosling or one of the other plastic assholes prancing across our screens. I had a crooked nose, high cheekbones, a jaw that would've have made Abe Lincoln jealous and lips that were a bit too thin. But my eyes were my redeeming feature – they were large, corn-blue and dreamy.

That was my take on it; my buddies had a totally different perspective. They were of the opinion that I needed some serious reconstructive surgery to remedy the perpetual 'I-just-woke-up' look. Hmmm, but then the bums drink too much, and most of them think that Michelangelo is a kick-ass, pizza-loving turtle.

Let's get back to the dame – she was about five-ten, blonde, had a face that was straight out of a '50s Hollywood movie and a rack that Lindsey Wagner would be proud of. Who is Lindsey Wagner you ask? She was my childhood obsession – the Bionic Woman! I was ten and would religiously watch the reruns, wondering why she didn't live next door to us instead of the dorky Peggy Burns. Peggy Elizabeth Burns! Now there's a fucking contradiction if there ever was one, but I'll get to her later. The dame who made me drool and wish I was Gosling or one of the other pretty boys waltzed into my life and, sister, nothing has been the same since.

It was a slow Monday. I was on my lunchbreak at the park across the street from where I worked. I was minding my own business wrestling with a sandwich that Rico, my buddy's pit bull, would have had a hard time getting down and trust me, that mutt has the digestive tract of a Great White. I was about to toss what was supposed to be a ham-and-cheese when she walked by me. Her strut was something to behold; hips swaying, tits jiggling, body undulating to some primordial rhythm and that face! Mama Mia, I thought I had died and gone to heaven!

I must have flat-lined for a minute or two because I don't recall a thing – nothing! No synapses, neurotransmitters or whatever it is that allows me to function as a semi-rational human being. If she had stopped to talk to me, I would have choked on my tongue, but thankfully she walked right on by.

I watched that tight little butt wiggle past me for about ten yards or so before she sat down on an adjacent bench, crossed her long legs and casually fished out a cigarette. Some women just have a way of smoking that makes you imagine things. I swear, it looked like she was giving the damn thing a blowjob and when she pursed her lips to exhale, my cock twitched like a jimmy jamboony on a trampoline! Now, don't go looking up 'jimmy jamboony' – I made that shit up.

She sat there for a while, lost in her own world until she finished her smoke, then stood up and nonchalantly flicked the butt away. She walked back past me without a glance, but whispered in a low, husky voice, "Left you a note."

A note? I thought I had gotten past that in junior high. I could hear my mama's voice imploring, *"Ignore her! Don't take the bait, kid, she's trouble!"* but I couldn't resist. If curiosity killed the cat I'd have been dead a long time ago, so I must be the one with nine lives.

I waited for a bit, and after she disappeared, I walked by the bench and picked up the neatly folded piece of paper. It had nothing but a handwritten phone number scribbled across it. Okay, so she must be married or have a jealous boyfriend, something I could relate to. I wouldn't let that broad out of my sight if she were mine. I'd put a dog collar on her and make sure that she was within arm's reach twenty-four-seven. But this smelled like trouble and that was one thing I didn't need.

If it weren't for Covid-19 and the ensuing bullshit, I would most probably have chucked the note, but my bank account was edging precariously close to double zeros and my dead-end job was killing me. The hours were long, the pay bordering on slave labor, and working as a foreman in a small machine shop was as boring as it could get. The message from my landlord bitching about the overdue rent was the last straw. So that evening when I got back to my cramped and messy one-room apartment, I popped open a beer and called her.

Two rings and she answered in the same husky voice, "Hello?"

I tripped and almost spilled my beer. She had the sexiest voice I've ever heard and phone-sex with this gal would have lasted all of ten seconds at best.

"You left me your number," I squawked, trying to compose myself and sound like Barry White. If you don't know who Barry White is, you're living under a fucking rock. Go Google him.

"Ah, yes. The sexy man who sits on the park bench every afternoon," was the breathless acknowledgement.

Did I tell you she had a sexy voice? Well, damn, it just got sexier.

"You must be thinking of someone else," I tried the Barry White thing again, but sounded more like a duck being strangled.

"Oh, it's you alright… you have that Gregory Peck thing going on; very attractive."

Wow! We have something in common - Hollywood and the '50s except I don't suffer from the Dunning-Kruger effect, you know, that garbage about cognitive bias where a lack of self-awareness has you overestimating your capabilities or some shit like that. I'm a realist and this Gregory Peck reference wasn't going to cut it. I mean, Gregory Peck was fuckin' handsome, so damn handsome that I may have considered a sex change if I had been born early enough.

"Let's not play games. What do you want?" No more Barry White. I gave it to her straight in my normal voice that sounded a bit like Daffy Duck with a sock shoved down his throat.

She was quiet and I was sure my irresistible charm must have worn thin. Just as I was about to hang up, she spoke, "Okay, so you're not Gregory Peck but there is something very attractive about you. I'm sure you have no trouble with the ladies."

"Listen, baby, you didn't leave me your number so we could chat about my batting average and I don't play baseball. I repeat: what is it that you want? And please, no more sexy-man references. I flatter way too easy and that worries the heck out of me."

"Batting average; I like that." She paused letting it hang for a moment before continuing, "I can explain everything. Can we meet?"

"Sure, as long as it's after five. I'm not missing work. If I don't put in the hours this week, my rent won't get paid and my landlord is a heartless bastard. But if you want me to move in with you, I'll quit my job and be there in a freakin' New York minute."

She laughed a throaty infectious laugh and ignored my offer, "That's funny. Can we meet tomorrow?"

"Sure. When and where would you like to have our little tête-à-tête?" I asked, unable to hide the surprise in my voice. Hey, maybe I was sexy and not just delusional.

"How about 7 PM at the Ristorante De La Milano?"

Ristorante De La Milano? The lady was certifiably nuts.

"How about Dunkin Donuts?" I scoffed. I would have to sell a kidney, or maybe both, to afford De La Milano.

"Dunkin Donuts is fine but I'm buying so you might want to reconsider?" Now that's what I'd call being persuasive. I never had a gal pay for my dinner before and though it was flattering, I'm old school and it didn't sit well. However, Mama didn't raise no dummies.

I swallowed and swallowed again. This time it was my pride, and it tasted like puke, "In that case, De La Milano it is, and I'll be there at seven."

"Ciao," was the breathless response before the phone went dead.

The Ristorante De La Milano is a ritzy place, freakin' high class. Even the valet parking kids looked like they had popped out of a Burberry ad.

I tossed my keys to a baby-faced punk that bore an uncanny resemblance to Richie Cunningham from Happy Days, and walked up the steps to the front. You might have guessed by now that I like old TV shows and older movies. They just don't make them like they used to. Take the Fonz for example – now that's a character you could relate to. A real bad-ass but with a kind heart and… I'd better stop before I bore the heck out of you. Where was I? Oh yeah, I was at the Ristorante De La Milano.

The hostess, a tight-assed, snotty broad in a low-cut red dress, gave me the 'what are *you* doing here' look and asked, "Do you have a reservation?"

It must have been my suit, a wrinkled two-tone ensemble that hadn't seen a drycleaner in like forever, but it was comfortable and the only one I owned. I didn't mind the attitude – God knows, everyone has one these days but it was her fake British accent that really bugged me.

"You need to get it out, sis," I advised.

"What?" she asked with her nose up in the air, except it sounded like "Whott?"

"Whatever is stuck up your ass!"

She looked like I had smacked her and turned redder than a painted pomegranate; I mean the gal was pissed out of her mind. She looked to her side and said the magic word: "Alfredo!"

And what do you know? A trained gorilla turns up, except he's dressed in an ill-fitting tux, but I'm impressed – the monkey was wearing a fucking tux! He had a shock of prickly black hair cropped short, no forehead, a nose that had been flattened across his mug, a pair of tiny, deep-set eyes, cauliflower ears that stuck out, no lips and a receding chin. Damn, I'd hate to meet his mom - this guy was ugly, so ugly he made me look like, yeah, Gregory Peck. But Bongo had been a wrestler in a past life and it didn't take a genius to figure out what he did for a living, and I can assure you that it wasn't playing chess.

"Is there a problem?" he asked with a slight lisp. I was surprised; the big ape could actually enunciate. He was speaking my language though so I was thrilled. We could communicate, one ape to another.

"Fuck off!" I snarled. Okay, so I'm not very good with words, and in gorilla language, it's a way of saying "My dick is bigger than yours, so bugger off."

He obviously understood and disagreed, and for a moment I thought that he was going to whip out his wiener and that had me worried. I wasn't blessed with one of those gargantuan kielbasa sausages, and being embarrassed in front of that broad would have killed me. He grunted and stepped forward and came within a millisecond of meeting Salvador – that's my left fist, I'm a southpaw, when that voice, sexy as all heck, intervened.

"He's with me."

The primate turned, looked and made a noise, pure gibberish, which when translated meant: "Baby, you're one sizzling-hot mama and I'm your slave forever!"

He smiled a toothless grin, gave an obsequious bow and stepped away muttering deferential apologies. Now I was *really* impressed – this was one fucking trained monkey.

"Come on, our table's in the corner," murmured the goddess with power over man and monkeys, and led the way.

Fredo scratched his head and jumped up and down, and the pompous bitch in the red dress looked like she had swallowed a gallon of broken glass. I just smiled and followed the perfect bubble butt to our table.

I waited until she sat down before taking a seat across from her. I noticed that she was halfway through a bottle of Latour Chardonnay and had a book lying open and face down next to her plate. It was "Existentialism and Human Emotions" by Jean-Paul Sartre. I don't think I could spell existentialism without spellcheck so this broad was definitely out of my league unless, of course, she was faking it.

In college, I once carried around the hardcover version of War and Peace for a week, all one thousand four hundred pages of it, trying to impress a Russian gal I wanted to bang. It didn't work but I got her to notice me – she spat in my direction, gave me the finger and said something obscene before her boyfriend proceeded to kick the shit out of me. And that explains my crooked nose. I did learn one thing though - you don't mess with little Russian guys or their girlfriends. That fuckin' midget could fight! Ah, the good old days – but back to my '50s Hollywood blonde.

"So you made it. A man of his word," she said, looking into my eyes.

She had the bluest eyes I'd ever seen, so blue that I realized mine were closer to something else. She was perfect – flawless skin, pearly white teeth, small celestial nose, a full, pouting mouth and blonde hair, not the fake, dyed yellow but the real stuff. It made me feel like Alfredo and I might belong to a different species, and brother, that ain't a good feeling.

The thought that Fredo and I might have a common ancestor was depressing. That was low. I was contemplating committing hara-kiri, staring at the zillion knives, forks and spoons arranged neatly by the plate in front of me, when the waiter turned up.

"And what can I get you, sir?" And there it was again,

that fucking accent! Whatever happened to good old American?

He was older, maybe in his forties with a lipless thin face sporting horn-rimmed glasses, slicked back brown hair peppered with gray, a beak of a nose and a pointed chin. He was stiff and formal, and one look from him told me what we both knew: that I didn't belong there. But the highhanded bullshit never sat well with me.

"You can start by toning down your fucking attitude. Then get rid of all this hardware; it's confusing the heck out of me. I'm going to be getting a steak so leave a fork and a knife, that's all I need. Then loosen up your collar and get me a beer. And, Bubba, make sure it's American and not some imported tastes-like-piss shit!"

He stood frozen. From the pained expression on his face, you'd think I'd kicked him in the nuts, but she nodded and he did what he was told, walking away like his shoes were made of cement. A stiff-assed mother-fucker if there ever was one!

"You're charming," she murmured.

"Yeah, it's the secret to my success," I replied, still mesmerized by her. "You have the bluest eyes I've ever seen.

"Azure, and is that a line?"

"Did you say 'Are you sure?'"

She smiled a tolerant smile you'd reserve for a child. "Azure. It's a color."

"Never heard of it and even I can come up with a better line than that, sister," I replied, looking around the room.

The place was filled with filthy rich, pseudo-liberal assholes who looked at me like I was a flea-ridden mongrel dog, you know that 'Ooh, get him out of here' look. If this was what money got you, then mama was right; I wanted no part of it. I grew up poorer than dirt but everyone I knew was real, not play acting at being someone else. We didn't smell good, talk right or dress in silk but when the shit went down, we were there – you could count on us.

"You don't like us, do you?" she asked, smiling and making my heart skip a beat.

"Us? I like you, check that, I don't know you but I'd like to…," I hesitated. It was her face, it altered my thinking. I was going to say 'I'd like to fuck you' but that would've been too uncouth even for a bum like me. "I'd like to get to know you better."

"Mmm," she murmured. It conveyed all that needed to be said: *you don't have a chance in hell, buster!*

"You said 'us,' but you're not like them, are you?" I asked.

"Them?" She seemed genuinely surprised.

"Yeah, them. These rich, pompous, self-obsessed, reptilian motherfuckers! They're a bunch of fucking chameleons that would sell their mothers if it gave them an edge and got them another dollar!"

She laughed, a throaty laugh. "You are funny, Cal, very astute, but that's a broad brush you paint with."

Now, that shocked the heck out of me. No, not the astute, broad-brush part but how the fuck did she know my name? I played it cool like I was James Dean and everyone should know who Caleb Montague was. It was part of that delusional syndrome I suffer from called CDGS– Caleb-Don't-Give-a-Shit. I'm a bit like the Honey Badger, but bigger and nastier.

"I'm not being funny, I'm dead serious. The people who risk their lives so these assholes can enjoy their hundred-dollar bottles of wine, eat snails and act like their shit don't stink are guys like me – piss poor white, black and brown kids. We put our lives on the line so you can sit here and speak in phony accents and discuss the fucking weather. Now that's okay, I'm not looking for a thank you but don't go looking down your snotty nose at us; that's fuckin' hypocritical!"

She ignored the rant and asked, "So you were in the armed forces?"

"You know my name; I'm guessing you did your homework and know that I was booted out of the Navy."

"Yes, but I don't know why."

"It's a long story and boring as hell. Let's talk about you and what I'm doing here, and where the heck is Jacko? I could use a beer," I replied, looking for the waiter.

"You are direct; I like that. Okay, Caleb, we don't have to delve into the past if you don't want to. You're here because I have a proposition for you – one that can make you some money and solve a problem I inherited."

"And here I was thinking it was because I had that Gregory Peck thing going on."

She was on the verge of responding when the obnoxious motherfucker in the starched suit picked that precise moment to return with my beer, a Budweiser.

"Your beer, sir," he said with the fake accent. This dude was stiffer than an arthritic eighty-year-old. His demeanor changed when he looked at doll-face, and with all the charm in the world he asked, "Are you ready to order, Miss Swanson?"

I swear this bloke was smooth; he could dance better than Fred Astaire and Ginger Rogers twirling on a dime.

"I'll have the usual, Richard." She smiled and handed the menu back to him.

"The grilled sea bass with pasta and a side order of roasted artichoke hearts," he said with an obsequious smile. He turned to me while refilling her wine glass. "And what about you, sir, what would you like?"

Though he was being polite you could sense the disdain. It was palpable but I decided to ignore it. I mean, his life was almost as shitty as mine having to stick his face up the butts of these rich assholes, and most of them didn't wipe more than once if they wiped at all!

"Get me your biggest steak, cooked rare, and a baked potato with butter."

I pronounce butter like a real American: budder! But he acted like it was a foreign word and gave me a 'what the fuck are you saying' look. "We have garlic butter and butter churned with cilantro, and the house favorite – fermented butter with bacon and chives."

"Plain old BUTT-TER," I replied, making sure to roll the fucking T right into the ground.

He smiled with his lips, his face colder than ice. "May I recommend the chateaubriand – it melts in your mouth. All our beef is the best dry-aged American Wagyu and we reverse-sear our steaks."

I perked up at the American Wagyu bit though I had no idea what Wagyu was. But as long as it was American I was a happy camper.

"Is that your biggest steak?"

"No. Our largest is the 24 ounce prime rib served bone-in. But…"

I cut him short, "The chance of me coming back here are slim to none and yup, you guessed it, Slim just blew out of town. So, if you loosen up your panties and get the wax out of your ears, you would have heard me the first time – your largest steak, Jacko!"

"Thank you." He glared at me and reached for the menu, but I grabbed his arm, pulled him down and drilled him with a look that would have frightened King Kong. Okay, maybe not Kong, but you get the drift.

"Listen up because I'm only going to say this once. If you fuck with my food I'll nip those tiny little nuggets you call balls and feed them to my pet pig, and then I'll stomp you to a bloody pulp. So you go on back there and let those lads in the kitchen know that I'm not one of your genteel, cock-sucking, roach-eating, motherfucking clients! I'm a Neanderthal with a bad temper. You got that?"

He tried jerking his arm free, but the man hadn't seen the inside of a gym in his life. His lips began to quiver and I was sure he was going to lose control of his bladder. He turned paler than Casper but not quite as friendly.

"This is the Milano and we don't do that kind of thing here, sir. There are cameras all over and even if there weren't, I wouldn't stoop to do that," he croaked, his voice shaking a bit.

"Okay, old chap, then you have nothing to worry about. Just make sure the steak is rare – bloody rare and get me another beer. I'm hungry, so try and speed this up or should I say chop, chop and all that!"

She hadn't said a word during my friendly repartee with the waiter but sat there with a bemused look on her face and a smile, a Mona Lisa smile, except she'd make da Vinci's model look like a fat caricature of a demented hag. Hey, chill out before you blow Twitter up with your sanctimonious tweets screaming blasphemy. She was Euro-trash and my gal is a red-blooded American. It's a no-contest. I've been to France – crooked yellow teeth and pale skin, not my cup of tea. Wait a minute, I think that was England; oh, never mind they're all the fuckin' same.

"I guess you're beginning to wish we were at Dunkin' Donuts, right?" I asked fascinated by those lips and Azure eyes. Yup, I learnt a new word.

"Au contraire, mon chéri," she sighed, "you are everything I expected."

She picked at her food; dainty little bites while watching me wolf down what looked like half a cow - the tastiest steak I'd ever eaten. And while I savored the rib and guzzled the beer, she explained her predicament. It was an interesting proposition – dangerous but then anything worth something comes with strings attached. We talked about other things too, mainly about my life but I did find out that her name was Rachael Swanson and that she was related to the billionaire Swanson family from Montana.

After a couple of hours of small talk, she asked, "So, Cal, will you do it?"

"Let me mull it over and I'll let you know," I replied, totally noncommittal. Though I had risked my life in the past, this was different and even a lucky cat like me can run out of lives.

"I will need to know soon," she urged, forehead furrowed and a look of concern etched on that pretty face.

"You'll have my answer tomorrow," I assured her and stood up. "I've got to get going. Some of us have to work for a living."

"Oh, we all work, Cal, it's only a question of the type of work we do."

She bent over and collected her book and purse.

"I punched an officer," I said looking into those hypnotic eyes.

"What?"

"I got booted out of the Navy Seals for punching an asshole who was trying to assault a young girl. It was late and he and his pals had dragged her into the men's room of a pub. I stopped it and that was that. His buddies swore that it was consensual and that I was just jealous."

"Did she comes forward and testify?"

"Nope. She was young, no more than fifteen or sixteen, and was too frightened to report it to the police. She said her parents would kill her."

Rachael was quiet, studying me for a while, then said with a sigh, "You're a strange man, Caleb, but I think I'm beginning to like you."

"All because I punched an officer?" I was trying to be funny.

"That's partly it, but more so because you're not pretentious. I'm going to stay a bit and mingle with the pompous, reptilian motherfuckers," she said, keeping a straight face, and gave me a peck on the cheek and traipsed off to mingle with the rats and snakes and the cutthroat assholes that rule our world.

God, she smelled good. She had eaten only half her food so I asked the arthritic rabbit to pack it along with the bone. Rico would enjoy it, and just maybe he would forgo chewing on my ass. Hey, I'm not proud and a meal is not to be wasted, especially one from the Milano.

I was feeling good, so on my way out I picked a banana from the fruit bowl and tossed it to the snotty bitch. "Give this to your chimp."

When I got into my car, I could hear Bongo shrieking for his reward and that's when my cell phone rang.

CHAPTER 2

FRIENDS AND FOES AND A NASTY DOG…

Ronnie Archibald Griffith was my childhood buddy. His mother left Barbados for a better life and had moved to Brooklyn, and the first time I saw him, he was getting his ass kicked by a bunch of the neighborhood bullies. He was a skinny, frightened ten-year-old with no friends and looked like a hapless deer being set on by a pack of hyenas.

I despised bullies so I walked over and kneed Arlo Stevens in the nuts. He was the biggest hyena in the bunch, and when he dropped the others fled like their butts were on fire. That was it; we formed a bond closer than brothers. I was a couple of years older, but that didn't make a difference and we did almost everything together. I taught him how to hunt and fish and he showed me his stamp collection. Not an even trade but his mom and older sister turned me on to curry and spicy food and that made up for the difference.

But as we grew older, things changed. Somewhere along the line in high school he morphed into a black Georges St. Pierre and learned how to fight. He got tagged with the nickname Rags – not just because of his initials but mainly because all of his clothes were frayed and ratty. He wasn't crazy about it but it stuck, so he went with it.

Now, Ronnie wasn't very tall – maybe six feet if you skinched a bit – but he could get nasty and it wasn't a good idea to get him riled up. He once got into it with a three-hundred-pound offensive lineman and broke the big man's jaw and put him to sleep. After that, people gave Ronnie a wide berth.

He played pro football for a few years as a defensive back and quit when he blew out his knee. Now, when he isn't being a bouncer or bodyguard, he helps his sister with her restaurant. She swears he's eating her out of house and home and I believe her – he should have taken up competitive eating. This boy could eat.

He was one of those rare specimens who could chow down anything and still look great. He was blessed with a body that most men would kill for – shredded with zero fat. I know that's impossible but this boy is a freak, a fucking anomaly. He foraged all day and most of it was garbage, I mean some nasty shit, but it didn't seem to affect him. I once saw him down a tub of Rocky Road ice cream with a large everything-on-it pizza and act like it was a snack. I'm getting fat just thinking about it. But not Ronnie; he could digest a tin can. Michelangelo – not the turtle but the artist – should have used him as a model for the statue of David instead of that dope with the tiny chilito.

In any case, when the phone rang I grabbed it thinking it was the babe, but it was Ronnie. I tried to hide the disappointment. "Hi, what's up?"

"You don't sound too thrilled. You could fake it, bro. Where are you?"

"I'm heading home from dinner at De La Milano."

"Fuck you! You couldn't get past the front door," was Ronnie's sardonic reply.

"Well, I did. I had a gigantic Prime Rib and to prove it, I saved the bone for Rico."

"Who'd you go with?"

"A doll and I mean she's a dead ringer for Marilyn Monroe. She'd make a dying man's pecker dance the samba, brother."

"And you keep telling me that I'm the lucky guy! Come on over. Maybe the bone will distract Rico – he's been chewing on my shoes for the last hour."

"I can't. I've got to get some sleep and get to work early tomorrow. Jake landed a new contract from Cabot."

Jake was my boss and Cabot Pharmaceuticals was the company we made parts for. They were Jake's biggest customer. I hated the big pharmas – they poisoned the public and made money off of the sick but what are you gonna do? I had to work and Jake's machine shop was it.

"Fuck Jake. I think I've got a gig that will make us some money," Ronnie snapped, "come on. I've got some beer."

He said the magic word, and maybe now I'd have some options, so I headed over to his apartment.

Ronnie's pad was a few blocks from mine, a one-bedroom, messy shithole he shared with his dog, Rico. The mutt was one part pit bull and the other must have been Godzilla because the beast was big and nasty, and had more muscles than his master. The good news is that he liked me and I pretended to like him… the alternative was unthinkable. The apartment had a strange smell – a comingling of pizza, unwashed socks and dog sweat, but after a while you went nose blind and focused on keeping Rico entertained.

I wrestled with the beast, and when he started to get rowdy I tossed him the bone and took advantage of the distraction to get myself a beer from the fridge.

"What you watching?" I asked, taking a swig of the cold brew.

"Two Mexican dudes kicking the shit out of each other. Damn, this one cat is wild; I mean these boys are downright nasty. They don't pay these guys nearly enough. What's in the bag?"

"Leftovers," I replied, hoping he'd miss it.

"Let me see," he shot back and grabbed the fancy Milano's takeaway bag. That's what they called them – not take out but takeaway. There are no limits to their snootiness.

"Okay, turn it off. I'll tell you my proposition and you tell me yours and then we can decide," I said, dejected, knowing that my take out was history.

His deal was to babysit a rapper and his entourage from the west coast for a few days. For that we would get a couple of grand each, and if all went well, a bonus and the promise of more gigs like that. It wasn't bad but there was no way Jake was giving me time off.

"So what's *your* deal?" Ronnie asked, opening the fancy box and drooling over the Sea Bass.

I told him a bit about Rachael Swanson and the fact that she was rich. I mean you had to be if the waiters at the Milano knew your name and your menu preferences.

"She wants us to retrieve an attaché case from a locked storage near JFK," I explained.

"That's it? How much?" he asked while shoving a huge piece of fish into his mouth.

"Ten grand," I replied, watching as my "tomorrow's lunch" disappeared.

"We get ten grand for getting a bag from a locker?" He almost choked.

I liked the way he said 'we,' but then we did do almost everything together except when we were with the ladies. We weren't into the gangbanging, voyeuristic bullshit. Sex is a private thing and should be but unfortunately it's not. The kids these days are a bunch of hedonistic, lazy bastards and that's why the country's going to hell.

"It's complicated. Her brother snatched the bag from

a Chinese businessman in Vegas and now there are some dangerous types trying to get it back."

He kept watching the tube and working on the pasta and no, he didn't turn it off; combat sports were *his* thing.

"Well?" I asked.

"Hey, it's ten grand and we've done shit for a lot less. You remember that necklace we had to get from the penthouse on West 54th?"

How could I forget? It was a few years back and we were bouncers at a very chic nightclub when one of the regulars offered me five thousand to get a necklace back from his old apartment. He swore it belonged to his mother and her mother before her so there was a lot of sentimental yada, yada, yada. He'd give us a key to the place and tell us when it was unoccupied so it would be no problem at all. It sounded too good to be true and it was.

What he overlooked mentioning was the two attack dogs, a boyfriend bigger than Goliath and a pissed-off ex with a 9mm! It was a good thing the bitch couldn't shoot – she took out her boyfriend with a shot to the knee and one of the Shepherds before Ronnie grabbed her. I had the easy part wrestling with a 120-pound Cerberus. He didn't have three heads like the hound of Hades but it sure seemed like he had more than one – I got bitten so many times I was leaking blood like a freakin' sieve! But we did get the necklace.

"Let's not go there; bad fuckin' memories," I replied and added, "So, we're doing it then?"

"Fuck yeah, screw those west coast bums. I'm tired of their fucking attitudes. Those niggers think they're rock stars or something."

He could say that. He was black and if anyone understood what colored people go through it was Ronnie. He's had to face his share of ignorant bullshit. He was a sable-eyed, handsome devil, nice small features resembling something between Harry Belafonte and Denzel Washington. The gals dug him – it was his attitude, that 'I'm gorgeous and you're not' attitude and of course his freakin' body.

"They *are* today's fuckin' rock stars," I countered.

"Well, fuck them!" he retorted. He had polished off the leftovers and said with a satisfied look on his face, "Hey, can you get me a beer?"

"Go get it yourself!"

"Come on, man, you're up and closer to the fridge and I think my tummy's gonna bust."

I shook my head, gave Rico a quick look and made a dash for the fridge.

"Can we meet her tomorrow?" I asked.

He looked at me, scratched his head and said, "Not tomorrow, Cal, I promised Jenny I'd help at the restaurant."

"What the fuck do you do there? The last time I saw Jenny she said you sit in the corner of the kitchen and literally eat everything!"

"Let's do it the day after, okay? And Jenny always complains that's her thing. My help comes in many subtle forms and her cooking is amazing. You'd being doing the same thing so don't go John the Baptist on me," he retorted.

Ronnie was right. Jenny could cook and yes, I'd be doing the same thing if it had been me. And in his defense, no one did the 'dine and dash' thing when he was around. Not anymore. A bunch of college kids tried it once and got smacked so hard their grandkids will wear scars. Ronnie was like a mama bear. He could see, smell and hear better than you and he could run faster than you. And if you mess with what is dear to him, God help you. Unless you're a professional mixed martial artist, you were gonna get stomped and even those pros would have their hands full. Ronnie was one of those real badass motherfuckers you leave alone.

"I'll call the doll and let you know how it goes," I said, and made my getaway. I was lucky Rico was still gnawing on the bone.

The next morning, I called in sick and of course Jake wasn't happy. That fucker was never happy – no wonder his wife scooted off with the delivery man. I told him it might be a case of the Covid and since only two of his blokes were vaxxed it would be on his head if any of the others fell sick. I could hear the wheels turning and before he could come up with some 'pity me' shit I stopped him.

"I'm going to get tested, so hopefully it's nothing and I can get back to work," I lied, sniffling and wheezing like an asthmatic on Mars. "I need the money so believe me, Jake, this is not some weak-ass excuse."

"We're getting busy, Cal, and you're the only one who can run the Fehlmann 8-axis. I don't trust Frank. The last time he ran it he didn't set it up right. He rammed the fixture, broke the tool bit and fucked up the z-axis. I had to get the Fehlmann tech in to reset the damn thing... cost me a bundle," he complained, adding, "Frankie thinks with his dick!"

Frankie is a twenty-year-old kid, so what do you expect? Twenty-year-olds think with their dicks. That's a given. My dad had a saying: Don't put a donkey in a horse race and expect the donkey to win. And when the donkey loses don't blame the freakin' donkey! You're the ass that put him in the race.

"Jake, I've been telling you to send the kid for training but you don't want to spend the fucking money and now you blame him? That's lame, brother."

"Okay, fuck Frank. I need you in. When will you know?"

"A couple of days at most." I kept the lie going and was hedging my bet on the outside chance that Rachael's gig didn't pan out.

I still needed a job and keeping the peace at the nightclubs was getting far too dangerous. The kids these days are different and some of them can actually fight but it is the psycho nuts that you worry about. The assholes that get hammered and then come back with their friends, and I don't mean their drinking buddies, I mean friends like Smith & Wesson. Fifteen bucks an hour plus tips ain't worth risking your life for that kinda shit.

"Okay, do what you have to and get back in as soon as you can. I'll give you a bonus, Cal – a real bonus, not like the last time," he said sounding like Rover had just been run-over.

I hung up satisfied with the way it went, and called the babe.

Two rings and she picked up. "Hello Caleb, please tell me you'll do it."

That voice and the memory of her face did things to me, things only my computer screen and some porn sites were aware of, but I wasn't a total dork. I got myself together and said, "Okay, Rachael, I'll do it but there are some conditions. First, a lot more detail so I'm not flying blind. And second, I will need to get some help in case things go south and sister, things have a way of going south. That means sharing the loot and ten grand is not going to cut it."

There was a protracted silence during which I looked out the window and watched Rico taking Ronnie for a walk. Yeah, this pair had things backwards and if there was one thing Ronnie was frightened of, it was Rico.

And just as they disappeared from sight, she came back on this line, "How much more?"

I decided to test the waters, "Fifty grand. This type of reinforcement is expensive."

There was a short pause, "Fifty? That's unreasonable! I could get someone for a lot less."

"You could but they would fuck it up and spook the Chinaman and his cronies and you'd most probably lose the bag. With me, you're dealing with a pro, and I'll make sure the job gets done right."

I was a pro alright, a professional fuck-up but I could get her the bag, I was sure of that especially with Rambo by my side. Ronnie was the real Rambo, not some spiked-up, steroid caricature like Stallone.

She thought for a few moments before acquiescing. "Okay but I will need to see you again to give you all the details. We're not doing it over the phone. And, Cal, bring your partners with you. I like to know the people who are working for me."

It was time to push my luck, "I will need 50% up front and the balance when the job is done."

"No, that's not happening. I'll advance you five thousand and you'll get the balance when the job is done. That is non-negotiable," she replied.

This was the line in the sand; I could sense that the dame was as intransigent as that Russian broad I had wanted to fuck. She wasn't going to budge. A good negotiator knows when to compromise and it was a relief to know that she wasn't a total dumbbell. I gave in – five up front beat the heck out of my other options.

I hesitated like I was giving it some thought before answering. "Normally it's a third up front but that's cool, I'll make this the exception only because of your azure eyes. When would you like to meet?"

She laughed, a husky little chortle, "Tomorrow evening at 8 PM, is that good?"

"Are we meeting at the Milano?" I asked, sounding hopeful. I wanted to try the chateaubriand and give the chimp another banana or better, serve him a Jamaican sandwich – Salvador right to the kisser!

"No. We'll meet at P. J. Clarke's on the Hudson. Do you know where that is?"

"I'll find it. Just so you know, I'm not wearing a monkey suit again and neither is Ronnie," I informed her, so she didn't look out for two jokers dressed like clowns. I looked a lot better in casuals, and Ronnie preferred loose Havana shirts and jeans.

She laughed, "That's fine. It's on Vesey Street in the financial district overlooking the Hudson. It's nice and the food is decent and we can talk."

"I'll take your word for it," I said and hung up. I wanted her to think I was cool and busy.

The next evening, we arrived at P. J. Clarke's a little past 8 PM. Parking in lower Manhattan can be a bitch but we managed to find a spot near a sign that Einstein would have a hard time deciphering. I think the city does it intentionally so they can write you a ticket and interpret the BS any way they want. They were a bunch of bloodsucking leeches. I hate the fuckin' Government but I'd better not start or this story will never end.

Ronnie was wearing a pink polo shirt and a navy jacket with a pair of chinos. He looked like he had stepped out of Abercrombie and Fitch. I guess he wanted to impress the blonde. I, on the other hand, believed in grunge cool. I'll let you figure it out, but here's a hint: no jacket, untucked wrinkled shirt, jeans and fisherman's sandals in lieu of loafers.

"The reservation is under Rachael Swanson," I said to the hostess who was far nicer than that bitch at the Milano.

"Oh, Rachael called and said she couldn't make it but you were to go ahead and have dinner anyway. She's taken care of the tab," the tall feline smiled. She was a pretty African American gal, slender with all the right curves and a complexion I would kill for; a velvety, golden café au lait.

She extended her hand and introduced herself, "I'm Roxanne Nunn, and if there is anything you need you just let me know."

"Anything?" Ronnie asked flashing her his thousand-watt smile and holding on to her hand.

"Yes, anything," she purred and I swear she was ready to jump him right there.

She walked us to our table staring at Ronnie all the way, and when he smiled at her, I think the gal had a spasm. While we were studying the menu, she returned with a large sealed envelope and said to Ronnie, "She left something for you."

"Not for me. For him." He gave her another smile, slid the envelope across the table and quipped, "He de boss!"

She laughed like he was George Carlin and I was the dog he was making fun of.

There were two smaller envelopes inside. One had a note that said 'Sorry, Caleb, but something came up. I'll call you later and explain.' It was signed: RMS with a sad emoji and 3 Xs next to it.

The second was interesting. It had the five thousand dollars in it and a single coin in a small plastic pouch. It looked a lot like an American eagle, except it had some strange markings on the back. If it was real gold, that coin could be worth about two grand. Along with the coin, there was a small, folded piece of paper with some Chinese or Japanese on it, and under it was a eleven-digit number that began with 852. It was all fucking Greek to me.

I gave the coin to Ronnie and asked, "Is this real?"

He turned it over a couple of times and bit it gently before answering, "It's real." He shook his head and handed it back to me, "Man, this lady is loaded. Maybe fifty grand was too little. This shit could be a lot more dangerous than we think."

"We can back out?" I suggested putting the money and the coin away. "Messing with the Chinese mafia isn't like bouncing some drunken preppie out of a club."

"Back out? Are you fucking kidding me? I love this shit."

That's where we were different. I didn't and I was beginning to lose my appetite. Ronnie, on the other hand, was ravenous as usual, and got the clam chowder and the carpaccio for starters, and settled on the bone-in ribeye for the main course. I was beginning to feel nauseous thinking about the Chinese triad, but I wasn't going to pass on a free meal so I got the Cadillac burger with everything on it. Hey, the babe was paying and for all I know, we could be eating chop suey for a while.

When we were leaving, the lovely Miss Nunn gave Ronnie her phone number and whispered, "Call me."

It was amazing. Some guys have all the fuckin' luck. Maybe it was the bone, you know, pussycats love to bury bones, but whatever it was, it never ceased to amaze me.

"I will," he promised. She watched him walking away knowing that he wasn't going to call and had a look of sheer disappointment on her face.

He tossed the card into a garbage bin on the way to the car and said, "She cute but who's got the time?"

"What's the matter with you? You are doing nothing! Maybe she's the one, you know, the keeper," I said, feeling sorry for her.

"Then you call her," was the terse reply.

I was about to fish through the garbage for her card but who was I fooling? I didn't stand a chance. It must be nice to be able to pick and choose who you'd fuck and when. On the other hand, guys like me had to try and try real hard to bed a juicy broad. Life just ain't fair.

CHAPTER 3

SPEAKING MANDARIN AND GETTING LUCKY...

achael Swanson waited, staring at the phone while it rang. She knew who it was and wasn't quite ready to deal with it. She counted the rings in her head and after the twenty-ninth ring, she relented and picked up. Why twenty nine? She wasn't sure but maybe it had something to do with numerology and her life-path number. She was born on June 2, 1992, and this added up to 11 in numerology. Eleven was the master number of a born leader. It had to be subconscious because she didn't really think about it but 2 + 9 also added up to 11. Or maybe she just got tired of hearing the loud ringing of the phone.

"Where the fuck were you? I've been calling all evening." The voice was angry.

"I was taking care of things. This isn't easy, you know," she answered petulantly, almost childlike.

"My life is on the line and you're talking about easy? Where's your head at, Rachael?" the caller sounded more desperate than angry now. "Will he do it?"

"Let's get someone else. I don't have a good feeling…"

"You're not having second thoughts, are you?" the man cut her off. "What is it? Are you falling for this loser?"

"Don't be ridiculous! I'm not falling for anyone. He's a nice guy and has had a tough life. Why not pick someone else?"

"You've got to stop dragging in strays off the streets. Did you give him the money?" the man asked, his voice impatient.

"Yes, five thousand, as you instructed," she replied.

"Then what the fuck are you thinking? He's not giving the money back. He's it, baby, and fuck him, we've all had tough lives. Money doesn't make your life any easier and you should know that better than anyone else."

She was quiet. Money may have bought things but it sure as heck hadn't made her life easier; in fact, it often complicated things. And being born attractive with desirable looks came with another type of baggage, one only beautiful women could relate to or understand. As far back as she could remember, every male in her life had wanted to get into her panties – all except Eddie. If it hadn't been for her brother, God only knows what might have happened. He had taken care of her, keeping her safe and now, he was the one needing help.

"Okay. It's on and I'll let him know," she replied, giving in.

"Now that's my girl. They are getting impatient, Rach, we'd better get it soon. I don't want to end up like Frankie," the man said, and hung up.

The mention of Frank Bonadio was sobering. He was a mutual friend who ended up with cement shoes somewhere off of Cape Cod. Frankie had a gambling habit and it finally caught up with him when he couldn't repay the money he owed the loan sharks.

She sat staring out the window of her Fifth Avenue apartment. Edward Brandon Swanson was her step brother. He was seven and she was four when their parents decide to get married. And though he wasn't her real brother, he had been her protector from day one. Her mother was a poor Polish immigrant from the wrong side of the tracks, but she was gorgeous and that made up for a lot.

The debonair Alex Swanson fell head over heels in love with her and was more than willing to look past the difference in their social strata. After all, it was New York and the elite were into the egalitarian bullshit. There was nothing cooler than dating or marrying a gal from the bourgeois especially if she was an artistic bohemian, and Anna Bukowski claimed to be a struggling actress. However, the only acting she ever did was on her back with her legs spread.

Rachael was jolted out of her reverie by the ringing of her phone. "Hello, Cal. What a coincidence, I was about to call you!"

"Karma, baby, we are meant for each other."

Rachael laughed. "Maybe and maybe not. Can you

meet me for coffee and I'll explain the details so you won't be flying blind."

"Now? It's late but I can make it if you can."

"Meet me at the Ritz-Carlton on Central Park South."

"I'll be there in twenty minutes."

"I'll be waiting at the bar," she said and hung up.

I got to the Ritz a little quicker than I had anticipated, but the lady was already there and except for a couple of night crawlers, the place was deserted. The barkeep, an Irish troglodyte I knew from way back, smiled and nodded in her direction.

"Hobnobbing with the rich, are you, Cal?" he said as I walked by. "Watch your back then, mate, and count them fingers; you're swimming in the deep end now."

I had been swimming in deep end since I was fourteen and a guppy learns real fast exactly where to hide when the sharks are about. But I wasn't a guppy anymore; I was a grown-ass barracuda and cudas have teeth and are as fast and as nasty as the biggest sharks.

She got up and gave me a peck on the cheek and pressed her body against mine. I swear I felt a jolt, a zillion-amp current shoot through me. She must have a fucking Taser shoved between those succulent tits.

"Thanks for coming," she murmured.

The waitress was a young, dyed-blonde skank with

way too much muck on her face, a nose-ring, and a top that left nothing to the imagination. She placed the beer in front of me, batted her eyelashes and said in a fake breathless voice, "Compliments of the house."

It was an Amstel Light. This was the only foreign beer I'd drink and Mickey, the trog behind the bar, remembered. I turned and raised the bottle and gave him a nod of appreciation.

"I thought you didn't like 'taste-like-piss' foreign beers?" Rachael asked, smiling.

Wow! This babe has a memory like an elephant. Either that or she thinks I'm Friedrich Nietzsche and spouts that stuff to impress her pseudo-intellectual pals.

"There are exceptions to every rule, baby," I growled, trying that Barry White routine again.

"You know Mickey then?" she asked, looking slightly amused and nodding towards the bar.

"Yeah, we go back a few years. I was a cooler at a club where he danced," I said, looking around the plush, cozy room. It must be nice to live like this and not have to worry about making your rent each month.

"He was a dancer?" She was genuinely surprised and I don't blame her. Mickey dancing would be like me on ice skates – not happening.

"No, he was the bartender, you know, throwing bottles up in the air, catching them behind his back, twirling and stuff like that… dancing to impress the ladies."

"Oh, okay."

"Thanks for the advance and the gold coin. That was

unexpected but much appreciated," I said, taking a sip – not bad but I would have preferred a Bud or a Sam Adams.

"Gold coin?" She couldn't hide the surprise. "What gold coin?"

"There was a gold coin that looked a bit like an American eagle in there," I fished the coin out of my pocket and gave it to her.

She studied it carefully, her face a picture of concentration, then said, "This is not a regular gold coin. Look at the lion's head and on the flipside, the two daggers and the Chinese script – this is from the Chinese triad."

"I thought as much," I handed her the note that was with it. "I have no idea what this says but it was in the pouch with the coin. I thought you had placed it in there as a bonus and this note was a test to see how smart I was. I fail, baby! I barely speak English."

She handed the coin back to me and studied the note, and I could see her expression change. "It's Cantonese and it's a warning telling us to return the attaché case. The number is a number that we are to call; 852 is the country code for Hong Kong. This is from the Chinese triad in Hong Kong."

This is unreal. Not only is she gorgeous but she speaks Chinese! I played it cool like it was no big deal.

"Interesting, this shit gets more intriguing by the minute. I mean Hong Kong, the Chinese triad… what the heck is in the bag?"

She didn't answer me but sat studying the note. I looked at the coin with the lion's head and the two daggers, and the strange looking bullshit embossed around it. Now why couldn't they have given me a good old American eagle? Who the fuck wants a coin with some ching-chong hieroglyphics stamped on it? Not me, brother, that's for sure, but it's gold so I'm keeping it.

"Is it gold?" I asked, to be sure.

"Yes, it's gold alright. They will want it back, a sign that we are square. This is getting worrisome, Cal. They got into my apartment and I didn't even know it!"

Now it was my turn to be baffled. This Sherlock Holmes garbage was beginning to bend my brain and whenever that happens, it gives me a headache. And they're not getting it back. Fuck them!

"Why would they put it there? Do you think Roxanne is working for them?" I asked.

"No, not Roxy. I got her the job. Her mother worked for us for years… she was more of a mother to me than my own mother."

"Who else could have had access to the envelope?" I was puzzled. "I mean why would the Chinese triad give me or you a gold coin? And why not just call you and ask for the bag?"

"In the old days, they would include a copper coin with the note. When the note was from the local boss, the coin was silver. When the coin is gold, it means the request is right from the top. When you finish doing what they ask you to do, you have to return it. They must have entered my apartment *after* my trip to the bank. I don't carry cash, not that much anyway, so I had to go to the bank and get the money. I sealed the envelopes myself and left it in the dresser by the bed."

"They would need time to open the envelopes and reseal them. Does anyone else have a key to your pad?" I asked.

"No. And I had the locks changed after…" she paused, "after I broke up with Patrick."

"Are you sure no one else has a key?"

"My brother Eddie has one but he's in Holland, in Amsterdam. He's in hiding. I wasn't supposed to tell anyone but I trust you. I'm not sure why but I do."

She said the last part with a look of such helpless innocence that I was tempted to reach over and give her a kiss, but sanity quickly returned in the shape of a mako circling the waters reminding me that those fuckin' fish are nastier and faster than barracudas.

"It's possible your apartment is bugged," I offered, snapping out of my temporary insanity.

"I was at the Times Square Diner when you called me so there was no way they knew we were meeting at the Milano. They can't have the Milano and the Diner bugged. Do you think they're following me?"

"How did you get here?"

"My limo," she said, sounding like everyone had a private limousine service at their beck and call.

"How are you getting back?"

"The limo would have waited, but since it's late I'm staying here tonight."

"Well, this is making me nervous," I mused out loud, "the coin, the note and the triad. They most probably know that you are hiring someone to get the bag and wanted to make sure the message was getting through."

My curiosity about the attaché case had been building from the moment she made her proposition, and like a zit it finally popped, "I do have one question regarding the contents of the case. It must be worth a lot more than fifty grand or the freakin' triad wouldn't be tossing gold coins at us. So what's to stop me from making a run south of the border and living like a king?"

She smiled. "I was waiting for that million dollar question. It's packed with explosives. The tumblers of the dual combination locks have been replaced with a biometric keypad which requires your fingerprint and a sixteen-digit code. Once you activate the biometrics, you have exactly thirty seconds to enter the code. It takes roughly ten to twelve seconds to input sixteen digits carefully so in effect, you have two tries before it goes boom! There's enough explosive in there to send the Empire State Building into orbit. So unless there's a clone out there, my brother is the only one who can open the case."

I was impressed by her matter-of-fact manner. "That answers my question and I guess my kingdom in Tijuana will have to wait. You can't blame me for asking. This entire proposition, with the Chinaman, your brother, the coin, the triad… it is baffling and intriguing and makes me a bit nervous, especially this coin and the note."

"You're not backing out, are you, Cal?"

I looked at her and could see the worry on her face.

"No. I'll get the attaché case for you. I did accept the job and I've never backed out of a gig before… ain't starting now."

"Thank you. That means a lot," she said, her voice filled with relief. "I must confess that this has me frightened and worried."

I had a feeling that Roxy may have been involved. She had to be. How else could a bunch of Chinese dudes get into a building with security tighter than the White House? And though Ronnie was a heartbreaker, Roxanne was coming on pretty strong, perhaps a little too much.

"Can I keep this?" she asked, indicating the note and breaking into my Blade Runner fantasy.

I didn't give it a second thought. I don't speak Cantonese and I wasn't about to call Hong Kong and I'd be damned if they get the freakin' coin back.

"Sure."

She looked down into her coffee mug, absentmindedly swirling the grinds at the bottom, hoping to find the answers to all her questions. After a while she looked back up and directly into my eyes, "Will you do me a favor?"

I could hear Mama's voice screaming even louder: *run, baby, run. Get away from her while you still can.* But I rarely listened to my inner voice. I should have, but I didn't.

"Sure, as long as you don't want me to go to Hong Kong and return the coin to the triad. I don't think I'm ready for my version of Kung Fu Panda," I answered, trying my hand at humor, but she ignored the glib quip.

"I was wondering if you could stay with me tonight. I'm frightened, Cal, and I don't want to be alone." She sounded like a scared little girl. The circling mako had disappeared and in its place was a kitten, frightened and alone.

I couldn't believe my luck. I pretended like I was giving it some thought, staring out the window, acting mysterious and all, and maybe I gave off the wrong vibe because before I could answer, she said, "I'm sorry. I'm sure you have other plans. I'm being a baby. Don't worry, I'll be fine."

"No, there are no other plans," I blurted out, losing the practiced cool. "I'll stay with you. I was thinking about the gold coin; it could be a threat – sending you a message."

"Oh God! Now I'm really frightened."

"Don't be. No one's going to mess with you, not while I'm around."

It sounded good, like a line from a Charlie Bronson movie, but I didn't feel that confident. Anyone who can toss in a gold coin worth two grand wouldn't think twice about wasting a no-name bum like me, but I was in now, too far into the deep end to back out, and it wasn't all about the money either. I was beginning to fall for this dame and the thought scared the shit out of me.

We chatted for a while, discussing numerology and psychics and shit that I don't understand and somehow in the middle of all that, she took my hand and read my palm. I have never felt anything as sensuous as her fingers caressing the inside of my hand. It was a good thing we were seated or else my woody would have pecked a hole through my trousers and knocked my coffee over.

"Your lifeline extends way back beyond the bottom of your hand which means you'll have a long life, Cal," she cooed. And turning my hand inwards, she added with a soft giggle, "You also fall in love easily. See how your heart line starts under your middle finger; that means that you are a hopeless romantic."

"That's a lot of bull, but if you keep playing with my hand, I *will* be falling in love," I responded, gently extricating my hand from hers, trying like heck to quell the badger bouncing in my pants.

"You don't fool me, Cal; the tough guy exterior is just an act. I think deep down inside you're a sentimental romantic and I like that," she said, giving me a look that would melt a polar bear, and then added, "But it's getting late, let's leave the chiromancy for another time and if you want, I'll do your horoscope."

What the fuck is chiromancy? I acted like I knew and got up hoping she wouldn't notice the flag flying at half-mast. If I was a fucking romantic it was buried so deep inside you'd need an pickaxe and a shovel to dig it up, and my horoscope should have said *'for tonight, tape your dick to your thigh!'*

We took the elevator up to her room in silence. I didn't know it then, but she was in the Presidential suite, a two thousand-plus square foot den of extravagance that offered exceptional views of the park. It was more than twice the size of the little shithole I called home and it dawned on me exactly what Mickey had meant by swimming in the deep end. This was wealth that guys like me couldn't imagine, not in their wildest dreams.

I tried playing it cool, "Nice. A bit cramped for my liking, but nice."

"You make me laugh, Cal," she murmured with a big smile then pointing past the dining room, said, "Your room is through there. There's a wet bar with a pretty wide selection of drinks but you can always call down and they'll get you whatever you want."

"I'm good for now but I may indulge in a nightcap before I hit the sack."

We were standing next to each other, close, so close I could hear her breathing and smell the wonderful fragrance of her. I felt my head spinning with crazy notions concocted by a wild imagination. I thought about kissing her and making love to her right there on that incredibly plush carpet. I have never been shy with women; guys like me couldn't play coy and hope to get lucky. Rejection came with the territory and I was used to it, came to expect it almost, but this dame had me bamboozled. I was paralyzed, feeling like a sixteen year-old stumbling into his favorite wet dream only to realize that the two women making love to each other were dudes in drag.

She reached up and kissed me on the cheek, her body pressing against my side. "It's been a long day and I'm tired. I'm going to take a shower and go to sleep. Thank you for doing this, Caleb."

I watched that heavenly creature walk away and knew that the moment had passed; I had blown it and had missed the window of opportunity and in life, timing is everything. But sometimes, just sometimes, karma plays a card you don't expect and throws you a bone. The joker was alive and well.

I took a quick shower, changed into the pajamas that came with the room and had a nightcap of cognac with cream before I hit the sack. I fell asleep almost immediately and dreamed of sharks, barracudas and the beautiful dame except she was Grace Kelly in High Noon and I was the dumbass that was about to get shot.

It must have been two or three hours later when I felt her get into bed with me. I thought it was part of the dream until she spooned against me, her body soft and warm.

"I couldn't sleep. I've been thinking about you…" she whispered, her breath silky soft against my ear.

I felt her hands snake into the silk jammies and when her fingers wrapped around my cock, I was caught in that chimerical state between dreams and reality. I turned and kissed her and tasted the minty freshness of her mouth with but one thought. This was a night she would never forget and when she squirmed in some other lover's arms, it would me she would think of. I was going to make sure of that. I worked my way down between her thighs and feasted on the sweetest peach I'd ever eaten. And while I savored the delicacy of her being, I waited for the bomb to go boom and shoot her into space.

CHAPTER 4

CAIN AND UN-ABLE...

My dad died when I was fourteen. I will never forget that day. Mom came to school and told me that my father had been killed at work. He was a longshoreman and was shot while breaking up a fight. How fucked up is that? He was being a Good Samaritan and lost his life for his efforts. That night, the saying that no good deed goes unpunished echoed in my brain while I lay tossing and turning in bed, struggling with my new reality. And that's why I stay in my lane. I don't mess with others and as long as they don't mess with me, we're cool.

William Montague, my father, Wild Bill to his friends, was more Hemingway than Hemingway himself. When he was in college, he hitchhiked through Europe alone, scaled the Matterhorn, attempted to climb K2 and while he was in in Italy, participated in the Calcio Fiorentino held at the Piazza Santa Croce in Florence. You have to be a real man to survive the brutality of this event.

Despite being bruised and battered he headed for Spain to Pamplona in time to take part in the Running of the Bulls. He almost got gored but made it out alive. In his diary, he noted that he had never felt so alive in his life.

He could drink and sing and fight with the best of them, and not many of his friends knew this, but he was also a gifted writer. He kept a diary and would jot down notes and sayings expressing his take on life. He was a Renaissance man if there ever was one.

I have kept all of his diaries and treasure them more than life itself. There was a verse from his early notes that defined him to the core, and I quote:

> *"To be a man you have to make a little noise and stir up a bit of trouble.*
>
> *You must trample leaves under foot and break the branches to cut a path and let them know that you had been through there.*
>
> *You must laugh and cry, love and hate, forgive and be forgiven and let the gamut of emotions run their course.*
>
> *It is the scars earned in life's adventures, both emotional and physical, that will warm you when the chill of age has you imprisoned in its snare."*

He taught my brother and me to fight, hunt and fish, things that he felt every man should know. If there was one thing I learned from my father it was never to back down. His mantra was *physical bruises will heal but emotional scars will haunt you for the rest of your life.* He quoted Emiliano Zapata: "It is better to die on your feet than live on your knees" and that resonated with me. I have never backed down from anyone, anything or any challenge.

My brother, Dylan, was more like my mother, a sensitive introverted kid. He liked to read, write poetry and listen to music. When I was twelve, I shot my first deer and while Dad was showing us how to butcher the animal, Dylan fainted and had nightmares for a month. He was only nine and that was the last time he came hunting with us. My mother put her foot down with the assertion that two wild men in the family were enough.

My mother used to tell us that marriage for my dad was a form of prison and that men like him needed to be unshackled and free. Marriage had been her attempt to domesticate a wild and iconoclastic man and had succeeded to some extent, but the wildness was never far from the surface. He was a legend at the local bars, a man's man who lived life with an unparalleled zest – he used to say that life had to be lived with passion and a lust for adventure or we would turn into dogs wagging our tails to keep our masters happy. Eighteen years later, I miss him just as much – his booming laugh, wild stories and magnetic presence; I miss it all. After his death, I felt a sense of abandonment and if it weren't for Ronnie and his sister, I don't think I would have made it.

Dylan left home as soon as he graduated from college.

He got a job in San Diego doing something I'll never understand. It had to do with computer graphics and brain waves and he got paid a shit load of money for sitting on his ass and staring at a screen. I'm sure it's a lot more involved than that but the effect of abstract imaging on the frontal lobe was beyond me. He never explained and I never asked.

My brother and I rarely spoke but he called my mother often and sent her a check every month. I'll give him that, but it was me who stopped by her place every evening to make sure she was okay and took care of the day-to-day problems she encountered. Sending money was a form of appeasing his conscience; at least that is what I told myself because money is one thing I didn't have.

A year ago, when I made my customary stop, I was surprised to see my brother and a cute, mousey-looking broad at my mother's place. Surprised would be an understatement - I was shocked. I mean, it was almost ten years since I saw him. Dylan is as tall as me but slender. His face is more effeminate, soft and boyish but his eyes were unlike either of our parents. They were cold and unfeeling, reminding me of a viper.

"Dylan, damn boy, what a fucking surprise!" I exclaimed and went over to give him a hug but he stiffened and stuck his hand out. We shook hands and I turned to the lady, "And who is this pretty little thing?"

She got up smiling and gave me a warm hug, and said in a Tweety Bird voice, "Hello Caleb, I'm Angie, your brother's wife."

You could have bowled me over with a feather. I turned to him, "You got married? When? And you didn't think Ma and I would want to be there?"

He held my gaze, steady as rock. "Ma *was* there."

Then it struck me, that trip she took to see her sister, Aunt Mary, in Ohio. My mother's face was filled with sadness and guilt.

"I wanted to tell you, Cal, but…"

"We wanted you to be there," the Tweety Bird said rescuing my mom, "I told Dylan that it wasn't right but he wouldn't hear of it. I don't want you to think it was me, or mother, because it wasn't. We wanted you there."

"It was me and it's because I know you," my brother explained without the slightest remorse. "I know how you are. You'd come there and make it all about yourself, get drunk and create a fuss and I didn't want that, not on my day! Not on *our* day. Angelina and I had a quiet, wonderful wedding. No one got drunk or unruly, no one got punched in the face and all our guests had a great time and that's how we wanted it. You're like Dad, you can't help yourself, Cal, and I know you don't mean it but I wasn't about to let you ruin things for us."

The undercurrent of loathing in his voice hit me like a Mike Tyson right hook. We were never close but I loved my brother and had no idea he felt this way about me. This was some Freudian Cain and Abel shit he was dropping on me.

I stared at him for a while, trying to digest what he

had said and the fact that my mother hadn't said a word to me. She had lied to protect my brother, though in hindsight it was clear that the deception was to protect my feelings.

"I get it. I'm an embarrassment to you… okay, I'll let you have your evening with Mom. It was nice meeting you Angie, and it's too bad I couldn't get to know you better. I *am* like my father and I'm proud of that."

I turned to leave when my brother stopped me.

"Wait, you need to know this. We are taking Mom back to San Diego with us. We have a big house and we have created a place where she will be comfortable and will have her privacy but will also have access to the family. She won't be alone and the warmer weather will be easier on her arthritis. We've been talking about it for a while now, and Mom and I feel this is the right time to make a move."

This would be called 'piling on' in football and the penalty was fifteen yards. What the fuck was going on? They were discussing her move across the country and my mother doesn't say a word to me? This was far worse than Tyson's right. It was more like a giant saltwater croc dragging me under!

I addressed my mother. "You're okay with this? Leaving me and everything you know behind?"

"I'm lonely, Cal, and yes I know, you come by to make sure I'm doing well but that's not enough. You're a good son but you have your own life and Dylan is right about you – you are a lot like your father, God rest his soul. You cannot be caged and an old woman needs more than a laugh and a few minutes of company, she needs companionship and love and the warmth of a real home. One day you will understand, and maybe even forgive me."

Life doesn't indemnify you against emotional loss. There it was again, that feeling of abandonment. My mother was the only real family I had left.

"There is nothing to forgive, Ma. What about this apartment? All the memories…"

"It's too big for her to manage and most of the memories are not worth remembering. You romanticize our lives forgetting what it was really like. Dad was a drunk and most days…"

"Dylan! That's…" Angie started, but he cut her off.

"Stay out of this, Angie. This is between my brother and me. He needs to hear this."

"You say one more word about Dad and I'll forget you're my brother. Just one word, go on, give me an excuse," I snarled, stepping towards him, my face an angry mask.

"Yeah, of course, if you can't deal with something beat it into the ground. You haven't changed…" he riposted, not backing away, his eyes colder than chips of black ice.

It was my mother who saved his sorry ass. She stepped in and pushed Dylan back, "We don't speak ill of the dead. And your father wasn't a drunk; he liked his drinks and there's a difference. You are being disrespectful, Dylan. Now, we will be civil to one another or *all* of you can leave!"

"Sorry, Ma, I didn't mean that. I know father did his best," he said and turned to me. "About the apartment, we have decided to sell it and the money will be split. I will send you your half so you don't have to worry."

"You're okay with this, Ma?" I asked her.

"I just told you…"

"I'm not talking to you," I snapped at Dylan. I asked my mother again, "Ma, are you okay with this?"

She was quiet before nodding. "Yes, I am. There are memories here I cherish and memories that will haunt me but those will always be with me. I used to love New York in winter, the stores, decorations and the happy buzz, but now, the cold burns through my bones and chills me to my soul. I need to feel the warmth of family, Cal, to sit at a dining table and hear laughter and make small talk and hopefully be there for my grandchildren. It's time, son, for all of us to move on."

"I will send you your half of the sale," my brother repeated, his voice was gentler now.

"Don't bother. You keep the money. I don't want it."

I gave my mother a hug.

"I hope you'll be happy, Ma," and turning to Dylan's wife, "It was nice meeting you, Angie, you're a lovely gal."

I left without saying another word, and that was over a year ago. My mother and I talk every now and then and she seems genuinely happy, but surprisingly, it is Angie who calls me regularly and gives me all the news. She is kind and sweet and provides the warmth for the snake masquerading as my brother.

CHAPTER 5

SWIMMING IN THE DEEP END...

When I finally woke up, Rachael was gone. There was a note on the nightstand by the bed. It was in her neat, small handwriting.

"Caleb, I will never forget last night, it was wonderful, you were wonderful and I thank you for that. The key-card to get into the building is in the envelope next to the coffee maker in the kitchen. The key with the locker number is also in the envelope. I will text you the sixteen-digit code. The place is called Brookfield Self-Storage and it's on Brookfield Avenue in Queens about three miles from the airport. The address is on the card. Please be careful and call me when you have the attaché case. RMS xxxx."

That was it. I'm not sure what I expected, but reading the note left a sour taste in my mouth, like curdled milk. This was impersonal and aloof. Maybe she was right and I was a hopeless romantic and this was just a pity-fuck or what the boys called 'a slum-cum' for her. My feelings, however, were far deeper than that or so I thought.

It is what it is and there was work to be done – I wasn't about to lose sight of the end goal, the fifty grand. I checked my phone and sure enough she had sent me the sixteen-digit code. So now all that was left was to get the attaché case.

I couldn't stop thinking about the note and the number in Hong Kong and what that could mean. I took a shower, made a cup of coffee and called Ronnie.

"Hey, did you have breakfast yet?" I asked when he picked up.

"No. Where are you? What time is it?" he asked, sounding like he had just woken up. I could hear a sleepy female voice in the background mumbling something incoherent. This dude never slept alone.

"It's time to get up. Get rid of her and get your ass here. I'm at the Ritz-Carlton on Central Park South. Come up to the presidential suite, yes bubba, you heard me – the fucking presidential suite!"

There was a moment's silence and then he hissed, "I'm there. Don't you fucking move."

To say that Ronnie was blown away would be an understatement. He played pro ball and had stayed in some fancy places, but this was more than even he could handle.

"Fuck, Cal, you are the luckiest bastard I know!"

He went from room to room and came back smiling. "How long? How long can we stay?"

"Maybe a couple of hours," I replied and showed him her note.

"I say we stay until they kick us out," he announced, plopping back onto the soft, leather sofa.

"They won't kick us out. This is Rachael Swanson we're talking about. Do you remember Irish Mickey? He's working nights at the bar."

"Fuck him, he's a dick. Let's get breakfast."

"He's not a dick. He doesn't like you because his girl was flirting with you and you were encouraging her," I defended Mickey. I liked the big Irishman and Ronnie, well, Ronnie was being Ronnie.

"Whatever, dude, let's get breakfast."

We ordered up so much food I'm sure the kitchen must have thought we were hosting the New York Giants. We said very little while we wolfed down plate after plate of every possible item on their breakfast menu. And when we were done, you had two beached whales unable to move.

"That was best damn waffles I've ever had and brother, I've had them all," he groaned. "My stomach is going to burst…" and he burped so loud I swear the windows rattled.

"So when do we go and get the attaché case?" I asked, in case he had forgotten what this was all about.

"We do it at night, sneak in and out and hopefully without a bunch of cloak and dagger, Kung Fu bullshit."

"Sounds like a plan, brother. Let's go down and case the place."

"You go on, I'm going to lie here for a while and then I'm going to get a massage. It comes with the room," he said, picking up the phone and calling down to the concierge.

You'd think he was paying for all this but I figured it was okay; if we were going to risk our lives for Rachael, a massage should be the least of our worries.

The Brookfield Self-Storage was located in a section of Queens where walking your dog at noon would be considered suicidal. It was a gang-ridden, dangerous area and gun violence was an everyday occurrence – the Wild West on steroids and that was during the day. At night it was a fucking warzone where even the cops stayed away. Drug-lords, pimps and gangbangers ruled, and unless you were there for drugs or sex you had better get the heck out of Dodge. Sometimes I wonder if Ronnie and I should have our heads examined – the things we've done to turn a buck!

"This doll knows how to pick them. A million storage places in New York and she picks the one in fuckin' Bermel!" Ronnie hissed as we drove past a crew of obvious gang members.

His reference to one of the most dangerous places on earth, Bermel District in Afghanistan, seemed appropriate. If I had been nervous before, I was downright on edge now. I had my Sig cocked and ready, and if a fly farted, I would have obliterated the motherfucker to hell. Like I said, I was on edge.

"Relax, Wyatt Earp, the shit's not happening now. The party starts when we lift the bag," Ronnie said, trying to calm me down.

"Just keep your eyes peeled. I don't want to get jumped by these local motherfuckers."

We managed to make it to Brookfield Avenue without incident, which was a damn miracle in itself. It was dark and poorly lit, and as we drove by deserted graffiti-covered buildings, I got the feeling that we were going to earn every penny of the fifty grand.

Brookfield Self-Storage was made up of three long brick buildings behind a stone wall with steel fencing and welded razor wire on top. There were cameras everywhere and signs that said: *Patrolled by Dogs and Armed Guards*. I didn't see guards or dogs but the place was well lit, and surprisingly, there were a few cars parked in front of the first building. I guess we weren't the only lunatics risking life and limb.

There were two sets of gates about ten yards apart. I inserted the card and punched in the four-digit code and waited until the gate opened. I had to repeat the procedure at the second gate but it didn't open until the first one closed. Pretty nifty – it ensured that no one could sneak in behind us and if they did, they wouldn't get past the next gate. And while we waited, I caught sight of an armed guard and a dog walking towards the main building. The guard was carrying an AR15 and the dog was a German shepherd as big as a giant timber wolf. These fuckers took this security business seriously.

"Hi, how's it going?" I said to the two men behind the desk. They were both dressed in black. One was seated, keeping his eye on several monitors in front of him. The other was the dude with the dog, and he was standing with his hand resting on his gun. These were both big, troubled boys, either ex-military or ex-cons replete with tats and bad attitudes; not the kind you messed with. And that dog reminded me of the one that did a number on me some years back. The memory gave me shivers.

They ignored my greeting, and the one behind the desk growled, "You need to sign in and I'll need to see some ID."

"Hey, I know you; you're Ronnie Griffith… Green Bay Packers!" the guy with the dog exclaimed, recognizing Ronnie. "Hey, bro, what you been up to?"

Ronnie looked at him, and without batting an eyelid, said, "Getting fat."

The man laughed.

"I used to watch you lay them out on Sundays! For a little guy, you could hit. What are you doing here? Looking for a storage unit or a locker?"

"We're here to pick something up for the boss. It's in a locker," Ronnie answered.

"Not a problem." He turned to his buddy. "TJ, this here is *'the Ronnie Griffith,'* played for the Packers, man, I don't believe it."

His friend wasn't impressed. He gave Ronnie a glance and grunted and went back to staring at the monitors. His buddy, though, was obviously smitten.

"Wow! I don't believe it! Doctor Destruction in the flesh. They should've retired your jersey, man, and number 21 should be hanging on the rafters."

If he said 'I don't believe it!' once more, I'd puke. Okay, so Ronnie was famous at one time but this was pushing it. *I* couldn't believe it - a hard-ass in fucking Dodge City acting like a ten-year-old. I was surprised he didn't ask Ronnie to sign his shirt!

The man turned to me and said, "You play?"

Why do people assume that ball players only hung out with other ball players?

"Yeah, I played. I played hooky and that's why I'm a bagman now," I replied, my voice dripping with sarcasm.

"You should've stayed in school, bro," the man quipped, cracking a smile. "I've seen you around... maybe at the Horny Goat?"

The Horny Goat was a titty bar on West 77th on the Upper Westside, but I had never worked there. I would have remembered - the waitresses and strippers made the Playboy Bunnies look like rejects from a pimple ad.

"Not me brother, but I get that all the time. People mistake me for Brad Pitt and that's a bitch."

"Funny man," he hissed.

After signing in, I asked the dude behind the desk, "Where are the lockers?"

"Down those stairs and to your right, and don't get lost, Brad, a river don't run thru' this shit out here." He said the last part with a snicker and pointed to the stairwell with a finger that was twice as thick as mine.

"Hey Ronnie, you should be in Hollywood, dude! You're a good looking son-of-a-bitch and you could be like the Rock, you know, beating up bad guys and banging chicks."

Was this guy for real? Ronnie and the Rock, really?

"That's a thought, but I'll let Brad here do the acting," Ronnie replied, following me down the stairs. Now everyone was a comedian.

We got the attaché case, and on the way out, the guy sitting said, "You ladies have to drive around to the exit. There are two gates. We buzz the first open and you wait until it closes before the second opens, then you exit. Hang a left and that gets you back onto Brookfield. At that point, all bets are off and you're officially in the jungle and will have to shoot your way back to civilization. Dig?"

He laughed like he was funnier than John Belushi, and I swear I saw that damn wolf grinning – he had the biggest fangs I've seen on a dog.

"This wasn't so bad. We got to hobnob with some Desert Storm dropouts and experience life in the death lane," Ronnie mused as we drove onto Brookfield Avenue.

"You mean hobnob with your fan club, right? That guy was ready to polish your fucking shoes. Doctor Destruction, for God's sake!"

"Hey, you're not jealous, are you, Cal? So he happened to like football and it made it easier for us. Those retards would have given us a real hard time if it wasn't for his recognizing me. So, now what?"

"Let's get back to my place. I'll give her a call and we can arrange the exchange."

"Call her now. Why wait?"

"No. We are not out of this yet. This place is worse than the Bronx and stop playing with the fucking keypad. I don't want to be blasted into outer space."

Those boys weren't kidding; this was a bloody jungle and now there were many more predators on the prowl, gangbangers cruising in their cars looking to shoot up anyone and anything. Turf wars here were like brushing your teeth – it was a given and in fact, the kids enjoyed them. Adrenaline is the worst kind of drug, makes heroin seem like a strawberry milkshake. I should know, I come from a long line of adrenaline junkies.

Just then, a black SUV pulled up alongside us on our right. The driver of the Escalade was a kid no more that sixteen or seventeen. He was sporting a red, white and blue doo-rag and motioned for Ronnie to lower his window. We were coasting at eighty, so this dude wasn't kidding and if we had any doubts, the muzzle of the AK47 that appeared through the rear passenger window closed the deal.

"Keep your cool," Ronnie said, lowering the window and noticing me grip the Sig on my lap.

The kid gave Ronnie a long, hard look and then without a word, sped past us like we were standing still.

I let out a sigh of relief. "That was fucking nuts. That kid had the coldest eyes I've seen in a long time."

"Look in the mirror, dude, you have the same look," Ronnie said, lowering the backrest and closing his eyes. "Take 495… no tolls."

"Grand Central is quicker and now we can afford the fucking tolls!" I said, bothered by what he had said.

My mother had said the very same thing to me once when I dealt with a guy who had disrespected her. While we walked back to our apartment, she took my hand and said, *You frightened me, Cal. You got that look in your eyes – the look of a killer and you're still a baby.* I was seventeen, about the same age as that kid in the Caddy, and I was stoked that I had that look. Now, I know better.

The traffic was horrendous and it took us over forty minutes to get to my place, but the rest of the ride was without incident and that was a relief. The assigned parking that came with the apartment was in a lot about fifty yards down and across the street. You could park in front of the building, but that cost you extra and I wasn't paying diddly for that convenience.

We crossed the street to the three-story apartment building. My place was on the third floor. The emergency stairwell was a lot quicker than the lumbering old elevator, but Ronnie wasn't one to run up anything; his excuse was his bum knee and that he'd done as much exercise as a man can do in one lifetime. One day, and I hope it ain't soon; karma is going to turn him into a very fat man.

"I'm hungry. Let's call her and then grab a bite to eat," Ronnie said as we stepped into the lobby.

"Sounds good. How about pizza?"

"How about we get some Indian? It's been a while since I had some curry or Tandoori chicken."

"Let me call her. Maybe we can meet at the Bombay Bazaar," I said hoping that Rachael liked authentic, spicy Indian cuisine.

We were waiting for the elevator when a voice behind us commanded, "Don't make a fucking move, assholes, and don't even breathe unless you want to die here."

We both froze. Ronnie was relieved of the attaché case and I felt the tip of a pistol pressing against my occipital bone. I've got to admit, it never feels good no matter how many times it happens. These boys, all three of them, looked a lot like the two at the storage place except they weren't ex-cons – these jokers were paramilitary or CIA types, you know, the kind that can kill you with a credit card or a ballpoint pen. And the funny thing is that they fit the stereotype: dressed in suits and wearing shades in the middle of the night.

As soon as I opened the door to my pad, they shoved us in, and not gently, but with enough force to send both of us stumbling into the space I called my living room. I was pretty sure I would need a back adjustment if I got out of this alive.

"On your knees, shitheads," the one in charge commanded. His voice was hoarse and deep like Paul Robeson with a bad case of laryngitis.

We were both on our knees when Ronnie gave me look that said: *Well, here's another fine mess you've gotten me into!* Aww, come on now, you know that famous line from Laurel and Hardy? It's funny except I wasn't laughing. These clowns weren't playing, and the thought that they may try and open the case had me thinking of the space cadets and Neil Armstrong. Not exactly how I planned my exit from this life.

Captain Deep-throat must have been a mind reader because at that precise moment he ordered, "Open up the case."

"Not me, brother, it's packed with explosives so I wouldn't try. I don't have the…"

One of the three kicked me in the back so hard that I turned into an instant Bobblehead doll.

"Hey, he's not kidding. They've got it rigged," Ronnie protested, coming to my defense, and for his efforts he earned himself the same reward. Now we had two Bobbleheads.

There is a peculiar comfort in shared misery that is inexplicable. I smiled at Ronnie, a sort of commiserating smile, but he glared at me. I guess the comfort only applies to the one who got to misery land first.

I was trying to get my head to stop bobbling when one of the troglodytes picked the case up and began examining it, and after a few minutes muttered in a voice that was similar to the first guy, "Nothing. It's a decoy, a fuckin' fake."

These morons must attend the same voice training school. I made a mental note to find out how and where to enroll. It sounded sexy cool, the type chicks would dig, and if it weren't for our current predicament, I would have asked them for a reference.

"You need a sixteen-digit code and a fingerprint..." I started in a voice that sounded nothing like theirs but that's as far as I got.

The trog threw the attaché case against the wall and what do you know, it flew open and there was no boom! The case was empty except for a few blank sheets of paper and a large Ziploc bag filled with rice, white rice. I guess roughage wasn't an issue for these cats.

So I was wrong, you don't need sixteen digits or fingerprints; you just throw this shit against the wall. It also dawned on me that I was set-up and sadly, this wasn't the first time in history that a gorgeous gal used her charm on a cerebrally compromised Neanderthal. Remember Samson and Delilah? The difference here was she didn't cut my hair; she nipped my freakin' balls and that wasn't nice. Babysitting those fucking west coast rappers seemed like a far better proposition now.

"Call her," boss-trog ordered.

"Who?"

The designated case opener kicked me in the gut so hard that plans for Tandoori chicken and curry would have to wait for a year at the least.

"Call her," the boss-trog repeated.

"Okay, okay but no more foreplay. Just ask me out on a date, dude," I said to the trog number two, and readied myself for the inevitable. My mouth had a way of getting me in trouble.

His boot was aimed at my head, but I saw it coming and rolled and that saved me from a visit to the dentist. He got me in the back near the upper shoulder. It hurt like a motherfucker but it kept my looks intact. My delusion has no limits.

"Enough," boss-trog commanded. Trog number two stepped back and the boss bent over and whispered, "Call her or I can make this really painful and trust me, you *will* call her in the end."

I think the other troglodytes were hoping I'd resist so they could work me over but like I said, mama didn't raise no dummies. I called her, and to no one's surprise listened to that frustrating message: *the number you dialed is not in service, please check the number and try again.*

"Give me the phone," the boss-trog growled and grabbed my phone.

He scrolled through the calls list and threw the phone back at me. He stood there studying me for a while, not saying a word. I felt like a mouse that had just been dropped into a boa constrictor's tank. Dylan, my brother, once had a Peruvian red-tailed boa as a pet. It wasn't very big, but it gave me the creeps. I was thrilled when Mom got rid of the damn thing. Of course, he blamed me, but that's another story. Let's get back to the boss-trog and his groupies.

After watching me for what seemed like an eternity, he said, "We're going to keep the pretty boy here. I grew up a Giants fan and hated the fucking Packers. If you don't come back in twenty-four hours, this kid ain't going to be too pretty, capisce? You got twenty-four hours to find the broad and get the bag back to us. Twenty-four hours, dipshit, and the clock starts now!"

I turned to my buddy and said, "Hang in there, brother; I'll find her and I'll be back."

I was hoping to sound like the Terminator but it sounded more like Bugs Bunny with his nuts in a wringer. And, to make matters worse, on the way out I almost fell, tripping on my favorite beanbag.

Ronnie rolled his eyes and gave me a look that said: *Oh shit! Now I'm really fucked.*

CHAPTER 6

KINGS AND QUEENS, AND A JESTER...

Shika Sanchez was the one person who could help if I had any chance of finding Rachael in twenty-four hours. Shika was the name she gave herself. She was Emma Maria Sanchez when we were kids in school. She was a quiet, studious gal who happened to be pretty – well, maybe a bit more than just pretty. She was every sixteen-year-old's wet dream. She had those perky tits, hourglass body and legs that wouldn't quit, and add to that a face that filled your mind with lascivious thoughts and you had Emma. I think every red-blooded jock in school had tried to jiggle her knickers at one time or the other but got absolutely nowhere. This gal was locked tighter than a bar-headed goose's ass in winter. That was before she went to jail.

Our judiciary system has a way of punishing the victim and making a victim out of the perpetrator. When she was sixteen, her stepfather tried to rape her but she had managed to escape to a neighbor's place and called the police. The perp got a slap on the wrist and was told to get some counseling. Really, counseling for attempted rape?

Her mother blamed her, accusing her of wearing "provocative" clothing and flirting with the slob, and not surprisingly, three months later he did rape her. But Emma was not the forgiving kind so while he was sleeping, she stabbed him eighteen times and cut his dick off and stuffed it into his mouth. You would think that would have done the bastard in but against all odds, the fucking reprobate survived!

In the ensuing circus that was a trial he claimed that the sex was consensual and that she attacked him because he had refused to leave her mother. And of course, those self-righteous, liberal bastards sitting on the jury believed him and bought the tripe about the hardworking immigrant who was trying to provide a decent home for a misguided teen. She was tried as an adult and found guilty of malicious wounding and attempted murder. She got twelve years in Gladiator School. She would have gotten a lot more but as consideration for her age, the sanctimonious asshole who presided over the case thought twelve was an appropriate sentence for justified retribution. About twenty-five years ago, Lorena Bobbitt got off scot-free for pretty much the same thing, and that goes to show just how fucking crazy our judiciary system has become.

She went in as Emma, a quiet and gentle girl, and emerged from prison as Shika. She refused to answer to Emma or any other name. The day she got out, she called me and that was a surprise; not just the fact that she called me, but her physical transformation had me wondering if I had been smoking that funny weed. Gone was the long black hair and soft, pretty face, and in its place was a bob-cut, boned-out, hardboiled bitch, tough like a Japanese katana folded over a million times. She was still beautiful but in a dangerous sort of way. Her arms and upper body were covered in prison tats and her eyes had lost their innocence. They were cold and unwavering.

Early on in her jail term, I had gone to see her a few times but life has a way of getting in the way and the best-laid plans of mice and men often go awry. I had to steal that line from Robert Burns and a poem I read as a kid. I hadn't seen her in a while and felt a bit guilty about abandoning her.

"I'm sorry, Emma, I should have come to see you more often but life is a bitch and you know…" I tried concocting some lame excuse, but my conscience betrayed me.

"It's Shika not Emma and don't sweat it, bro, at least you called, and except for Sue you came to see me more times than anyone else," she replied, allowing me a way out.

"Where's Sue?" I asked, curious why Sue hadn't been the one to pick her up. Suesheila was Shika's younger sister. Everyone called her Sue and she had met a guy from Switzerland or Austria when she was in college.

"You were always nice to me, Cal, and I have no one else I could trust," she explained. "Sue moved to Zurich so you were it by default. I needed to see a friendly face on my first day out. You're not regretting it, are you?"

I didn't know that Sue had moved and that explained it. Emma and Sue had been pretty close.

"No, not at all, I'm happy you called. It's great seeing you again," I said and stood back, appraising her after giving her another hug.

"That's good to hear. I wasn't sure, Cal, I kept having all these crazy thoughts."

"What crazy thoughts?"

She was quiet. "I used to dream I was drowning and all the people I loved were watching, but no one raised a finger to help, crazy shit like that. But, forget it. That place does things to your mind. I'm just happy you came."

"You can count on me, you know that. Now, what's with this 'Shika' bullshit? I like Emma and Shika sounds like," I hesitated before adding, "like a freakin' dyke."

I thought that maybe prison had converted her to women. I know you can't just convert to being a lesbo but hey, I'm a Neanderthal retard, what do you expect?

"You're being anal. A dyke? Really, Cal?" she retorted and continued, "Shiva is the God of destruction and protector of women and Kali is the Goddess of death, and they form the yin and yang of creation and the balance of spiritual energy. So, I decided to combine them and came up with Shika. It suits me perfectly. I am the avenger of wronged souls. Emma died a long time ago."

She pulled back her sleeve and extended her arm, revealing tattoos of some foreign-looking characters dancing on fire with a multitude of arms holding swords and spears and severed heads, stuff that would give a grown man nightmares.

"But you're not a Hindu."

"Your name is Caleb and you're not really a Christian," she retorted.

"You're wrong. I am a Christian, a sinner for sure, but I hear you, it's the convergence of religious precepts." I paused, impressed by my own creative bullshit, but she seemed to ignore it. "It's not just the name… you've changed."

I was troubled by her transformation. There was a hard edge to her now and the incongruence of what I knew and what was in front of me was disconcerting. I didn't recognize the person I grew up with and treated like a sister.

"You'd change too if you were raped by your father. I thought of him as my dad and he did something that can never be undone. That incident haunts every dark corner of my mind. When I'm falling asleep, I see him grunting over me, telling me how great it is to finally fuck me. The smells, the noise, the pain, the panic… all of it is indelibly burnt into my memory. I struggled, God, how I struggled but I wasn't strong enough so I promised myself that I would never be weak again. My mother refuses to believe me even to this day. Twelve years and she never came to see me once. And jail is no place for a pretty girl. I had to change or turn into a slave-bitch to some real dyke. That hellhole is full of them."

"If you fill your heart with hatred, he wins. I will admit I have no idea what you are going through but you need to let it go and live your life. You are young and you are beautiful and…"

She cut me off.

"I can never let it go. The reason I survived is because I used it to motivate me and become strong. I fought every crazy bitch in there and worked out like I was possessed. After a while, no one wanted to mess with me. I wasn't the helpless little Emma anymore, I was Kali reincarnated, and I could sense that people feared me. The toughest bitches in there gave me a wide berth. I had regained control and I felt empowered. Unless you've walked in my shoes you wouldn't understand, but this is who I am now and there is no going back. Emma is dead. She died the day I was raped."

I felt sorry for her, for what this had done to the simple, lovely girl I knew but love transcends circumstance or it should. I didn't have a sister and if I could pick one, it would be her.

"I'm really sorry and just know that I love you either way. Now tell me what you'd like to do, maybe get a good meal and a huge slice of tiramisu at Kosta's little place? Or, do you want to catch a movie? We'll do whatever you want to."

I recalled that she loved Italian deserts and we used to frequent a small dive run by an old Greek that served the best damn tiramisu and cassata this side of the Atlantic.

I was mentally debating the virtues of both dishes when she asked in a soft voice, "Can we go somewhere beautiful, Cal, away from the noise and the traffic? If that's a drag we can go get something to eat."

I drove her to Bear Mountain, to a place my dad took me trekking. It was a long drive, and for most of it she was quiet, but the look on her face when we sat on the ledge of a large rock that overlooked the lake with an incredible view of the Bear Mountain State Park made the trip worth it. She stared out at the panorama, quiet as a church mouse with tiny teardrops streaming slowly down her face. I resisted the urge to put my arm around her shoulders and give her a reassuring hug. She needed her space to let it all sink in, that she was now free and that the past was done and that there was still beauty in the world if you knew where to look for it.

It was strange how her stepfather turned up dead, his throat slit from ear to ear a month after Shika returned, but they couldn't pin it on her. She was with Ronnie and me when it happened; at least that's what we swore to. We were playing poker with a bunch of other disen-franchised bums and every single one of them swore on their mother's graves that she was with us that evening. Karma is a fucking bitch and that slime-ball is roasting in some superheated corner of hell. I could picture Kali with his head in her hand dancing on his sorry ass.

Shika now had a boyfriend, a Russian ex-Spetsnaz hard-ass with a reputation as a killer. Together they ran almost every nefarious activity in their neighborhood. When she decided to go rogue, she went all the way – but if there was a redeeming quality left in her it was her loyalty; she was loyal to a fault.

I found her with her boyfriend, Andros Bychkov, in a derelict, tumble-down, rat-infested building that served as their office. Andros was known as Andy the Bitch but no one in their right mind said that to his face. I had to get by a few low-IQ drones to get to the queen bee, except these fuckers were born with stingers and no brains. They were more likely to shoot first and ask questions later but as luck would have it, a few of them recognized me and let me in without too much of a fuss.

After I had explained my predicament to Shika, it was Andros who answered, "Why you come to us, eh? Who the fuck you are? Shika don't need your problems so get the fuck out of here before Andros do something nasty."

This was not what I had expected. My track record with angry Russian men wasn't too encouraging but I have a serious learning disability when it comes to shit like this. I got up and was about to introduce him to Mike, my right fist, when she stepped between us. I had better explain. Salvador Sanchez was my Dad's favorite boxer. He was the featherweight champ with an incredible left hand, so I christened my left Salvador as a tribute to him. My right was named for the hard-hitting Mike Tyson. I was a lefty but my right wasn't all that shabby and I was just about to drop the hammer on the retard when Shika intervened.

"This is the Caleb Montague I told you about. He's a friend, baby, and his trouble is my trouble," Shika explained, diffusing the situation.

The angry grizzly morphed immediately into a cuddly teddy bear. "Oh, I am sorry, my friend, your trouble is my trouble and that means trouble for bastard who is giving you trouble."

I was having trouble understanding the alliterative accent-laced mumbling, but the fact that he had a smile on his ugly mug was comforting. That's when he got up and slapped me on my back. If you're one of the few that managed to survive being hit by a eighteen wheeler doing ninety, you'd understand what that felt like. Damn, it hurt worse than a kick from an angry mule. But he got me a cup of coffee and smiled again and sat next to me.

The coffee was bad, the crooked smile was worse and the cologne he reeked of took you straight to a cheap whorehouse in Bangkok but I'll be damned if I was going to complain.

"Explain to Andros exactly where and what happened. First step is not to find girl. First step is to find your friend. That is easier and safer."

His referring to himself in the third person was a bit disturbing. It made sense though - with her money, Rachael could be anywhere; she could be in Timbuktu for all I knew. Those CIA types would most probably still be at my apartment. I guess Andy the Bitch was smarter than I thought.

"What about those assholes who have Ronnie? They look like a rough bunch."

"Andros will fuck them up. Andros knows how to take care of bad boys," he replied with another scowl that passed for a smile.

There it was again, the illeism but I was relieved he was on my side. It was like dropping the deuce after being constipated for three days and yes, I've been there. I thought about renaming him Ex-Lax but I don't think he'd go for it and I didn't want to risk another love pat on the back.

I showed Shika the gold coin. "This was in the envelope with the money she advanced. There was a note with it in Cantonese and a phone number in Hong Kong. Rachael has the note."

She was on her computer scrolling through pages about the Swanson family. She looked at the coin and tossed it to Andros.

"It's gold alright and it's from the Chinese Triad based in Hong Kong or Macao. It's a warning," she said. "Your girl and her brother are quite a pair, especially her brother. Edward Brandon Swanson has always been in trouble. He was a problem even in school… some private school in Switzerland. He was kicked out for supplying cocaine to the principal's daughter. She was fifteen. He likes to gamble and loses way more than he can afford and has the worst taste in women; beautiful losers looking for a sugar daddy. His latest stomping ground is Las Vegas, and his main squeeze is a redheaded call girl named Satin."

"You got all that off the net?" I was impressed.

"You can find pretty much anything about anybody. It's all out there. You just need to know how to look," was her smug reply. "The twelve years wasn't a total waste. I spent time learning the science behind computers and how they function. It's not that difficult once you understand the programming. And, Andros has shown me a few tricks. He's a wiz with at hacking."

I looked at the big oaf again with newfound respect – a hard-ass with a brain. He was getting himself a refill and damn if he didn't resemble a Kodiak Grizzly bear.

"Love must be blind," I said with a smile, nodding towards the big Russian. "Talk about Beauty and the Beast."

She smiled back, "He treats me well and he cares for me, Cal. That beats the heck out of any pretty boy who lies, cheats and treats you worse than shit."

"I get that but do you love him?"

"Love? My mother loved my stepfather and what did it get her? She was so in love that it affected her thinking. She blamed me for everything. You can have love. I'll take what Andros gives me, and if that's not love then I'm okay with it," she said, morphing back into Emma for a moment.

"Hey, what the fuck do I know? I'm not Dr. Phil and my life is so messed up, I wouldn't know love if it kicked me in the ass," was my somber observation. This was especially true after what Rachael did to me. You don't fuck someone and then feed him to the wolves.

"You talk to Andros and be nice. He's a genuinely nice guy when you get to know him. I'm going to make some calls and see if I can track Miss. Swanson down," Shika said and left the room.

Andros and I made small talk for about twenty minutes; by that I mean he talked and I pretended to understand. What I gathered was that they met at the local gun range; I mean where else would a Russian psycho meet the Goddess Kali? It was love at first sight for the big Russian. It took Shika a bit longer but their friendship soon blossomed into something more. He swore eternal love and dedicated his life to making her happy. It dawned on me then that it wasn't Shika who sent her stepfather to the great inferno but Andros. I was impressed and a bit jealous. In this shithole, he had found love and a purpose.

But what intrigued me was why someone like him would leave the motherland. "Why did you leave Russia? Were you in trouble with the law or what?"

He gave me a look that said I was crossing a line

and it could cost me some pain, but after a moment's silence he smiled.

"Shika, she love you like brother, Cal, so I tell you. I treat you like my family so I will give you reason. It is the fucking Russian government. They steal from the people. The oil and natural resource of country belong to all but they steal it. While my mother, father, sister all stand in line for a small loaf of bread, those bastards live like kings in big mansion with chauffeur, and body-guards, and maid with French chef cooking fancy foods, while we eat shit like little piggy."

He spat out the last bit and I felt for him. I too had an intense dislike for government so I got it.

"But you were in the Spetsnaz, the Special Forces, so why leave?"

"I was in special detail to look after Putin's buddy, an oligarch and big asshole. One evening, I was taking some chicken pieces for my mother, scraps left on table, and he say something stupid to me so I tell him to fuck off. That was it. They throw me in jail and try and to break me but I am from mountains of Koshtan. Andros kick many, many ass in jail!"

One look at this ogre and I believed every word. He would and could kick your ass if you messed with him! He was standing by the window and turned back to face me.

"They use us and keep us down like slaves. And Putin, he is the big crook, the eight hundred pound gorilla. So one day, after I get out, I say 'fuck it' this little piggy had enough. I talk to my close friends and we decide to leave together. That is reason I come here. So now you know why Andros is American."

I put my hand on his shoulder in commiseration.

"Do you think they will come after you and your friends?" I asked. I had heard stories about reprisals for those who crossed Putin or his buddies.

"Andros will kick their ass. Some of us are in England, some in Canada; some are in Holland and some here in this great country. We are all brothers with only one rule. If one has trouble, all of us will come to help. If the big gorilla with white back…"

"You mean the Silverback, Putin?"

"Yes, yes, if he comes here or he send people here, I send bastards back in body bag! They know where I am and I know where they are so it is better they leave Andros alone, you know, you don't poke sleeping dog! I will tell you one more…"

That's when Shika returned. Her expression told me everything I needed to know – things were bad and she was concerned, real concerned.

"I don't know who the CIA types are but there's a bounty on your head by the Chinese triad. These guys are either from Hong Kong or Macao. They want you alive and trust me, Cal, it's better to bite on the pill before they get to you."

I was about to drop another deuce. There were two problems with Shika's suggestion. One, I didn't have a suicide pill and two; I wasn't the type to "bite" on anything that would terminate my sorry existence. Granted, I wasn't living the easy life but I was like every other slob hoping for better things to come. There's something to be said about hope, you know, hope springing eternal and all that. Well, that applies to me. I clung to a glimmer of hope that things would work out for Rachael and me and that there was some logical explanation for us being set up. Yeah, I'm delusional, but hope is like a bulldog and when it bites your ass, it doesn't let go. I knew I was clutching at straws here.

"Fuck the Chinese. Call me a fucking xenophobe but I don't like won-tong, fortune cookie bastards who subjugate their people and try and take down our way of life while profiting from it."

"When did you turn into a racist?"

"Screw you! I'm not a racist and you of all people should know that. I love my country and I don't like anyone who doesn't. It's called Dissuasive Patriotic Dissonance." I made that stuff up. I'm good at that, you know, making up shit that sounds real.

"What? You're so full of it and stop kidding around. This is some serious shit you've gotten into," Shika retorted, then grabbed my shirt and pulled me closer to her and her tone changed, she was Emma again.

"Get away from here, Cal. This life is not for you. I've known you since we were kids and that tough-guy, macho exterior doesn't fool anyone. It can't cover what's in your heart. Stop trying to be your dad. You don't want to hear this but Dylan is more like your father than you'll ever be. The sad thing is that you try so hard to be like him and Dylan tries so hard not to but it's in the genes. You are a decent, sensitive soul. Leave this fucked-up business for the likes of Andros and me. Go somewhere far away and find yourself a nice country girl and settle down, have kids and lead a normal life. The life I've chosen ends only one way but I can deal with it. You hear me, bro, as soon as we get Ronnie, you leave."

I was quiet, taken completely by surprise by the intensity of her emotions. She wasn't the type to give advice or get into other people's business. Her saying Dylan was like my father was a shock, a revelation. He despised the way Dad was and wanted nothing to do with him. I was the one who was more like him, but even I had to admit that my father was self-centered and, in many ways, selfish. I guess, in that respect, Dylan was more like him. Maybe I was wrong all this time and maybe wanting to be is not being.

"Listen to her," Andros growled in his heavy Russian accent. He placed a cup of that awful tasting tar in front of Shika and gripped my shoulder with a hand the size of fucking Texas. "Andros know how to read people and this is not for you, my friend. Soon as she finish her coffee, we leave. We get your friend and then you listen to Shika. If you don't, Andros kick your ass."

What is it with these Russian retards? All they seem to want to do is to kick my ass. Now she was the second woman to tell me that I was a sensitive soul. I'm not even sure what that means but with all these people wanting to kick my ass, maybe I *should* move to Katmandu or someplace up in the mountains. Get away from here and live like a mountain man but I would have to find myself a mountain woman first if I wanted to spawn a bunch of tough-assed mountain brats. And that would mean that I had to find Rachael before the triad found me… or worse, her.

"Let's get Ronnie first and then we can discuss my exodus from this wonderful cesspool we call home," I suggested, not liking where the conversation was heading.

Shika gave me a look that washed away the years. It was a nostalgic trip to the past. "You're as stubborn as your old man and that's where the similarity ends. Think about what I said."

She chugged her coffee down and checked the 9mm Glock holstered by her side and the Taser she kept strapped to her ankle before we left the sanctuary of her dark, crummy office.

"Are you carrying?" she asked me.

"Of course I'm carrying. I'm the meanest motherfucker this side of Dodge, sister."

Shika and Andros exchanged smiles and the big Russian shook his head. On the way out, the queen bee spoke to her drones and several of them jumped into their souped-up Mustangs and Supras parked in the shadows and roared away.

We got into her five-series BMW and before I could shut the door, Andros floored the gas pedal. I heard the tires screeching and felt like Michael Schumacher at the Monza in Italy, except I doubt that Schumacher ever wet his pants.

CHAPTER 7

FLY HUMMINGBIRD, FLY...

The room was located in the basement of a dingy, gray walk-up in the low-rent district of Iao Hon in Macao. Low-rent was a nice way of saying slums. The curtains to the only window were drawn, and except for the dull hue of the table lamp, the periphery around the table was covered in shadows. The diminutive, elderly man behind the desk was Kuok-Bai, the leader of the largest and most powerful triad society in Macao. He was also known as Gold Tooth for the gold crowns on several of his front teeth.

As a homeless orphan, he had wandered the streets of the Portuguese district around Largo de Senado and had to scratch and fight for every morsel of food. And as he grew older, his reputation as a tough streetfighter caught the attention of the local triad, and not surprisingly, he was recruited into their ranks. He worked his way up the hierarchy using his propensity for violence to eliminate those who posed any threat to his ascension to power. He had a brilliant mind honed sharp by the years lived on the streets.

Like Hong Kong, Macao was a Special Administrative Region (SAR) of China and the local government was as corrupt as any in Asia. The corruption wasn't a surprise – money has a way of eroding ethics and morality, and greed was something Kuok-Bai understood. He used his guile to pay off several key officials within the government, and in return it provided him with a certain amount of immunity from the local police.

The international gambling scene had shifted from Las Vegas to Macao and with that came the arrival of the mega casinos. Money flowed into the local economy and the triads exploited all the verticals, from food and drink to protection, prostitution and money laundering. Paying off the right people was just the cost of doing business.

There were three men seated in front of Kuok-Bai, and a woman, partially hidden by shadows, was standing behind him. The men were nondescript, small, wiry street-thugs but the woman was anything but that. She was stunning; a tall, exotic beauty with flawless golden skin, large sloping eyes and a rosebud mouth. Her hair was long and straight and blacker than the blackest coal. Her presence had a sobering effect on the three men. Her reputation as a mystical assassin with supernatural powers was common knowledge within the underworld, and though these were hardened criminals they were deathly frightened of her.

Her past was shrouded in mystery and intrigue. There were rumors that she was raised in the Himalayas by Buddhist monks and learned sorcery from passing Indian mystics and that she lived in both worlds – the real and the supernatural. The stories of her exploits had a life of their own and people began believing the myth. The truth, however, was far less romantic. She had been trained by the MSS, the Ministry of State Security (also known as Guoanbu) – the ultra-secret police of the Chinese Communist Party – and when she left their services, her classified files had been sealed and every detail of her existence had been wiped clean.

Very few knew her real name or where she came from. Her parents were both presumed dead. When they had tried to get their only child back from the authorities, they were interred in a camp for "reeducation" (the Government's term) and were never seen or heard from again.

She was twelve when she was selected, along with several other boys and girls, and sent to a school for gifted children. The school was tucked away in the remote foothills of Changbai Mountain in the northeast province of Jilin. From there, the boys and girls with potential graduated to the next level, a highly secretive training center hidden in the Xinjiang province near the Kazakhstan border. At this training school, the young men and women learned a wide array of skills from mastering martial arts and computers to human psychology. Their final training involved the killing game and the most effective forms of wet-work. This included the use of sophisticated potions and powders that were undetectable except by the most skilled of toxicologists.

From this select group, the attractive girls and boys were sent to Beijing and trained to use charm and sex as tools to entice and deceive foreign operatives and people of interest. She had excelled in almost every category.

To the rest of the triad world she was known simply by the mononym, Hummingbird, and like the incredible little bird that boasts of many shades, she had a thousand disguises and went by a thousand different aliases. Except for Kuok-Bai, very few knew who the real Hummingbird was or whether there was indeed a real Hummingbird. Her real name was Lienna Quan, but he affectionately called her Jade after his favorite semiprecious greenstone.

"Where is Steven Chang now?" Kuok-Bai asked in Cantonese, his voice surprisingly high-pitched like that of a chirping sparrow. His face was small and round and he had a habit of constantly adjusting his glasses. The innocuous appearance was dangerously misleading; the old man was a stone cold killer.

"We have him. He is with Christopher Chen in San Diego," answered the man with crooked, tobacco-stained teeth and a scar running from the right corner of his mouth down his chin. He was seated on the left.

"What did he say about the attaché case?"

"He blamed the redheaded bitch, the one named Satin. He said she stole it from him after spiking his drink. We are closing in on Swanson, her boyfriend." He paused and added as an afterthought, "Steven Chang is a bumbling idiot, a liability. Why don't we get rid of the motherfucker? Why are we keeping him?"

Kuok-Bai's face turned cold and he adjusted his glasses and pinned the man with an icy stare. "You let me worry about Steven. You do your job unless you are having a problem with that. Are you having a problem, Fai?"

The answer was immediate and deferential, "No. No, boss. I just thought…"

Kuok-Bai cut him off, "Don't think. If I let you do the thinking, we'd be eating conjee and pickles from the sewers in Beijing. You let me do the thinking."

The man looked down and remained silent. Kuok-Bai had a mercurial temper stoked by deep-rooted insecurities stemming from his early life on the streets, and this in turn led to a healthy paranoia. Those who questioned him were often found floating in the Pearl River.

The man in the middle was older than his two associates and he decided to run interference for the younger man.

"We think we know where Swanson is. We had a tip that he is in Amsterdam in the Red Light district. I have instructed our people to find him but not to do anything. It is certain that he left the attaché case in New York. The problem is there are hundreds of locations in or near the city where he could have stored it. He will surely ask his sister to retrieve the case. She is the only one he trusts."

"I thought he was in Vegas?" Kuok-Bai was surprised.

"He was and that is where he got together with the whore. And, that is also where they met Steven. It is common knowledge that Steven likes to gamble and has an obsession with pale-skinned redheads. Once they got the valise, Swanson and the whore separated and he flew to New York. From there he took a flight to Amsterdam. We grabbed the whore and worked on her but she knew nothing except that Swanson had dumped her."

The man seated on the right felt compelled to add to the conversation. "I have no idea what he saw in that ugly gwaipo. Her skin was pale like that of a pig's belly and had spots all over it. Her eyes were ghostly, translucent and blue, and that hair was blood red. She resembled a she-devil straight from hell. I wouldn't fuck that bitch if they paid me a million dollars!"

"You would fuck a goat for ten cents!" was the sarcastic retort from the man named Fai.

"I'd fuck your mother and she's uglier than a go…"

"Enough!" Kuok-Bai snapped; he wasn't one for jokes or useless banter. The conversation ceased immediately and he continued, "What did they do with her?"

"She was an addict. They shot her up with a cocktail of carfentanil and fentanyl. The maid found her body in her room at the Casino. The cops think it was a drug overdose. They don't give a shit; she was a whore – one less bitch to worry about."

"What about Swanson's sister?" Kuok-Bai asked.

"Swanson has been calling his sister regularly so we think she has the case or knows where it is."

"Swanson needs money; that is why he did this in the first place. Has he contacted Chang for money?" Kuok-Bai inquired.

"No, there has been no contact. Are we planning on paying him?"

"We don't pay people who steal from us. Get the briefcase back and we will deal with Swanson and his sister, if she is involved."

"We have her under surveillance and she hasn't retrieved the case as yet, but she was seen speaking with several local hoods so it won't be long. Because of who she is, we have not tried to extract the information from her. We can grab her and get her to talk. Just say the word and…"

"No, don't do that," Kuok-Bai interrupted, "we don't need a political shit-storm. The family is connected all the way to the White House. We don't do anything until we have the valise. Have you found out who the people are that she was talking to?"

"They are some local guys; nothing to be concerned about. We are working on their backgrounds and will have a better picture shortly. We *will* get the bag from them if and when they retrieve it. Our people are watching them closely."

"Do not underestimate the fucking Americans. They are a bunch of cowboys and before you know it, you will have John Wayne shooting up the fucking moon. You find Swanson, he is the key; all this nonsense with the sister could be a diversion to distract us. He could have someone else retrieving the valise as we speak."

The men were quiet. They knew better than to question the boss – Kuok-Bai was usually right and even if he wasn't, contradicting him was a bad idea.

"We searched the sister's apartment and found a card key but it requires a code. We couldn't find that anywhere so we left a warning and Hwang's number in Hong Kong."

The triad in Hong Kong was run by Hwang Hak-Kun, a protégé of Kuok-Bai. Though the triads functioned independently, they worked collaboratively whenever it was required. Kuok-Bai held sway over matters that concerned both mobs.

"That locker could be for her jewelry or something else," Kuok-Bai said and contemplated the situation for a few moments before continuing, "Find out who else the whore knew. Her friends at the casino, maybe some of the other girls… she may have confided something in one of them. We don't need a string of dead whores leading back to us. Use someone with a brain. A little money works with most people. Killing the whore served no purpose. Are we still using Akira Hirai?"

"Yes, boss, we use him for complicated assignments. I did not know this but they call him the Ghost Who Kills.

Hirai's father was a devout Catholic who was estranged from his son. He passed away a few years ago."

Kuok-Bai was quiet, lost in thought. He disliked using outsiders but Akira Hirai was different. His father was Chinese and had moved to Japan from Beijing. He had changed his name in order to assimilate and had married a Japanese woman. His son, Akira, grew up hero-worshipping Bruce Lee and the samurai.

"Wei, you take control of this. We need to know where Swanson is now. If you find him, tell your men not to hurt him. He is weak and will hand over the bag without much trouble; that is, if he has it. I have a feeling that the sister will be a bit more difficult but we will deal with that later. I doubt the whore spoke to anyone but we need to cover all the angles," Kuok-Bai said to the man in the center.

"Do you want me to use Akira Hirai?"

"No. For now we will keep it within our people. Do not kill or hurt Swanson or his sister, is that clear?"

"Yes, boss."

The old man concluded their meeting with a precursory nod. "Now leave us and get back to me as soon as you have something. What is Swanson's sister's name?"

"Rachael Swanson."

"And the redheaded whore?"

"She called herself Satin but her real name is Ciara McMann." He mispronounced the name 'Kee-a-ra'.

The woman leaned over his shoulder and whispered in his ear, "It is an Irish name and is pronounced 'Keera' not Kee-a-ra."

Kuok-Bai wrote the names down on a pad then commanded, "Go! Go now and let me know when your men have Swanson."

Once the men had left, he turned to the woman and switched to Mandarin, "What do *you* think, Jade?"

She had been standing expressionless and silent behind Kuok-Bai throughout the entire discussion. Now that the men were gone, she relaxed and drew up a chair.

"I don't think," she replied. "I do what you instruct me to do."

He held out a cup of tea for her before pouring one for himself.

"Stop that! It's only you and me now. You know that I trust your judgment. Do you ask yourself why you are with me and why it is that I have not slept with you? You are far more beautiful than all the bitches who share my bed."

"You like ugly women?" she replied, and smiled.

"Now that is disrespectful. I will tell you. It is because I think of you as my daughter. From the moment I saw that little girl practicing her kicks and moves long after all had left, I felt a connection. The Hindu sages speak of reincarnation and lives lived before. Maybe in a past life, you were my daughter. So, now that we have settled that, what you do think about all this? And do you think we need to use Akira Hirai?" he asked, taking a sip of the strong tea.

Unlike most Chinese, Kuok-Bai had a predilection for Assam Tea, a strong dark brew that he drank with an ample serving of condensed milk. It was a habit he had picked up on his many trips to Singapore.

Jade disliked the tea but would never think of offending him. Like most Chinese she usually drank white tea or green tea without adding anything to augment the flavor. She took a dainty sip of the overly sweet tea before speaking.

"I don't think we need an outsider right now. I think I should talk to Steven Chang first and then I will look into Ciara McMann's family and friends to see if they were privy to any of this. And, of course, I will speak with Swanson. The sister may be the key but I will deal with that once I have more information," Jade replied.

"And what of the people she is hiring?"

"That could be a problem. Americans are not like us. They are unpredictable and independent and can be dangerous especially if they are ex-military."

"And that is why I trust you. It is exactly what I was thinking," he said. "You must act soon, Jade. We don't have a lot of time. Wang Jie is not a patient man and we don't want the Ministry of Defense poking their noses into our affairs."

"I lost my parents a long time ago and had become a ship without a rudder sailing in turbulent waters until you came into my life. You have been a father to me. If it wasn't for you, I would still be working for the miserable bureaucrats at the MSS. I cannot forget what you have done for me. I will retrieve the valise, father. I will not disappoint you."

She knew that addressing him as father pleased the old man. Kuok-Bai nodded. She got up and bowed and was about to leave when he stopped her.

"Daughter, you do not have to pretend to like the tea. It is a peculiar habit of mine, this sweet dark nectar that I have grown fond of." His voice was soft and gentle now.

"I will learn to like it, father," she replied with a smile before leaving.

Though his expression hadn't changed, he felt a warm glow inside him. Jade made him happy and she was the one good thing he had done in his life. She was like him, an orphan with no one to love. He had used his considerable influence and wealth to extricate her from the MSS. It had cost him a fortune but he didn't regret the decision for a single moment.

The first stop for Lienna Quan was to her two-bedroom apartment in a modest low-rise in Toi San close to the administrative border that separated Macao from the rest of China. She used the rear entrance and made a couple of calls while packing. She fished out several passports that she kept hidden under her dresser, and after picking the ones she wanted, placed them in a false lining of her handbag.

She then removed the paneling in the rear wall of her kitchen, revealing a secret chamber. Here, stashed away, was a canvas duffle full of various currencies – mainly euros, British pounds, dollars and the Chinese renminbi. She counted out what she needed in each currency, returned the bag to its hiding place and carefully replaced the panels. She studied the kitchen to make sure nothing was out of place before going into the bedroom.

She pulled on a skullcap that fit tightly around her head and tucked her hair in. A wig, false teeth, round granny bifocals and a bit of makeup along with an over-sized dress completed the disguise. The transformation was dramatic. Gone was the young, exotic beauty and in her place was an old, frail woman with slightly protruding front teeth, poor eyesight and ivory hair. She smiled at the reflection of the prototypical granny smiling back at her.

Zhuhai provided an oasis for the menial workers in Macao. The cost of food and supplies were much cheaper and many of the older generation crossed the border by bus or ferry to do their shopping. When the old woman boarded the crowded bus, a young man got up and offered her his seat.

"Here, grandmother, you sit here." He spoke in Cantonese.

"Thank you, my son; you are so kind," was the tinny, trembling reply.

When they arrived at the Macao Portas do Cerco bus stop, the same young man helped Lienna off the bus. The bus terminal was always bustling and the crowd pressed by them, jostling each other to get to the crossing into Zhuhai.

"Do you need help with customs, grandmother?" he asked, trying to shield her from the people rushing by.

"Thank you, my son, can I hold onto to your arm? People are always in a hurry and I have been knocked over a few times."

The young man held her arm and helped her while they were pushed along by the crush of the crowd towards the customs and immigration queues. Once they were done with the border formalities, the young man stood by her and asked, "Do you need help getting to the market?"

"No, my daughter will be here any minute but thank you, my son, you are most kind. I know you have things to do so go, go with my blessing."

"Thank you, grandmother."

She watched the polite young man walk away, swallowed up by the throng, and waited until he had disappeared before flagging down a taxi. She took it to her apartment in a modest two-story walk-up brick building on a private road.

The three large rooms that made up the upper floor were meticulously clean and sparsely furnished. The middle room had a thin mattress that lay on three tatami mats and in the corner was a small dresser with a mirror and a three-legged wooden stool. A connecting door on the left led to the bathroom that had a western-style toilet, a small sink and a bathtub. The porcelain tiles of the backsplash were stained and chipped in places but like the rest of the apartment, they were sparkling clean. The room to the right of the bedroom was her kitchen. It had a small gas stove with a single burner, a tiny fridge and a sink with a drying stand next to it. The stove sat on top of an old teak wooden table made without nails but held together by wood dowels and dovetails.

The ground floor was boarded shut with locks on every door. Except for a set of Bluetooth speakers, the basement was empty. There were no other tenants in the building which gave her the privacy and anonymity she demanded. The landlord was indebted to Kuok-Bai and knew better than to interfere or pry.

After removing her disguise she changed into a loose tee and tights, and went down to the basement, turned on the music stored on her phone and began her workout routine.

At first, the soothing strains of a soft classical number set to a slow three-four beat filled the basement. She began her routine with the stretches of tai chi but as the music changed and the tempo quickened she transitioned effortlessly, moving faster and faster until she was a blur. She leaped, twirled, kicked and punched in a dazzling array of precision and speed, a whispering shadow of a hummingbird in motion. After thirty minutes of explosive, nonstop ballet, for it was more dance than combat, she stopped, her face and body glistening in a golden sheen.

She turned off the music and continued with her workout using a rattan Bo staff, and once again, she started slowly increasing the tempo until she was a shapeless silhouette of a thousand doppelgangers blending loosely together in fluid nonstop motion. Her workouts were several hours long, and she often repeated moves until they were perfected and she was satisfied.

For the finale, she drew a black, satin cravat and used it as a blindfold before performing a series of katas that were complex and precise and required the utmost concentration, impeccable balance and flawless timing. She was lithe and strong and fast with a seemingly limitless well of endurance, and when it was over, she sat cross-legged on the floor, regulating her breathing until her body had fully recovered.

She drew a bath, soaking her body in the warmth of the water, and after changing into a loose fitting kasaya robe, she lit a candle and glided down the stairs to the first floor. The soft patter of her bare feet and the jangle of keys created a ghostly symphony that echoed eerily in the hallway. She unlocked one of the doors and stepped inside the dark room and lit several incense sticks before assuming the lotus position in front of a black, marble statue. It was Kali, the goddess of destruction. Alongside the statue was a handmade wooden cross and next to it, a small stone carving of Buddha. Lavender and jasmine filled the air accompanied by the euphonic murmur of her chants. It was only after her meditation that she went back up and ate a simple meal of rice noodles with vegetables and a small piece of dried fish.

She fell asleep almost as soon as she lay down on the hard mattress of her bed.

CHAPTER 8

THE KAMIKAZE BROTH-ERHOOD...

The drive to my apartment was way beyond scary and made the Kingda Ka rollercoaster at Six Flags seem like a walk in the park. I don't think they have traffic lights in Russia or if they do, I don't think they pay attention to them. Andros ran every red light, blitzed through stop signs and drove down one-way streets, all the while singing along with some disturbing Slavic music blaring on the radio. I'm not ashamed to admit that there were times when I shut my eyes tight and prayed for divine intervention.

When we arrived at my apartment, I was the first to jump out of the car, a few shades paler and surprised to be alive. I swore to myself that I would never drive with that lunatic again.

"You get used to it," Shika said, noticing the look on my face.

Andros had pulled up right to the front door and parked in a reserved parking spot.

"You can't park here; this is for…" I started but was summarily cut off.

"Andros will park anywhere. Fuck them, what they gonna do?"

They gonna get pretty pissed off and tow your fuckin' car, that's what they gonna do! The thought had just buzzed through my mind when the pain-in-the-ass from apartment 2B rushed outside and said, "Hey, Bubba, you can't park here. Move your fuckin' car. This is a reserved…"

"Go fuck yourself!" Andros suggested in the globally accepted language of Neanderthals. You could be from Outer Mongolia and you would have no problem understanding him.

"I've got a better idea; I'll fuck you, you foreign retard!"

The man was big – big and fat and stupid. He took two long strides towards Andros and got his trachea crunched. The strike was so fast that I missed it. What I saw was the fat man grabbing his neck and crumbling to the ground.

"That was mistake. You never make move with your hands down." The Russian helped the man up and dusted him off. "Go drink some water. You will feel better but stay in your lane. If I see you again, Andros will kick your ass."

And that was that. The guy from 2B took the elevator up with us but didn't say a word. He kept making strange gurgling sounds like there was a giant goober stuck in his throat, and shook the big Russian's hand before getting off at his floor.

"Remember, drink water. You feel better soon," was Andros' parting advice.

I guess this was his version of Dale Carnegie's 'How to Win Friends and Influence People'. I looked at Shika, bewildered, and she smiled. "You get used to it."

We found Ronnie seated on the couch, watching the tube with an empty pizza box on the coffee table. He was alone and didn't seem worse for wear. The three CIA types were nowhere in sight.

"What happened?" I asked, but got no answer.

Ronnie had jumped off the couch and was hugging Shika. He stood back holding her at arm's length. "Damn, girl, you look freakin' amazing. Cal told me that you had changed but this is what I'd call a real change - all butched out and stuff but gorgeous! I like the new look, Emma, like Xena, the Warrior Princess."

"You didn't come to see me once, Ronnie, and that was hard. Cal came to visit almost every week for a while. In the early days, I lived for those visits. It was lonely and frightening in there."

I felt a guilty pang shoot through me. I could have gone to see her more often. I had tried to get Ronnie to go with me a few times but he always had an excuse, so I assumed he didn't want to see her behind bars, and pretty soon I began making excuses myself. Damn, I'm such a loser.

"I couldn't. The thought of you in there was too much and… and, I just couldn't." Ronnie looked pained, and though he was known to be a pretty good fibber, this time I think he was being sincere.

"It doesn't matter. Emma is dead. Call me Shika."

Ronnie looked relieved. He smiled and repeated, "Shika? Okay, Shika it is." He looked at Andros, "Who's the bully?"

"I am Andros Bychkov," the big Russian introduced himself, and put his arm around Shika, making sure there was no doubt just who her man was. "You are Ronnie, the pretty-boy, football player."

"I *was* the pretty boy, football player," Ronnie quipped shaking the big man's hand, "now, I'm just plain old Ronnie Griffith; brother to Caleb and Emm… Shika." He paused for effect and added with a big smile, "And now, I am a brother to you, Andros Bychkov."

The big man grabbed him in a bear hug and said, "You my brother from different mother! We are like the Black Russian – I am the vodka and you are coffee. Or maybe more like the Brothers Karamazov except we not fight and get crazy, eh?"

"I have no idea who the fuck that is, but I like you and I think we're going to be buddies," Ronnie replied. And while the two men were playing at some twisted Dostoevsky parody, Shika took a quick look around the apartment.

"What happened here?" she asked, looking at the empty attaché case.

"I don't know. The boss man got a call, he listened and they disappeared without a word. They left that behind. That's the attaché case we got from Brookfield Storage. I tried calling Cal but got no response. I figured he must be halfway to Montana chasing after the elusive Miss. Swanson so I went out and got me a pizza." He looked at me and added, "I had to swipe twenty bucks out of your jar… didn't have any cash on me."

"You haven't changed a bit - the same old Ronnie!" Shika said with a smile. "You were always mooching off Cal and me."

"He's a born moocher. If he paid me back what he owes me, I'd be rich and wouldn't have to chase after the elusive Miss Swanson."

"Hey now, give me a break. You guys have short memories… remember the Rolling Stones concert? I had to buy the tickets for both of you and Peggy Burns! You do remember Peggy, don't you, Cal?"

Shika and Ronnie both laughed. Just the mention of Peggy's name brought back some embarrassing memories, ones I'd sooner forget. It was October of 2006 at the Beacon Theatre – I will never live it down. This was a few months before Emma was assaulted and our world changed.

"Oh God!" I looked up at the ceiling and rolled my eyes, "Not that damn Rolling Stones concert again! That was the only time…"

"What we do now? You still want to find the girl?" Andros cut me off. I guess a trip down memory lane wasn't his thing.

"I have no idea where Rachael is so, yeah, what now?" I asked, looking at Shika.

"I'm hungry and I know Andros is too. I'll put the word out on the streets and hopefully we'll get something in a day or two."

"Hey, how about some Tex-Mex?" Ronnie suggested, "I've been thinking about tacos and margaritas. That little Mexicali cantina is right around the corner, so what do you say?"

"You just ate a fucking pizza and from the looks of it, a very large one!" I exclaimed. And just a short time ago, he wanted Tandoori chicken. This guy is Garfield on steroids.

"That was nothing. An appetizer is all it was," Ronnie replied with a big smile.

"You really haven't changed. But Mexican sounds good," Shika said and the big Russian concurred with a nod.

So we headed out and yeah, I ended up paying. Shika and I watched the Brothers Karamazov chow down enough food to feed a small nation and with it, enough tequila to keep Jose Cuervo in business for the next ten years.

I had no idea that Ronnie spoke Russian, and he most probably didn't, but after a few shots of the mescal the two of them were singing songs from the old country and swearing eternal friendship and brotherhood and whatever else they could toast. It was bad enough with Ronnie screeching gibberish off-key, but when Andros got the other patrons, waiters, waitresses and busboys to join in, it was beyond anything I'd seen. It was a raucous fuckin' sight.

I looked over at Shika. "Don't say it! I know, you get used to it."

I was just about to turn in when my phone rang. It had to be Ronnie or Shika calling from the crash site, but it wasn't. It was Rachael.

"Cal?" She sounded frightened.

"Rachael! Where the heck are you? Are you okay? " I was so happy to hear her voice that for a moment I forgot that she had set us up.

"I don't know," she paused, "Cal, I'm so sorry about..." and then she started to bawl.

"Okay, easy now. You need to calm down and stop crying. We can figure this out," I said, trying to assuage her fears. "Where are you?"

"I'm here... in New York. I was supposed to go to London but I got scared." She sniffled a few times then added, "Cal, are you angry with me? I couldn't stand it if you were angry with me."

"Yeah, I'm mad! You could have gotten us killed, Rachael; that was a fucked-up thing to do. I dragged my buddy Ronnie into this because I trusted you and using me as a decoy wasn't cool, not after what we shared."

I could hear her crying softly and it was too much for me. I was one of those dopes who couldn't stand to see women cry. I often wished I was more like Ronnie when it came to women; his mantra was *'It's good for them to cry; it's an emotional release and it helps them cope. Also, after a good cry they want to cuddle and that leads to some good sex or they want to feed you, both good options.'* But I wasn't like him.

"Hey, stop crying. It's okay. Except for a few bruises we didn't' get hurt. Are you at the Ritz?"

"No. I'm staying at a friend's. Can you come over? Please, Cal, I know I don't deserve it but give me another chance. Please?" she asked, in a little-girl voice.

The ferrets were running wild, doing cartwheels in my head, screaming: *Don't be a moron. This broad is trouble. Run for cover. Fool me once, shame on you, fool me twice, shame on me!* But I was a sucker for a pretty face.

"Give me the address."

"I'll text it to you," she replied.

The 'ding' from my phone told me that she had sent it. It was in Armonk and that was about forty miles from where I was.

"It's going to take me an hour or so to get there. Can your friend drive you halfway so we can save some time?"

"She's not here. Sarah is in Spain with her family. I'm alone. I took a taxi to get here. I can call and Uber it if…"

"No. Just sit tight. I'll be there as soon as I can. Keep the lights off and don't open the door until I get there, okay?"

"Thank you, Cal! I feel so much better now. Please hurry and call me when you are close."

I thought about calling Shika and the Brothers Karamazov, but decided to go it solo. After all, this was *my* mountain woman and maybe we could run off together and leave this mess behind. That would have been too easy - I had no fucking idea what I was getting into.

CHAPTER 9

DANCING TO THE PIPER...

Edward Swanson was sitting in his car on the Chunnel train. He was heading from Calais to Folkestone in the UK. He had a feeling that the woman who ran the brothel in Amsterdam had recognized him, and he wasn't taking any chances. His first mistake was getting involved with Satin, but compounding this folly by rolling that idiot, Steven Chang, and snatching the attaché case was bordering on insanity.

The only reason he agreed to Satin's crazy plan was his desperate situation; he was in dire straits. He owed a considerable sum of money to a sadistic loan shark, a sum that involved far too many zeroes to be left unpaid. Satin was sure Chang's attaché case was full of diamonds or cash and it would be easy pickings. The Chinaman was one of the high rollers staying in a reserved suite and it made perfect sense that he would have a bag full of dough. At least it made sense then.

They had taken advantage of Chang's overt fascination with Satin and after a wild night of cocaine, sex and erotic games, they had tied Chang up and made off with the attaché case. It was a good thing the Chinaman called them the next morning and informed them that the attaché case was rigged with explosives because they were about to force it open. He also warned them that it belonged to the Chinese triad and they wouldn't take it too kindly if it blew up and sent them orbiting into space.

"Listen, last night was fun but this is no game. Just return the damn thing and let's party again, huh, what do you say?" Chang had pleaded.

"I don't know what you are talking about. What attaché case?" Swanson replied, denying any culpability.

"Listen to me, Eddie, there is no money in the attaché case. The only things in there are a few hard drives and a stack of papers. You have no idea who you are dealing with. Your father and his money won't save you. This is way beyond some silly game. These are fucking animals of the worst kind. I have a few thousand left; return it and I'll give it all to you. I am in as much trouble as you are… believe me, they will skin us both alive!" The man was pleading, almost begging Swanson.

"What hard drives? And why is this so fuckin' important?"

There was a long silence so Edward asked again, "Steven, why would they be so desperate to get it back?"

"It is the latest Artificial Intelligence research with the test results of the simulation and beta models. It is for the Department of Defense. The Chinese Government wants it and they are using the triad. I'm just a pawn. Listen, you don't…"

"Fuck off, Steven; don't call me. Go tug on your little puddle-maker! I don't know anything about any attaché case." And with that he hung up on the poor slob. The news wasn't what he had hoped for, but now he had to figure out how to maximize this opportunity. He would find out who would pay the most for the contents and make sure he survived the exchange.

When Swanson found Satin dead in her room, he freaked out and bolted, running as fast as he could to the only person he trusted – his sister, Rachael. He left the bag with her and that, in hindsight, was also a mistake. Now she was in danger too.

He needed the money to pay off the loan shark, so the plan was to take the attaché case to an expert he knew. Paul Kloet was an old friend and could open almost anything from locked doors and small safes to huge vaults. His claim to fame was the botched robbery of the Central Bank of Belgium in 2014 that had cost him three years in jail.

A few calls to some mutual associates and Swanson learned that Kloet had relocated to England. He contacted the Belgian only to find out that his friend had gone straight but much to his relief, the safecracker was willing to help him out for old times' sake and for some monetary compensation. Now all he needed was for Rachael to reach him the attaché case.

It was bad enough that there were a bunch of Chinese hoods looking for him but Swanson's primary concern was the loan shark. The last few messages from Ricky Di Santi weren't too pleasant. He was getting impatient and that could only mean that a visit from Big Moses was pretty imminent – and that scared the piss out of him. He had better come up with the money or he was more than likely to get his nuts clipped. The thought that he could be singing soprano in a boys' choir frightened him more than the triad did. He had watched Moses pull out a man's fingernails using a pair of pliers before he kneecapped the poor bastard with a ball-peen hammer. The screams and whimpers of that horrific event had left an indelible impression on him. Like his namesake from the Old Testament, Big Moses had a set of commandments but instead of the original Decalogue, he had only two: pay Ricky. And the second: pay Ricky now or else!

He tried calling Rachael again but got her voice mail. This was the fifth message he had left her and he was getting concerned. Unlike him, Rachael was dependable and had always been there for him. From the moment they met, the step siblings had formed a bond. At first, he had been her protector, making sure that no one hurt her, but as they got older the roles reversed and it was Rachael who took care of him. He had lost count of the number of times she had covered for him or sent him money or helped him recover after a night of binging on cocktail of booze and drugs, and how does he pay her back? He gets her involved in a scheme that could get her killed – how fucked up was that? But this was it. Once this was over, he was determined to make it up to her; he wasn't sure how, but he would figure out a way to make amends.

The drive from Folkestone to Chelmsford took longer than the two hours the GPS had originally indicated. The M20 was backed up and the M25 was only slightly better. And though it was smooth sailing once he got off the orbital and onto the A12 in Brentwood, it was late into the night when he arrived at the Swanson mansion. It was appropriately named "Eden's Harbour".

Alex Swanson, his father, had purchased the huge stone Tudor in the early '80s when he was hobnobbing with Clapton, Jagger and the rest of the British rock scene, but now it remained mostly unoccupied. John Aston, the caretaker, had been in the employ of the Swansons for over thirty-five years. He and his wife, Helga, lived in the small cottage that was located on the periphery of the 100-acre estate.

Swanson had called the caretaker the previous evening and instructed him to get the place in order. It had been a while since he had stayed at the mansion and he wondered whether they would recognize him. A lot can change in eight years.

When he pulled up to the front door, he was greeted by Aston and his wife. They looked pretty much the same, a bit older maybe, but he would have recognized them anywhere.

"It's good to see you, Master Swanson," John said, scurrying down the front steps. He was of medium height, thin and sprightly with thinning hair, high cheekbones, a square chin and a ruddy complexion.

"You look well, John, and please drop the Master Swanson bit. Call me Edward or Eddie."

"Whatever you say, Master Edward; here, let me get that," Aston said, and relieved the young man of the small, leather duffle.

Swanson bounded up the gray granite steps and hugged the woman and said, "You haven't changed at all, Helga, it must be those Nordic genes. You look younger than ever!"

She laughed and stood back. "Look at you, Edward, you're all grown up. So dashing… like your father."

Swanson liked the compliment. His father had the reputation for being a debonair playboy and the comparison bolstered his rather fragile ego. Edward was tall, about six-two, lean and looked athletic but was as uncoordinated as they came. He had avoided sports in school and instead dabbled in drugs and booze, and soon earned the reputation as the person to party with. He loved Rachael to death but her amazing looks made him the ugly duckling in the family.

"Why, thank you, Helga. I'll take that as a compliment," he replied, and put his arm around the older woman as they walked into the house. He could hear the crackling of the fireplace and welcomed the embracing warmth, a change from the clutches of autumn's enduring cold.

"I need to use the restroom," Swanson said and headed for the powder room that was adjacent to the foyer.

Once inside the bathroom, he took a long piss and then pulled out a small plastic bottle from his jacket. He tapped a little of the white powder into his palm and snorted the coke using a rolled up dollar bill.

"I needed that," he said to himself, studying his reflection in the mirror. He waited a few seconds, checked his reflection to make sure there weren't any telltale signs, before washing up and returning to the living room.

The caretaker was using a pair of bellows to stoke the fire. He looked up and smiled. "Ah, Master Edward, you look refreshed. Which room would you like to use, the master bedroom or your old room by the rear portico?"

"I'll stay in my room, but I'm starving and would like to have dinner first."

"It's ready; Helga is warming up the stew. I'll place your bag upstairs and turn down the bed. I took the liberty of selecting a bottle of Cabernet Sauvignon to go with your meal. If you would prefer something else with the lamb, I can get it from the cellar. Your father has a rather wide and eclectic selection so you can opt for anything you'd like."

"No, that won't be necessary. Your choice, like you Brits would say, is splendid."

The large, ostentatious dining table with the twelve rosewood chairs drove home the reality of his pathetic existence. He was alone once again; alone and lonely and in trouble. His family's wealth had done little to mitigate the immutable purgatory that his life had become. He was tempted to ask John and Helga to join him but remembered his father's words: *the help are just that: help. Don't blur the boundaries or make friends of them or they will lose respect for you.*

He finished dinner in silence and feigned his appreciation for the lamb stew with biscuits and mushy peas. It would have served no purpose in hurting Helga's feelings. He would have much preferred a steak with potatoes, but hungry as he was, he polished off several servings of the stew.

Once the caretaker and his wife had retired to their cottage, he moved to the living room and sat by the large ornate fireplace. He threw a few more logs onto the fire and watched the flames rising from the black metal grate licking at the fire-screen and tiled hearth, and contemplated his circumstance. He had to get the attaché case to Kloet; it was his only chance. Hopefully the contents would provide him with enough cash to pay off Di Santi. He had burned through his stipend for the year and had borrowed from friends to the point of embarrassment, and Rachael had no more money left to give him. This was it and if this failed it would be a date with Big Moses. They would come after him; there was no doubt in his mind, and the thought made his balls shrivel up and sent a shiver running down his spine. He would deal with the triad later.

He finished the bottle of Joseph Phelps 'Insignia' and chased it with a goblet of Vecchio Amaro del Capo. The bitters from the southern region of Italy helped settle his stomach and assuage the nagging worry that accompanied his every waking moment. He smoked a joint and, feeling pleasantly buzzed, decided to try Rachael again, but his sister's taped message only raised his level of concern.

"Shit! I hope she's okay," he said aloud. His concern was partly for Rachael but more so for the attaché case and himself. If they got to her, she would be forced to talk, and he might as well kill himself.

It had been a long day and he was tired – it was time to shower and turn in for the night. He stood by the bedroom window looking out over the vast, manicured estate, and though most of the topiary was covered in darkness, he felt the familiar comfort of home wash over him. He wished that Rachael could have been there. As kids, they had spent days and weeks exploring the house and the property, and playing hide-and-go-seek and other silly games. Now, Rachael was half a world away and he had thoughtlessly drawn her into his mess.

He checked his laptop for messages but there were none, and so he began scrolling through a few of his favorite porn sites with the thought of pleasuring himself. He needed to take the edge off of his frayed nerves and what better than a leisurely pull on his pleasure pud. He had an obsession with threesomes, especially when spit-roasting a woman, and it was turning into some kind of fetish. He browsed through several pages before he found what he was looking for - a pretty blonde on all fours with a cock stuffed in her mouth and a second man fucking her from behind. He unzipped his fly and pulled out his cock, and began stroking it.

"Yes, yes, fuck her mouth. Suck him, you bitch, yes, suck his cock and make him cum..." He closed his eyes trying to picture her lips around his cockhead, "Suck me, baby, yes, yes, suck me..."

But try as he might, his coochie wiggler refused to cooperate and he remained flaccid. He closed his eyes and tried reliving his recent real-life threesome with Satin and Steven Chan – she had him in her mouth while Chang had pumped her from the rear. He began to respond, his pecker twitching and showing signs of life but then the image of her lying lifeless in her own puke came rushing back and put an abrupt end to his fantasy.

The embellished moans and groans and sordid images on his laptop failed to resuscitate his intransigent passion, and instead he was filled with a despondent revulsion. He stared blankly at the screen and after a few minutes, slammed the laptop shut. He zipped up, grinding his teeth and blamed his dysfunction on being too tired and too preoccupied. Without thinking, he rolled another joint, lit up, and inhaled deeply.

"This is some good fucking shit," he said as he held the smoke in his lungs, and it wasn't long before his worries began to fade.

He would deal with it all tomorrow. Mañana: it was his anthem; things always looked brighter in the light of day.

The scraping of a chair on the mosaic floor jarred Swanson awake. He sat bolt upright and was about to scream when he felt the cold edge of the blade pressed against his neck.

"Shhh, don't make a sound. I would hate for Goran to slit your throat," said the man who was seated by the bed. His voice had a velvety, smooth quality to it; a soft caressing tenor.

Swanson could feel his heart thudding against his ribcage while a million thoughts raced through his sleep-addled brain. Was this Ricky Di Santi's men or the triad? How did they know where to find him? And how did they get into the mansion? He had locked the front door and checked the windows and all the other doors, making sure that they were secured. He had also locked the door to his bedroom, so how the fuck did they get in? And what of John and Helga, were they okay or had they been compromised, or worse? Could it be that they were in on this? Not many people knew about the family's vacation home in Chelmsford so it had to be John or – and his heart lurched – or could it be Rachael? He shut that blasphemous thought out and looked around him.

In the muted golden halo of the table lamp, he identified a total of four men in the room. The man with the knife to his throat, Goran, was tall and lean, sporting a scruffy week-old growth that covered his angular face. His dark, piercing eyes were unblinking and cold. The other two, who were standing by the window, were similar in size and appearance – these were tough men, hardened by war or circumstance, who wouldn't think twice of ending his life. All three were dressed in black paramilitary outfits. However, the man seated by the bed was the anomaly; he was a good-looking East Asian dressed in a white cashmere suit and a light pink, silk shirt. He had lit a cigarette and was eyeing Swanson with studied indifference.

"You know why we are here, so let's set aside the pleasantries and get straight to the point; where is the bag you stole, Edward?"

The man's accent was a subtle Anglicized American, possibly an English transplant now living in the US.

"How the fuck should I know? Some slant-eyed wogs grabbed it from me in Amster..." Swanson started, but that was as far as he got.

The blow to his solar plexus drove the breath out from him and had him doubled over, and gasping for air. He was pulled upright by his hair and made to face the suit.

"Let's try this again. Where is the bag?" The man asked in the same emotionless, silky-smooth voice.

"I... I can't bre... I can't breathe," Swanson gasped, fighting for air.

He was struggling to get his breath back when Goran struck him again, this time with the heel of his hand. The blow to the temple was strategic and precise, and knocked the smaller man unconscious.

"What about the caretaker and his wife?" Goran asked the suit.

"Are they up?"

"No, Damir is still by the cottage. They are fast asleep."

"Let them be." The man nodded towards Swanson. "Get him into the car and take him to Adam's place. Leave a note on the dining table. Something like 'I've gone to London' and sign it with an ES. Run the shower for a bit, wet the towels, pee in the toilet but don't flush and leave the bed undone. The rich are messy by nature; lazy and messy. Lock all the doors and windows except the front door. Wipe the place down and get rid of anything suspicious. And don't forget to get his bag, phone and the laptop. I'll meet you there."

The three men sprang into action while the suit casually put out his cigarette, walked down the stairs and as quietly as he had arrived, disappeared into the night.

CHAPTER 10

MAKING LIKE MCQUEEN...

On my twentieth birthday, my mother handed me the keys to my dad's Ford Mustang 390 GT. Though I had gotten my license when I was seventeen, she didn't trust me with the car and I didn't blame her. I would most probably have wrapped it around a pole trying to impress the chicks. It was the same exact model that Steve McQueen drove in Bullitt even down to the Highland green. It was my father's pride and joy and he often said it would be mine one day. I remember dashing over to Ronnie's place and taking Jenny and him for a ride. I had asked Dylan if he wanted to join us, but he declined muttering something about not having a death wish. He was predictably dejected and unhappy even though he had no interest in the car - he just resented the fact that Dad had wanted me to have it.

My beat-up old Grand Cherokee was my everyday ride but I decided to take the Mustang to rescue the damsel in distress. Rachael would be impressed; at least, I hoped she would and if we had to run from the bad guys, this baby would give us a leg up.

Her friends obviously swam in the very deep end of the pool. The place was the fuckin' Taj Mahal with manicured everything, including the damn trees that were perfectly coiffed. The cobblestone driveway was wider than the I-10 in LA and snaked past tennis courts, a swimming pool and a miniature golf course, and led to a huge stone, 5-tier Tulip fountain located in the front of the mansion. The architecture and the lighting that colored the jet streams and waterfall would have given the Bellagio in Vegas a run for its money. Yup, these people certainly weren't living on Spam or struggling to make the rent.

I had tried calling her when I got off the exit to Bedford Road but she didn't answer, and that had trouble written all over it, and when I saw the black SUV race past me in the opposite direction, my worst fears were confirmed. I caught a glimpse of Rachael's blonde hair in the back seat and spun the Mustang around, tires screeching, rubber burning and barely missing the outer skirt of the fountain - it was McQueen all over again except I wasn't as cool and the bad guy driving the SUV was probably a pro.

I came close to losing them several times as we raced along poorly lit backroads and dark narrow alleyways that curved through quaint little New England towns, but I managed to keep them in sight. Though I had the advantage of driving a muscle car, the dude in the SUV was good, a lot better than me, and as hard as I tried to channel my inner McQueen, I couldn't seem to catch up. He must have also been related to Andros because one-way streets, stop signs and red-lights meant nothing. The only thing missing was that godawful Russian music.

It was like a fuckin' movie. I had several close calls, barely missing an oncoming car once and jumping the curb another time, giving an old man walking his dog a heart attack. If that pooch didn't want to take a shit before, he certainly did after his near-death experience. I looked in the rearview mirror and saw the man waving his fist at me – a feisty old bastard. But it was late and the traffic in the towns, for most part, was light. I was gaining on him when he cut across oncoming traffic to a crescendo of blaring horns and got onto the interstate.

I-95 heading north is always busy and it was just outside Stamford that I lost sight of him. I had to admit, the guy was slick. He used the eighteen wheelers for cover and weaved his way ahead, merging into the ubiquitous stream of cars, trucks, pick-ups and SUVs. I was about to give up when I hit the jackpot, or maybe it was more like a blind squirrel finding a nut - lady luck, that fickle bitch, threw me a bone in the form of a traffic jam. The highway was gridlocked near a town called Westport, jammed tighter than a virgin's thighs on prom night.

I parked the Mustang on the off ramp at Exit 17 and had walked about a hundred yards or so, scanning the vehicles, when I spotted a commotion in the back seat of a Chevy Blazer – it was Rachael and she was struggling to get out. I ran towards them and when the guy in front passenger side stepped out, gun drawn so, without thinking, I fired a shot in his direction. I'm pretty good with a pistol and my goal was to scare him but it didn't work. He fired back and I felt the susurrant tickle as the bullet whizzed past my head. Damn, the fuckin' son-of-a-bitch! He was actually trying to kill me. I was about to let him have it when I caught sight of Rachael running towards me. She was being chased by a second bum who was gaining on her, so I shot him and saw him stagger. He caught himself and headed back towards his buddy.

There was a volley of gunfire from the SUV, forcing me to duck behind a large van. I fired back, blindly, and wondered where the fuckin' police were? With all the cell phones around, I would have thought the National Guard would have been here. I mean, granted this was close to New York and there's some serious gang violence there, but it wasn't every day that you had the gunfight at O.K. Corral taking place on the I-95!

I inched my way towards where I had last seen Rachael, staying low and using the cars for cover, and found her huddled behind the wheels of a semi, her face pale and her eyes as wide as saucers.

"Quick, my car is parked on the ramp. It's the green

Mustang; get in and wait for me," I yelled at her over another hail of bullets and pushed her towards the exit.

The sound of sirens blaring in the distance must have spooked the bastards. The driver rammed the car to his left and forced his way onto the shoulder. I saw them drive away and it didn't take a rocket scientist to figure out that it was time to hightail it out of Dodge. I ran back to my car and we took off down the exit, hung a left at the light, and headed into the town.

"God! That was crazy! You are amazing!" she said, leaning over and giving me a kiss. Her face was flushed from the danger and excitement.

"Later, girl; we're not out of the woods yet." I checked the rearview mirror and saw headlights racing towards us and was about to floor it, but it wasn't them. It was a cop car and I was certain we were going to get stopped but he went by me, glanced at the Mustang or maybe it was the broad, and kept going.

"Are they looking for us?" Rachael asked.

"I doubt it. Not too many 390GTs around so he'd have stopped us if we were on his radar."

"It's a beautiful car. Is it yours?"

"Naw, I rented it from Hertz. You can get them for 39.99 a day," I replied.

She let out a soft giggle, "You're so full of it, Cal, but you *are* my knight in white armor. Thank you for saving me."

"Do you know who they were?"

"No. They were Asian; maybe Chinese… it was hard to tell. They were speaking English."

"You mean they all look the same to you?" I was kidding but she looked like someone had slapped her.

"No, they don't all look the same to me. It was dark and the man in the back was trying to rape me. He spoke English and told the others to drive to a deserted place so they could take turns with me. That's when they saw you give chase."

"I was kidding, but I guess the triad is not kidding and they want the bag back. How many in the car?"

"Three - there were three of them; the guy in the back was the leader."

She was quiet. I could see that the abduction had rattled her and she was debating whether to come clean with me. So far it had been all innuendo and cloak and dagger stuff – this was her first direct experience with the bad guys and it had frightened her. The degrees of separation had vanished and she was face to face with her predicament.

I drove around until I found a quiet spot near the Saugatuck train station and parked in the shadows. I cut the engine and turned the lights off and said, "Let's stay low for a while. Give things a chance to cool off. We need to come up with a plan. You need to return the attaché case; you realize that, don't you?"

"I can't. I have to get it to Eddie. If he doesn't get it, they are going to hurt him."

"Who's going to hurt him?"

"That's the scary part. He doesn't know. It could be the triad or someone else… Eddie thinks it might even be the CIA," she replied.

"What's in the bag, Rachael? If you want me to help you, you have to tell me what these dangerous types are after. I could get killed, so no more secrets."

She was quiet and then looked at me and said, "All I know is that it has something to do with artificial intelligence. It is the next generation of AI that will make everything we have now obsolete. Steven Chang stole it from a small company contracted by the DOD. That's all I know. I swear… I really didn't want to know any more. I tried to talk Eddie into giving it back but he needs the money. He needs a lot of money to pay off his gambling debts, so he's going to try and sell the contents to the highest bidder. It's risky but it's his only chance."

"Wait, your family is the one of the wealthiest in the US and he has to steal a bag that could get him and you killed? That doesn't make sense."

"My father has pretty much disowned Eddie and I have no more money to give him. I don't even have the balance of the fifty grand I owe you!"

I looked at her shocked. It was Salvador and Mike doing their thing – except they were pounding on my fucking jaw! What the heck am I doing? Am I that desperate for attention from a pretty gal that I would risk life and limb? Rhetorical questions, these, no need for answers. I know I'm an idiot.

I guess she sensed my 'welcome-to-the-light' moment and said, "I will pay you in full as soon as I get my stipend. I promise, Cal, I will sell my apartment if I have to but I *will* pay you."

She had grabbed hold of my arm and the look on her face melted my heart. There was no way I could say no to her – it was that Samson and Delilah syndrome all over again.

She leaned closer to me, "Eddie is in Chelmsford and once I reach him the attaché case, I'll be done with all this; I'll be free." She paused, and seeing that I wasn't about to respond, asked, "Will you come with me to England? Please, Cal, I'll do anything you want me to, just help me with this. Please say you will? Please…"

The voice in my head was now banging on my temples, ricocheting through my cerebellum: *Don't do this, dude, this is trouble and no matter how beautiful she is, it means nothing if you're dead!*

"Sure, why not. I've always wanted to see Buckingham Palace and Madame Tussauds… I hear they have a wax statue of Elvis which is pretty amazing. And, I think we'll have a bit of fun before we get whacked by the triad or the freakin' CIA and end up in the Kensal Green Cemetery!"

"Why the Kensal Green?"

"It sounds nice and I hear there are some fine folk buried there. Sure beats the heck out of a sewer in the Bronx!"

She was quiet for a moment, looking down at her hands, lost in thought. I was about to ask her if she was okay when she leaned across the center console, grabbed the back of my head and pulled me towards her and kissed me. She pushed her tongue into my mouth and tasted sweet, like minty licorice, and we spent the next several minutes lost in a desperate tongue-wrestling contest before she broke free.

"Put your seat back," she instructed, breathless, her voice soft and husky, and I felt her fingers tugging at the zipper of my trousers.

"Rachael, let's wait…"

"Shhh. This is not for you; it's for me."

She drew me out and sucked me into the warmth of her mouth, her tongue swirling around the ridge of my cockhead, sending jolts of pleasure shooting through my body. She knew exactly what she was doing and the effect it was having on me.

This was a throwback to my teenage fantasies jerking off to images of Grace Kelly, Marilyn Monroe or some random Penthouse centerfold, imagining them suckling on my cock. It was an adolescence reminiscent of Portnoy's Complaint, Philip Roth's ground breaking story about a teenager who jerked off to every imaginable thing, except, unlike Portnoy, I had no religious hang-ups.

I tried sitting up to get a better look, but she pushed me back and whispered, "Just lie back and enjoy it."

Her hair formed a shimmering, golden veil around her face as she bobbed up and down over my crotch, sucking for all she was worth. The soft mewling sounds and moans that accompanied her salacious oral manipulation sent me to another place, and I knew that the pleasure-riddled torture wouldn't or rather, couldn't last. I tried to distract myself by thinking about the Chinese triad, the CIA and even dancing blue monkeys but none of it worked. All too soon I felt my orgasm build, I moved her hair out of the way so I could watch those luscious lips wrapped around me and that's all it took.

"Rachael, oh God, baby, don't stop, don't… I'm cumming! I'm cumming!" And with that, I thrust my hips upwards and pumped my juices down her throat. I could feel her sucking and swallowing almost as quickly as the jets of cum filled her mouth until there was nothing left.

She kept nursing on me long after I was done, her fingers stroking my shaft, coaxing the last drops out and whisking them away with the tip of her tongue. After what seemed like an eternity, she looked up at me with those baby blues, dark with passion, opened her mouth and said with a sigh, "All gone, baby!"

I was basking in the aftermath of my climax when she sat back, closed her eyes and taking my hand in hers, murmured, "You taste divine. I want to do that again tonight."

If I had wanted her before, I now knew that I would do anything to keep her. And, if it meant going into a den of badass Philistines, then so be it.

CHAPTER 11

IN THE DEN OF PHILISTINES...

When Edward Swanson opened his eyes, he found himself tied to a chair in the basement of a strange house. A single overhead incandescent bulb shed just enough light for him to realize that he wasn't alone. There were two dogs, Dobermanns, sitting motionless just beyond the ambient arc and studying him, their eyes unwavering and glowing ghoulishly in the semi-darkness. He struggled against the bonds, trying to relieve the numbness in his hands but to no avail. The bastards, whoever they were, knew what they were doing.

He felt groggy like he had been drugged, and shook his head in an attempt to clear the fog and get his bearings. He could hear footsteps walking on the floor above accompanied by the indiscernible voices of a man and woman engaged in a vociferous argument. After a few back-and-forth exchanges, the woman screamed obscenities and he heard a door being slammed shut followed by footsteps coming down the stairs into the basement. The dogs hadn't moved a muscle – they remained frozen, never taking their eyes off of him.

She was tall and slim with auburn hair cut short and a friendly face, nothing remarkable, except for her hazel eyes; they were large and wideset, speckled with blue and amber.

"I see you're awake. I'm sorry they treated you badly, Edward, but you've gotten yourself in quite a pickle." Her voice was soft and melodic.

"Where am I? And who are you?"

"It doesn't matter who I am or where you are. What matters most is that you give them what they want. They will be here shortly and the last time it took me a week to clean up the mess... blood, poop and piss everywhere. I seem to end up with the short end of the stick, so do us both a favor and just give them what they want."

Swanson was frightened, but like most of the privileged he had a defiant streak bred into him from a life of getting what he wanted and doing as he pleased.

"I don't have it. I don't even know where it is and even if I did know, I wouldn't be telling you or anyone else. Do you know who Alex Swanson is? If you think you will get away with this, you had better think again. My father will hire the best men and make sure that every single one of you is held accountable. You will pay, all of you. Your fuckin' basement will be filled with…"

"Tsk, tsk, tsk, Edward, Edward, you don't have to be like that," she cut him off. "You're being reactive and a bit delusional. Your father couldn't care less. He thinks you're a loser and I do think you are overestimating your importance. After all, you are a drug addict with a gambling habit; do you really think anyone would care if you were to disappear?"

He didn't answer but sat staring sullenly at her. He was such a fool to think he could get away with this. She was right – no one would care. Rachael would shed a few tears but other than her, no one gave a shit, least of all his father.

Getting no response from her captive, the woman continued. "Right now, I'm the only friend you have, so it would be wise to listen to me. The men coming here are a bunch of animals. They are from the mountains in Serbia or Croatia or some godforsaken place like that; at least that's what I've been told. Believe me, I've dealt with nasty boys my entire life but these men fall into a category that is all their own. Once they get here, it's out of my hands, so think about what I said."

Swanson didn't answer. He had been frightened before but now her matter-of-fact demeanor and the memory of the assailants who had grabbed him from his house only heightened his fear.

"Let me make a few calls. Maybe I can trace the bag…" he started, when she interrupted him again.

"See, that's more like it. We've tried calling your sister but she's not responding, gone AWOL like you yanks like to say. I hear the two of you are very close, so maybe she will respond to you."

The snapping sound of the switchblade startled him.

"My, you're a jumpy lad, aren't you? Relax, I'm going to cut you free now so don't make any sudden moves. Remain seated when you make the call. Any effort to escape will be disastrous. Crosby and Nash will attack, and tear you to pieces. I mean literally – they *will* tear you to pieces."

She went behind the chair and cut the ropes that bound his ankles and wrists. He caught a whiff of perfume, a subtle potpourri reminding him of a rose garden, an allegorical surprise considering his current situation. He was rolling his wrists and clenching his fists when she stepped in front of him.

"I think you should take a look at this. It will help with your presentation and ability to convince your sister or whoever has the attaché case." She handed him a cell phone and instructed, "Hit play."

What he saw made him shudder. Steven Chang was naked and bound and strung up by his arms from a hook in the ceiling. His face was a bloody mess and his body was covered in cigarette burns. He was babbling in non sequitur, pleading and begging for his life when a man wearing a full-face ski mask and wielding a chainsaw appeared on the screen. Chang's expression changed to unmitigated terror and he lost control of his bodily functions. His screams fell on deaf ears when the man began cutting him from his ankles up. The urine and feces trailing down his legs mixed with the blood, flesh and bone created a gruesome sight and by the time the man got to the thighs, Chang's head lay lifeless against his chest – he was either dead or had mercifully passed out.

The grating sound of the chainsaw cutting through flesh and bone and the grisly visual of blood and gore splattering all over were far more horrifying than anything Swanson had witnessed or ever imagined. Though he wanted to look away, he couldn't - the bizarre compulsion in the human psyche that finds fascination in the macabre kept him focused on the video. He watched the grotesque charade to the end and felt sick to his stomach. He dropped the phone and puked, and kept retching even when there was nothing left.

When he was done, she lifted him up from the floor and helped him back onto the chair.

"Now do you believe me, Edward? These are not your usual run-of-the-mill criminals." She paused and studied Swanson with a look of compassion before adding, "Steven Chang was an addict – he gambled way too much, liked his drugs and he indulged in kinky sex. But he didn't deserve that. He was an innocuous little fellow, quite charming really. Your actions are the reason that he died in such an awful manner. So unless you are into some medieval, masochistic bullshit, you had better convince your sister to deliver the bag here and soon."

She backed away and instructed the frightened man, "Sit still until I get back."

She was midway up the stairs when she stopped and said, "There's a mop and bucket in the far corner and water in the sink – clean up your mess. Go on, I'll make sure the boys behave and don't make a meal of you."

She waited by the Dobermanns while he cleaned up the vomit. "Make sure it's thoroughly cleaned. We don't want to agitate the boys."

He wasn't sure if she was referring to the dogs or the men who were to arrive soon but it didn't matter; he was in a state of psychological disrepair. His fingers were trembling while he mopped up the smelly, regurgitated stew and peas and used paper towels to make sure the cement floor was spotless. He kept scrubbing the floor over and over, his mind numb, until she stopped him.

"That's fine, Edward, you can stop now. You did a brilliant job. I may have to recommend you for the janitorial duties around here!" she laughed and added, her tone turning serious, "Sit and wait until I return. Don't make any sudden moves. I'll get your phone so you can call your sister."

Rachael and I spent the night at a low-cost motel run by a very nice Indian fellow named Freddy Patel. The name was a bit peculiar, but he explained that Americans found Pradeep, his real name, too difficult to pronounce; so to makes things simpler, he changed his name. I guess it made sense from a business perspective - as a people, we Americans prefer simplicity and Freddy was a lot easier to pronounce than Pradeep. I'd say that was a smart move on his part and may explain why the Indians are such successful businessmen.

We were both tired and went to sleep almost immediately and it was well past 9:00 AM when I woke up. While taking a shower, I heard a cell phone ring. It had to be Rachael's because mine was turned off. She let it ring for a while before she answered. I couldn't hear much but I heard her getting agitated so I turned off the water, grabbed a towel and walked into the bedroom.

"Are you okay? Did they hurt you?" she asked and gave me a quick glance, covered the phone and whispered, "Edward."

I got a bit closer and heard a male voice on the other end, prattling quickly and sounding desperate, but couldn't make out what he was saying and then it went silent before a woman spoke. Rachael quickly put it on speakerphone.

"Your brother is unharmed and as well as can be expected. Listen to me carefully, Rachael; these are not men you mess around with. Return the bag and you might save his life and yours. I say might because that is not a given. If you need a bit more convincing I can share a video of what was done to Steven Chang, but you're a smart lass and I'm sure you know how a chainsaw works."

Rachael swallowed, her face turning pale, "Please don't hurt him. I'm in New York and need a bit of time to get the bag and get to London. The big question is how? The attaché case is wired with explosives so how do I get on the plane with it?"

"You can hand it over to an associate of mine in the US, which would be the most expedient way to handle this."

"And how do I know for sure that Edward would be safe?" Rachael asked. This girl was no dummy.

"You wouldn't. You would have to trust me."

I shook my head and whispered softly, emphatically, "No!"

"That's not happening," Rachael said, countering the woman. "I have to be sure and the only way is to arrange an exchange. I give you the bag and you let my brother go. Why don't you come to the US with Edward and we can handle the exchange here?"

"First, I set the rules and we are not coming to the US. Second, who told you that the bag was wired with explosives?" the woman asked.

"Chang told my brother."

"And that is why Chang is dead. He was trying to scare your brother. The case has a modified lock and is not easy to open, but there are no explosives. Listen carefully; we will get the bag one way or the other. It is only a question of time. But the people I'm dealing with are getting impatient so if you care about your brother's welfare, get me the fucking bag!" The last bit was a hiss.

"Don't hurt him, please. I'll return the briefcase to you, I promise... I just need a bit of time."

I motioned to Rachael with 4 fingers and mouthed a silent, "Four days."

"I'll need four days, that's all I need," Rachael pleaded when the phone went silent. The woman had obviously hit the mute button.

After a few seconds she was back on the phone, "You have two days. You will receive your instruction via text. I'm also sending you a link so you can watch Steven's last few moments on earth. It is pretty convincing and I might add, revolting. And, Rachael, please don't get imaginative and stupid. If you talk to the police or any of the authorities, your brother will be mailed to you in bits and pieces. And that is a promise."

With that, the call ended. Rachael began sobbing. I sat down next to her and tried to console her, "He's alive and our job is to get him out unharmed but you need to hold it together. Where is the attaché case?"

She sniffled into my chest a few times and then answered, "In my apartment."

"In your apartment?" I was shocked. "How come the Chinese didn't find it?"

"It's not very big so I slit open a large throw pillow and slipped it in and made sure there was stuffing around it before stitching the pillow back again. There are several pillows lying by the bed and they all look pretty much the same so I guess they didn't figure it could be out there in the open."

"Are you sure it is still there?"

She nodded, "Yes, I checked before leaving for Sarah's place."

"That was smart. Okay, we need to act fast. Let's get the attaché case first and talk to Shika. She will know people in London who can help us make the exchange so no one gets killed."

"I know people in London too," she offered, trying to be helpful.

"Not those kind of people. I mean the dangerous kind."

I called Shika but it was Andros who answered. "Cal, where you disappear? We are worried. We try calling but you do not answer. Don't do like this, little brother, or Andros will have to kick your ass."

I wasn't in the mood for his nonsense and got straight to the point, my tone a bit brusque, "Hey, Andros, let me talk to Shika. It's important."

"You speak to Andros. Why you not like me anymore? Show Andros some love, huh?"

I was about to scream at him but thought better of it. "I'm with Rachael and we have to go to London to return the briefcase. I need to talk…"

"London?" he interrupted, "Andros like London. I have many friends there. You come here and we will make plans. Don't worry and tell Rachael not to worry - everything will be fine. Come here and we take care of things. You hurry."

The phone went dead and inexplicably, I felt better. Something about Russian's tone and manner made me feel like everything would be okay. Now that was a bit worrisome.

I looked at Rachael. "That was Andros. He's a friend… he's Shika's man. I'll explain everything on the way. You need to get ready."

She came over, put her arms around my neck and gave me a kiss. Not a peck on the cheek but a hot, suck-on-the-tongue kiss and I responded. Her hand snaked down between us and pulled the towel away, her fingers wrapping around the throbbing member pressing into her.

"Baby, we don't have time, let's save it for later…" I started but didn't sound very convincing.

"I need this," she said in a throaty whisper and began making her way down.

I wanted to stop her, knowing that this wasn't the time, but I couldn't. I closed my eyes and let nature take its course and waited for the blissful moments of oblivion to wash over me.

CHAPTER 12

THE HUMMINGBIRD'S TRAIL...

The Water's Edge Bar and Grill was a small popular dive near the harbor in San Diego. It was known for its ginormous burgers and fish sandwiches and for being relatively affordable. The decor was '70s retro with a convivial ambiance, pretty waitresses and a juke box playing soft rock. They catered to a healthy mix of tourists and locals.

Jason Polashock, the owner, was also the bartender, and Big John McCray, his buddy, made sure things didn't get too unruly. Big John had been a football player in college and a celebrity on the professional wrestling circuit before the rigors of that profession sent him into early retirement.

It was late on a Tuesday night – a little past 2 AM, which would make it (technically) early Wednesday morning – and except for the four men seated in the corner, the rest of the crowd had left. They were tough men, lean and hard, with dark penetrating eyes and scary dispositions… the types you left well alone. They had arrived a little after 10 PM, ordered burgers and fries and sat in the corner, huddled together, conversing in a foreign language that neither Jason nor Big John understood. They had also been drinking steadily through the evening.

"We're closing up, boys; it's time to call it a night," Jason said to the men while clearing plates and glasses from an adjacent table. The waitresses had all left for the night.

"Last round; we do one more round," the man seated in the corner chair facing the bar said in a harsh, staccato tone that affects most Central Europeans. "Four more, Smirnoff."

He was in his early thirties with wavy brown hair combed back and an unshaven face. His eyes were dark bordering on obsidian, and his aquiline nose gave him a swarthy, hawk-like appearance. He was the oldest of the lot, and seemed to be their leader.

"Come on, man, I have to shut the bar down; it's the law. I can get you some snacks or soft drinks if you like," Jason said, trying to be reasonable.

"Fuck your law and fuck your food. It tastes like shit! Bring one more round. Do it now," the man countered, his tone turning confrontational.

Big John was helping clear the tables at the other end of the room and overheard the man's demands. The surly attitude was an obvious sign of trouble.

"You heard the man, we're closing up. Finish your drinks and be on your way." There was no mistaking the intent or implied threat in the bouncer's deep rumbling voice.

He had moved closer towards the men and was a fearsome sight, standing well over six feet with a shaved head, a long beard and dark, bushy eyebrows. His thick chest, huge arms and powerful legs were testament to his physical puissance. If he were dressed in a bear-skin, he would resemble his Gaelic forefathers from the hilly coastline of Scotland. His sheer presence was intimidating.

The two men whose backs were turned shifted their chairs so now they were all facing the bouncer. The man in the corner was the one who spoke. He gave the big man a steady look and said in Croatian.

"Fucking asshole! Florijan, you need to teach this big monkey a lesson."

The man named Florijan smiled and got up without any hesitation, and walked up to Big John. He was as tall and almost as big as the bouncer but leaner.

He addressed the big man in English, his voice low and harsh, "You bring the drinks or I cut your fucking heart out and feed it to my dog!"

There was an edge to the man, a cold, hard edge that comes with supreme confidence. He showed absolutely no fear on his face or his demeanor. The flattened bridge and scars over his eyebrows and jawline validated a life of violence and were worn as badges of honor. Big

John knew that this was no false bravado; this was more trouble than he had anticipated but backing down wasn't in his DNA. He was about to respond when his boss intervened.

"Hey, hey, no need for all that. One last round, okay?" Jason said getting in between the two men. "It's alright, John, one more round for our friends. It is not a problem."

Jason Polashock wasn't a small man but he looked diminutive standing between the two giants.

"Whatever you say," the bouncer said and gave the man a parting glance before going back to what he had been doing.

"Fucking pussy! I make you my bitch." Florijan hissed in English, his eyes boring through Big John.

"Hey, man, I don't want any trouble. I'll get your drinks, okay, no problems," Jason said, sounding amicable and trying to placate the man.

He was smart enough to realize that these men were different and Big John didn't have a chance, but his friend wasn't one to yield, and the last thing he wanted was for anyone to get hurt. Not to mention the potential damage to his establishment and having to deal with the insurance company and the law - headaches he didn't need. Things were just getting back to normal and he wanted to keep it that way but the big Croat wasn't having any of it. He pushed Jason aside and made a move towards the bouncer when the man in the corner called out to him in English.

"It is okay, Florijan, come back. We don't make trouble tonight."

Florijan stopped midstride, smirked in the direction of Big John and returned to the table. The men reverted back to their native tongue; the buzz of their conversation was interspersed with laughter and backslapping and disparaging looks cast in the bouncer's direction.

When Jason brought the men their drinks there was a momentary lull in the conversation. He placed the glasses on the table and said, "This one's on the house."

The men, ignored him, raised their glasses and toasted in unison, "Živjeli!", then threw back the drinks in a single gulp and slammed the glasses on the table top.

True to their word, they squared up their tab, paying in cash, and ambled towards the exit; that was when Florijan broke away and walked over to the bar, "You are lucky man, John, very lucky. Now my dog will go hungry."

He waited for a response, but the bouncer held his tongue. The Croat grabbed a handful of peanuts from a bowl before joining the others. He said something to them and they all laughed as they headed out into the night.

Once the men had left, Jason locked the door and jammed the deadbolt home, "That was fucking scary! Those boys are trouble with a capital fucking T."

"You should've let me handle that dude. That would have settled…"

The bartender interrupted his friend, "John, you know I love you like a brother and would bet on you against almost anyone; but not those boys. There was something creepy about those motherfuckers."

There was a moment's silence, an agonizing moment, when both men struggled with the truth of what had transpired. It wasn't often that someone could intimidate Big John; in fact it had never happened before, but Jason had recognized the subtle change in his friend's demeanor, a hesitancy which had led him to intervene.

And deep in his heart, in a place where self-deception is trumped by the truth, the bouncer was just as relieved that the men were gone. Thirty eight was too old to be taking on four hard cases like them. His reflexes weren't what they used to be and his knees were shot from years of abuse and punishment. His addiction to painkillers and opioids certainly wouldn't help him in a fight with the likes of Florijan.

"Fuck them! Let's close up. I need to get some sleep," was the terse reply and both men went about clearing the tables and cleaning up.

The Croatians, having arrived late, had parked at the far end of the parking lot and were still joking and exchanging playful barbs when they caught sight of the woman. They fell silent and came to choreographed halt. They studied the woman, and then strolled casually closer to the van before stopping again.

"Fuck, what do we have here?" the leader, Bogdan Ivanović, said.

Standing with her back against the side of the Ford Transit was a tall, slender oriental woman dressed in a loose fitting, full-length gown, the white satiny robe a stark contrast against the dark navy blue of the vehicle. Her hair was a black, velvet blanket surrounding her face, and her dark eyes shimmered in the dim fluorescence of the parking lot. She was beautiful, a delicate apparition, altogether incongruent with the surroundings.

"She must be a fucking whore looking for some late night action," Florijan suggested, leering at the woman.

"Well, the cunt has come to the right place and the right time. I need something new tonight. Boleslav's ass is rubbing my cock raw!"

"That's because you fuck like a rabbit," Boleslav replied, his quip met with muted laughter.

The men were captivated by the vision in white, by the strangeness of her and her apparent lack of concern.

Bogdan Ivanović was the first to address her. He spoke in English, "Who are you? You speak English?"

The woman said nothing. She remained motionless with a slight smile playing on her lips. She looked at them, not at anyone in particular but collectively; a wolf studying a flock of sheep.

He tried again, "You speak English, yes? What is it you want?"

She remained silent watching them, unmoving

except for the wisps of hair that fluttered across her face, ruffled by the Ocean's breeze.

"Hey, maybe she is Chang's bitch?" Boleslav chirped, facetiously, laughing at his own attempt at humor. He was young and good looking and naïve.

"No. This cunt needs a real cock like my ten inch bushmaster not that little pickle Chang had hanging between his legs," Florijan retorted and began rubbing his crotch in a lewd and suggestive manner.

"Your snake is going to have to wait until she tastes my dragon from the mountains of Zadar," another man chimed in.

The woman continued to smile neither ignoring nor acknowledging the vulgar exchanges.

"You want to fuckee, fuckee?" Boleslav asked in English making the lewd sign with his fingers.

"Okay, enough of this shit. Grab her. We can fuck her in the van," Bogdan said and made a move towards the woman.

Their judgment had been impaired by too much alcohol or they might have questioned the presence of a beautiful woman, alone, in a deserted parking lot at 2 AM. Or maybe it was their overconfidence that was their undoing but it was too late when they saw the flash of the katana blade. The rest was a blur, the thousand arms of Kali slicing and slashing, twirling and twisting, floating effortlessly from man to man until all was still again.

The Hummingbird wiped the blade clean and picked up the chainsaw. Her work wasn't quite done.

Jason Polashock was in the process of closing out the cash register, tallying up the receipts, when the grating sound of a chainsaw made him look up from his laptop. *Who the fuck was cutting logs at this ungodly hour?* Each night, before going home, he rationalized the sales numbers while Big John sorted out the tips jar and placed each waitress's share in an envelope. It was a force of habit for both men.

The bouncer came around the bar, "Did you hear that? It's gotta be those fucking assholes. This time they're gonna get it!"

He drew his handgun, a Glock 17, from his waistband and headed for the front door. He was determined to make amends and set right the earlier confrontation. No more backing off and no more hesitation – this time he would settle it, bad knees and all.

"Wait, John, use the back door. They may be waiting out front," Jason said and retrieving a shotgun from under the counter, followed the big man out.

The two men walked by the bouncer's pick-up truck parked in the rear, rounded the corner and cautiously made their way along the side of the building to the main parking lot. They could see the van and hear the sputtering of the chainsaw but the rest was cloaked in darkness. As they inched slowly forward, the silhou-ette of the bodies lying motionless came into view. Once the initial shock and surprise had worn off, Big John hurried over to assess the extent of the carnage while Jason stayed behind. He scanned the fencing and trees that bordered the lot, taking his time to make sure that there was no one secreted in the shadows. The trees provided perfect cover for an ambush and he was not about to let someone surprise them. The confrontation with those foreign men had him on edge.

"What's up, John? What's going on there?" Jason called out impatiently.

"Call the cops," Big John said stepping back from the dead bodies. "Damn! Whoever did this did a number on them."

There was no trace of the perpetrators. No footprints, no fingerprints, nothing except the grisly sight of four men with their throats slashed and Florijan, the big man, sawn in half, his chilling demise evidenced by the sputtering, blood-soaked chainsaw.

CHAPTER 13

D-DAY AT HEATHROW...

The flight to Heathrow Airport was a fucking nightmare. The seats in coach weren't designed for tall men; add to it the kid behind me and you had a flight from hell. The banging and kicking on the backrest started almost as soon as we reached cruising altitude and was pretty much non-stop. I swear that kid must have been related to the Energizer Bunny! And through it all, the father sat there with a smug expression on his face and said nothing, not one word. He seemed totally engrossed in whatever he was reading on his Kindle and each time I'd turn around he'd look at me with that "what are you going to do, he's a kid" smile and go back to his book.

About three hours into the flight and I'd had enough; I was ready to strangle the fucking bunny. I stood up into the aisle, leaned over the kid and grabbed the deadbeat father hoping he'd say something so I could smack that grin off his face but, he didn't.

"One more kick to my backrest and you'll need to see a dentist when we land. You hear me? Just one more and you will regret it for the rest of your miserable, fucking life!"

I let him go and turned to the kid and snarled, "You kick that backrest one more time and I'll beat the shit out of your dad, I'll send him to the fucking hospital and then I'll strangle you with the seatbelt, get it?"

The kid started bawling and of course, it's Murphy's Law, just then the flight attendant turns up. "Is something wrong?"

"Yes, this man just…" the father started when karma stepped in. The plane lurched and dipped as it went through a pocket of turbulence, and flung the attendant against me.

I grabbed hold of her and smiled, Sir Galahad and a damsel in distress. "Hey, we've got to stop meeting like this."

She was a young gal and had no idea what to do, so she stepped away using the adjacent backrest to keep her balance, blushed and with a look of chagrin said, "Sir, you need to sit down and put your seatbelt on. Now!"

And with a final look of indignation, she walked away, ignoring the petulant father and the crying bunny. Damn, whatever happened to the friendly skies! I noticed the father admonishing his boy and returned to my seat. I wasn't about to beat up the father or hurt the kid – I'm not that kind of guy. I closed my eyes and hoped for the best.

And, what do you know? No more kicking the back-rest. I don't blame the kid, he was bored, but it is up to the parent to make sure he behaves and has something to keep him occupied.

I began nodding off and in that semi-somnolence, I thought about my father. One of his underlying precepts was to respect others. If this had been him, the very first time I kicked the backrest intentionally, he would have made me apologize. If I did it again, I'd get a look, yes that "don't make me smack you" look. And if that didn't work, trust me; I'd be busy rubbing my butt for the rest of the flight. My parents didn't give a hoot about Child Protective Services etc. etc. They believed in *not* sparing the rod, and a good thing or I'd be wearing pin stripes and playing hide and go seek with Bubba and LeRoy in some fucking joint in Alabama.

What young boys and girls need is discipline and boundaries and that's what's missing these days. But I'm not a parent so what the fuck do I know?

Why am I flying to Heathrow alone? It was part of *the* Master Plan as Andros called it. Actually, he called it "Andros D-Day Master Plan" – it sounded hilarious in his Russian accent but I guess you had to be there. The plan was simple. Ronnie and I would take an earlier flight and wait for Rachael, Shika and him. Their flight would arrive two or so hours after ours which would give us enough time to scout the Arrivals Hall. Shika and Andros would be met by his 'comrades' while Rachael would follow the instructions the woman had sent her.

She was to go to the passenger pick-up zone outside and look for Edward. He would be standing by a green Range Rover with a guy that looked like Godzilla. She was to hand her suitcase over to the muscle-head and get into the back seat. Once the contents of the attaché case had been verified, Edward and she would be set free.

The Andros Master Plan was for Shika and him to wait near the Range Rover and grab Edward during the exchange and along with Rachael get the heck out of Dodge. His 'comrades' would make sure that the shit didn't hit the proverbial ceiling and if things did go south, they would provide cover for the getaway. Seemed simple enough, right? Not!

So where was Ronnie? I'm surprised you have to ask because by now you should have guessed. He got bumped up to First Class by the gal at the counter who also gave him her number. I used the kiosk but then I'm not Ronnie Griffith. It was one of life's ironies: the little guy sits in the big seat enjoying the perks of upper class while the big bloke gets scrunched into the little seat with a manic kid kicking a hole in his back! But who said life was fair? Not me, brother, I grew up knowing life was a freakin' prankster and all you can do is to grin and bear it.

Once I cleared Immigration and Customs, I wandered through the arrivals hall with a coffee in hand channeling my inner Holmes, by that I mean Sherlock Holmes and not the big-dick porn star John C. Holmes; though, as a teen, I had often wondered what it would be like to walk around with a 14-inch bazooka concealed in my pants. Hey, don't blame me, it's the American culture; boys are obsessed with two things - the size of their penises and the size of women's boobies. That's just how it is.

I was about to invest in a delicious-looking walnut scone with strawberry jam and clotted cream when I caught sight of Ronnie, and there he was, seated at a table with a bevy of pretty girls chatting them up. We ignored each other on the outside chance that the Chinese thugs who tried to abduct Rachael, or their associates, were there and put two and two together – it was all part of the Andros D-day Plan. I think I said this before; this cloak and dagger stuff strains my brain and gives me a fuckin' headache but Andros was in charge and I was just playing along.

About an hour and forty minutes later I caught sight of Rachael and she looked simply amazing – hard to believe that she had been in a plane for eight hours. She looked like she stepped out of Vogue magazine and I'm not sure how she managed that because I looked like shit. My new navy jacket and gray chinos were crumpled, the bristles on my face were itching and my briefs were sweaty, making me wish I'd gone commando. I had a flashback to De La Milano and Bongo and the possibility of our common ancestry made me shudder at the thought. I guess good genetics and traveling in first class makes up for a lot because every man with a tickle of testosterone, and within fifty feet of her, had their tongues hanging out.

I noticed a chubby Asian dude dressed in all black with a bright yellow jacket hovering close by, behind Rachael. He had a rolled up newspaper in one hand and seemed as nervous as a mouse in a snake pit. After several quick glances around, he made his move and went straight for the suitcase. The ensuing struggle was short and frantic before Mr. Bumblebee wrenched the bag free, turned and made a beeline for the exit with the casters on the suitcase squealing like a pig being grilled alive.

"Stop him! He's got my bag!" Rachael screamed, chasing after the man but she was handicapped by the six-inch stilettos.

The little bumblebee was running as fast as his stumpy little legs could carry him but he didn't get too far, fifteen yards at best when he ran smack into Salvador. The straight left to the man's chin laid him out, stark cold, and that's when all hell broke loose.

It was the storming of Normandy all over again – Operation Overload played out at an airport in London a lifetime later. The Chinese, Russians, Brits and Airport Security, and a bunch of unknowns were shooting at each other and at anything that was perceived to be a threat. And I thought there were no guns in England! Wrong!

It was chaos, total bedlam, with people screaming and dropping to the floor for safety while some folk ran, pushing and shoving, heading for the exits, and others scrambling helter-skelter in every which way possible.

And through this madness I caught a glimpse of Andros and Shika with Rachael. Andros had a gun in hand and Shika was following close behind, leading Rachael away.

I was crouched low looking in their direction, feeling a sense of relief that Rachael was safe, when I heard, "Psst!"

I looked down and saw the pudgy little bumblebee smiling up at me with the rolled up newspaper pointed at my belly. It was odd and comical and made me smile but the next thing I heard was a "zzztt" and felt the prongs of the Taser hit me in the chest. I was jerking and shaking uncontrollably, like Elvis on Red Bull, as the zillions of volts coursed through me when a whack to the back of my head turned out the lights.

When I came to, I was scrunched up in the trunk of a car. So there you have it, you're all caught up now; but hold on, there's more and if you want to take a break, now would be the time because it gets really crazy from here.

It took a while for the cobwebs to clear, leaving me with a throbbing headache. I thought my head was going to explode but the events that led to this predicament came seeping back, frame by frame, ever so slowly. Rachael and the bumblebee, Shika and Andros, bullets flying all over and the Taser; the fucking Taser! He wasn't a bumblebee after all, but a Chinese yellow jacket and it stung like a motherfucker. So this had to be the triad and I recalled Shika's warning: *"They want you alive and trust me, Cal, it's better to bite on the pill before they get to you."*

Though that should have concerned me, it didn't. What I was concerned about was the way my knees were pressing into my face; it was unnatural, and what I could have used were a couple of aspirin with a shot of bourbon. Make that two shots of bourbon, a whiskey and a keg of beer.

It was about two hours before the car came to a halt. I heard the windows roll down and a voice ask in a clipped accent, "Where's the Yank?"

"Dead," the driver replied.

"Maggie's not going to like that."

"I know but it was fucked up right from the get-go. We caught another one though... a big motherfucker. He's in the boot."

"Leave him in there. Maggie's waiting so you'd better get your story straight."

The quantum of time is often distorted by circumstance. I think that was Einstein's theory in a nutshell. Take my predicament for instance. The additional thirty or so minutes that I lay bent-up and twisted like a contortionist seemed to drag on forever while I contemplated the irony of my situation. I had always wanted more than just being a foreman in a small machine shop. I dreamt of running with the bulls in Pamplona and climbing the

Matterhorn or setting out on the many other adventures my father described. I wanted to be Hemmingway and Jeremiah Johnson, the famous mountain man, rolled into one. And that's when Rachael Swanson walked in and things went into overdrive – crazy overdrive. Now I was in England trapped in the trunk of a car with my knees playing diddly-do with my chin.

I was dozing off to sleep when I was unceremoniously dragged out and stood up. There were four of them, three men and a woman, standing in an arc. The men were a scruffy looking bunch, two that were average height and the third a big dude with a John L. Sullivan mustache. Behind the group, near a structure that looked like a barn, was a man with a dog, a big fucking beast of an animal. I'm not an aficionado of dogs but this mutt was bigger than Rico and just as scary.

The woman was tall and slim and plain, but her eyes were spectacular. They were the lightest brown speckled with blue and amber – unfathomable pools of intrigue. Ah yes, I have a thing for eyes, the windows to your soul and all that.

"And who are you?" the woman asked. Her voice was surprisingly friendly.

"My name is Caleb Montague. What am I doing here and what do you want with me?" I stretched my arms and rolled my neck to get some feeling back.

One of the smaller thugs, a short stocky bulldog with an abrasive attitude, gave me poke in the ribs and hissed, "We'll do the questioning, asshole!"

He didn't pronounce it as 'asshole but rather, 'arse-hole', which struck me as rather peculiar; what the heck is an arsehole? I know what it is – it's another of those rhetorical questions.

My legs were still a bit cramped and the love pat was all it took to send me stumbling against the car. It was a Bentley, a shiny, new one at that and I certainly didn't want to put a dent in it.

She said to the man, "Get his wallet and his phone."

I started to reach inside my jacket when he grabbed my hand, "Stay still or I'll crush your fuckin' nuts."

Neanderthals speak the same language no matter what the accent. I stood still while he fumbled inside the coat pocket and retrieved both items and handed them to the woman. She rifled through the wallet first and found a dog-eared photograph.

She studied it for a while, "Your father?"

"Yes."

"He's a handsome man," she commented, putting the photograph back.

"So what the fuck happened to you?" the irascible bulldog next to me quipped.

"You happened… ugly is contagious," I quipped back and noticed the big fella smiling through his handlebar mustache. But little thug didn't have a sense of humor and dug an elbow into my gut. He nicked my liver and that doubled me over.

"Enough," the woman commanded and the pug backed off.

There was a short silence while she scanned my driver's license.

"Well, Caleb, you are not very photogenic." She handed me my wallet back and continued, "If I saw you in a pub, I'd say to myself, now there's a handsome lad. That is, after a few pints."

The men laughed and big one slapped my back like we were old buddies. Granted, the mugshot on my driver's license wasn't very flattering, but then I wasn't posing for GQ and it wasn't like these four would win any beauty contests either, but I kept my mouth shut. Liver shots are not particularly pleasant; in fact, they are downright nasty and I wasn't about to give that little monkey another excuse to play the Marquis de Sade.

Next she checked my phone and I was thankful that Andros had the foresight to get us all new phones with new sim cards. He had insisted we leave our old phones behind on the outside chance that someone got a hold of one and connected us through our call history.

"How do you know Rachael Swanson?" the woman asked, handing the phone back to me.

"Who? What are you talking about?" I sounded and looked surprised, a performance that Robert De Niro would've been proud of. I hadn't called Rachael on my new phone so I knew this broad was taking a stab, a shot in the dark.

"Don't play games with me; you know exactly who I'm talking about. She's the one you helped… the pretty one."

"Oh, you mean the dame in the purple dress. She was a doll. I wasn't the only one ogling her. I don't know who she is… just that she's a looker. I see this little Asian dude, dressed up like a bumblebee, attacking her and I went to help her. That's all I know. I swear it. I didn't expect World War III to break out."

She studied me for a long time, long enough to make me uncomfortable, but I held her gaze making sure not to waver.

"So, you've never met her or talked to her before? Careful, Caleb, if I find out that you are lying, the consequence will be dire. There are degrees of pain that my boys can inflict – pain like you have never imagined."

Now that didn't sound good but I continued with my take on De Niro and gave her my best 'honest, ma'am, I'm just a country bumpkin' look.

"I don't know her, never met her or talked to her. I'm here on vacation. Ever since I was a kid I've wanted to see the Buckingham Palace, walk down Carnaby Street and have a few beers in one of your pubs. That's all I'm here for. I'm a foreman at a machine shop in New York… business being what it is, COVID and all, I decided to take a trip. You can check this out."

"I'm going to make a few calls. Take him to the back and make sure he doesn't get away. Whoever was behind this, shot Janis, John and Richard," she paused, and took a breath before continuing, "Janis and John are dead. They also nabbed the suitcase. Without Edward or his sister, we have nothing."

"Where's Edward?"

"He's dead. No one's sure who shot him. It could have been an accident considering the clusterfuck this turned out to be."

"Where's Richard?" It was the big man who asked. He had moved and was standing behind me.

"We've got him in a safe house. Dr. Raymore is taking care of him. You had better be telling me the truth, Caleb Montague," she said, giving me a quick look before walking back towards the large stone cottage that must have been the primary residence.

The obnoxious guy followed the woman and the remaining two led me down a narrow flagstone walkway to a small, dark toolshed in the back, away from the large cottage. It was damp and cold and my legs felt like Jello. I stumbled a few times but the big man steadied me.

"Easy there, Yank."

Once inside, they tied me to a cast-iron garden chair, making sure I was properly secured. These boys had done this a few times because there was no way I was wriggling free.

"Any chance I could get something to eat?" I asked.

"Let's see what Maggie has in mind. If everything is cool, we'll feed you and you can be on your way; go see Buckingham Palace and say hello to the queen." He was about the same height as me but he had me by about twenty pounds and none of it was fat.

"How about a drink of water then? My throat's dry."

"Sure." The big bloke motioned to the smaller man, "Get him a glass of water."

He studied me for a few seconds and asked, "So you're from New York, eh?"

"Yeah, the city that never sleeps."

"I'm Gordon Aitkens."

"Caleb Montague, but you know that. My buddies call me Cal."

"And my mates call me Gordy. Pleased to meet you Cal, and I only wish it was under different circumstances. You know, have a pint or two and bother the ladies. You look like an interesting bloke so I'm hoping I don't have to work you over."

"I'll second that, brother!"

The smaller man returned with the water and held it to my mouth.

"This here is David. He's proper gentry, this lad; he graduated from Oxford and all but don't let that fool you. He's a mean cunt, you know, one of those ninja types." He made some awkward, chopping motions with his arms.

I finished the glass of water and said, "Thanks, David, and just so you don't go all Kung Fu on me, I hate violence and I hurt easy."

"Gordy's exaggerating. I took a few lessons in Brazilian jujitsu and learned a few chokeholds. I'm not Royce Gracie by any stretch of the imagination." He paused and then asked, "Is New York as..."

The rasping creak of the door interrupted the conversation, and in walked Maggie and a new man.

This wasn't the pugnacious bulldog who was with her earlier. This guy was different - tall and lean with a face that was cut from stone. His eyes were dark and emotionless. He looked menacing, scary menacing, not the kind you want to meet in a dark alley.

The mood in the room went south in a hurry – the convivial nature a minute before was now cold and impersonal. Maggie was the one who spoke.

"I made a few calls and it seems that you're not telling me everything. You do work in a small machine shop and you are from New York but you also know Rachael Swanson, so why the lie?"

"I'm not lying! I have no idea who she is and whoever told you that I know her is either lying or misinformed," I replied, sounding as earnest as I could. Apart from the people closet to me, no one knew about Rachael and me so I was pretty sure she was playing devil's advocate.

She studied me again and after what seemed like forever, she said, "I guess we'll need to find out for sure."

She turned and walked towards the door, stopped and said to the scary one, "Goran, find out what he knows."

And with that she left. This wasn't going to go well for me. Even if I were free, I doubt I could've taken Gordy or this dude, and then there was David with his chokeholds – I would have bet against me.

"Close the door," Goran growled, sounding like Arnold Schwarzenegger except his voice was a couple of octaves lower.

David closed the door and stood there with a pained expression on his face. Gordy had stepped back to give the monster from Transylvania a bit of room. The scary dude didn't say a word and I didn't see it coming; the punch was short and fast. I felt my head jerk back and tasted the blood in my mouth. Ouch!

"How do you know Rachael Swanson?"

I shook my head and squinted, "You hit like a pussy. I don't know any Rachael Swan…"

Whack! It was his left. He knew what he was doing, just hard enough so I wouldn't pass out. I saw stars and exploding lights together with jumbled geometric patterns before I opened my eyes again.

"How do you know Rachael Swanson?" He sounded like the Terminator, and believe me, if it weren't for the current state of affairs, I would have seen some humor in this.

I spat out blood and offered, "You don't listen too good. I don't know any…"

Whack! This time the blow was to my ribs. Shit! That hurt like a son-of-a-bitch. Ouch, ouch!

"How do you know Rachael Swanson?"

"I told you, I don't…" I groaned, but that's not what he wanted to hear.

Whack, whack! Ouch, ouch, ouch ten times over!

"Okay, okay, I give! I'm married to her," I said, spitting out more blood.

"You're funny man."

Whack, grunt, whack, whack, grunt, whack, whack, whack.

"I swear I have no idea…" I stuttered through split lips.

There were many more whacks followed by the same question, "How do you know Rachael Swanson?"

This sadistic charade went on for a while, I'm not sure for how long because I lost track of time. I passed out a few times and he brought me back with buckets of ice cold water. After a while your mind goes numb, and I know it's hard to comprehend but you don't feel a thing.

At one point I asked my tormentor, "What do you want me to say? I'll say it. Yes, yes, Rachael Swanson and I are friends. We went to school together… is that good?"

And then through the fog I heard Gordy, "Hey, that's enough. He doesn't know her and banging on his head is not going to change the story."

"For tough man you have soft heart, like little girl. Not good for this business," Goran retorted, his breathing heavy from the exertion of rearranging my face. "Maybe you should be in caregiving business, eh? Like nurse… carry shit and piss from room to room and smile at all sick assholes."

"Fuck you, you Albanian cunt, you're a fucking animal. He doesn't know her and beating on him any further is not going get you anything!"

"You are ignorant. I am not Albanian, I'm Serbian. Bring me hammer," he instructed David, "I make this fucker talk."

Gordy shoved the Serbian back, "I said, that is enough!"

The squeal of the rusted hinges interrupted what promised to be an interesting distraction. The two men backed away from each other. It was Maggie and this time she had a good looking Asian man with her. He was wearing an ivory silk suit with a light blue shirt and a mauve cravat. A fucking dandy if there ever was one, and these are the ones you have to watch out for – they never get their hands dirty but have men like Goran do their dirty work.

She asked, "Anything?"

"No. He doesn't know her. There's nothing to beat out of him," Gordy answered matter-of-factly.

The man in the white suit walked over to me, lifted my face by the chin and said, "So Americano, what do you think about the hospitality at the Lamb's Head Farm?" It was rhetorical and I knew better than to answer. He studied my face before turning to Goran and chuckled, "Tsk, tsk, tsk, you are losing your edge, Goran, he looks way too good!"

Goran spat and walked closer to where I was seated.

"I don't know for sure. Maybe he's hard man. There are few, not many, they are hard to break. I can use hammer but I don't think he know her," Goran said, turning away from me.

"No, there's no need for that," Maggie said.

So at the least there was a certain satisfaction knowing that I'm one of the few nuts that are hard to crack, though the hammer bit had me wondering: would I have held out? I doubt it. As things stand, I may require some serious reconstructive surgery but that's okay - that was also the general consensus among my buddies.

"What do we do now?" Gordy asked.

"He's a bloody liability. We need to get rid of him and find the attaché case. That's the priority," the white suit commented.

"Take him into the woods and finish it," Maggie said nonchalantly like she was swatting a fly.

Just like that? And that too, after my Oscar winning performance! That's just not fair. I wasn't in any state to protest but could sense that Gordy wasn't into this.

"He doesn't know her!" he exclaimed, "Let's drop him off somewhere in town. He's a Yank and we don't need the…"

"What is the matter with you, Gordy? He's beaten to a pulp. We let him go and he's headed for a hospital and that means the coppers and then what do you think will happen? Abducted from the airport, held against his will, tortured, and add to this the fact that he knows what we all look like. I swear you are getting soft in the head. Take him into the woods and finish it."

It was hard speaking with a mouthful of blood but I had to try, "Wait! I won't say…"

"I do it," Goran said, cutting off my protest, "I take care of this motherfucker."

Now, I don't have too many people on my shit list but this retard was slowly but surely making his way to the top.

"No. You go and meet with Adam and take Gavin with you. We need to find the attaché case and he will know what to do next. Gordy, Damir and Paddy can take care of it," the woman commanded. She looked over at the young man who was by the door and said, "David, we are taking a short trip. You're driving."

The white suit gave me a final look before he followed Maggie and David out.

"You are lucky, Mr. American, very lucky. I would use hammer. First toes, then knees and end at balls. Make you sing like Sinatra." The Serb grabbed my hair and shook my head before turning to Gordy, "I will send Damir. He make sure so you don't fuck it up. You can dig the hole and watch. That is something you are good at."

"Go fuck yourself, Goran, you're a sick, fucking cunt and one of these days you and I are going to settle it," Gordy growled and waited for a response, but the Serb refused to take the bait and walked away. I don't blame him. In a fistfight, my money's on Gordy.

When the door squealed shut, the big Englishman came over and said, "I'm sorry, mate, but I'll make sure it's quick."

He cut me free and handed me a rag; I guess he figured I wasn't going anywhere in my condition. And while I gingerly dabbed my face, I thought about my dad and my mom, of Shika and Andros, and Ronnie, and of all people, my brother Dylan.

CHAPTER 14

ADONIS ON THE RUN...

Ronnie Griffith had watched the man in the yellow jacket snatch the suitcase and run, and was about to give chase when he saw Caleb deck the little guy and that's when things went nuts. The first sound of gunfire that reverberated through the Arrivals Hall was met with disbelief, and a moment later, sheer panic. People were screaming and scrambling for cover, running helter-skelter, leaving luggage and bags strewn all over the place.

Once he had recovered from the initial shock, Ronnie jumped into action. He pushed the table over, yelling at the three ladies seated across from him, "Down! Get down and stay down!"

In his peripheral vision, he caught a glimpse of Andros, Shika and Rachael making their way towards the exit and turned his attention to where he last saw Caleb, but there was no sign of his buddy.

"Shit! Where the fuck did he go? And where's the suit-case?" He looked around, but both Cal and the suitcase were gone. *Cal must have grabbed it,* he thought to himself.

He waited, crouched down behind the table until things had settled down and the place was crawling with uniformed ARP (Armed Response Personnel) – Britain's version of SWAT.

"You gals stay here and don't move until the cops clear the place," he said, and got up.

He was going to call Shika and try and arrange a rendezvous somewhere safe, hopefully before he was detained and questioned by some over-enthusiastic law-enforcement officer. He was navigating his way towards the far end of the terminal when he spotted the bumblebee heading into the men's room. The man was dragging Rachael's suitcase behind him. *What do we have here? And where's Cal?*

The restroom was deserted except for an older guy taking a leak. He was tall and thin, and was wearing a blue, short-sleeved shirt over khakis.

The man turned and said, "Can you believe that shit? It was fucking Hamburger Hill out there! I was about to wet my pants when some bearded asshole pushed me down behind a barricade. This is the last time I listen to my wife. Let's go to England, she says, it will be nice, she says, get away from…"

The bumblebee ignored him and walked into a toilet stall, maneuvering the suitcase into the cramped space, and was about to shut the door when it flew back, slamming into him. The impact knocked him backwards and he had a look of surprise when Ronnie stepped in and cracked him with a quick left-right combination. He followed that with a hard right to the bumblebee's jaw and eased the unconscious man onto the toilet seat and propped him upright.

Ronnie gave the old coot a hard look to make sure he didn't pose a threat. "Beat it, old timer. Now! Get the fuck out!"

"Hey, take it easy. I'm gone…" the petrified tourist at the urinal exclaimed. He zipped up, hands shaking, and rushed out as fast as he could.

The suitcase was locked so Ronnie placed one edge against the bathroom wall and kicked the opposite corner as hard as he could. He heard a cracking sound and checked it, and saw some give at the bezel. A few more strategically placed kicks and the hinges in the back broke away from the polycarbonate shell. He wrestled it open, rummaged through Rachael's clothing and got the attaché case out.

"Okay, so far so good. Now, I need to locate Cal."

He heard a soft groan and noticed that the bumblebee was just coming to, eyes blinking, and attempting to stand up.

"Unh-ah, not so fast, little man!"

Ronnie went back into the toilet stall and hit him again. "Go to sleep, Irene, its nappy-nap time!"

The man's head bounced off the back wall and lolled cataleptically to the side. A quick wipe down of the suitcase with a tank top and Ronnie left the men's room. He hurried back to where he had left his duffle bag behind the overturned table. The ladies were gone but his bag was still there. He slung it over his shoulder and sauntered casually towards where he had seen Andros, Shika and Rachael.

He was almost at the exit when a voice in a distinct, no-nonsense tone commanded, "Hold it right there."

The man, a stocky fellow in military fatigues armed with a semi-automatic approached him cautiously. "Let me see some ID. Take it slow, mate, and don't do anything silly."

"No problems, sir," Ronnie answered, handing over his passport, "It was crazy and I was sure this was it. Can you..."

"What are you doing in the UK, Mr. Griffith?"

"I'm here for some R and R and a bit of business," Ronnie answered.

The man looked at him carefully and asked, "Are you in the film business?"

"I wish but I can't sing or dance and my acting isn't much better." Ronnie smiled before adding, "I'm in computer sales, boring but necessary."

"With your looks I'd give the movies a try. Half the blokes can't act anyway so what's the difference." He handed the passport back to Ronnie and pointing to the duffle asked, "What's in the bag?"

"Clothes, toiletry... you can take a look if you'd like."

"No, that's fine. And, what do you have in the briefcase?"

"Work stuff. Papers, hard drives, stuff I'm working on."

The man studied Ronnie, and satisfied with what he saw, said, "Alright then, go out and take a right, there's a shuttle that will take you to the other terminals. You can get a taxi or take the underground into London."

"The underground?"

"Yes, the train… I think you Yanks call it the subway. You don't have much luggage so the underground would be the cheapest way to go. Get off at Terminal 2 or 3 and buy an Oyster card; it will save you a few pennies." And with that the cop walked away.

Ronnie tried Cal but got no response so he tried Shika again and got her voice mail. He left her a message and boarded the coach, and decided to find a hotel close to the airport. He would lay low until he could reach either Shika or Cal and figure out what the contingency plan was. The Andros Master Plan was now defunct and it was the time for improvisation.

When the shuttle stopped at Terminal 2, most of the passengers disembarked and Ronnie couldn't believe what he was looking at: there he was, the bumblebee, sitting at the front of the coach, face swollen, looking at him with a crooked smile.

The man waved to Ronnie and said, "Hello, Yank. Going somewhere?"

CHAPTER 15

A DATE WITH DEATH...

I had this surreal feeling as we trudged across a small meadow, plush and green, and moist underfoot. I couldn't believe that this would be the end of my journey and I had yet to do all those things I had wanted to do. My bucket list had literally nothing checked off but it dawned on me, an epiphany of sorts, that the things I thought I wanted to do were the things my father had done; I had been so busy trying to be like him that I didn't know what it was that I *really* wanted to do. Now, that's a mouthful of thoughts but that, my friends, was a rude awakening. Who the fuck was I? Caleb Montague? Thirty-two, clueless and about to die – heck, that was a rather depressing realization.

I'll say this for Dylan; he didn't try to be like anyone else. He had no heroes and he rarely listened to Dad's stories and when he did, he usually rolled his eyes in disbelief. He was a peculiar young boy and grew to be an even more peculiar man. But he was his own man. There was no getting around the fact that he was an unmitigated asshole but he was an original - a fucking I-don't-care-what-you-think original. And Rachael, what about Rachael? Did I really love her or was it all about tapping that luscious pussy? I didn't really know her and for all I know, she could be using me as bait for some Chinese gangsters or worse, those CIA types. Well, it didn't matter anymore; I was done and I guess I should be thankful that I got to experience some incredible stuff in my rather short and crazy life.

We were pretty deep in the woods when they stopped. Damir was a lot like Goran, maybe not as big or scary, but with very similar personality characteristics. Paddy was the one who had walked behind me. One look at the muscles under the rolled up sleeves and you knew this guy was strong as an ox.

According to Gordy, Paddy could bench five hundred and fifty pounds. That's a lot of weight to be bench pressing, and if true, it was impressive. But experience has taught me that speed beats power and timing trumps both speed and power so he didn't worry me as much as Gordy or Damir. I wasn't going down without a fight; I was going to have to suck it up and make a play but I would have to wait for the right time. Like I said, timing is everything.

Damir tossed me the shovel and said, "Dig!"

I stumbled a bit when leaning over to pick it up, and Gordy ran interference. "He can't dig, he is too messed up, mate. We'll be here all day if he digs – why don't you dig?"

"Not me, I don't do that shit. I will kill the motherfucker but I don't dig holes," was the Serb's terse reply. He lit a cigarette, and taking a deep drag, blew the smoke up in the air.

"Well, I'm not digging." Gordy spat back, "Let's pick straws, what do you say?"

"Fuck your straw! I'm not breaking back for this dead bastard."

"Hey, you cunts, stop bickering like two old biddies. I'll dig. Give me the fucking shovel," Paddy retorted and grabbed the shovel from me and began digging.

This was working out better than I had expected. I was going to wait until he was pretty much in the hole before I decked Damir and then would deal with Gordy and with some luck would still be standing to take on Paddy. It wasn't much of a plan but it was the best I could come up with. Who was I kidding? It would be a fucking miracle if I could deck a one-legged, arthritic octogenarian in my condition.

When the trench was about three feet deep, Paddy stopped and was in the process of getting out when Gordy said, "That's not deep enough. The animals will dig him out."

"Let them. Who the fuck cares," the muscle man riposted. He was covered in sweat and his muscles were gleaming in the diffused light streaming through the branches and leaves.

"You want someone strolling by here to see a half-eaten body and report it? There are kids and hunters out here all the time."

Paddy was silent for a few moments, giving it some thought before asking, "Okay, how deep then?"

"A little deeper… maybe another meter or so would be safer."

"Shit! You're buying me dinner!" Paddy said, and began digging again.

We watched in silence as Paddy dug for a few more minutes, maybe five or so. I could sense Damir's impatience. He tossed the half-finished cigarette and stepped on it.

"Stop, that is deep enough. We put stones on top and it will be fine," he said and drew his pistol.

"Yeah, I agree, let's get this over with," Paddy said, tossing the shovel over the edge and climbing out of the shallow grave.

"Okay then. Give the bloke a chance to make his peace," Gordy intervened again, stepping between Damir and me. "Do you need a moment to pray, Caleb?"

It seemed unreal. *Is this it? I wasn't particularly religious but now was the time to tell the man upstairs that I wished I had been a better person…* I was about to kneel when I caught a movement in the shadows behind the men. There was a whisper of feet, the hushed trampling of leaves, and the next thing I saw was Damir's head flying through the air.

What the fuck!

The shadow was an ethereal blur in black, twirling and spinning, seemingly floating on air, feet barely touching the ground in what can be best described as poetry in motion. Though that sounds contradictory, it's not. There is poetry even in violence. I don't mean the coward sneaking up under the cloak of darkness and unloading his pistol into the back of his nemesis, but the warrior who stands his ground when facing insurmountable odds even when it means death. There is beauty in that – sometimes tragically so.

I was mesmerized by Damir's head. His eyes blinked a few times while the horror of his condition registered on his face. No, this isn't some concocted BS, he actually blinked at me! It was fuckin' freaky!

The next thing I saw was the katana blade slashing across the muscleman's belly, slicing him open, and with a seamless pirouette she drove the blade through Paddy's heart. The speed and ferocity and effortless brutality seemed to transcend the boundaries of time and space. It was as though there were several of her moving in tandem. He let out a groan, his face a picture of disbelief and surprise, before falling backwards into the hole he had dug. *Talk about poetic justice!*

Now it was just Gordy and me. The Englishman hadn't moved. He stood staring at Damir's headless body twitching near his feet; the shock and astonishment were etched in Gordy's wide-eyed stare.

There was a flash as the sunlight reflected off the blood-mottled blade, and the woman was about to strike again when I shouted, "No! Please! Please don't kill him."

She hesitated and stopped in mid-motion, the sword's edge resting firmly against Gordy's neck. The woman stood still, eerily still; the bloody tableau vivant played out to the symphony of birds chirping noisily among the trees.

The image of the tattoo on Shika's arm flashed through my mind – *Kali!*

"Please don't kill him… he's a friend," I pleaded. I'm not sure why I said that because it was possible that I was next but Gordy was the decent sort and deserved better.

"Take your gun out and toss it to the ground, and any other weapons you may have," the woman instructed in perfect English but with a strange accent. It was her enunciation; it was almost like French.

Gordy did as he was told. She flicked the gun away from the Englishman with the tip of her foot.

"Sit," she instructed and watched Gordy drop to the ground before turning to me, "Are you alright?"

"I'm okay," I mumbled, "a bit messed up but I'll live. Who are you? And how did you know I was here?"

"It's not important who I am. It is important that you get your friends to return the attaché case to me; as to how I knew about Maggie Walcott and her shenanigans, that is none of your business. You should be thankful that I did decide to intervene."

"I think Damir and Paddy would disagree but thank you, mysterious stranger," I replied, partly tongue in cheek and partly from the overwhelming relief I felt. If she had meant to kill me, I would have been dead already.

"You don't move," she commanded Gordy in a soft but firm voice, then said to me, "Sit, so I can take a look."

She came over and examined the damage. Up close I could sense that there was something different about her, something mystical with a strong yet delicate aura.

Her skin was golden and her eyes wideset and slightly sloped. She had small dainty features and a heart-shaped face. She was an exotic beauty, the kind you see on postcards and book covers and in dreams. Her black hair fell forward and tickled my neck while she continued to gently palpate the bones around my face. I was intoxicated by her scent, a muted synthesis of rose and lavender and sandalwood with hints of cherry blossom that had me drifting off to some sunny island far away. This had to be a dream.

She pressed her fingers against the side near my left temple and I winced, "Ouch! That hurts." The pain snapped me out of my reverie and back to reality.

"Your orbital bone is fractured but other than that you will be fine. You will need a decongestant and maybe some antibiotics but it should heal on its own. You have good bones, Caleb."

"And you, you have 'good' everything, Madam X," I quipped back.

"Madam X? Do you even know what Madam X was about?"

"No. I'm not as smart as I…"

She interrupted, "It is a story about a wife and mother who was mistreated by her husband for her indiscretions. It has no bearing on our situation."

"So what do I call you?"

"You can call me Jade," she offered and looked into my eyes. Did I tell you that she was fucking gorgeous? What about Rachael, you ask… Rachael who?

"Hey, you two lovebirds can fly away together but what about me? And what happens when Maggie gets back?" Gordy cut in.

"You be quiet," Jade said to Gordy and then to me, "You should have let me cut his head off. He would have shot you."

"Maybe but he's a good guy; trust me, I know stuff like that."

"You don't and that's why you are in this predicament." She looked at Gordy, "I will take his word that you are a decent man. You need to get away. Maggie and her men will not survive this. They will pay for what they did to Steven Chang."

Gordy didn't say anything but sat still, studying her. "Can I get up?"

"Yes."

He rose slowly to his feet and hesitated before picking up his gun, a Glock 17, and said, "I had nothing to do with what happened to Chang and I don't think Maggie could control Bogdan or Florijan or the others even if she tried. They were a pack of wild dogs and did whatever they pleased." He paused before adding, "Now I know how they died... it was you."

She didn't acknowledge the accusation; instead stated, "You are guilty by association."

Gordy didn't reply. He stood still for a moment before walking over to the shallow pit and studied Paddy. The brawny body was contorted oddly in death. It was bizarre – disturbingly so; Paddy had been digging a hole one minute and in the next, he was lying dead in the very same hole he had dug.

He turned away and said, "Goran was right about one thing – this is not the business for me. I have a sister in Glasgow and I think it's time for a long overdue visit."

He gave Damir's body a final look and came towards me extending his hand, "Thank you for saving my hide, Cal. I doubt we'll be seeing each other again but if we do, it will be my privilege to buy you a few pints."

"I'll hold you to that. Life is strange and you just never know," I replied while we shook hands.

He took a few steps, then stopped and turned back towards Jade. "I have no idea who you are, lady, and I don't want to know but I have never seen anything like this and it frightens the piss out of me."

With that he disappeared into the woods away from the cottage, and despite my words I knew I wouldn't see him again. I felt a strange tug at my heartstrings; Gordy was the kind of guy you could share some laughs with... a mate, as the Brits would say.

I turned to the mysterious lady in black. "What now?"

She was studying me, her expression, inscrutable. "Why do you like him?"

"I don't know... you meet some people and you just hit it off. He's one of those. It's an energy thing, you know, kindred spirits, karma and stuff."

"Karma?" she asked with a smile.

"Yes. Take you and me – a Japanese woman in an English forest with an American. I mean what are the chances?"

"Chinese," she corrected.

"Chinese?" I was confused, not really sure what she meant.

"I am Chinese not Japanese."

"Oh, sorry… you all look the same to me," I said and when I smiled, it hurt like a son-of-a-bitch.

She noticed my grimace. "Let us go. We will go to my cottage and I will tend to your injuries. A few tablets of ibuprofen and some rest is what you need now. And you should learn to be more polite. Chinese and Japanese may look alike to the foreign eye but we are not the same."

"Sorry, I was trying to be funny."

"It is funny when both parties find humor in it," she said in that soft, enticing voice, "but I am not offended. I just wanted you to know where I am from."

She took my hand and led me through the forest. It was amazing, the way she moved, silently, gliding catlike, while I plodded behind her making more noise than a water buffalo trampling through the thicket.

I felt intrinsically connected to this woman, something I couldn't explain, and for the first time since my father passed away, I felt like I was home. I know it makes no sense but in some strange way, our lives were intertwined and cemented by fate. Predestination, karma, and other existential angst weren't things I normally wrestled with but maybe there is something to it and maybe soulmates do exist. Yeah, I know it seems ridiculous, a Chinese ninja who is Kali reincarnated and me, but I swear, there was an emotional synchronicity, a beating of hearts so to say - a fact that couldn't be denied.

So, what about Rachael then? Damn, I'm so confused, but I'll let you in on a secret; I never felt connected to her. The sex was spectacular but no matter how good the sex is, after a while, without love, it's bound to get jaded, no pun intended. And, deep down inside I knew that her world and mine were so far apart that I was clinging to some distorted fantasy. I mean, let's get real: what could I offer her? I lived in a shitty little studio with friends who drank beer, farted and scratched their balls without apology or embarrassment. And her world was the De La Milano and hundred-dollar bottles of wine, and people with fancy accents who discussed politics and hedge funds – the type I abhorred. We lived in the same country but in two very different worlds.

I sat in Jade's little MINI Cooper and though I was cramped a bit, I succumbed to the tiredness and found myself slipping into the outer realm of dreams, an intruder incapable of discerning reality from fantasy. Here, I was covered in rose petals, their fragrance titillating my senses and transporting me to white sands, blue skies and sunshine with palm trees swaying in the ocean breeze… and Jade and Rachael in bikinis, looking outrageously beautiful, while they played volleyball with Damir's head. Fucking unreal!

CHAPTER 16

YOU GET USED TO IT...

When Ronnie got off the shuttle, he exited from the rear door and noticed that the bumblebee stepped off too but through the front door. When he stepped back onto the bus, the bumblebee followed him, smiling broadly. They played this game a few times, getting on and then off, on and off, on and off, until the driver had pretty much run out of patience. He was a gray-haired, heavily built man with a jowly face, sad eyes and a hangdog expression, a bit like that anthropomorphic mutt, Snoopy, from the Peanuts comic strip.

"Make up your mind. Are you in or out? I'm closing the fucking door," he said, exasperated by the silliness.

The two men stood on the sidewalk and watched the coach leave and it was when Ronnie took a step towards the little man that he found himself surrounded by five, tough looking Asian men who were nothing like the guys at the local chop suey take out. These fuckers would make perfect pin-ups for the Chinese Elite Special Forces. They were tall, lean, and with cold demeanors. They dressed in jeans and t-shirts but there was no mistaking what they really were: dragon warriors in human form and he felt like Po.

Damn! This is fucked up. Ronnie thought to himself and then made his move. He was back on the football field, a free safety taking on the offensive line spearheading a 250-pound running back. He lowered his shoulder and tackled the biggest of the bumblebee's men. They went tumbling together in a heap, knocking over a luggage cart before he was set upon by the rest of the dragons. It was a free-for-all, a wild melee with kicks and punches, grunts and groans, and a lot of wrestling around until he felt a hand tugging at the attaché case.

Ronnie fought as hard as he could to retain his grip but he was at a disadvantage, and just when he thought he was losing the tussle, he heard a roar, "Andros kick your ass!"

He heard another voice with an English accent snarl, "Go shag your Beijing buddies, arseholes!"

It was music to his ears and then, as quickly as it had begun, it was over. Bodies were flying every which way - the Russian Spetsnaz had come to his rescue. Ronnie felt himself being dragged up to his feet.

"Damn, Andros, you're a sight for sore eyes, brother!"

The big Russian grabbed him in a bear hug, "Fuck those slant-eyed bastards. We drink some tequila tonight, huh?"

The men watched the Chinese brigade retreat into the terminal and just before they disappeared, the bumblebee turned and called out, "We'll see you soon, Yank, this isn't over."

"Fuck off, you little cunt!" another of the Spetsnaz yelled back.

"Where's Shika? And, Rachael, where are they?" Ronnie asked as they were ushered towards the cars waiting at the passenger pick-up zone.

"They are in Terminal 3. They wait for you," Andros replied. "Come on, we go there. Grigori will drive. He is ugly bastard but he is my cousin and he take care of stuff."

Grigori was a scary bloke. He was tall, taller than Andros, with tattoos running down his arms and neck. He had tow-blond hair cropped short; pale skin and ice blue eyes, and a small nose that had been broken more than once. The scar running down from forehead to his chin and the hard set of his mouth added to his frightening demeanor. He was the leader of the ex-Spetsnaz team and it was obvious that he deferred only to Andros.

The drive to Terminal 3 was stop and go - the traffic worse than Fifth Avenue on a weekday. Andros and Grigori were speaking in Russian, shouting over some foreign-sounding hip-hop blaring through the car's speakers. Andros was asking the questions and Grigori providing the answers. The loud persiflage went on for a while until they fell silent.

"What happened in there?" Ronnie asked Andros.

"It was shit!" Andros replied. He was looking out the window, seemingly preoccupied, and turned back to look at Ronnie and added with a wry smile, "Shit happened. Some fuckers from MI6 and Chinese triad, and some we don't know. All after fucking bag. How you get the bag? I see you talking to some bitches and then it was crazy shit from hell."

"I took it from the little guy, the one in the yellow jacket. He had Rachael's suitcase."

"He is from Chinese Triad. Those bastards are bad news but Andros know how to deal with them. Grigori think MI6 is involved… that is not good news."

"I told you; those guys in Cal's apartment were like the CIA."

"Okay, we will figure out. First we get Shika and Rachael; then we find Cal."

"Yeah, where the heck is Cal? The last time I saw him, he had tackled the guy in the yellow jacket." Ronnie was concerned. He had tried calling but got no response.

"We make some calls and we find out. Don't worry, little brother, Andros will find your friend."

When they arrived at the passenger pick-up zone, Shika was waiting for them with two of Grigori's men. She came over to the car, leaned into the window and said to Ronnie, "I knew you'd be okay. It was Andros, he was worried about you. What a cluster fuck! Edward is dead and the suitcase is gone."

"It's not gone. I've got the attaché case. Where's Rachael?"

"Rachael was upset, I mean she witnessed her brother getting shot," Shika replied. "I don't think she cares about the attaché case anymore. She…"

"We find Cal then we go back. Fuck the bag, it is bad trouble. We go home," Andros interjected.

Ronnie looked around before repeating, "Where's Rachael?"

"She called a friend, a guy named Peter. I didn't get his last name. They talked for quite some time. He came here in a white Lexus about ten minutes ago and they left to get Cal. He knows where Cal is."

"She didn't say anything about knowing anyone here."

"This is Rachael Swanson we're talking about. The rich know people everywhere."

"Then why did she need us?" Ronnie asked, perplexed.

"That I don't know. She said she would call once they got Cal. The guy looked like he had money. He spoke with an accent, you know, that Boston, private school, old money accent."

"I don't get it. This whole thing with Cal and Rachael is fucking strange."

"You're not jealous, are you, Ronnie?" Shika asked with a smile.

"Fuck no! She's beautiful but Cal is my brother and I don't want him getting hurt, that's all."

"Grigori has place for us, come on, let's go. The cops will be looking," Andros cut in, "We go there, eat some food, rest a little and wait for Cal."

"Sounds like a plan," Ronnie said and slapped the big Russian on the back. "Maybe we can get some curry here in London, what do you say? Does Grigori know a good Indian joint?"

"Grigori know every fucking restaurant in London. He eat like you... enough for ten men. We get some coffee now, freshen up and then he take us to a good curry place. Is that okay, Shika?"

She took Andros' hand. "Why don't we do curry later, maybe for lunch or dinner. I'd like to try Bangers and Mash."

Grigori smiled, "I will take you there. Little place with best bangers and mash."

"Okay, now we're talking," Ronnie quipped as they bundled into the waiting cars.

CHAPTER 17

ON THE WINGS OF A HUMMINGBIRD...

I wasn't sure where I was when I woke up. I lay still, staring up at the ceiling with a hint of peppermint tickling my nostrils. If I had to venture a guess it was peppermint tea or maybe it was chamomile or both… who the fuck knows and who drinks herbal tea anyway? Not me, sister, I'm a coffee man and the stronger the better and I could use a cup right now.

I was about to get up when the door opened, a tentative crack at first, and then a vision in white waltzed in. For a second I was confused but the events of the past came rushing back in a flood of cluttered memories. Maggie, Gordy, Damir and Paddy, and the exotic beauty with the sword! Here she was dressed in a loose white gown sans the sword.

"You are awake, Caleb. That is good," she said in that soft, sweet-sounding accent. Her hair was pulled back in a thick ponytail accentuating the high cheekbones and delicate bone structure.

She sat bedsides me and gently felt around my eye and then proclaimed, "Better. It is healing well."

I was fascinated by her and ogled her like a ten-year-old at the zoo seeing a Bengal tigress for the first time. There was awe tinged with that incredible feeling of being in the presence of something very beautiful and very dangerous.

"How long was I sleeping?" I croaked.

I had wanted to sound like Barry White to impress her but it fell a bit short. Okay, maybe it was more than a bit short. I sounded like a constipated frog with its nuts in a wringer. Wait! Do frogs have nuts? Dylan had a pet frog once and I don't recall…

She cut into my delirium. "Three days."

"Three days?" I was more than shocked. I was one of those nocturnal creatures who rarely slept more than three or four hours a night.

"Yes, Caleb, your body needed the rest."

I liked the way she said Caleb but suddenly I had to this unbearable urge to pee. I was about to get up when she pushed me back, "You need to rest some more."

"I need to use the toilet, that's what I need. I think my bladder is about to burst!"

She got up and fetched a bedpan from under the bed. Every move she made was effortless and graceful, and so very feminine.

"Use this." She handed me the metal utensil and left the room to give me some privacy.

It was then that I noticed that I was naked under the sheets. Wow! Don't get me wrong. I'm not one of those shy, self-conscious men but for reasons beyond me I felt embarrassed. *Did she undress me? I weigh over 220 pounds and how in blazes could she have managed that?*

It's strange how the oddest of thoughts cross my mind at the most inappropriate times. The bedpan was sparkling clean but I must have peed several times in the past three days. And, did I drop a deuce? Damn, this is fucking weird because if I did, she must have assisted me. I didn't recall any of it but now that I was awake, I wasn't about to use the damn thing.

I struggled to my feet and looked around for my clothes but they were nowhere in sight. The room was sparsely furnished but immaculate – there wasn't a single thing out of place. The dresser in the corner had a vase with fresh flowers on top next to the mirror and except for a dainty painting of a lotus flower the minimalist décor was reflected by the pure, barren white walls.

I staggered unsteadily and opened a door that I assumed led to the bathroom, and it did. It was spotless and had the distinct but mild odor of soap and disinfectant. I took care of my business, the longest pee in man's recent history, and felt a sense of relief that is hard to explain unless you've been there yourself. I flushed before checking my face in the mirror – not bad, the swelling was all but gone and except for the bruising around my left eye, I looked pretty much like myself. I was leaning forward over the sink, in the process of feeling the injured orbital bone, when the bathroom door swung open.

"You are a stubborn man, Caleb Montague. You should be in bed."

I jumped like a startled jackrabbit and grabbed the towel from the towel rack, and after fumbling a few times I managed to get it wrapped around me.

"Whoa! You need to knock, girl!"

And there it was, that smile – somewhere between playful and I-know-something-you-don't.

"I've seen you naked before," she said, smiling knowingly and trying to reassure me.

"Not while I was awake you didn't!"

She walked over and placed an arm around my waist, "Let's get you back to bed. I have some night clothes that may fit you. And your phone has been ringing almost non-stop."

"Where is it? And where are my clothes?"

"Your phone is charging. It went dead yesterday and your clothes are in the hamper. They need to be washed. I will do it today."

"No need for that. I like them smelly."

"You need to be quiet and trust me; rest is what your body requires. I will bring you some lunch, after which we have to discuss the attaché case. It needs to be returned to me."

I was sitting on the edge of the bed and she was standing in front of me when a sense of an unreasonable disappointment, a dolorous dejection of sorts, came over me. So that was it; that damn attaché case was what it was all about. I'm not sure why I was so freakin' disappointed; I mean, she didn't really know me and I didn't know her and just because I was attracted to her and filled my thick skull with some crazy, wild notions of soulmates and karma didn't mean that she felt the same way.

"That's all you care about, right, the attaché case?" I asked, sounding like a petulant child.

She was quiet; studying me with what I perceived was a sad expression. It was hard to read her.

"You know so little," she chided gently, "have you not wondered why I did not kill you," she said but it sounded like a question.

"Because I look like Gregory Peck?" I thought I'd give Rachael's original bullshit a try. I waited but she said nothing so I continued, "He's a very handsome actor from the fifties."

"I know who Gregory Peck is. I saw 'To Kill a Mocking Bird' and you do not look anything like him."

Well, so much for that.

"Damn, girl, you are one cold mama. So why did you spare my sorry ass anyway?"

"I knew you didn't have the attaché case and I had a pretty good idea who had it." Her voice was almost a whisper and she brushed back the hair from my forehead, gently, almost tenderly. "From the moment I saw you at the airport, I knew we were connected from lives lived many, many years ago. I could have followed that fat little pig, Dishi, and secured the suitcase, but you were in trouble so I followed Maggie's men instead and at the cost of neglecting my duty."

I was taken aback. *Lives lived many, many years ago?* I have enough trouble figuring out what day of the week it is so the thought of lives lived in the distant past is way beyond my cerebral capacity. I was thrilled though that she felt the way I did – that we were connected.

"Who is Dishi?" I asked.

"Dishi Guan. He was the one in the yellow jacket."

"Oh, the bumblebee!"

She smiled, "This bumblebee will sting. He works for the MSS and is dangerous. Don't let that little incident at the airport mislead you. He is tenacious and cunning."

Things were beginning to make some sense now. I was about to ask her what the MSS was when she leaned down and kissed me on my lips. It was a quick kiss, soft as satin's sybaritic caress. Why was my heart pounding? And, my head, it was spinning like a juvenile experiencing his first kiss. This was beginning to get strange and I don't mean funny strange.

She had moved back a bit, looking deep into my eyes, and I forgot about the bumblebee and the MSS. My thought process had been short-circuited and all I could come up with was a weak excuse for what I was really feeling.

"You could have intervened a little before Goran rearranged my face, couldn't you?"

"No, I couldn't. There is a reason and time for everything," she responded while gently pushing me back on the bed.

"What do you mean?" I asked, lying back.

"You will see," she said and pulled the covers over me. "I will bring you some lunch and then we can talk about the attaché case."

It was only after she had left that I realized I was aroused. My cock was harder than a freakin' high pressure hose and all she did was give me a peck on the lips! What would have happened if she had really kissed me? I'll leave that to your imagination. And the incredible thing was that the ferrets in my head had stopped running around, screaming *watch out!* In fact, I think the ferrets were gone for good.

CHAPTER 18

THE GAMES PEOPLE PLAY...

The white Lexus had just exited the airport. The driver, Peter Rudd, was the same good-looking man who had abducted Edward. He turned to Rachael and smiled.

"You get more beautiful every year, my darling."

The traffic was at a standstill, giving him the opportunity to study the woman's profile. She was perfect, gorgeous, and it still amazed him that she was his. He tried to kiss her but she pushed him away.

"You promised me that Edward wouldn't be hurt and now he's dead."

"Edward was in a lot of trouble long before this latest harebrained scheme of his. It was only a matter of time before Di Santi or one of the other degenerates he dealt with whacked him. Things would never have gotten this fucked up if he hadn't been so stupid and I'm sorry, I know you were close, but even you have to admit that this was sheer madness."

She remained quiet, looking down at her hands abstractedly, so Rudd continued, "It wasn't easy exchanging the original attaché case with the fake one but we managed to do that without raising Chang's suspicion. And then Edward had to go and stir up the proverbial hornet's nest."

"You didn't know Eddie like I did. He wasn't always a drug addict and a compulsive gambler. He was sensitive and kind and took care of me when I was young and naïve, and helpless. It was you who told me that desperate people do desperate things. Eddie was desperate and easily influenced and that…" she stopped herself from using the derogatory term, "that woman, Satin, took advantage of him."

"My point exactly; your brother was gullible and an addict. He was addicted to drugs and gambling and that is a bad combination. He refused any help and was enabled by everyone he knew, including you. He was on a one-way ticket to hell. If it hadn't happened now it would have in the very near future. You couldn't save him, Rachael, so stop blaming yourself and others for your brother's innate stupidity. He wasn't a victim – Edward Swanson was afforded every opportunity in life and instead of taking advantage of them, he embarked on the path of self-destruction. This may sound cruel but you are well to be rid of him."

She was quiet, knowing that what Rudd said was true. Edward's addictions had changed him. He was no longer the brother she loved but a stranger desperate and capable of doing things without consideration for the consequences. He didn't care who he hurt as long as he got what he wanted. She felt sadness but under the fragile veil of filial love was a sense of relief. She had sent him hundreds of thousands of dollars in the last few years but it was never enough. Now that was over. Her stipend from her father's estate and the money Peter and she would make from this caper would be more than enough for them to live in the manner she was used to. The severing of the fraternal cord had brought closure and a rebirth of sorts.

"What exactly was in the original attaché case? It must be something really important if everyone is after it."

"Do you remember Phillip Harrington, that geeky looking guy we met at the New Year's Eve bash at the Governor's Mansion?" Rudd asked.

"Vaguely."

He smiled, "I'm surprised you don't remember him. He was tripping over himself to impress you. He spilt his drink when you…"

"I said I don't really remember," she interrupted, a bit irritated by the non-sequitur and the fact that she had no idea who he was talking about.

"Well, he is the head of the R&D team at e-Paradigm, a small company that works with the DOD on developmental programs. They had just completed a three-year project called D2X2 involving something called Gray Artificial Intelligence. This generation of AI is far more advanced than what is currently referred to as 'super' AI."

"You mean like the technology used in self-driving cars?"

"Yes. The project name was later changed to 'Erebus' because some bigshot at the Pentagon thought that D2X2 was too much like Star Wars, you know, R2-D2."

"Erebus, the Greek God of Darkness?"

"Yes, the very same, and appropriately so considering the applications. This Gray AI is light-years ahead of anything anyone has, and would give the US a distinct advantage in space and in interstellar weaponry, especially the manner in which nuclear warheads could be deployed and manipulated. Not to mention pilotless flight, drones, autonomous vehicles, robots… it has the potential to change everything and would leave the Chinese and the Russians playing catch-up for the next ten years."

"Why is it always an arms race? Why can't we use it to help people everywhere?"

"There's no money in that. And it will eventually find its way into the commercial world and that in turn will filter down to the communal one. The microchips that were developed to process the incredible amounts of data required by the Gray AI will end up in our phones and computers and trust me; the do-gooders will at some point figure out the altruistic applications."

"What does all this have to do with Steven Chang and the attaché case?"

"Steven's cousin, Eleanor Dunn, worked at e-Paradigm on the Erebus program. Miss Dunn's real name, we came to find out, was Caihong Lin. She was one of the senior engineers with high-level security clearance. She's an American citizen with very confused loyalties."

"But didn't she have to go through a mandatory background check?"

Rudd smiled. "Of course she did and when questioned, she said the name change was simply to assimilate and be more American. A western name that was easy to pronounce – I mean, Eleanor Dunn or Nellie as she's known to her friends and colleagues, is easy enough for everyone. It seemed reasonable and innocuous and there was nothing in her background to suggest otherwise."

He paused when the traffic began moving again before resuming, "When she told Chang what she was working on, he convinced her to steal the information and she did. She copied everything, including the simulation packages, along with some of the detailed technical procedures and gave it to Steven. It took her over six months to do this."

"And no one suspected anything?"

"No. Nellie is a brilliant lass and very resourceful. Her boss, the very same Phillip Harrington, and coworkers thought the world of her and she usually worked late so no one gave it a second thought."

"So how did they come to know find out?"

"Ah, my dear, we have our fingers in every pie. This game is far from one-sided. Steven Chang was on the payroll of the triad in Macao. The head of the triad is a fellow named Kuok-Bai. The Chinese triads have connections to the MSS, the Ministry of State Security, and when Chang contacted Kuok-Bai with the news of what he had in the attaché case, our mole within their inner circle let us know."

It was beginning to make sense to her.

"Who is the mole?"

"I don't know. Very few people do and for good reason. If the Chinese ever found out who this person is, they would be eliminated almost immediately."

"But why did you have to exchange the real attaché case with a fake one? I mean, why go through all that trouble when you had all the stuff back and could have Nellie arrested?"

Peter Rudd smiled, "We had to let the Chinese think that the fake was the real thing. The data on the fake hard drives was manipulated; most of it is stuff that exists but with some incremental improvements. This would prevent the Chinese from trying to steal the real thing, at least for now. And as for Eleanor Dunn, we use her to feed garbage to the Chinese. They have replaced Chang with a fellow named Henry Liao who, as it turns out, is also related to Nellie. Makes me wonder if all one and a half billion of the Chinese are related!"

"But why is this so important, I mean this AI?" Rachael asked. "Why can't the Chinese just develop the AI themselves? They are smart people so why resort to stealing this?"

"They *are* smart people and they learned from the mistakes made by the USSR. It was before your time, dear girl, but the USSR tried to compete with the US during the Cold War and lost. They went bankrupt and fell into an abyss of poverty and crime; long breadlines, no jobs, drugs, prostitution, and every squalid curse that follows the poor was what they got for their foolishness. The Chinese weren't about to make the same mistake. They figured out that technology was the new frontier and stealing it was a lot easier and cheaper than developing it."

Rachael fell quiet. She found the incidents with Nellie, and especially Chang, to be disturbing, and deep down inside her, where lies and half-truths are laid bare, she knew that what he said about Edward was true. Sooner or later he would have crossed the wrong person and would have ended up dead. He couldn't help himself. On the other hand, Cal was an innocent bystander who got involved because of her.

"What about Cal?"

"What about him?"

Rachael looked away, their brief but intense relationship swirling in her brain, and after a while, said, "Caleb is a really nice guy and he got involved because of me. I feel responsible, Peter."

"I couldn't intervene without Maggie getting suspicious. I am hoping that Gordy can handle Damir and Paddy."

"That's not fair. You should have helped him; you could have at least stayed to make sure they didn't kill him."

"My, my, my, Rachael Swanson, you're not developing a conscience, are you? Hmmm, maybe it's something more; are you falling for this loser?" The last bit was said tongue in cheek.

She smiled and looked at him. "He's not a loser and no, I'm not *falling for him*. He's had a shitty life and we took advantage of him."

"People use people all the time – that's life. Let's keep our eyes on the prize. We need to get the stuff back to the Chinese. It seems that one of your friends waylaid Dishi Guan and snatched the attaché case."

"They should have sent someone more athletic than Guan. And how was I to know that Cal would be right there to intercept him?"

"Thorough planning takes into account all contingencies, my love; letting that Russian oaf take the lead was the first mistake."

Rachael was quiet. She wasn't the type to take the lead in something like this. She had been sure that Cal and Ronnie would be bored or otherwise occupied and when Guan snatched the suitcase, the deed would be done. Peter would speak to Maggie and let them know that the triad had the attaché case, and, with some persuasion, have Edward released.

"It wasn't Andros or Shika; they were with me and it couldn't have been Cal so it must have been Ronnie unless that creep from the MI6 got to it," Rachael countered.

"Well, that's what we need to find out."

"So where are we going now?" she asked.

"I'll drop you off in Chelmsford. You will be more comfortable there and out of the way if things get sticky."

"I can help and can deal with sticky situations, in case you haven't noticed."

"I'm going to see Maggie and hopefully bring our knight in white armor back home. The less she knows about us the safer you'll be. And it will give me a chance to explain things to Caleb and set things right. Monetary restitution is best handled by those not involved, my dear, and it makes up for a lot. I don't know what transpired between the two of you, and I don't care to know, but emotional ties only complicate things. Let me handle this."

Rachael wondered if Peter had guessed that she had slept with Cal. There was an unspoken understanding that whatever happened in the course of their work remained within those constraints and was above reproach or curious delving. She liked Cal but had known all along that their worlds were too far apart and after a while she would tire of him like she had with Patrick, her ex-boyfriend.

Peter Rudd was different. He came from affluence and an upbringing very similar to hers. He was the kind of man that could take care of her and make her happy and who really didn't care if she strayed every now and then. They made a perfect pair, so why did she have this nagging feeling that Peter was just a step on her journey? She would deal with it when they were on vacation and she had time to think about things but right now, getting Caleb out of Maggie's place was the priority.

CHAPTER 19

MAGGIE AND THE MAGPIES...

The mood in the room was palpable; it was heavy with anger and disbelief. Maggie Walcott stood by the window staring out across the meadow and at the woods that bordered the property, while Goran stood by the door nonchalantly leaning against the frame. The two other men in the room were seated in front of a large mahogany desk and were engaged in a hushed conversation. The older of the two was noticeably rotund with a bald head, round face and sporting horn-rimmed bifocals. His mustache and beard were trimmed short and streaked with gray. The other was younger and bigger with dark, curly hair and a lean, gaunt look. His aquiline nose, deep-set eyes and prominent chin gave him a hawk-like appearance.

It was several minutes, five or so, before Maggie turned towards the desk and said, "Whoever killed

Paddy and Damir took Gordy hostage, I'm pretty sure of that. Or maybe he got away. I find it hard to believe that Gordy would have been involved in any way. I've known him for over ten years and he was loyal to a fault - like family."

"Gordy was nothing… a pussy! He was not happy to work on the American." Goran spat out.

"That doesn't mean anything. He didn't enjoy the messier aspects of our business but that doesn't mean he was working for someone else," Maggie countered. She was fond of Gordy and didn't want to believe that he would betray her.

"If he had escaped, he would have contacted us by now, so if he's not with them then he's being held against his wishes," the bald man opined with a solemn look.

"Maybe the people who committed these heinous acts were the same that did Bogdan and his team," the younger man seated at the desk suggested. "Florijan was a tough biscuit so they had to be professional killers."

The bald man shook his head and countered, "No, not killers but killer. There's only one assassin I know who could do this and he uses a sword - Akira Hirai. This is his modus operandi. He fancies himself to be a ninja and the Croats weren't shot, they had their throats slashed. What happened to Florijan was retribution for Steven Chang – a clear message that there are consequences. If we don't get to the bottom of this, we will be next. The only part I find puzzling is Gordy - why would they kill

Damir and Paddy and spare Gordy? Why not kill him? Which raises the question: was he working with the triad? And what became of the American?"

"I would bet everything I own that Gordy wasn't working for anyone. And as to why they didn't kill him? I don't know. The American had the misfortune of being in the wrong place at the wrong time. I doubt he had anything to do with all this." Maggie paused then added, "I've heard of Francis Hirai… the ghost who kills. I'm assuming that this is the same person."

"He answers to both names but Akira Hirai is his real name," the bald man replied, stroking his mustache and beard.

"Adam, what do we do? And who would be behind this?" Maggie asked, sounding concerned for the first time. She was not one who was easily frightened or intimidated but the terrible spectacle of Damir and Paddy brought the war to her doorstep and that had never happened before.

"He has worked for the triads in Macao and Hong Kong and it is possible Kuok-Bai thinks that Edward handed the attaché case to us," answered the bald man; he got up and poured himself a drink. Adam Barnett was a cunning mastermind who operated within the dark underbelly of society. He enjoyed a symbiotic rela-tionship with Maggie in which he provided the brains while Maggie supplied the brawn.

"This is waste of time. We find Gordy and he will tell us everything," Goran suggested and straightened up. "I take Dejan, Viktor and Darren and we will look. What do you say, Maggie? And this ghost – fuck him! If he comes here, we cut *his* head off."

The woman turned away and looked out past the forest into the distant skyline. The hills formed a soothing silhouette that tempered the augury of the danger to come. She didn't trust Goran or his crew – they had their uses but there was no way to control them. They were a pack of Hyenas; once they smelled blood and brought down the prey, they would tear it to pieces. Gordy wouldn't stand a chance. But she also knew that if Gordy was alive, he could shed light on the situation. The other and more pressing worry was the Japanese assassin. Goran and his crew could come in handy, and with her dogs, Crosby, Stills and Nash, she felt relatively safe. Crosby and Nash were trained Dobermans while Stills was a two-hundred pound Rottweiler with a nasty disposition. Even a ninja would think twice before dealing with him.

"I can do it, Maggie, don't worry, I bring Gordy back without problems. I want to know the killer of Damir, that is all I want to know," Goran said reading her thoughts, "I do not hurt Gordy."

She was still undecided when Barnett urged, "Maggie, we have to act and soon. We don't have a lot of time."

"Okay, Goran, start at the Fox & Hound. Ask for Darin Colter; he is a bouncer there and Gordy worked with him off and on, and they were good friends. If

Colter doesn't know anything the only other person he'd turn to is his sister. Her name is Kayli Aitkens and she lives in Scotland, in East Kilbride I think, you could check there. I want to talk to him so don't hurt him and if he did in fact betray us, you can have him."

The big Serb smiled, a wolf smacking his lips, "I know Fox & Hound and I have friend in Glasgow. I bring him back, Maggie, don't worry."

And with that assurance he left the room.

The curly haired young man stood up, "Maybe I should go with him, Mum, to make sure they don't hurt Gordy?"

It was more a question than a statement.

"No, Brian, you stay here. This is far from over and should Akira Hirai come calling, it is a lot better if we are together… all of us. Bring the dogs into the house and check all the cameras."

Maggie waited for her son to leave before she turned to Adam Barnett, "Call Peter. We need reinforcements here now! I am not going to have my son butchered like a pig."

CHAPTER 20

THE CHANGING
OF THE GUARD...

Before the transfer of sovereignty to China by the Portuguese in 1999, Macao had been divided into two municipalities and seven civil parishes. In 2001, the Chinese government abolished the two municipalities, but for symbolic reasons they maintained the seven parishes. Kuok-Bai's sprawling mansion was located in the parish of São Lourenço close to the southwestern tip facing the Inner Harbor, and not far from the ancient A-Ma Temple. It was a huge modern building that defied history and had becomes a landmark of sorts.

He had five maids who took care of the house and the kitchen and several armed guards patrolling the walled periphery of the property. The ubiquitous cameras reflected Kuok-Bai's cautious nature, and to some extent, his paranoia. One of the maids, an old woman named Li Xiu, had been with him for over thirty years. She took care of the kitchen and planned all his meals and except for an estranged daughter, she too had no family. She was the only one of his personal staff that lived at the mansion and not the servant's quarters.

This morning he was on the computer scanning the messages from Jade. The death of the Croats in San Diego pleased him but the reprisals would not end there. Steven Chang's murder, especially the vicious nature of the killing, needed to be avenged. Chang's cousin, Caihong Lin, would be an asset and he would continue to cultivate her. Once Jade had taken care of Maggie and her son, and the bald demon, Barnett, she would bring the attaché case back to him. Of that he had no doubt.

"The tea arrived last evening, my son," Li Xiu said in Cantonese, placing the cup of hot tea next to Kuok-Bai. It was sweetened with a generous helping of condensed milk.

"How many boxes did they send?" he asked absentmindedly, his attention focused on the screen.

"They sent two boxes this time. I placed the bigger box in the pantry and opened the smaller one. There are sufficient tea leaves for next year's Tun Ng Festival."

Kuok-Bai was an avid fan of the Dragon Boat Festival, and attended the boat race each year. He took a sip and closed his eyes as the sweet amrita warmed his body. Every year, his Indian associates sent him boxes of Assam Tea leaves as a token of their alliance but this year, due to local flooding, the shipment had been delayed. He had been waiting patiently and was happy that it had finally arrived. This particular tea was one of the few indulgences that he allowed himself.

"You make it just the way I like it, godmother; I will take another cup in about twenty minutes. Also, pack some of the tea and give it to Hao so I can take it to the office."

Hao Jing was his personal bodyguard and driver.

"It is already done. Hao has the package. I will have your breakfast ready once you have finished your tea," the old woman replied, fussing around the table.

She was twenty or so years older than Kuok-Bai, bent from the years, with thin boney fingers and teeth stained by a lifelong habit of chewing betel leaf. And though she had slowed down and had occasional lapses in memory, she still managed everything to his liking, and he was fond of her, so the thought of replacing her had never occurred to him.

"That is good, very good; now I have to finish some work so you must leave me alone," he said the last part gently and with a smile.

"Yes, yes, of course," and with that she ambled off to the kitchen muttering to herself.

After approximately twenty minutes, she returned with the second cup and placed it next to him with the admonishment, "You stare too long at that thing. Take a break, my son, and do not work so hard. Go walk in the gardens. It will lift your spirits. I will make your breakfast and call you when it is ready."

He smiled and took a sip of the freshly brewed tea. Nothing had changed from the day he had hired her – she had mothered him from day one and for reasons that only orphans can understand, he cherished and needed that.

Thirty minutes later when Li Xiu came back to call him for his breakfast she found him slumped over the computer's keypad. The cup had been knocked over and lay in a small puddle of tea. Kuok-Bai was dead. The tea leaves, laced with several different toxins, had done their job.

The old woman felt his neck for a pulse and then used her cell phone to make a call, "It is over. He is dead. Now let the boy go."

She was sad but such is life. They had kidnapped her grandson and no matter what, blood is thicker than water.

In a small brick house, not far from the center of town, Fai Wong put away his phone and ran his finger along the scar on his face. It was an old habit. He was now the new head of the Macao triad. And though it wasn't his cunning that did the old man in, he claimed credit and would make sure people feared him as they had Kuok-Bai. He fought hard to contain the joy that coursed through him. But before he called Wei and the others and celebrated, there was one important call to make. The attaché case needed to be brought to him and the Hummingbird had to be neutralized and there was only one person who could do this - the Ghost Who Kills.

CHAPTER 21

THE FLIGHT OF THE HUMMINGBIRD...

I woke up to the soothing sound of a flute playing in the distance, a melody that was foreign to my ears – maybe Indian or Chinese or something else but it wasn't Jethro Tull, that's for sure. In my teen years I must have listened to Aqualung and Thick as Brick a million times. I can still recite the words to Cross-Eyed Mary and of course, my favorite: Locomotive Breath. But this flautist was different. He or she played a magical tune that conjured images of distant hills where snake-charmers and cobras and mystical, dusky women danced, swaying enticingly to the slow sensual refrain. It was hypnotic.

I followed the haunting strains to the living room and stood by the window looking out past the patio to the small garden and there, beyond a pond, on the green lawn was a stone shrine. Jade was in a seiza position, sitting on her heels in front of a cross and a statue of Buddha with her head bowed. I watched her, fascinated by the anomaly – killer and proselyte, lost in meditative prayer. She was a vision in a white kimono, beautiful and serene, and I wondered about the cosmic coincidence or whatever it was that brought us together. It began with Rachael and the park bench, and the note she left for me. Rachael! She seemed irrelevant now and so, so very distant.

Yeah, I know what you are thinking: *what a shallow bastard! One moment he's madly, head over heels in lust with the beautiful Miss. Swanson and the next, he's swept away by an exotic and beautiful killer. How is it possible unless he's just a seedy, shallow, male-chauvinistic pig looking to get his rocks off?*

I'll give you two out of three. Seedy I'm not. Am I a shallow, male-chauvinistic pig? Most probably but in my defense, I didn't plan any of this. Rachael set the ball rolling and like the song, Locomotive Breath; *old Charley stole the handle and the train it won't stop going…* I was 'invited' along for the ride. The fact that I got off at Station Jade is not my fault. Blame it on Rachael or old Charley, or maybe Jade was old Charley, saving my sorry ass from Damir and Paddy.

I looked at Jade again; she hadn't moved and except for strands of hair fluttering across her face with the occasional gust, she sat motionless. Then, as though she could feel my eyes on her, she turned, saw me and smiled. I felt a lump in my throat and I swear my heart skipped a beat when our eyes met.

I walked out onto the patio and as I got closer, I noticed the tears. I was at a loss – why would she be crying? I reached out and pulled her to me wanting to comfort her and was surprised when she melted into my arms, offering no resistance. She placed her head against my chest and sobbed silently.

"Hey, what's the matter? Am I dying and just don't know it?" I asked, wiping away a tear from her cheek.

She smiled, a sad smile, "No, Caleb, you are not dying. A person close to me was murdered and I wasn't there to protect him."

"Who was murdered and how did you find out?"

"He was like a surrogate father - an old man who took pity on a child."

I held her tight and kissed the top of her head. After a while the soft sobbing ceased and she stepped back, taking hold of my hand. "Come, I will explain so you know everything before we take the next steps to our relationship."

While I sat at the kitchen table watching her, she brewed a strong black tea with some exotic spices and sweetened it with condensed milk and my first thought was *'Yuck, condensed milk and tea?'*

She placed the cup in front of me and said, "Try it, this was Kuok-Bai's favorite beverage."

I had no idea what a Kuok-Bai was and took a sip, and it didn't taste half bad, "Not bad. What is it? I mean the tea, is it Chinese?"

"No, it is Indian from Assam. We Chinese have a long history with the Indians – not always pleasant but we are like siblings who do not always get along."

"I noticed you have a cross and a statue of Buddha in your little altar. Are you a Christian or a Buddhist?" I asked, curious about her religious beliefs.

"Does it matter?"

"No, I'm just nosy," I replied and smiled.

"I believe in one God. We call Him by different names but He is the same – the universal creator of all things. Buddha was a saint, an enlightened being, and his teachings were very similar to that of Christ." She stared into her cup, lost in thought, and then continued, "The Hindus have several avatars of their version of the Father, Son and Holy Ghost and the one I can most identify with is Kali – the goddess of death."

I almost fell off my chair. Kali! Damn, what are the odds? Shika had a tattoo of the same goddess and now here she was again, though Jade was more Kali than Shika could ever be. I was about to say something but held my tongue.

I sipped the tea and found myself enjoying the sweet, ambrosial taste, a bit like sweet chai with hints of cardamom and clove and spices that challenged the western palate.

"Tell me about the old man and his death and tell me about yourself. I want to know everything," I said, feeling like the petals of the Venus flytrap were closing but it was exactly where I wanted to be.

She sat sipping her tea and looking at me for a while, not saying a word. And just when I began to feel uncomfortable, she spoke.

"When I was twelve I was taken from my parents and sent to a school for gifted children. It wasn't a regular school but one with a very specific goal – to create a group of highly trained assassins and spies that would be at the government's disposal. Kuok-Bai saw me when I was a child at the academy and took an interest in me. When I was older he bought my freedom from the MSS, the Ministry of State Security. This was not easy and cost a lot of money but he persisted, and after a few years, I was set free."

"You mean the government had no problems letting you go after all that training?"

"Money can buy you almost anything, even your liberty," she answered.

"Did you have to pay him back?"

She smiled, "You mean did he expect to be paid in kind since I had no money. The answer is yes, but not in the way you are thinking."

I took both her hands in mine and lied, "I'm not thinking anything."

"Oh, you are such a liar," she laughed and squeezed my hand, "but it matters not, I will tell you everything."

She got up and poured herself some more tea before continuing.

"He did not want sex from me. He used me to neutralize those who would usurp his power or those who did his people harm, like the animals who killed Steven Chang. And I was only happy to oblige. I had no direction and no home; I had nothing. He was like a father to me. He was patient and gave me direction and a purpose... he was the closest thing to a family that I had left."

"What happened to your real parents?"

"I found out, with Kuok-Bai's help, that they had tried to get me back from the MSS and were sent to a camp for re-education. My mother was a beautiful woman, sensitive and loving, who loved art, dance and theatre and most of all, her family. My father was an engineer devoted to my mother and me. I was an only child and losing me broke my mother's heart, and she died shortly after. My father had lost his reasons for living and took his own life."

"Oh my God, how awful! I'm so sorry, Jade."

I could see tears beginning to cloud her eyes, a vulnerable side that got to me. I couldn't associate the head-lopping ninja with this fragile creature, and wanted to hold her to assure her that no one would ever hurt her again, and that's when she continued.

"I had a picture of my parents, an old picture taken a few days after they were married. They looked so happy, but one of the instructors found it under my pillow and confiscated it. They wanted us to have a singular purpose, to swear loyalty solely to the State, and nothing else was permitted."

"I would have killed the motherfucker!" I blurted out before I could control myself.

She laughed, "Yes. I was very angry but I was a little girl and later, when I was older, I knew that there was a purpose and a plan and that all these bridges that I had crossed would lead me to my destiny."

"And that is?"

"To bring me to you," she said. It was a simple remark said with the sincerity of a child.

"Or maybe it was to bring *me* to you," I replied reaching for her hand. She seemed so vulnerable.

She nodded, looking into my eyes, sending me tumbling headlong into those dark liquid pools, drowning in her mystical aura.

"We are twin flames, Caleb, a soul split and shared by two physical beings. I think the West calls them soulmates," she said.

I had no idea what all that meant but I knew one thing for certain, I was meant to be with her and she with me. It didn't matter that she was Chinese and I was an American. We belonged together and of this there was no doubt.

"I have never felt anything like this before," I told her honestly, "I never imagined that my mountain woman would turn out to be a beautiful Chinese flower."

"Mountain woman?" she was confused.

"Never mind, it's just more of my nonsense… the bridges I've had to cross."

She smiled and kissed my hand and held it in both of hers.

"I have to take care of some things for Kuok-Bai, but I will come back, for we have a life to live and other bridges to cross, but we will cross them together."

I had this dreadful feeling that if she left I would never see her again.

"Don't go, please don't go," I implored her. "Or, take me with you, I can help…"

"Don't worry, Caleb, I *will* come back, I promise you that. You cannot come with me; it is far too dangerous." She paused before saying, "Let us not dwell on this - we must take advantage of the time we have now."

She took my hand led me towards the bedroom. My mind was racing, filled with anticipation of what was to come. I considered myself to be somewhat of an expert at pleasing women, a savant of sex, but for the second time in my life – the first was with Peggy Burns – I felt like a rookie about to step into the big leagues.

And just as we walked past the living room, we were accosted by a small Asian man, who seemed to have materialized out of thin air. He was dark with leathery, brown skin and black hair cropped short, and was dressed in all black. He had an air of supreme confidence, standing straight as an arrow with his hands behind his back. To say we were shocked would be an understatement. Jade stepped in front of me and was still.

He ignored me and offered her a short, stiff, bow and said, "I am Francis Akira Hirai. Maybe you have heard of me; I have been tasked with taking your life."

What the fuck! Hey, asshole, I'm standing right here. You just threatened my woman and that means you're gonna get your ass stomped!

I stepped around Jade and snarled, "I'm Caleb Montague and I'm going to kick your sorry little…"

I'm not sure what happened but I was lying on the ground with his foot pressing down on my throat. I grabbed his leg and tried jerking it off of me but I swear the guy must have weighed a ton! I couldn't budge the fucking thing. The next thing I know, Jade and the little man were engaged in what was obviously some form of combat except it looked like a complicated dance. They were twirling, ducking, weaving, spinning… I know this sounds ridiculous but it seemed like they were floating on air. This was Crouching Tiger and Enter the Dragon all rolled into one. They took turns striking and blocking and just when Jade seemed to gain the slightest advantage, the little man stepped back and bowed.

"Stop, please. I did not come here for this. I came here to warn you. I take my task and responsibilities seriously but I also live by a code, a code of honor. Lienna Quan, you have been warned." And with that he disappeared. I mean, it was like 'swoosh' and he was gone out the back window.

"What the heck was that? And who is Lienna Quan?" I asked and reached for her.

"My real name is Lienna Quan. Not many know that. This can only mean that he has been hired by the MSS or the triad. The MSS would not use an independent contractor to do their killing. This had to be the work of Fai Wong, the man who is responsible for Kuok-Bai's death."

"Who was this guy?"

"Akira Hirai is a Japanese assassin. We must go; you are in serious peril. Call your friends and stay with them. I will come and get you once I take care of things."

"You're kidding, right? I'm not leaving you, Lienna Quan. I'll deal with this asshole ninja. Don't worry, he took me by surprise. The next time…"

"The next time you will be dead, Caleb, and I will not permit that," she interrupted and led me to the bedroom. "Change," she instructed, "your clothes are in the dresser, and call your friends. There is no time to waste, we must leave now. I will…"

"Lienna, Lienna!" I let the name roll off my tongue, loving the sound of it, "What a lovely name," I pulled her to me and kissed her hard and felt her open up. I slid my tongue into her mouth and tasted the sweetness of her, like peppermint and spiced candy. I would have stood there kissing her all day and all night but after a few lingering moments, she broke away, breathless and eyes bright with passion.

She took my hands in hers, "We will have time to consummate our desires but not now, my love, now we have to leave. So trust me and get ready, and call your friends."

CHAPTER 22

SNAKES AND LADDERS...

Kayli Aitkens lived in a small, one-bedroom apartment that she shared with her boyfriend, Raymond Cross, and their 3-year-old daughter, Sarah. Things had been a struggle ever since she lost her job at the local supermarket and they had to make do on Ray's paycheck, a paltry amount stretched to every penny that was far from sufficient. She was mulling over the unpaid bills when the doorbell rang.

"One moment, I'm coming," she called out and couldn't keep the surprise from showing on her face, "Gordy! My God, what are you doing here? Why didn't you…"

He grabbed her in a tight hug and kissed her on both cheeks, "You're a sight for sore eyes, little girl. I had to leave London in a hurry and really didn't have time to make plans."

It had been several years since he had seen his little sister so he stood back and gave her a once over. "Let me look at you. You look as pretty as ever."

"Come on in, it's cold," Kayli said opening the door wide, "I'll put the kettle on. Come on, you old goat, I can't believe you're here. You should've called, you know."

He placed his small, leather satchel near the umbrella stand and walked into the living room.

"Nice; it's a cozy little place you have," he said following her into the kitchen.

"It's alright - better than staying with Beth," she answered.

"How's old Bethany doing? Is she married?" Gordy asked, a bit curious about the girl he used to date.

"She's with a Muslim boy now. Mohamed Aziz and a proper ass he is. He has her wearing a burka no less. She's changed, Gordy, the fun-loving Beth is a Muslim now and runs with a very different crowd. She's not permitted to speak to us unless he is present – can you believe that?"

"Can't say I blame her, she had no luck with the local boys."

Kayli made a face. "I don't like them. They are a frightening lot, every one of them, and especially Mo; that's what he calls himself. The men stare at us like they're going to do something. It's creepy."

"Hey, that's not like you. I remember when father used go on about the Polish immigrants and you called him a xenophobe. What ever happened to tolerance?"

"That was different. The Polish are a lot like us. They speak a different language but culturally they believe in the same things we do. The Muslims are a horse of a different color, Gordy; these people are strange and act in ways that frighten me. Ray hates them."

"Where is Ray? And where's the little princess? The last time I saw her was at the christening."

"He's gone to the park and took Sarah with him." Kayli fell quiet and after a few moments, added, "Ever since I lost my job, things haven't been good. It's been hard. We fight all the time. Ray spends a lot more time with his mates at the pub. Money is tight and it's like he doesn't want to come home. He's changed."

"Is he seeing another bird, you know, a little distraction from his main squeeze?" he asked.

"No. I could live with that but it's Sam and John and the same old bunch of morons. They've never grown up. They stand around the pool table, yapping and getting drunk and rowdy."

"Boys will be boys. You've got to cut him some slack."

"What about me, Gordy, don't I get to have an evening out with the girls? I've been stuck here for…" and she broke down and began to cry.

He put his arm around her and gave her a squeeze, "Come on now, there's no need for that. Of course you do; everyone could use a break. Come on, stop crying, little girl."

She sobbed into his chest, and after a while stepped away. "I needed that. It's been so hard these last few months."

He looked at the bills on the table and picked one up, skimmed through it and put it back with the rest. "Are you having problems with the bills? How about the rent, are you behind?"

"No. I pay the rent if that's all I do. Sit. Here, this will warm you up." She poured the hot water over the tea bag. "Mum helps but I hate asking her, Gordy, they don't deserve this. They are just about making ends meet and you know how they feel about Ray. Dad never liked him."

"How much do you need?" he asked, taking a sip of the tea and sensing her concern. She was eight years younger than him, and growing up, that age difference precluded the usual sibling squabbles. He had always looked out for her and she, in turn, had run to him with all her problems.

She looked at him and looked away before answering, "A few hundred quid."

"Exactly how much do you need?"

"A hundred and eighty quid. Give or take a few pence."

He counted out five hundred pounds and handed it to her. "Here, take care of it and keep the rest for yourself. Don't tell Ray about it."

He counted out another five hundred pounds and pressed it into her hand. "This is for Sarah; you buy her something nice. Now stop worrying and I'll help until you find a job. Okay?"

She got up and hugged him, enjoying the warmth and comfort his presence gave her. "I'm so glad you're here. I've missed you, Gordy. Mum and Dad… we've all missed you!"

"Don't you worry, things will be different from now on," he reassured her. He didn't like seeing his sister unhappy.

"Do you mind sleeping on the couch? It's a bit small but that's all we have."

"It will be fine. I've slept on worse."

"Gordy, promise me you won't do anything to Ray. He doesn't mean half the things he says… it's only when he's drunk."

"Hey, what's between a man and woman is not my business. He doesn't get physical, does he? That's where I draw the line. If he hurts you all bets are off and I'll break the skinny little cunt!" The last bit was an ominous growl.

"No!" she exclaimed, protesting. "He's not like that and don't frighten me, Gordy. I still remember what you did to that policeman. It gives me the shivers to this day."

Alex Dunmore was a local constable who had a reputation with the ladies, but he made the mistake of shoving his hand up the skirt of sixteen-year-old Kayli and that didn't go over well with her brother. Gordy beat the copper so badly that the poor man spent six months in the hospital and moved out of East Kilbride as soon as he was able. After that, the local boys knew better than to take liberties with pretty Miss Kayli Aitkens.

"Maybe it's better if I stayed at the Purple Drake. It's still there isn't it?" he asked.

The Purple Drake Inn was a small bed and breakfast not too far from her apartment.

"Yes, it's still there but I want you to stay with me, Gordy; I've missed you and it will be nice having you here."

But things seldom go quite as planned. From the very beginning, Ray wasn't happy with Gordy crowding *his* space but what he resented most was the change in Kayli. Ever since Gordy arrived, she was sassier, more critical, and openly confrontational. And in a strange way, it annoyed him that she was happy again. Then there was Sarah who doted on her uncle, crawling all over him. She would sit on his lap and tug on his handlebar mustache and giggle. Well, he had had enough.

Late one evening, Ray and his friends jumped Gordy in the parking lot and found out that courage from a bottle is never any good. As soon as the fur began to fly, his friends vanished, leaving him to deal with a major problem, one he was woefully unprepared for. He took a beating. A broken nose, busted jaw and several bruised ribs had him laid up for weeks. And, predictably, while taking care of her man, nursing him back to his feet, Kayli reconciled her differences with Ray. He swore eternal love and promised never to drink again and Kayli basked in this newfound devotion. Gordy, poor soul, took the fall. He was the bad guy and after days of hearing his sister's rant, *'I told you not to hurt him'* - he moved out.

It didn't take long though for Gordy to land on his feet. He found a job as a waiter and handyman at a pub called the Nueva Scotia off of A78 in Largs, a coastal town about an hour west of East Kilbride. The pay was modest, not quite what he made working for Maggie, but it was less dangerous and gave him time to contemplate his future. He found a studio apartment, a bedsit to the locals, near the pub and made some new friends and all things considered, life was going well for Gordy; that is, until Goran and his crew showed up.

It was late and the night was cold with swirling winds and a misty rain whipping across the coastline. It was the only thing he disliked about Largs – the weather. It was always cold and damp and no matter how many layers of clothing he wore, it chilled him down to the bone.

Gordy pulled his slicker tightly around him and shivered, "Fuck! I should've moved to Madrid."

The streetlights reflected a shimmering golden-yellow off of the wet cobblestones, and the clatter of his footsteps echoed into the quiet of night. He was thinking about Kayli, Sarah and Ray, and Maggie and the others until the image of Damir's head being lopped off strangled his thoughts. It was the one macabre sequence that haunted him most.

His bedsit was on the upper floor of a two-story home and he was halfway up the stairs when old Mrs. Cairns, his landlady, came out and said, "I let your friends in, Gordon. They seem like lovely lads."

It took him a moment to digest the implication of her words and just as he was about to question her, a voiced called down to him, "Hey Gordy, come on up, mate. We spoke to Kayli. Come up, we have a lot to catch up on."

Gordy was a big, tall man and towered over the diminutive fellow who had spoken to him, the same one who had elbowed Caleb in the gut. His name was Darren Wallers and a nasty piece of work he was. He had a reputation for having a quick temper and being a wizard with a switchblade.

"Well, well, well, if it isn't Tweedledee and Tweedledum! What do you boys want?" Gordy asked, nonplussed by their presence. He knew that sooner or later, he would have to deal with Maggie.

Goran was seated on the sofa in front of the TV and didn't move. He watched Gordy with cold, unfeeling eyes. It was Darren who was the mouthpiece.

"Maggie needs to see you, Gordy. You know you can't leave without saying goodbye," Darren informed him.

"I don't like goodbyes but I like Maggie and have always been loyal to her." He stopped and looked at both men then said, "What happened to Damir and Paddy will haunt me for the rest of my life."

"That's what we're here for, mate, to find out what happened."

He took off his raincoat, "I'm done with all that. You can inform Maggie and Adam. I'm going to settle down and be a good, churchgoing lad."

"What happened to Damir? That is only what I want to hear," Goran asked, getting up and taking a step towards Gordy. Though he was as tall as the

Englishman he wasn't as broad in the shoulders or as heavily muscled.

Gordy's face turned hard, "You better think twice about stepping up to me, cunt, or I'll break every fuckin' bone in your body!"

"Easy, Gordy-boy, easy. Dejan and Viktor are with your sister and that sweet little girl. Sarah; her name is Sarah, right?" Darren intervened, his hands up in a defensive, nonthreatening gesture. "All Maggie wants to know is who killed Damir and Paddy and how you managed to get away. I swear, Gordy, that's all."

"If you hurt my sister or my niece…"

"Nothing is going to happen to them as long as you tell us what happened," the small man interjected. "Now, who killed Damir and Paddy?"

"I have no idea who she was. She appeared out of nowhere and in seconds Damir lost his head and Paddy lay dying in the grave he dug for Caleb."

Wallers and Goran exchanged a quick look.

"You said 'she', are you sure it was a she?" Wallers asked.

"Yes, I'm sure. She was an oriental lass; tall and beautiful, and dangerous. I've seen some shit in my life but I've never seen anything like what took place there."

"So why she spare you? Why you are not dead and where is the American?" Goran quizzed.

"She came to rescue Caleb. I don't think he knew her so I'm assuming that she was hired by someone to get him out. Maybe it was the Swanson girl – she has the money to hire someone like her. And, the only reason I'm not dead is because Caleb intervened on my behalf. Trust me, she was about to take my head off when he pleaded with her to spare me. That's all I know."

"It is funny that you live and tell crazy story about some fucking ninja woman. I think you kill Damir and Paddy and let the American go. That's what I think. This is bullshit," Goran hissed.

"You are a blithering idiot! If I wanted to kill someone, I'd use a gun. I don't know how to use a sword and I certainly don't have the skill to kill two people like Damir and Paddy in a few seconds. Damir's head was sliced clean off and do you really think I did that?"

"Okay, okay. There's some stuff I don't get. We were told that there is a Japanese fellow, a ninja, who is involved and that is why we're confused. If there is a woman out there then we have two problems and Maggie needs to know that. You *have* to come back, Gordy, those are Maggie's orders," Darren Wallers said.

"I want to speak to my sister first, and now," Gordy replied glowering at Wallers, "so get her on the phone."

The smaller man hesitated but he wasn't going to risk pushing his luck, "No problems, mate, I'll call Dejan."

He called his associate and spoke tersely, "It's me; put the woman on." He waited and then handed the phone to Gordy. "Here you go."

"Hey little girl, are you okay? They haven't hurt you have they?"

"I'm fine, Gordy, but I'm scared. What is going on? I was about…"

"Don't worry, sis, I'm going to take care of it. You sit tight and when Ray comes home, tell him to mind his manners and not to be stupid. I'll take care of things."

"Gordy, what is…"

"Just sit tight, Kayli, I'll explain later."

Wallers grabbed the phone and hung up. "I told you, she's okay so now we need to get going. It's a long fuckin' drive and the M6 is always a bloody mess."

CHAPTER 23

THE TOUCH OF THE HUMMINGBIRD...

I wasn't happy with the plan. I was to stay with Shika, Ronnie and Andros until Jade or more appropriately, Lienna, came back from taking care of business. I tried to reason with her but she wasn't listening. Her come back to every suggestion was: *You have to trust me in matters like this, my love; this is what I have been trained to do.*

After a while I realized that there was no point in pressing the issue and called Shika. Once we got past the *'where have you been'*, *'why haven't you answered your phone'* and *'we were worried sick about you'* phase, I got the address to Grigori's place. It was in Colchester, which was about an hour or two from Lienna's cottage.

The drive there was accompanied by the drumming of the rain and the rhythmic swishing of the windshield wipers. The overcast sky was covered in fluffy, dark clouds and made for a gloomy presage matching my mood.

Lienna glanced over at me and took my hand in hers, "Don't be cross with me. I am doing this for us."

"I'm not cross," I replied, parodying her words. "I just don't understand why I can't come with you. Look at me, I mean really look at me, Lienna, do I look like I can't take care of myself?"

She smiled; it was that tolerant smile. "You are a big, handsome man and I am looking forward to our life together but, this is not a barroom disagreement or a fight in the cage," she glanced over, "Is that what it's called? No, I think it's called a cage fight, yes? It's not a cage fight. Akira Hirai is dangerous, more dangerous than any of the MSS trained killers, and that includes me. There are no rules in his kind of fighting."

"Then why are you pursuing this? Why don't we just disappear to some faraway place?"

"Because, my love, he will find us. And, it would be in my favor to choose the place rather than wait for him to pick his spot and time. I will have the advantage of surprise. And then there is the retribution for Kuok-Bai's murder. Fai Wong and his pack of rats will be held responsible. It is a debt I must repay to the man to whom I owe so much."

I was struck by the matter-of-fact manner in which she spoke about all this. She had major challenges in front of her having to deal with the Japanese ninja and the Chinese triad but she seemed unperturbed and determined. She had clarity of purpose, which was something I lacked my whole life. I looked at her and tried to rationalize this delicate and beautiful creature to the killer who beheaded Damir, but couldn't. So I did what any male chauvinistic pig would do, I resorted to being physical; psycho-physical!

"Pull over," I told her.

"Pull over where? What is wrong?" Concern etched on her face.

"Pull over! Right here on the shoulder."

She glanced at the rearview mirror and did as she was told.

"What's the ma..."

That's as far as she got. I leaned over and in one svelte swoop, pulled her to me and kissed her. She was startled, eyes wide and hands against my chest, but after a few seconds of gentle oral persuasion in the form of deep, sensual kisses, trailing from her forehead to her neck and to her lips, she closed her eyes and gave in. Her fingers ran through my hair, caressing the back of my head.

Now, making love in a MINI Cooper is almost impossible, especially for a big man like me but, if you recall, I had mentioned before that I was somewhat of a sexual savant and a creative one at that. I know my buddies would disagree and say that I was a sexual deviant and certainly *not* a savant but we'll get to that later; right now, all I wanted to do was to make love to this gorgeous woman. We could do it if I could get her to straddle me especially since I knew that she was nimble as hell, I mean, she had to be or there was no way she could have performed all those crazy gyrations – spinning, twirling, and whatnot.

She was wearing a blouse and long skirt which made it perfect. I began dragging her across the center console and that's when I think the realization of what I had in mind dawned on her. She hesitated but when I ran my tongue across her nipples, sucking gently, it sealed the deal – she was sold.

"Put the seat back," she whispered, her voice muffled with desire and lifting her skirt, she straddled me.

I could feel the moist heat through her panties searing the length of my shaft. And, as I unbuttoned her blouse she lifted herself off of me to free my cock. I felt her fingers guide me into her and lost myself in the tight, moist warmth of her. I closed my eyes, savoring the incredible sensations, as she sank down engulfing me inch by inch until we were fused at the crotch. She sighed and let out a soft moan and did something incredible; she squeezed my cock using her pussy – it was like nothing I'd ever felt.

She began riding me, slowly at first, staring into my eyes, up and down, up and down, making soft mewling sounds, going faster and faster, bouncing on my lap, her head thrown back, hair rolling in waves and flailing about her in a black, silky storm. Our groans and moans and salacious whispers only added to the heightened intensity of the union. This wasn't just fucking; it was an intimate physical experience, carnal and spiritual, driven by the need to possess the other – to be one; a karmic joining of souls.

The newness of her combined with the urgency of our tenuous situation proved to be too much. I could feel my orgasm building and at that precise moment she leaned over and kissed me, her mouth cold and hot all at once. And when she pushed her tongue deep into my mouth, it signaled the end; I couldn't hold back and crested the waves of pleasure, tumbling mindlessly into euphoric oblivion while pumping my juices deep into her. It seemed to go on forever, the writhing and thrusting, clutching and grinding, the orchestrated rhapsody complemented by the hiss of our labored breathing.

The silence that followed in the sybaritic aftermath hung heavy with echoed whispers of desires now spent.

When I finally opened my eyes, her face was nuzzled into the curve of my neck and we remained still, basking in the languid afterglow of our lovemaking. The slushy cacophony of the traffic and the relentless pitter patter of the rain were reminders of where we were and the reality of our transient state.

And all too soon, she stirred, raised her head and whispered, "We have to go, my love."

"No, not yet… just a few more minutes," I protested. I could have stayed there, holding her, while the rest of the world disappeared.

"We have to go." She was firm.

She sat up and reached behind her for the tissues, and slid back onto the driver's seat. Her every movement seemed effortless and graceful, and though this sounds repetitive, she was feminine to the core. She turned away to clean herself, and under the circumstances I found her modesty to be endearingly cute.

"Do you need help with that?" I teased.

She was shy and embarrassed. "I can manage, thank you."

I moved her hair aside and kissed the back of her neck, inhaling deeply. Her skin felt warm and silky smooth with a faint redolence of sandalwood and jasmine. "You are amazing, baby."

"I will never forget this moment," she murmured, cheeks blushing pink. She fussed with her clothing buttoning up her blouse and straightening her skirt, and then with a quick kiss she got us back on the highway.

I reached across and placed my hands on her leg, sliding it between her thighs, resting against the warmth of her mound. She was my mountain woman and everything felt just the way it should.

Francis Akira Hirai

THE GHOST WHO KILLS...

Akira Hirai waited, concealed behind a cluster of thick brush under the leafy canopy of a large, imposing beech tree that stood a few yards away from the cottage gates. He was a patient man, and despite the rain, hadn't moved in over an hour. When he saw the MINI Cooper driving past, he left the sanctuary of the cathedral-like boscage and raced swiftly to his car, a Volkswagen Golf that he had parked along a narrow grassy track.

He ignored the tiny rivulets of raindrops trickling down his forehead and cheeks and dripping onto his lap. His sodden clothing clung to his body with stubborn persistence, but he was unwavering in his focus. The contract was to neutralize the Hummingbird, kill

Maggie Walcott and return the attaché case to Fai Wong, the new head of the triad.

He could have killed the woman and the big American earlier but he needed them to lead him to the attaché case and the truth be told, he rather enjoyed the cat and mouse game being played. The Hummingbird was said to be a ghostly revenant of Kali herself, skilled and dangerous, and a worthy foe, but he, Akira Hirai, *was* the ghost who kills, and he had dealt with dangerous foes before.

He stayed several cars behind, shielded by the traffic and a veil of misty rain. He avoided changing lanes making sure not to raise any suspicions. When the MINI stopped on the shoulder, he drove past, going another five hundred or so yards, and around a slight bend, before easing over onto the shoulder. He wasn't sure why they had halted but he would wait – there was nowhere for them to go and experience had taught him that all things come to the one who waits.

CHAPTER 24

WAR DOGS...

Peter Rudd smiled to himself. Rachael was safe at her family's estate in Chelmsford and Maggie Walcott was losing her mind. She sounded almost hysterical over what had happened to Damir and Paddy. *Perfect; the plot thickens and he wouldn't shed a tear for those two bastards!* The more complicated things got, the more he enjoyed it. He had worked for MI6 and with the CIA before becoming a freelance operative – a facilitator of sorts for international espionage dealing with sensitive political situations. His years working for the British Secret Intelligence Service had taught him that no one was to be trusted and that a healthy paranoia was the key to survival in this treacherous arena. Question everything and trust no one – this was the advice his father had given him when he was recruited into the agency.

His father was an ex-MI6 operative, and his mother a beautiful Indonesian diplomat from whom he inherited his honey-golden skin and boyish good looks. Though his physical attributes had helped, it was his astute mind and his ability to assess the complex nature of the business that had brought him success.

Dishi Guan did not have the attaché case and had offered an outlandish tale about a debonair Black man who, with the help of the Russian mafia, had stolen it from him. Dishi Guam was an incompetent fool and not the person he would have chosen for this assignment but there was nothing he could do about that. The key now was to make sure that the triad or even better, the MSS, took possession of the attaché case. That would complete this mission, and Rachael and he could embark on their planned trip to Bali. He was looking forward to sipping margaritas by the crystal blue waters, making love and soaking in the sun.

Rachael would be calling her friends to locate the attaché case and once that was done, it would take but a few discrete phone calls to his contacts within the MSS. He chuckled and hummed tunelessly to himself.

Rudd was aware that Lienna Quan, the Hummingbird, was in the country and so too was Akira Hirai, but he wasn't sure which one of them killed Damir and Paddy – the modus operandi could have been the work of either assassin, or maybe both. His contacts in the MI6 had received information that the two assassins were working independently but he wasn't quite as sure. He hadn't ruled out the possibility that they could have colluded for this assignment. Akira Hirai held a Japanese passport but he was of Chinese descent. He recalled a conversation he had had with the head of the MSS, Wang Jie, who had told him: *You should never trust the Chinese, Peter. We are a bunch of xenophobic assholes.*

He chuckled again and pulled up outside the large cottage. He flipped the sun visor down and checked his reflection in the mirror, furrowed his brow, pushed back his hair, and said with a satisfied smile, "You're a handsome devil, Peter Rudd, a fucking heartbreaker!"

The grating crunch of the gravel under his feet should have alerted the big Rottweiler. Rudd stood by the car, looked around and called, "Hey Stills, where are you, boy?"

Rudd liked dogs and he was one of the very few that the big Rottweiler had bonded with. The giant dog was cunning and smart. He would lay low to ambush anyone he didn't recognize and God help the poor slob when that happened. He had witnessed the dog catch a red fox that had strayed too close to the cottage and within seconds there was nothing left but fur and shredded pieces of the unfortunate animal.

"Come on out, boy, papa's here!"

A man armed with an AK47 stepped out from the wooden barn that was located a hundred yards from the cottage and called out, "He's in the house with Crosby and Nash. They are all there. I'll let Maggie know you are here; she's expecting you."

He gave the man a thumbs-up and headed for the door. When he got to the office on the upper floor, Stills was the first to greet him. The big Rottweiler almost knocked him down.

"Now there's my boy! Come here you big, nasty rascal," Rudd said and got down on his knees to play-wrestle with the huge animal.

The others watched patiently, amused by their shenanigans, until Stills got riled up and rowdy and began growling and nipping at Rudd's arms. That's when Maggie stepped in.

"Okay, that's it for now. Come here, Stills, come here now!" she commanded and the Rottweiler promptly turned and trotted off to be with his comrades. The two Dobermanns hadn't moved a muscle. They sat by the woman like statues carved from stone.

"You've ruined that beautiful suit, Peter. Do you really have to get him worked up?" Maggie Walcott admonished.

Rudd dusted himself off, his white suit wearing the drool-soaked remnants of their tussle. "Hey, he's my favorite buddy and I do want to stay on his good side. So, what's the emergency?"

"What's the emergency?" Maggie was incredulous, her words rolling out with staccato speed. "Damir was decapitated and Paddy was skewered like a pig. Two of my best men are dead and the American is nowhere to be found. And as if that wasn't worrisome enough, Adam tells me that Akira Hirai may be responsible and will be after us to exact his pound of flesh, and you have the audacity to ask me what the emergency is?"

"Easy, old girl, it is a bit more complicated than that. Have you heard of the Hummingbird?"

"I have," Adam Barnett answered, "she's Kuok-Bai's private killer. She's said to be a succubus existing in both the real and the supernatural world, and one who possesses mystical powers. I always assumed that the rakshasa bit was a myth."

"I'm not sure about the voodoo stuff but she is no myth – she is as real as you and me. She was trained by the MSS and believe me, those killers are a handful. They make the Russian Red Sparrows look like kids at armature hour. If you've ever studied the Japanese ninja, these assassins are as close as you can get to them," Rudd said.

"So what are you saying, we now have two dangerous killers after us?" Maggie was in shock.

"That's a possibility. They could be collaborating though in the past both have preferred to work alone. The boys in San Diego were killed in very much the same manner, but Akira Hirai was still in Japan, so that spectacle in the parking lot had to be the work of the Hummingbird. One woman took out four battle-hardened veterans and those four were as tough as they get."

"That sounds preposterous," Maggie said, almost to herself.

"Preposterous or not, those are the facts." He let that sink in before he continued. "Now the two are in England, and I ask myself, why would two killers, both of whom have ties to the triad, come here at the same time? There are two possibilities – one is that they are here, working together to avenge Steven Chang and retrieve the attaché case, and two, they are here working independently and were hired by two different organizations with the same objective. There in no way to know for sure. However, what is irrefutable is that butchering Chang precipitated this and was a bad idea; you do acknowledge that, don't you, Maggie?"

"I had no idea that Bogdan and Florijan would lose control and get all medieval. That entire crew... they were a pack of wolves!" the woman protested.

"Now they are a dead pack of wolves. I don't think the triad cares. You are the head of this house and they hold you responsible. You also had Bogdan send you a video of the gruesome affair so pleading ignorance would hardly hold water." He gave the woman a piercing look. "They didn't come here to play checkers with you or to negotiate; they came here to finish the assignment. You should be flattered, Maggie, these assassins are the best available and cost a pretty penny. The triad must think very highly of you."

"For the record, I didn't ask for that video; Bogdan sent it to me," Maggie snapped back. "And I am not flattered; I am deeply concerned."

"You should be. This is going to be tricky."

"That is exactly why we pay you the big bucks, Peter, to take care of the inconveniences of our business."

"This is a tad bit more than an inconvenience, dear girl."

"Oh, I get it, you want more money?" Maggie asked, her tone laced with sarcasm.

"I'm not the one they are after so if you want to stay alive, I will need to ask for favors and bring in reinforcements, and that costs money. I will also speak to my friends in the MSS and see if they can stop the madness. Monetary compensation usually solves these problems."

"How much are we talking about?"

"The Chinese have gotten greedy, so the days of paying them with crumbs are gone. I have no idea what it will take, but the last thing you should be concerned about is how much. A fat bank account will be no good to you if your head gets lopped off. I will make a few calls and tally it all up. In the interim, bring the boys into the house. Leaving them in the barn is like leaving goats tied to a tree where tigers roam. They will be dead before sunrise."

Maggie's son, Brian, had been listening to the exchange. He stood up and said, "I'll go speak to the men. I think except for Colin, Milo and Fredrick, the others are with Goran. I agree, having them in the house makes more sense; out there, they are far more vulnerable."

"David's gone to see his mum and Gavin' wife is having a baby so we have two less. This is making me nervous. Hurry up and get back in here," she said to her son then turned to Barnett, "Adam, call Goran and find out where they are. We could use them here."

"I'll get you some additional men who can deal with this, I mean serious blokes who know what they are doing." Peter Rudd said, and got up. "The part I haven't figured out yet is where Caleb Montague fits in? Why wasn't he killed and where is he now? He was badly beaten so whoever did this must have him. There may be more to that boy than we thought."

"And where is Rachael Swanson?" Maggie asked.

"Honestly, I have no idea," Rudd lied, "but I'm not worried about her, she'll surface soon enough if she wants to barter for the attaché case."

"If she saw her brother getting shot she would have no reason to strike a deal, would she?" Maggie asked.

"When the shit hit the proverbial ceiling, she was ushered off by her friends, so I doubt she witnessed Edward's death," Rudd answered.

There was a short silence while they pondered the ramifications. It was Maggie who broke the silence.

"I need that attaché case so you need to find out where she is but for now, let's focus on keeping us alive."

Rudd smiled and said, "That's the plan. Don't worry; we'll have this place locked down tighter than Fort Knox. And with your dogs from hell, I think we can keep those killers at bay, at least for a while."

He walked over and gave the big Rottweiler a pat on his head and left, saying, "Hasta la vista, baby!"

Maggie waited until she heard the Lexus start up, "He makes me very uncomfortable. Don't let the choir-boy looks fool you. He's a very dangerous man. He was spawned by a reptilian monster and a nympho bitch. His father, Patrick Rudd, was a stone-cold killer and his mother, Seema Dassel-Rudd, was the great manipulator in her day. She used her looks and her cunt to win favors and bedded everyone from British royalty to the princes in Europe and Arabia – a real calculating, over-sexed bitch if there ever was one."

Adam Barnett was surprised by the resentful fervor in his partner's tone.

"Sheath the claws, Maggie. We'll keep a close watch, and when the time is right, we can deal with him the old-fashioned way," Barnett replied and walked over to the liquor cabinet. "I could use a drink. What would you prefer, scotch or vodka?"

"Ballantine's on ice. Vodka gives me a headache."

And while Adam poured the drinks, Maggie stood by the window watching the men and her son troop back towards the cottage. *I should never have gotten Brian involved in all this.* The sense of perdition that welled up in her was suffocating. Her son was the only thing she loved more than her precious dogs.

She could use that drink.

"Make it a double, Adam," she said and walked back to her desk.

CHAPTER 25

FRIENDS AND LOVERS, AND FOES...

"It is possible that Akira Hirai has followed us," Lienna said to me as we drove into the driveway of Grigori's large brick-and-stone Tudor.

"What do you mean?" I wasn't thinking about that little ninja, I was thinking about what the meeting between Rachael and Lienna would be like. I would have to break the news to Rachael that there was only one woman for me and that it wasn't her.

"After..." she paused, blushing before continuing, "After we made love, I noticed that there was a car, a black Volkswagen Golf that was parked on the shoulder. With people like Hirai and me, you have to assume that we are one step ahead of what you are thinking."

"I was thinking about making love to you again and if you are one step ahead then we need to find a hotel soon, don't you think?" I said with what I considered a sexy, mischievous smile, and squeezed her thigh. My hand was still lodged between her legs.

She slapped my wrist and freed my hand from its warm confines.

"Be serious, my love. This is not a joke. This man is very dangerous and he could be watching us right now. He is like the wind; I can feel him but I cannot see him."

I've got to be honest; this ninja bullshit was way beyond me. I don't go for all the smoke and mirrors crap. Let's take it into the back alley, face off and go, and let the better man win. But I realized that these killers were far more dangerous than anything I had dealt with.

"Okay, so what do you sug…" that's as far as I got when a shout split the air.

"Cal! Damn bro, where the fuck have you been?" It was Ronnie with Andros trailing behind him. He opened the door and dragged me out and gave me a hug. "I swear, man, we thought you had bought it! Why didn't you answer your phone? And your face, what the fuck happened?"

He peeked inside the car, while I was being crushed by the big Russian, and said, "Whoa! And, who is *this* lovely lady?"

"My name is Lienna Quan. I am…"

"She's my mountain woman," I interrupted, sensing her uneasiness. I put my arm around her and continued with something that was pure, unadulterated gibberish. "She saved my sorry ass and we are souls destined to cross our bridges together."

I knew that sounded pretty ridiculous. Andros and Ronnie exchanged glances and did their best not to burst out laughing. The bit about souls and bridges made no sense at all but that shit just rolled off my tongue. I wasn't sure how else I could explain my destiny with this exotic siren.

There was an awkward silence following my proclamation. I knew exactly what my friends were thinking. *WTF! What about Rachael?* Good question. Where the fuck *is* Rachael? And, where is Shika?

I looked past Grigori, who was standing on the upper landing of the stoop with two of his goons and a German shepherd, but there was no sign of the either woman. I was about ask the million-dollar question when Andros stepped in and in his inimitable manner, took over.

He gave Lienna a quick gentle hug and said, "Welcome! If you are with my brother here, then you are my family. Yes, yes, I know, we don't look same. He is from different mother, much prettier mother, no? Come on, we celebrate. Come on, all of you, we go eat, drink and talk of good things! My brother is back and he is safe, and that is good."

Lienna took me aside before we went up the steps and confided, "He's here, Caleb, I can feel his presence. This is not good. I am going to stay here and your friends and you have to leave. I will take care of him and call you when it's done."

I could see the concern on her face. This wasn't the time for a smartass quip.

"I don't think Andros or Grigori will leave. These guys are all ex-Spetsnaz and not afraid of anyone or anything. I mean these are guys who said 'fuck you' to Vladimir Putin and are still alive," I replied.

"You must convince them. And if they refuse then I will have to lead him away. Too many of your friends will die if I don't."

"I will try. Come on, I'll talk to Andros."

Who was I kidding? There was no talking to Andros. Everything I said was met with a "Fuck him! Andros kick his ninja ass."

"Where is Shika?" I asked, frustrated and hoping she could talk some sense into her lover.

"Rachael, she call. Shika is with her. She went with two of Grigori's men and with attaché case. They are safe. Don't worry, Cal, I tell you they are safe."

When I told Lienna about Andros' intransigence, she was annoyed.

"You men!" she hissed in frustration, "your egos are going to get you killed."

I was about to reply when a booming voice cut in, "Come, we have some tea and Russian cookies – it is very tasty and nice. Like mama make."

How can you not love this guy? I just told him there was a killer ninja on the loose and his answer was *let's have some cookies*. He had a way of making me feel that there was nothing to worry about, and that life was good. And this feeling, it was contagious; I sensed Lienna's mood shifting. She smiled and we went into the house holding hands.

Ronnie gave me a strange look but didn't say anything. I'm certain the curiosity was killing him. I had to smile; for once Adonis wasn't the one with the gal!

From beneath the cover of the trees, Akira Hirai watched the Hummingbird and her friends enter the home. The dog didn't bother him – poison darts always worked. But this wasn't the time or the place, he thought to himself. There were too many of them, and they were dangerous, a bit too dangerous. These Russians were not the type to be taken lightly and he would prefer to deal with the Hummingbird alone, a one-on-one confrontation with no intrusions or distractions.

He would focus elsewhere for now.

CHAPTER 26

DISCOVERY...

It was late, well past midnight, when Gordy, Goran, Darren Wallers and the boys arrived back at the Lamb's Head Farm. To their surprise, the place was cloaked in darkness except for the golden streaks of light piercing through the slats in the barn door. None of the external lights that usually lit up the yard were turned on and there was no one patrolling the property, and that was odd. Maggie always had one or two men walking the yard.

They had spoken to Adam Barnett about an hour ago and nothing seemed untoward, only that Maggie wanted them at the farm and to hurry back.

"I don't like this one bit," Gordy said rolling down the window. He whistled a shrill double inflected call, a signal for the big Rottweiler to respond, but it was met with silence.

"Maybe they go somewhere to be safe," Goran suggested.

"No, they wouldn't do that without telling us. There is something amiss here," Gordy replied.

They remained in the car peering into the darkness beyond the hazy glow of the headlights until Wallers spoke up. "Gordy, you'd better go and check. I don't fancy having my throat ripped out by that beast. He's a cunning bastard he is; a real fucking piece of work."

"Okay, but something isn't right," he reiterated. "Call Maggie."

The big man stepped out of the car and looked cautiously towards the barn. The grating crunch of gravel would have given him away but he needn't have worried, there seemed to be no sign of life.

Gordy called out again, "Stills! Hey boy, come on out, it's me, come here, boy." He got no response so he leaned over the open window and said to the men, "He's not here. Did you call her?"

"No answer. It keeps ringing. I tried Adam's phone but he's not answering either."

"One of you stay with the car, the others go and check the cottage. Turn the lights on in the foyer," he instructed the men.

"I'll stay," Darren Wallers volunteered and asked, "Do you want me to come with you, Gordy?"

"No, you stay in the car and keep it running just in case we have to get the bloody heck out of here. This is giving me the fucking willies," Gordy replied, and with gun drawn began trudging noisily towards the barn.

None of them noticed the shadow hidden in the darkness watching them with a smile on his face. Akira Hirai enjoyed his profession and delighted in the way his traps played out.

The Serbs led by Goran entered the stone cottage and stopped at the top of the stairway. Lying motionless near Maggie's office door were both Dobermanns. They were either sedated or dead. These dogs never left Maggie's side and Goran had rarely seen them quiescent and never so when others were around. They were trained attack dogs and the sight of them lying still made the hairs on his nape bristle.

Dejan said in Serbian, "This is not good, boss, let us leave… we can come back in the morning."

"We are not leaving. We are not pussies! I am not worried about some slant-eyed bitch," Goran hissed, recalling Gordy's story about the oriental woman. He motioned to the room adjacent to Maggie's office and commanded, "You look in that room, and Viktor, you check downstairs. Make sure there is no one there. Keep your back to the wall and shoot anything that moves."

Without a word Viktor made his way back down the stairway.

"Listen Goran; we have been friends, no, more like brothers since we were kids. I am asking you as a friend and your older brother to leave. We can come back in the morning. What we are dealing with is not normal, I can feel it, and it is not what we are used to. Listen to me, brother."

Goran studied the older man. He had known Dejan for as long as he could remember. As children they had been inseparable and though he had taken lead in their relationship, their bond exceeded the limitations circumscribed by the hierarchy of work. Dejan had never resented his leadership. And for his part, Goran was well aware of his friend's strengths and weaknesses. Dejan had a soft heart and was more of a dreamer than a warrior.

"Alright Dejan, you go and wait in the car with Darren. I will check the rooms and if Maggie is dead, we go back to Palić. Fuck the English and this cold, sunless country."

His friend hesitated for a moment then nodded and made his way down the stairs. Goran waited until he was gone, then with his back against the corridor wall, he inched towards the office. He felt blindly behind the door for the toggle switch and turned on the lights. What greeted him was a scene even his war-hardened senses couldn't fathom. The awful smell of feces and urine was overpowering and he had to hold a hand up to cover his nostrils.

Maggie was dead, her body propped up against the liquor cabinet and sitting in a pool of her own blood. Her throat had been slashed and her face held the ashen hue that comes with severe hemorrhaging. Roughly five feet from her was Adam Barnett - he was lying face down with his bald dome facing the desk. He too was dead. The manner of his demise was evidenced by the scarlet ring and sanguinary puddle around his neck, and the feculent stain on the back of his trousers was a clear indication that he had soiled himself in death.

Lying across the doorway was Colin Sears. It was hard to tell how he had met his end but the frozen expression etched on his face was indication enough that he was as dead as one can get. Goran stepped over the body and looked around the room and noticed a pair of feet sticking out from behind the desk. It was Brian, Maggie's son. He too had met his end. What was puzzling to Goran was that all four had been killed and none of them did anything to stop the carnage. Add to this the fact that there was no sign of Milo or Fredrick and it bordered on the bizarre.

Goran felt uncertain and fearful, feelings he hadn't experienced since he was a boy and his grandfather would tell him stories of Ala, the demon, who would come out at night to eat the hearts of little boys. A shiver ran down his spine.

Maybe Dejan was right and they were dealing with something beyond the scope of their capabilities; maybe those stories of Ala and beings that dwell in the quantum realm were real. And just maybe these tele-plasmatic creatures who take human form and possess supernatural powers do visit the living to mete out their form of justice. His father's words echoed in his ears: *You have to know your boundaries, Goran, and set your limits within them.* It would make sense to come back the next day during daylight when demons and such take refuge.

He stood by the window staring down at the front yard. The soft rumbling of the Jaguar's engine and the scalloping smoke from the tailpipe offered him some comfort. *At least we are alive,* he thought to himself. And, just as he was about to turn away, the loud crackling sound of breaking glass stopped him in his tracks. He looked out and saw Viktor's lifeless body lying near the car, face contorted in horror and eyes wide open, staring blindly at the night sky. Viktor was a big man standing six-two and weighing well over two hundred pounds. It would take an inordinately strong person to hurl him through a window.

He swore, "Fuck!" and ran down the stairs just as the shrill klaxon of a car horn rent the silence.

"Dejan!" he screamed above the brassy din, "Dejan, run... run!"

It was too late. From the doorway, the reason for the blaring horn became obvious to him - Darren Wallers was slouched forward with his face resting on the steering wheel, and on the passenger's side, Dejan was slumped sideways against the door. He didn't have to investigate to know that both men were dead. He ran past the car towards the barn and though he disliked the big Englishman, Gordy was his last bastion of refuge. Terror raged through him like a wildfire and the only thought he had was survival.

CHAPTER 27

DANGEROUS LIAISONS...

Peter Rudd was happy with the way things were progressing. He was on his way to Chelmsford to meet up with Rachael and hopefully locate the briefcase. He assumed her friends must have it, and it was imperative that it get to the MSS via the triad or directly through one of his contacts within the organization. Maggie's failure in dealing with Steven Chang in a manner that would have been acceptable was one of the reasons the project was in the state it was in. All she had been tasked to do was to get the original briefcase from Chang and instead she butchered him *after* the replacement was stolen by Edward and his girl, Satin. Two mistakes were more than you could make in this business.

Maggie and her crew are dead, they just don't know it yet, he mused. He was a realist and though he had liked the woman, there was no saving them. Assassins like the Hummingbird and Akira Hirai were not easily discouraged, and the cost far outweighed the benefits of intervention. It was time anyway to assemble a new team for his many complicated and often devious schemes. He made sure never to get too close to his associates and for good reason – sooner or later they would become competition or end up dead. This was a nasty business and with very little margin for error.

He liked to refer to these assignments as his "projects". The Project Erebus would soon be over and once the Chinese got their hands on the AI, he could focus on the next one.

Maggie and Adam were getting greedy, digging into my business dealings. The queen bitch was attempting to bypass me. She was too smart for her own good. He had a few people in mind who could replace her, and once Rachael and he returned from their planned holiday to Bali and Phuket, he would begin preparing the new crew.

When Rudd arrived at the Swanson mansion, he had expected Rachael to be alone so it came as a surprise when he saw Shika and two burly men with her. His first thought, contrary to most, was *'the more the merrier!'*

"Hello Rachael, I had no idea you had friends over," he greeted them with a dazzling smile. He recognized Shika from the airport but the two men were new to him. "Ah, beauty and the beasts! So, who are the dangerous looking blokes?"

Rachael gave him a quick peck on the cheek and put her arm around Rudd's waist, "You met Shika at the airport; she's the beauty and this is Denis and next to him is Alexey. They are dangerous, yes, but I wouldn't call them beasts." She then introduced Rudd to the others, "This is Peter Rudd, a dear friend."

Shika shook Rudd's hand but the two Russians merely nodded and walked back to the window where they resumed their conversation. Alexey was tall and pale with tattoos covering his neck and arms. He had soft, brown hair and a long, gaunt face. Denis was a tad shorter but was much thicker in the chest and arms. He had black hair cut short, a trimmed mustache and beard, thick dark eyebrows that offered a striking contrast to his sky-blue eyes. *'These boys weren't to be mucked with'*, Rudd thought to himself and decided to turn his attention to Shika.

"Shika! What an unusual name. What is it, Spanish? Or is it Japanese or Indian maybe?" he asked amicably.

"It's just a name," was the blunt reply. She instinctively distrusted Rudd and looked him right in the eyes. "I am here to make sure that nothing happens to Rachael. There's a lot of shit going down."

"Ah, yes, there have been some unusual occurrences and you can never be too careful these days," Rudd paused, taking out a cigarette. He used an ivory-inlaid gold lighter to light up and took a deep drag, holding the smoke in his lungs and enjoying the pleasant burn of the menthol before blowing a vortex of smoke-rings into the air.

The others watched him with the curiosity reserved for dangerous reptiles – it was like watching a King

Cobra or a Black Mamba. Apart from his good looks, there was something intangible about Rudd that caught people's attention, something that set their nerves on edge.

"Is there any news of your friend, Caleb?" he inquired, looking across at Rachael.

"He's with Andros and Ronnie. They'll be here soon," Rachael answered. "Shika spoke to Andros and it seems a mysterious Chinese woman saved him from Maggie's merry men. Could she be the one you spoke about, the one they call the Hummingbird?"

Rudd hid his surprise and shrugged. "She could be. No one really knows what the Hummingbird looks like so it's hard to tell. All the intel we have on her is pure conjecture – smoke with no fire. I'd like to meet her if that is possible."

He took another deep draw on the menthol when Denis came over.

"Cigarette?" he asked and extended his hand.

Rudd studied the tall man, his attention drawn to the tattoos covering the Russian's arms. These weren't prison tats but some really intricate stuff done in Japan or Thailand.

"That's some fine ink you've got there, mate," he complimented and offered Denis the pack. "Here you go, keep it; I've got more in the car."

The Russian took the cigarettes, nodded and went back to his friend. The two conversed briefly before he turned to Shika, "We go out to smoke, is okay?"

"Sure. Don't go too far," Shika answered and watched the men leave. "Caleb, Andros and the rest will be here shortly. Do we have enough for dinner or are we going out?"

"I checked with John and Helga. We have plenty. They're busy with dinner so we'll stay in, sit by the fireplace and share some wine and good company," Rachael said. "I'll be hap…"

"Where's the briefcase?" Rudd interrupted. "If they have it then they need to bring it with them."

His tone had changed. It was more of a command than a request. His friendly demeanor was replaced by a hard edge.

"I have it and it stays with me unless Rachael tells me otherwise," was Shika's terse answer. She looked over at Rachael expectantly.

"Thank you, Shika, but it is okay. Give it to him. He knows what to do with it."

"Do you want to wait until Caleb gets here?" Shika wasn't convinced that Rudd could be trusted. It was her intuition and she had rarely been wrong.

"No, we don't have to wait. The sooner all this is over, the safer we will all be. Edward is dead and I have no use for it."

When Shika left to get the attaché case Rudd lowered his voice, "How much do they know? I mean about us?"

"That we are good friends, that's all."

"Keep it that way. I'll get rid of the briefcase and then we can leave for our holiday."

"I can't wait. This entire thing with the attaché case and Edward has been too much. I want to move on, Peter, I want to lay down roots somewhere nice and have a simple but glorious life."

"And I promise you, you will have just that. Bear with me for a few more weeks and all of this will be behind us," Rudd reassured her.

He never tired of looking at her. She reminded him of a swan, graceful and beautiful. Rudd got up and went over to where Rachael was seated and was about to give her a kiss when they heard the muffled tread of shoes coming down the stairway.

"Here you go," Shika said tossing the attaché case onto the sofa near the fireplace and added, "All this killing, lying, and deceit and for what? Money? Power, what is this all for?"

"I don't know what rocks your boat, sister," Rudd replied looking directly at Shika, "but I need a certain amount of money for the lifestyle I've chosen. And since I lack any real talent for theatre and am as uncoordinated as a three-legged goat, this is all I know. It's a complicated game that requires nerves of steel and brains. It's a game with no rules and killing is part of the game. One wrong move and it could be me who ends up dead. However, that doesn't faze me - I'm willing to sit at that table because the higher the risk, the greater the reward. And truth be told, I enjoy the thrill of it."

Shika didn't say anything; his honesty took her by surprise. He had no moral compass but at least he didn't pretend to be anything else. He was a creep but he wasn't a hypocrite. She studied the man, knowing that she played in the same arena. Maybe not the same game but her dealings were mostly with dangerous and/or desperate people. Andros and she ran every nefarious trick in their neighborhood – drugs, booze, prostitution, protection; you name it and they were into it. Maybe they weren't that different after all. Maybe she was just like Rudd. The thought had a sobering effect on her.

She looked out the window at the two men smoking and making small talk. Their comradery was obvious and it brought back memories of Caleb, Ronnie and her, and how they would stay up late talking about their dreams and aspirations for the future. Nothing had worked out as they had planned. Ronnie's NFL career was cut short by a devastating knee injury, Caleb's Navy Seals ambition was thwarted when he decked an officer, and her own dreams of becoming a restauranteur ended that fateful day when her stepfather raped her… it seemed like they were jinxed. But that was when she was Emma and it was before the rape and before prison.

Where was Emma? Was she really dead? She felt an inexplicable sadness in her heart. She needed to put the negativity of her circumstance behind her and start afresh – go someplace new and open a small coffee shop. She had always wanted to do that. They had enough money and Andros would be happy to help her with that. She needed to resurrect Emma, to rediscover her and bury Shika once and for all. She would forgive her stepfather and those who…

Her thoughts were interrupted by the two cars pulling into the driveway. It had to be Andros, Caleb, Ronnie and the others. Her mood lifted instantly and she smiled.

"They're here," Shika said and headed to the front door to greet them.

CHAPTER 28

FLIGHT OF THE HUMMINGBIRD...

When Goran entered the barn, he saw Stills hanging from the rafters. The huge Rottweiler had been disemboweled with his entrails piled under him in a bloody, spiral soufflé. The foul stench emanating from the dog's stomach pouch and intestines took him back to his youth when he worked in his uncle's butcher shop. It was the odor of death and smelled worse than the slaughterhouses he had visited.

He noticed Gordy standing against the back wall seemingly mesmerized, staring past the hanging dog at something or someone behind him. The tall Serb turned, a rubberneck reflex, when the katana slashed across his neck severing both his jugular vein and the external carotid artery. A misty, maroon geyser sprayed high and far as the gun dropped from his hand and he clawed at his neck. He stumbled drunkenly towards the dark shadow when the sword was driven through his heart. The last rational thought he had was of his family in Palić, and that he would never see them again.

A loud gasp escaped from his lips and echoed over the faint sputtering of the Jaguar's engine, before he fell to the floor with a resounding thud. His body twitched and jerked in a final act of defiance, and then it was still.

Gordy hadn't moved. He was as tough as they come but panic and fear, those uncompromising imposters, had paralyzed him. He sank slowly to his knees and bowing his head, he prayed. Thoughts of his childhood, his parents, and Kayli raced through his mind in jumbled, blurry sequences. He needed to make peace with his maker, and after a whispered petition for forgiveness, he ended by reciting the Lord's Prayer.

"Our Father, who art in heaven,

Hallowed be thy name.

Thy Kingdom come…"

Akira Hirai stood over Gordy with the katana raised high. He stood still, every muscle taut and ready, but he did not strike. He listened to the solemn incantation then lowered his sword, studying the huddled form bowed in frightened obeisance. Hirai's father was a devout Christian and he couldn't bring himself to kill the Scotsman while he was in prayer. Without a word he turned and left through the side door.

The soft rustle of the assassin's clothing and the ensuing creaking of the door jarred Gordy's eyes open. For a moment he couldn't believe he was still alive. He looked around to make sure the threat was gone, and that it wasn't a ploy or some sort of a sadistic trick to prolong the game. But he needn't have worried. Akira Hirai was gone, disappearing like the morning mist on a sunny day.

He made the sign of the cross and looked skyward and whispered, "Thank you, Father. Thank you for giving me another chance."

He got up and went outside and stood by the barn door. His hands were trembling and his throat was dry, and as he looked at the stars and moon he was overcome by a salmagundi of emotions, emotions that ran the gamut of elation, fear, grief and relief, but most of all, he felt a sense of thankfulness. Though he had no idea why the killer had spared his life, he was grateful and was convinced that the Lord had interceded on his behalf. How else could he have survived the encounter with that beautiful siren, and now this brush with certain death? There could be no other explanation. If this wasn't divine intervention he didn't know what was. He was being given another chance, and this time he was going to take full advantage of it.

He took a deep breath before walking over to the Jaguar. He studied Viktor's body and the bodies inside the car before turning off the engine and shook his head in disbelief. And though he wasn't particularly fond of Goran, the manner of his death was frightening. The Serb didn't stand a chance at all; he was cut down like an inanimate mannequin. Gordy was quite certain that there would be no survivors in the house.

"Oh God, what a fucking nightmare!" he muttered to himself over the cacophony of crickets and frogs serenading the creatures of the night.

It was going to take him some time but he was determined to clean up the mess, and bury every last one of the people he had known and had worked with. He started with the ones who were nearest to him, lining their bodies next to the car - Goran, Dejan, Darren and Viktor. He cut the big Rottweiler down and placed him outside the barn before going into the cottage. He found the bodies of Milo and Frederick in the utility closet located under the stairway. He felt a sadness he couldn't explain. Milo was only twenty and was the nicest of the Serbs. *He was just a curious kid and way too young to die.* He dragged their bodies out and laid them next to the others and wiped his blood-soaked hands on his trousers before going back into the house.

One by one, he brought the bodies of Maggie, Adam, Colin and Brian down the stairs and into the yard, and laid them in a neat row adjacent to their friends. And finally, he dealt with the Dobermanns, and after arranging them alongside the Rottweiler, he stood back and sighed. He was fond of dogs and the sight of Crosby,

Still and Nash lying dead pushed him over the tipping point. The anguish and turmoil he had bottled up burst free and he began sobbing uncontrollably. Perhaps it was a catharsis or maybe an overwhelming sense of relief knowing that amidst the carnage he was lucky to be alive, and try as he might, he couldn't control the tears. He leaned back against the car, face buried in his hands, and let his emotions run their course.

In all, that shadow or ghost or whatever it was had taken the lives of ten people and three dogs and did it before they knew what hit them. That was awe-inspiring. *I will never kill or hurt another living creature again,* he thought and began the tedious task of burying the dead.

It was nearing dawn when he finished. He sat by the graves and prayed for the departed, then took his gun out and threw it as far as he could into the nearby brook. He stood silently basking in the glimmer of the early morning sunlight, looking over at the silhouette of the distant cloud-capped hills. He had often seen Maggie standing where he stood now, watching the migrating birds and talking on her phone. It was a beautiful spot and she would have wanted to be buried here.

He was covered in sweat and blood and grime, and was exhausted, but decided to drive home, back to Largs, back to the comfort of Scotland. He wanted to get as far away from this madness as he could.

Sisters, brothers, friends, and lovers, and death...

The meeting between Rachael and Lienna was not at all what I had expected. They were cordial and for her part, Rachael was warm and convivial. She hugged Lienna and said, "Welcome. Welcome to my family's home and thank you for saving Caleb."

Lienna was more reserved. I noticed her cheeks flush slightly before she stepped back and answered, "Thank you. That is most kind. I am Lienna Quan and..."

"The Hummingbird!" Peter Rudd exclaimed, interrupting her and stepping forward, "Lienna Quan, I've waited years to meet you. There are many who think you are just a myth. Let me..."

"If you know that I'm the Hummingbird then you know that Akira Hirai is here and that you are all in danger," Lienna replied, interrupting Rudd.

I figured that this was the best time to set the record straight, and seeing Rudd again only brought back memories of the beating I took from Goran. I didn't like this good looking, slick motherfucker and walking up on my woman was certainly a no-no.

I pulled Lienna to me and gave him my best "fuck you, asshole" look and shoved him hard and hissed, "Hey buddy, don't ever do that again. The next time I'll break you fuckin' neck, get it?"

Rudd stumbled back, caught his balance and protested, "Hey, easy mate! I know exactly why you're angry and I don't blame you. I wanted to help, truly I did, but they would have been suspicious. Come on, Caleb, you know that Goran is a nasty piece of work. I was trying to get you out of there. You can ask Rachael; I was, really, I was."

Rachael intervened, corroborating the asshole's account. "He was, Cal, he called several people he knew to get you out."

To say that the ensuing silence was awkward would be the understatement of the year. I felt a bit foolish but having Lienna next to me, holding my hand, reassured me. I still didn't like the bum but maybe he was telling the truth, and it was my unfortunate stint with Maggie that brought Lienna into my life. In some convoluted way, this asshole was the facilitator of our karma.

It was Andros, in his inimitable manner, who eased the tension, "Come. We are all friends. My brother, Cal, he don't like people getting too close to his woman. He slap my face because I give her hug! But I am bear and it don't hurt; it is like fly with elephant, no!"

And then he let out a loud, bellowing guffaw. It was contagious and soon we were all laughing with him, even that slimeball Rudd.

Ronnie smiled, nudged me with his elbow, and added, "I'll bet that's the first time anyone has called you a fucking fly!"

"So if I'm a fly, what does that make you?" I retorted. I was a lot bigger than Ronnie.

"Fly shit, that's what it makes me," Ronnie replied with that mischievous smile. He then got serious. "Hey, bro, why don't we go home? It's been fun but I miss Ricco and I'm getting homesick."

"There's nothing more I'd like to do than go home but Lienna has some unfinished business and I want to be here in case she needs me. We'll talk it over and make plans soon. Why don't Shika, Andros and you go home? I'll follow as soon as I know that Lienna is okay."

"You're an asshole, you know, a real fuckin' asshole! I'm not leaving you here. We'll see this through together. Come on; let's go in before Andros eats everything in sight."

Trust him to worry about food at a time like this but I felt better with Ronnie by my side. I could always count on him – brothers to the end.

When we got inside, Shika and Lienna had found a quiet corner away from the others. I have no idea what they could be discussing but it was obvious that they were comfortable with each other. They were huddled together, glancing in my direction on occasion, and giggling conspiratorially like schoolgirls.

I was about to go over when Rachael intercepted me.

"Peter didn't mean anything by it, Caleb, and I'm so happy you've found someone. She is so beautiful – exotic and graceful. You deserve to be happy."

"You're not mad?" I asked, bewildered by her nonchalance.

"Mad? No, not at all! What we had was wonderful but I think we both knew…"

The high-pitched scream from the kitchen cut her off and ended any plans we had for an uneventful evening.

Lienna was the first to react and got to the kitchen ahead of the rest. We followed willy-nilly, in a schizophrenic crush of fear and adrenalin, and were greeted by the ghastly sight of Denis's head, lying on its side; his striking blue eyes staring lifelessly back at us with a neatly folded piece of paper protruding from his mouth.

Lienna retrieved the paper, wiped it clean, and was reading the note when I peered over her shoulder. It was written in Chinese or Japanese script and looked like art but it was Greek to me. I studied her face for clues but she was expressionless.

I heard Helga's strident voice.

"It rolled in from the back door like a bowling ball..." she stuttered. Her husband John was holding her, trying to calm her down, but she was near hysteria. "I didn't see or hear anything until it..." she shuddered, "Oh, God, have mercy on us!"

"Shhh. You need to be quiet," Lienna said. "Quiet! Now!"

And though it was a whisper, there was no mistaking the urgency in her voice. She wasn't Lienna Quan anymore, but had morphed into the Hummingbird.

"Stay here. Lock the doors and form a circle. Don't let your guard down for a moment. It is me he wants. He is not after you but he will do anything to get my attention." She looked at Rachael. "Where's the valise?"

There was a moment's silence when Rachael looked confused so Lienna asked again, "Where is the valise, the briefcase?"

"It's in the living room, on the couch by the fireplace. I'll get…" Shika answered.

"It's mine!" Rudd interrupted, stepping back towards the living room, "I'll deal with it. You are not getting it."

"It is not yours to keep and you are lucky that my benefactor, Kuok-Bai, thought you may prove to be useful or I would have ended your miserable life long before now. I know all about you, Peter Rudd, and I am familiar with the machinations of your father and your mother. You need to reconsider your ways."

"Kuok-Bai is dead," Rudd mumbled, almost petulantly.

"I know and I will settle that score, but now I need the valise. Akira Hirai wants it, and unless I bring it with me, more of you will die."

Rachael decided to step in. "It is mine. I was keeping it for my brother but he's dead. I am now giving it to you, Lienna Quan, because I trust you." She turned to face Rudd. "Peter, you stay out of this."

And with that she brushed by Rudd and went into the living room. She returned with the briefcase, and extended it towards Lienna. "Here, it is yours and I am hoping and praying that you will end this insanity so we can all go back to living normal lives."

The Hummingbird took the attaché case, and came over to me, and took me aside. She squeezed my hand and whispered, "I love you, Caleb Montague, I have always loved you, even before we met. You were a thought that I clung to when things were desperate. I know you don't understand this, but one day you will."

I was lost, drowning in the dark pools of her eyes and for a moment I felt my heart stop. I couldn't believe how deeply I cared for this woman who I barely knew. It defied logic but logic be damned – love is beyond any rational explanation and I was in love. I know what you are thinking; I said the same thing when I was with Rachael, but this time it's real, trust me.

"Where are you going?" I asked her.

"I'm going to end this once and for all," she answered.

"Yes, but *where* are you going?"

She hesitated, and I could see that she was ambivalent. There was a part of her that wanted to tell me everything so I pressed her before she could change her mind.

"Please Lienna, don't leave me hanging. Where are you going?"

She handed me the note.

"The address is in there."

"I'm coming with you," I said to her, trying to sound convincing.

"No, Caleb, he will use you against me. This, I must do alone. They need you here, so wait for me. I will return after I end this and if I don't, we will meet again in another life." She paused and then said, "Promise me that you will not follow; listen to me, Caleb, I do not want to lose you now. Promise me that you will stay here."

I nodded. "Okay, have it your way."

She rose up on her toes and gave me a soft kiss on the mouth, and before I could stop her she was gone, melting into the darkness. I heard the car start up and watched the taillights disappear and was filled with a feeling of inevitable loss. After searching for so long, I had found my soulmate only to lose her now. She was headed into the eye of the storm, and though I knew that this was her destiny, I was riddled with doubt and a premonition that I may never see her again.

I looked absentmindedly at the paper in my hand and it remained indecipherable, but then it struck me, Rachael! Yes, Rachael could read Mandarin. I *could* find out where Lienna was going to meet Akira Hirai, and just maybe help her slay the monster. That was the predestination for both of us, no, the three of us, because Akira Hirai was woven into the fabric of our saga.

CHAPTER 29

THE METAMORPHOSIS...

The Levington Textile Mills was located a few miles off of the A14, a stone's throw from the Ransomes Industrial Estate in Ipswich. In the early 1960s and '70s it had been one of the largest garment manufacturing centers in all of Britain, but with the advent of globalization and the de-industrialization of England, it declared bankruptcy in 1985 and shut its doors for good. The abandoned factory was about a fifty-minute drive from Chelmsford and was the perfect venue for what Akira Hirai had planned.

He hid his car under a cluster of trees that fringed the parking lot located behind the building farthest away from the entrance. He was certain that the Hummingbird would come alone, but he was a cautious man and wanted to be sure. His strategy would be a lot different if she arrived with her friends, especially the Russians who were all ex-military. He needed to get this assignment wrapped up before he could return to Japan and his secluded life. He missed the beauty of his garden and the familiar warmth of his bed.

The textile complex consisted of five large rectangular structures and three smaller cottage-style buildings that served as the offices at one time. The roof of one of the smaller manufacturing buildings was all but gone. The tiles and rafters had caved in and the interior had been scavenged by the weather, and everything except the skeletal stone walls of the exterior was ruined. *What a waste!* He thought to himself, *these could have been converted into homes, schools or hospitals but the owners would rather see them rot than have them put to a charitable use. The western concept of capitalism was baffling.*

He went from building to building locating the fuse boxes and turning on lights that were still functional – it would be interesting to see how the Hummingbird would deal with the uncertainty of this dangerous game that they were about to play. From the moment he had met her, he had this uneasy feeling that she was his equal, maybe more, and this would be the ultimate challenge he would face. *She was said to have supernatural powers, to be able to read the minds of her enemies, and see into the future. Well, this will be the true test.* He tried to shut out any doubt - *I am the Ghost Who Kills and she will discover that I too have powers; powers far greater than hers.*

While turning on the lights, he did a quick reconnaissance of each building and chose the largest to wait in. This had been the manufacturing hub of the mill.

There were a few dust-covered looms, several cloth-finishing machines, some knitting and sewing stations, along with transporters, forklifts, conveyors and other auxiliary equipment that had been left behind when the factory had closed down.

He walked by the manufacturing area, past the various staging cells, to the southeast corner of the building and took the stairway leading to the upper floor. After assessing the advantages and disadvantages of the location, he chose a spot near the banister at the top of the stairs – this would give him a view of anyone who entered the building. He sat in the sukhasana meditative pose and closed his eyes. He was a patient man and while he waited, his thoughts wandered back to that fateful night when his life had changed without recourse. It seemed like only yesterday…

Osaka, 1998

Akira Hirai and his best friend, Daiki Higashi, had been planning this for months now. They had slipped out, without their parent's permission, to go to the red-light district in Osaka. After absconding from their homes, the young teens crossed the Ebisu Bridge and entered the Shinsaibashi. They turned off the main road, taking a narrow passage leading to a labyrinth of smaller streets filled with sex shops, sex clubs and bars, all catering to every fantasy a man could imagine.

Though it was late, the streets were packed with curious tourists and locals looking to satisfy their carnal needs. The boys followed along with the throng, excited by the nature of their illicit adventure and the anticipation of what was to come.

"Look, school girls! Let's go here," Daiki exclaimed looking up at the large sign that showed a young woman in a schoolgirl's uniform with a come-hither look on her face.

"If I was going to fuck a schoolgirl I don't have to come here," Akira rebuffed. "Let's find one where there are beautiful women who are experienced, and will show us everything! You lose your virginity only once, Daiki, so it has to be special."

"I'm not a virgin," Daiki announced shyly.

"Who did you fuck?" Akira exclaimed; he was the leader and Daiki had always been the follower so this came as surprise.

"Our maid, Nozomi," Daiki replied.

"You fucked her?" Akira was incredulous, "Man, she's beautiful!"

"I was pleasuring myself in the bathroom and forgot to lock the door. She came in and saw what I was doing and used her hand to finish me," Daiki explained, feeling slightly embarrassed. He was a good-looking boy with sensual, almost feminine features.

"And then you fucked her, right?"

"No."

"You fucked her later?"

"No, I never fucked her. When I tried to get her to do it again she threatened to tell my mother. I think she felt bad about what she had done. She's married…"

"Then you're still a fucking virgin, you idiot. Jerking off is not fucking!"

"Hey, at least she jerked me off. All you do make love to your hand!"

"And that's why we have to find the right women for tonight, and make sure we will remember this day forever! We will become men."

"I don't care about all that, Akira; all I want to do is to get laid. I'm so fucking horny!"

The boys laughed, and after passing a few buildings with bawdy advertising they were met by a very pretty young woman standing at the entrance of a brothel. She smiled at their audacity – *these boys couldn't be more than fourteen or fifteen.*

"Do your parents know you are here, little boys?" she asked Akira.

"We are not little boys. We are sixteen and I don't need my parents to tell me what to do," Akira hissed, his face flushing in anger.

She laughed a soft sexy laugh and asked, teasingly, "So, what is it that you want to do?"

The boy studied her carefully. She was beautiful, the kind he had dreamed of.

"We are here to lose our virginity. This will be our first time and I want it to be special," Akira told the woman without the slightest hint of shyness.

He's a bold one, she thought to herself. She gave them a thorough once-over, noting that they were well dressed and not the run-of-the-mill young street punks.

For their part, the boys were taken by her looks and unsure of what she was thinking. She couldn't have been more than twenty but it was obvious from her bold confidence that she was experienced and accustomed to dealing with men.

"The first time *should be* special," she said, and stepping towards them, she lowered her voice. "How much money do you have?"

When Akira disclosed how much they had, he could tell from her expression that it was far too little. The woman hesitated, then smiled and said, "Give it to me and wait here."

They waited anxiously, hands in pockets, shuffling from foot to foot. Neither could believe that this was actually going to happen but after several minutes when the young woman didn't return, suspicion and worry replaced their anticipation.

"I knew it! It was too good to be true. She was a fucking thief!" Daiki fumed.

"Then why didn't you say something instead of trying to hide your boner?"

Daiki blushed and glared at Akira. "I was…"

"Okay, boys, this is going to be a night to remember," the pretty young woman interrupted Daiki. She appeared quite suddenly from behind a large, ornate room divider that hid the interior of the brothel from the street. With her was an attractive older woman who was tall and voluptuous.

The young woman looked at Daiki, "This is Yoshika

and she will be taking care of you. My name is Tamiko and I will take this rogue to the stars tonight!"

And with that she took a hold of Akira's hand, and the four actors in this Cyprian play disappeared down the corridor.

It would be close to two hours before the boys reappeared and began their walk back home. For a while they were quiet, each lost in his own thoughts, reliving their favorite moments, and feeling like they had crossed a major milestone to becoming men. The innocence and naiveté of yesterday were irrevocably gone, replaced by the carnal knowledge gained from the acts of pleasure they had indulged in.

A quote from the Bible that his father often recited echoed in Akira's mind: *"When I was a child, I spoke as a child, I understood as a child, I thought as a child: but when I became a man, I put away childish things." Corinthians 13:11*

It was Daiki who spoke first, "Oh my God! It was fucking amazing. I had no idea women did things like that. As soon as we got to the room, Yoshika took me in her mouth! I couldn't believe it; it felt so incredible. She made me cum and she swallowed it. Can you believe that? Then she showed me how and where to touch a woman and how to use my tongue..."

"What did I tell you?" Akira interrupted, "School girls are a waste of time; they know nothing. Women, man! Experienced women are what we should be fucking!"

"She was beautiful, like a soft pillow and she felt…" he stopped, shivering at the memory, and then asked, "When do we come back? I want to see Yoshika again."

"As soon as we can save up more money, that's when. It took us three months for this. I just hope my father doesn't find out that I am not home. He wants to send me to a Catholic school and that would mean going away from here."

"My father is too drunk to know if I'm there or not and if my mother checks, she won't tell him. She will scold me but I won't get a beating," Daiki offered.

"I keep telling you to learn martial arts. If you know how to defend yourself, no one can beat you, not even your drunken father."

"Not everyone is like you, Akira, and I could never raise my hand against my father. He has had a difficult life and…"

"So he is allowed to beat you and your mother?" Akira riposted.

Daiki was quiet, suddenly sad. "It's not him; it's the whiskey and the sake. I know he feels…"

"Fuck that!" Akira reviled. "If my father, who I love dearly, ever raised his hand and hit my mother, I would interfere, and if it meant subduing him, I would, without hesitation."

"You mean you would hit him?" Daiki was astonished. This was blasphemy.

"I would kick his righteous ass right out of the house! My mother means everything to me – she gave me life."

Akira slowed and pointed to a smaller, cobblestone lane to the side. "Here, let's go this way; it's a shortcut."

"Are you sure? It looks dark."

"Stop worrying. I'll keep you safe, Daiki."

They took the lane and walked through a dark underpass that led to a poorly lit street. There by the stoop a few houses down were two men. It was obvious from the tattoos covering their arms that these were yakuza, ruthless gangsters who were to be avoided.

"Let's go back," Daiki said, "we should take the other way."

"Don't be frightened. Keep walking and don't pay attention to them."

When they got closer the bigger man stepped into their path. He was thickset; about five foot eleven with tiny, cruel eyes and a slit for a mouth. His shaved head and goatee added to his frightening demeanor. His cheeks were pockmarked and scarred.

"Where are you faggots going?" He asked, blocking their way. "This is a private road and if you want to pass through, you have to pay the tax."

"What tax?" Akira asked.

"A road tax, you pisser; you pay a fucking road tax!" he snarled. He was looking at Daiki when he added, "You're a cute bastard. I used to fuck boys like you in prison."

Daiki shifted back so he was behind Akira. He was terrified and could barely breathe.

"We don't have any money," Akira said, his voice even and steady.

"Well then, your cute little friend is going to have to pay."

"What do you mean? He has no money either," Akira questioned, unsure of the implication.

The man didn't say anything but surprised the boys by moving fast for a man his size. He pushed Akira aside and grabbed Daiki. "Come on, pretty boy, it's time to play the bitch."

For a second the boys were shocked and confused by the sudden turn of events. Akira stumbled backwards, thrown off balance but he caught himself and the years of training kicked in - he attacked. He came in low and threw a front kick to the thug's torso but the man reacted quickly, slipping sideways, blunting the impact. It was obvious that he knew how to fight. Without letting Daiki go, he smacked Akira with the back of his hand. It was quick and timed perfectly. The blow caught the boy on his temple and sent him sprawling to the ground, stunned, and as he struggled to get up, he felt the sharp edge of a knife pressing against his neck.

"Don't move or I'll slit you throat from ear to ear." It was the smaller man. He was wiry and quick and he had his knee pinning Akira's body.

"Keep him here. I'll be back soon," the big man said, his voice low and hoarse. He dragged Daiki up the short flight of stairs into the house.

The smaller man waited a few minutes then got up and using a rear wrist lock, he held Akira by the arm. It forced the boy to lean forward to ease the strain on his shoulder. It was a painful maneuver often used by cops.

"Stay still and you won't get hurt," the man said matter-of-factly. "It will be over soon and you boys can go home."

The man didn't say or do anything. He held him against the side of the stoop while he continued to smoke his cigarette. They heard a scream followed by more muffled screams. Akira fought to get free but the man forced his wrist further upwards, towards his shoulder blades, and that put an end to the struggle.

"Please, let me go. Let me go and help my friend. Please…"

"Shut the fuck up and wait. You shouldn't have come this way. Now, you're just going to have to wait. There is nothing I can do and there is nothing you can do."

The ensuing fifteen minutes were the most agonizing that Akira had endured in his young life. He was frightened for his friend, and for himself. He had no idea what these thugs had in mind for them. His imagination was running wild and it was almost a relief when he saw the door to the house open.

The thickset man came out, buttoning up his trousers, his forehead glistening in the dim light, "I've got him ready for you. He was a good fuck. Go on. I'll keep this little bastard here unless you want to fuck him."

The smaller man shook his head, "Not for me. I like the feel of a woman's cunt."

"Hey, there's always a first time and that ass was tighter than any pussy I've fucked. You should try it."

"No, I'm good," the man replied and let Akira go. "Go on, get your friend and beat it, and don't come back here."

Akira rolled his fist trying to get the blood flow back into his arm. "What did you do to my friend? Where is he?"

"Fuck off!" the big man snarled and cuffed him on the back of his head.

The smaller man grabbed Akira and pushed him toward the door, "Go on. He's inside."

Akira glared at the men and quickly went into the house. He took a few tentative steps and stopped. He had to wait until his eyes had adjusted to the dark interior. He could feel his heart pounding in his ears.

"Daiki?" he called tentatively, "Daiki, where are you?"

There was no answer, just an eerie silence. He had a sudden premonition that maybe the man had killed his friend. He looked around, frantic at the thought, and saw a hazy yellow light shrouding a partially opened door that was located across from the living room. He rushed towards the light, and in his hurry, stumbled and almost fell.

"Shit! Daiki, where are you?"

When he entered the room, he saw his friend lying curled up in a fetal position; he was naked from the waist down. His pants and underwear had been ripped off of him and had been tossed on the floor besides a futon.

The boy was crying softly, his whimpers and sobs hardly discernable. Akira watched him for a moment, his mind numb. *Why? Why did this have to happen? Why did he take the shortcut? Why? Why? Why didn't they go home the usual way? Oh God, what am I going to do?*

He didn't say a word but knew that he had to get Daiki away from there. He helped his friend up off the floor and got him dressed, and then with Daiki's arm around his shoulders, they made their way slowly down the stoop. With every step Daiki would grimace and let out a soft cry.

Time had stalled, dragging in infinitesimal snapshots of conjured images, violation and despondency, anger and hatred ticking like a time bomb. And as they passed the men, the perpetrator laughed and slapped Daiki on his behind.

"Hey, pretty boy! You can come back anytime. Once you get fucked a few times you will enjoy it."

Akira turned and gave the man a look. It was a cold, bitter look. *I won't forget you. You will pay, you fucking animal. You will pay.*

"What are you looking at? Do you want some cock too?" the big man snarled and began getting up.

The smaller man grabbed his friend by the arm and barked at Akira, "Go on, get out of here and don't come back, you hear, don't ever come back!"

And through the amalgamated confusion of anger, frustration, fear and regret, Akira could hear his father's voice, "… *but when I became a man, I put away childish things.*"

Weeks after the assault, Daiki refused to see or talk to anyone. Akira had tried, almost every day, but each time Daiki's mother would say the same thing, "He doesn't want to see you, Akira-chan."

On this occasion, she had quizzed him. "Tell me what happened. Did the two of you have a quarrel?"

"No, Obasan, we did not fight. He is upset about something and I wanted to find out why he is upset."

"He is a sensitive boy," Daiki's mother said, then asked, "Where did the two of you go that night?"

It caught Akira by surprise, "Which night, Obasan?"

"Don't get smart with me, young man. You know which night." Her tone had changed.

"We didn't do anything, Obasan, honestly we didn't. We walked around and ate some gyoza and it did not sit well with either of us. We both felt a bit ill," Akira answered, and looked away.

He knew that she knew he was lying. He wasn't a good liar. After a short pause, he looked at her and said, "Tell Daiki that it will be okay. I am going to take care of things."

"What do you mean? What are you going to take care of?"

"Just tell him that, Obasan, please. He will know." And with that he turned and walked away.

On his way home, he realized that martial arts had its limitations and he had to learn the use of weaponry, poisons, disguise and others ninja-like skills. He would find a suitable sensei to train him. He had heard of Hiroki Masashige, a descendent of the great samurai, Kusunoki Masashige. He would approach him and do whatever it takes to enlist in his school.

Within three months, Akira had mastered the use of the katana, the tachi, the tanto and the wakizashi, and was far better than all the other students in Masashige's classes. In eight months he was as good as his sensei and after a year, he had reached the pinnacle of expertise, surpassing even the most skilled. His prowess with weaponry astounded even the masters, so much so that Masashige acknowledged Akira's prowess in front of all the students, something he had never done before.

After one particular class, Masashige called him into his small office to speak to him privately. "There is no need for you to be in this class anymore, Akira, no need at all. You have mastered every weapon and know more about poisons than I do. You are truly Samurai and Ninja in your capabilities but you lack the spirit of bushido, the code of the warrior and that is something I cannot teach you." He paused and handed the boy a piece of paper on which was written in neat script: Courage, Frugality, Righteousness, Respect, Sincerity, Honor, Loyalty, Benevolence, and Self-control.

Akira scanned the list and placed it back on the desk without saying a word.

"You must seek this on your own. I don't know what is driving you, and I do not want to pry. Remember that choices we make have consequences that can affect the course of our lives. You are a truly gifted fighter, better than any I have seen, but your anger creates disharmony within you. And disharmony and turbulence are counterproductive to inner peace, and this will cost you in one way or the other. I urge you to seek a spiritual path, the path of the true warrior."

Akira was quiet, contemplating his master's words.

"And what if someone has hurt you or the people you love?" he asked.

Masashige studied the boy before answering, "Anger and grief transcend reason and are subjective. I cannot tell you how to deal with this; it is your reality and only you will have the answer. What I can tell you, from personal experience, is that compassion and kindness and forgiveness are nobler than revenge."

That is not what the boy wanted to hear.

"May I leave, sir?"

The older man nodded, and when the boy reached the door, he stopped him. "Akira, inner peace can only be attained through the spiritual path. Vengeance may provide temporary satisfaction but it will not grant you peace. That is all I will say to you, my son."

The boy bowed and left without another word.

A month later, the police found the body of the big man.

The neighbors had complained of a foul smell emanating from the man's house. His throat has been slashed and he was disemboweled. His genitals were stuffed into his mouth and seven fingers had been sliced off.

A yakuza tradition required a soldier to cut a digit off his own pinky finger if he had done something wrong or hadn't fulfilled an important task. The seven fingers was a parody mocking their tradition, and what no one knew was that it was also Daiki's lucky number.

Two weeks later, the police found the smaller man; his body was lying by the roadside near the tunnel. He had been decapitated. His head was found skewered on a pole by the stoop of the house. In his mouth was a folded piece of paper, and on it was written in neat script: *Guilty by association.*

The police didn't care to pursue the murders. As far as they were concerned, society had two less thugs to worry about. They called the vigilante 'The Yakuza Killer" and despite political pressure, made little or no effort to solve the case.

At first, the yakuza were convinced that rival gangs were involved but that premise led nowhere. Things soon settled down and returned to normal until more yakuza turned up dead. The killings seemed random and took place from Tokyo all the way to Naha in Okinawa.

The yakuza leaders offered a reward of ten million yen, roughly a hundred thousand dollars, for any information leading to the killer or killers' identity. And despite hundreds of calls and leads, the murders remained a mystery. It was the yakuza that gave the killer the name: The Ghost Who Kills.

It was five years after the rape that a knock on the door interrupted Akira's dinner. His first thought was that it was the police or maybe the yakuza. He was prepared for either, and Katana in hand, he opened the door without hesitation. Standing in the hallway of his apartment was a tall, good looking man dressed in a navy blue suit. It was Daiki Higashi. Though Akira had tried many times to get in touch, Daiki had avoided him and the best he got was a quick nod when they passed each other on the street. This was certainly a surprise.

"Do you want to come in?" Akira asked. It was the expected courtesy.

Daiki glanced at the katana and then studied his friend before he spoke.

"No. I have something to say and then I must be on my way." He paused, his gaze unwavering, and continued, "This is difficult but it must be said. I know it's you, killing these yakuza, how many? Ten, twelve… do you even know?"

"I know exactly how many," Akira replied, his voice unemotional.

"Killing them means nothing. You can kill them all and it changes nothing. I have come to terms with what happened and though I struggle with the memory of it, I have moved on. And you must do the same. I forgave you a long time ago, Akira, and I hope one day I can forgive the man who violated me. But I have come to realize that there were two victims that night; you and me. We were victimized in different ways but we were both victims all the same. I used to blame you for my rape but I don't anymore. I did not have to take the shortcut; I did not have to follow you, I chose to do so. It was my decision and only I am responsible."

"I swore to protect you…"

"Rubbish! It was a childish notion that makes no sense," Daiki responded. "No one can really protect another. You were right when you said I should learn to protect myself; no boy or girl should ever have to go through a nightmare like that. In any case, I have found a beautiful, sensitive woman who knows everything and is willing to assume the burden of loving a wounded soul, and it is indeed a burden," he smiled, his expression changing, softening a bit. "I love her deeply and we will get married soon."

"Does she know it is me?" Akira asked, paused, and then added for clarity, "That I am the one who is responsible for the killings?"

"No. That is the only part she doesn't know. I left you out of the entire evening. I will take that to my grave so you don't have to be concerned."

"Is that all then?"

Daiki studied his childhood friend, and was saddened; it was obvious that Akira's suffering and inner turmoil had changed him. This was a stranger, someone he did not recognize.

"That night and that horrible event are indelibly burnt into my mind. I struggle with it every single day and can never forget it. But, I know that if I live a good life and create a happy home, my life will not be defined by that one atrocious act."

Akira said nothing but stood expressionless.

Daiki reached out and placed a hand on Akira's shoulder. "Forgive and move on, Akira; don't let that night define you. Stop the killing; it is madness."

The words of his sensei, Hiroki Masashige, came back to him clear as day: *compassion and kindness, and forgiveness are nobler than revenge.* It irritated him that Daiki was able to forgive and move on. It insulted his concepts of justice and retribution, and of what was right and what was wrong.

"Is that all?" Akira's voice was brusque.

"Yes. Goodbye, my friend, I will try and remember you as you were, not as you are." And with that, Daiki Higashi walked out of his life.

CHAPTER 30

THE THINGS WE DO FOR LOVE...

It's hard to get a word in when you have a room full of very angry Siberian troglodytes yelling at one another in some gobbledygook, profane-laced language, but I don't blame them. I would have been really pissed off if someone had wasted two of my buddies and my dog. It was Grigori who was the loudest and most upset, not so much for Alexey and Denis, but for Sasha, his beloved German shepherd. We had found Alexey and Sasha in the yard a little after Denis' head rolled into the kitchen.

I turned to Ronnie and Shika. "Come on, let's go. I have the address and we have to hurry. God know what that little ninja prick is up to."

"Okay but whose car do we take and can you drive here? I mean, sitting on the right and driving on the left? Fucking confusing!" Ronnie replied.

"Good point," I acknowledged. I hadn't thought of that. I found myself looking the wrong way when checking the traffic. The Brits had it ass-backwards.

"Don't worry, I'll speak to Andros," Shika said, and left to end the Battle for Leningrad or whatever it was that the ex-Spetsnaz were still squabbling about.

After they exchanged some words, Andros nodded and took charge. He slammed a huge fist on the table and screamed in Russian, "Enough! Everyone shut the fuck up."

Helga and John were horrified, and Rachael took an involuntary step backwards, but it worked and the room quietened down. Andros waited, and then proceeded in English.

"Look, it is bad that this man kill my friends and Grigori's dog but it is done. This may be ploy to separate us. He is tricky man, this Akira, and dangerous. If some go chasing pretty Chinese woman…" He turned to me. "Sorry, brother, I forget her name…"

"Lienna," I said, "Lienna Quan."

"Yes, if some go to Lienna, then he comes here or maybe he still here watching us, waiting for us to separate. What do you say, Caleb? She is your woman and I will do as you say."

I looked around the room at these tough, hardnosed men and felt a sense of gratitude – these guys had gone beyond the call of duty to help us and they had paid the price.

"First, let me thank you all for what you have done for us; you guys have are the best. But enough is enough. I can't ask you to risk your lives and those of your men anymore. You have sacrificed a lot. Now it's up to Ronnie, Shika and me… we will take care of this."

Andros grunted and looked pained, like someone had punched him in the gut.

"What are you saying?" He came over and grabbed my shoulders. "You are now my family and we do not let our brothers fight alone. Do you not listen to what I said earlier? When one has problem, we are all the solution. Your war is my war. We are nothing without family and friends."

He turned and looked at Grigori and his men, and they all nodded solemnly, muttering, "Yes, yes, of course. It is as it should be."

"So it is settled then. We are team of brothers and sisters, yes? We will live and die for each other." He stopped, as though he recalled something, and gave Rachael a quizzical look, eyebrows raised, "Rachael, you are with us, no? Or do you go with this man? He is not good for you. He is without backbone and lies like motherfucker… I will leave it at that because Andros don't like to insult people."

I had to subdue my impulse to laugh. He just called Rudd a lying, spineless motherfucker and if that's not insulting him then I want to hear exactly what is!

"Hey, watch that mouth. I'm not…" Rudd began but was summarily cut off.

"Oh, quiet, Peter," Rachael admonished her lover. "For the first time in my life I have met people who really care about each other and are not out for themselves. I envied that about you and your friends, Caleb, and I recall what you said a lifetime ago, and you were right. All my life I've dealt with rich, pompous, self-obsessed, reptilian motherfuckers who were only out for themselves! No more. I am with you, Andros, with all of you and if it means risking my life, so be it. Just tell me what you want me to do. I can't fight and I'm not very good with guns but I have other skills, so what do you want me to do?"

She was beautiful. Golden hair, azure eyes and that gorgeous face; her expression said it all, passion and sincerity, and she had that Joan of Arc thing going on - commitment, that fearless commitment. You wanted to believe her. I could tell that the Russians were ready to follow her into battle. Damn! I was ready to follow her into battle and she didn't know a damn thing about fighting! And that's what a pretty face with passion gets you.

"Hey, I dig the brotherhood of man moment but let's get real here for a minute," Ronnie obtruded, breaking the spell Rachael had cast. "We have a fucking ninja on our hands. He's already killed two very scary dudes and an attack dog. So for what it's worth, here's my suggestion. Shika, Andros, Caleb and I will go to help Lienna. The rest of you stay back here with Grigori and his men so we limit the casualties. And there will be more, trust me. What do you say, Shika?"

"No! No, no, no!" Grigori was emphatic. "He killed

Sasha and nobody kills my dog and get away." Grigori gave Shika an apologetic look and added, "No disrespect but I say Shika stay back here and I come with you."

Shika was about to respond when Rudd spoke up.

"I must be losing my fucking mind, but I will come along. I know where it is – I had considered buying the place when they declared bankruptcy. The Levington Textile Mills was huge at one time. I remember the buildings well. There are quite a few and he could be holed up in any of them. I can help."

This was met with silence. We were all a bit startled and nonplussed by his words. The metamorphosis was surprising. Did I misjudge this asshole?

Rachael was the first to react. Her surprise followed by delight showed clearly on her face. She hugged Rudd and said, "I was worried, Peter; I thought this would come between us…"

"You mean you were worried about a rich, pompous, self-obsessed, reptilian bastard?" Rudd interjected, smiling broadly.

"Reptilian motherfucker, if you want to get technical," she replied, tongue in cheek.

"Shhh, I would never let that happen. You stay here and wait for me," Rudd replied and kissed her forehead. "This thing, whatever it is, must be contagious. I'm going to have my head examined if I survive!"

They were beautiful together but they made an odd couple. Rachael, despite all her money and experiences, was an innocent at heart and this guy? He was a wolf, cigarette dangling from the corner of his mouth, prowling through the mess he had manipulated; a slick Willie, the kind that would huff and puff and blow your fuckin' house down without a second thought. I couldn't put my finger on it but there was more to him than he was letting on – he reminded me of a blacktop bandit dressed in a suit. I wouldn't trust him any more than I'd trust a snake but there was no denying that Rudd's knowledge of the place would be an asset.

"Alright then, it's Andros, Ronnie, Grigori, Peter and me. Can we fit in one car?"

Andros, Grigori and I were all big men and there was no way we'd squeeze into a regular sedan.

"We'll take my Lexus. We can all fit in it and I'll drive since I know where it is," Rudd said.

"Okay, before we go, we drink some vodka and say toast, yes?" Andros suggested with a big smile; a suggestion met with raucous enthusiasm; with hoots and hollers and a lot of back slapping.

Andros was quick to add, "Don't worry, Caleb, we make it quick. Then Andros kick ninja ass!"

Shika had wanted to come along but Andros convinced her to stay with Rachael. Someone who knew how to deal with dangerous situations needed to stay back on the outside chance that Akira Hirai decided to circle back. She wasn't happy but after some of that intangible Andros charm, she agreed.

And so it was that this motley crew of Panglossian brothers, strangers and a disingenuous rat headed into the fray, all of us with the intent to help the Hummingbird. Little did I know how ill-prepared we were for what was to come.

CHAPTER 31

THE HUMMINGBIRD AND A WOUNDED TIGER...

She parked her car outside the industrial estate behind an old, rundown, stone guardhouse and used the cover of darkness to reconnoiter the buildings. The property surrounding the factory was heavily wooded and hadn't been maintained in years. There were fallen trees with hedges, and brush that had grown high and wild, spilling onto the asphalt and crawling up the walls of the buildings, obscuring some of the windows on the lower level. The spiny shrubbery should have hampered her progress but it was as though she was a shapeless, amorphous being, a wraith effortlessly gliding through the trees and stumps and clumpy undergrowth. She was calm and unconcerned, and considering that this was a zero-sum game, she was filled with anticipation, with a feeling that this confrontation was preordained.

Lienna had picked up on Akira's energy as soon as she entered the complex. She had located his car with little effort and stood behind it with her eyes closed. She cleared all thoughts from her mind and focused on a single one - the Ghost Who Kills. Her natural psychic ability had been honed by the hours of meditation each day and the years spent in dark rooms, blindfolded and attacked at random as part of her training. It was her extraordinary ability to see with what the Shaolin monks termed as the third eye, or the sixth sense, that had saved her life several times over.

Life is energy. The beating heart, the pulsing blood coursing through the veins and arteries, the hundreds of synapses that make up a single thought; they are all forms of energy. She had learned to sense this life force in every living thing around her. She could feel it as palpably as the average person senses heat from a fire.

She knew exactly where he was, and like a shark honing in on a wounded fish, she zeroed in on the Ghost Who Kills. She used the cracks and crevices in the stone walls to scale up the side of the building and through a back window to gain access onto the second floor. She was silent and invisible in the darkness.

Akira Hirai opened his eyes from the meditation. He couldn't comprehend why he was beleaguered by thoughts of Daiki. It was a long time ago and he had tried to forget the words spoken during their last meeting but they haunted him: *"Forgive and move on, Akira, don't let that night define you."*

However, either by choice or by chance, the tentacles of memory had held him prisoner, fomenting in him the miserable turmoil of anger and pain.

How can that night not define me or you? No matter what you do or say, Daiki, it has defined you. We are all products of our collective experiences, are we not? The very fact that you struggle with the memory of that night is evidence that it has molded you, at the least, to some extent.

The past is often blurred especially when dealing with negative, autobiographical experiences. The declarative aspects of recollection when viewed through the lenses of deception and convenience, and occasionally, self-preservation, are distorted but Akira's memory of that night was as clear as the day it had occurred. His sensei, Hiroki Masashige, had been right: revenge and retribution were temporary salves and hadn't healed his emotional wound; in fact, it had festered. The emptiness and deep discontent he experienced after killing Daiki's rapist had led to an irrational anger, and his solution was to kill more yakuza but that too proved to be unsatisfying. By then, the labyrinth of twisted emotions that had enmeshed in his psyche were too complex and convoluted for his young mind to process, so he ventured deeper and deeper into the dark morass of the killing field until there was no turning back. The protective cocoon of youth had been compromised and a dangerous synthesis had emerged – a highly skilled killer with no conscience. The transformation of the naïve boy to the Ghost Who Kills was complete.

That incident has burned a hole in the core of my being, and that night has turned me into what I am – a killer. I cannot forgive and I will not forget, and without the killing, my life has no meaning. I have eschewed wife and family because I do not wish to bring disgrace and ignominy on any woman or child. I am a lone rōnin, the rogue Samurai, and the dealer of death. There is no light in my life, only darkness.

An intuitive feeling made the hairs on the back of his neck stand up and jarred him out of his agonizing reverie. She was here – the Hummingbird had arrived. He didn't know exactly where but he could feel her presence; she was somewhere in close proximity to the building. The feelings of doubt began to creep in: *Did she know where he was? Did she really have supernatural powers? Was she able to read minds? Was this the day he would die? He was ready for that eventuality – death would be a welcome release from this hell.*

He forced the charlatans of fear and caution out of his thoughts and focused on the Hummingbird. He was the Ghost Who Kills and he would be ready for her. He stood up and was about to make his way down the stairs when a voice from the shadows stopped him.

It was a whisper spoken in Japanese, "I am ready, Akira-san."

He spun around, katana in hand, every nerve and muscle on alert. All other thoughts were banished. He didn't question how she had made her way to the upper level and managed to get behind him. She was a dim silhouette in the shadows, a specter from another world. Akira could feel his heart pounding in his chest. *She is not real!*

He had to make sure that it wasn't his imagination.

"Step forward, lady, and let me see you."

She stepped out from the shadows and into the nebulous glow of the diffused light. She was tall for an Asian, and the black, silk jumpsuit knotted at her waist made her seem taller. Her face glimmered incandescent, eerily pale against the raven shroud of her hair. A shroud that was blacker than night and fell to her shoulders in a silky veil. She was a vision so beautiful and yet so dangerous that he was mesmerized for a moment.

The soft thud of the attaché case drew his eyes away from her and when he looked back up, she had drawn her sword. It wasn't a katana or tachi, or a tanto; it was a hybrid the length of a katana, folded twenty times over and curved like a Turkish Kilij. She waited, motionless, a statue cast in alabaster and cloaked in stygian myth. Her eyes, large obsidian pebbles, remained focused on him, boring though his soul.

She is not the spirit of Kali. She is not Kali, control yourself. She is real and only a person! She will bleed if you cut her so stop thinking of her as a myth.

In a move that would have surprised most, he pivoted, spinning, the flash of the katana's blade swishing at her abdomen, but she wasn't there. She appeared to his left, a few feet from where he was, a smile playing at the corners of her mouth. He slashed again and again, lightning-fast, moving forward, but he was in pursuit of an elusive revenant. She would appear and disappear and was always a step beyond his reach.

Why doesn't she fight? Stop running and fight!

With his anger and frustration mounting, he chased after her – lancing and thrusting, downwards and forwards, upwards and horizontally; the susurrant hiss of the blade creating an interlude to their dark symphony. But in this Pas De Deux, his speed and impressive repertoire proved inadequate.

She was every metaphor, an illusionary dancer, the seraphic ballerina, a vacuous mist, moving effortlessly, and yes, even as the hummingbird floating on air, she seemed weightless. She was the quintessential counterpoint to the attack of a powerful tiger.

He paused, exasperated, and snarled, "Let's fight. The dancing is for fools and geisha."

She said nothing but smiled and decided to engage him, to probe and test his skills. When he attacked again, she stood her ground and used her sword to parry the strike, deflecting his blade harmlessly to the side. And in a seamless move, she struck at his temple with the kashira, the pommel of the sword, but he blocked the blow, quick as a boxer, and sprung back to reposition himself.

They circled each other, striking and defending, thrusting and parrying, taking turns to test the other with frenzied but skilled attacks, the clangorous sounds of their blades ringing through the empty warehouse. They were evenly matched in speed and skill. He was a raging storm personified, and she the opposite; calm as a gentle breeze sifting through green meadows on a sunny day.

They fought their way down the stairs and into the aisles, and around the old machinery until they reached the back wall. It was here that for the first time in his life Akira Hirai knew, without a doubt, that he had met his match and more. He could feel the sweat dripping down his face, his clothing clinging to his body, and his lungs burning for air. His strikes and movements had slowed and fatigue had let doubt creep back in. His mind began to accept the inevitable:

> *She is toying with me. She isn't even breathing hard. It is not possible! Bruce Lee had said, 'Be water', but she was more; she was light as smoke and shapeless as water. She is indeed the mythical Kali incapable of being defeated. I am lost.*

He decided to make one last desperate attempt to end the fight. Feigning a stumble, he came at her in a mad rush, low and fast, his strike arcing towards her neck but she parried the blow, allowing the katana's blade to ride up the curve of her sword, trapping it against the bend of the tsuba only inches from her face. Their eyes met and in that fleeting second, with immaculate timing, she spun, wrenching Akira's weapon from his hand. It clattered on the concrete, and came to rest a few feet from them. To her surprise, he made no attempt to go after it and instead, lowered himself to the floor.

He looked up at her. "Why do you wait? Finish it. Kill me."

"I kill only my enemies. You are not my enemy, Akira-san."

"I would have killed you."

"I am not you," she replied softly.

"Enough! Enough of this! Then I shall die with honor and dignity. Grant me this."

She smiled at him – not gloating or condescending, but a benevolent smile. "What do you wish, Akira-san?"

"I am samurai and wish to die as one."

"You father is Chinese like me and a devout Christian. You cannot be samurai."

"My spirit is my mother's. I am samurai; rōnin, maybe, but samurai."

"Okay then; what is it that you wish?" She wasn't going to argue with him.

"I wish to commit seppuku and with your assistance," he said and sat in the traditional fashion. He unbuttoned his shirt, baring his abdomen, and laid the wakizashi in front of him. "Take your place, lady, I will need you to do your part; you will be my kaishakunin, my second."

"I am familiar with the ceremony of seppuku and know what my role is, but before you disembowel yourself and before I decapitate you, I have a few questions. Will you answer them?"

He didn't hesitate. "I will."

She retrieved the katana and returned it to him. Akira nodded, acknowledging her kindness and his appreciation. A warrior without a sword would wander aimlessly in the afterlife.

"First, I have a favor to ask," she said, sitting back on her heels, facing him with head bowed in the graceful manner of a geisha. It was a posture denoting respect.

A look of surprise crossed his face but he said nothing.

"Fai Wong hired you after he had Kuok-Bai murdered. The old man was the only family I had – he was like a father to me." She paused and waited for him to respond, but he remained silent so she continued. "I can deal with Fai but I have found the man I wish to live my life with and would like to leave my past behind me. I have a chance at happiness, Akira-san, and I know you understand what that means. Karma has dealt you and me this life that demanded sacrifice above all else, and now, fate has intervened again and brought this man, my soul's flame, into my life."

He remained stoic, and after a few moments spoke.

"It wasn't Fai who murdered your father but another - one who is more dangerous. Fai is a puppet and a very stupid man and could have never tricked Kuok-Bai. He did as he was instructed to do. I am sorry for your loss.

But what is the favor you seek?"

This was news to her. Her sources were usually very dependable and none of them had mentioned anyone but Fai.

"Who is the man that is responsible for my father's death?"

"I regret that I cannot divulge that. I am sworn to secrecy. What is it you wish of me?"

She was still coming to terms with the news of a mastermind.

"I wish to hire you to avenge Kuok-Bai," she said without further preamble.

He was surprised but remained expressionless, and sat studying her. *She was beautiful like a swan, but it was her eyes that betrayed her; they were that of a killer, and right now, she seemed more dangerous than ever.*

"Was this your plan from the beginning?" he asked, suddenly overcome with the suspicion that she had spared him only so she could use him to avenge her father's death.

"No. You give me too much credit, Akira-san. I am incapable of such foresight. I had no plan. I was tasked by Kuok-Bai to retrieve the attaché case and to avenge Steven Chang. It was when you arrived at my cottage that I knew our destinies were intertwined."

"And what of the attaché case?" he asked.

"As long as it gets back to Wang Jie, you can have it."

He sat still, contemplating what she had said. The situation had taken a very different turn from any contingency that he had anticipated, and he was filled with conflicting thoughts.

Death is never an easy choice and that is why we cling to it. But maybe I too have a chance at happiness.

"I never liked Fai. He is a man without honor. I knew Steven Chang. He was a harmless fellow, a bumbling and likeable simpleton. He did not deserve what was done to him. And when Fai explained that you were a liability, it piqued my interest. I had heard of the Hummingbird and her mythical skills. Finally, I could test myself against a worthy opponent. And, Lienna Quan, I feel no shame in my defeat. It is not because of you that I wish to end my life but because of the darkness that surrounds me. I have lived in anger and turmoil for so long that I need to find peace. I…" he stopped, looking down at the dagger.

She could sense his indecision and inner struggle. She knew that what she said next could mean life or death for this troubled man.

"You can find happiness, I am sure of it now. I thought I was destined to live a meaningless life, but I now know that this is not true. I too was lost, Akira-san, but there is hope for the likes of us." She was gentle, not wanting to offend him in any way. He was older than her and in a fragile state.

"Is it the big American, the one who was at your home?"

"Yes."

"He is ugly. You are far too beautiful for him and need a handsome man like me. We could journey together."

She laughed. "I do not find him ugly. And, attraction cannot be defined; it is intrinsic to your soul and he and I are meant to be together. I feel it here." She placed a hand over her heart and added with a smile, "You will find your soul's flame, Akira-san, maybe there is an ugly, golden-haired gaijin in your future!"

The last bit brought a smile to Akira's face. He had a predilection for dark, dusky women, so the thought of a blonde westerner as a soulmate was unimaginable. It was the first time in many years that he had smiled. It surprised him and he felt awkward and quickly suppressed the smile. He sat still, ruminating on the genesis of this journey as an assassin from the moment of Daiki's rape to the present. It had been a difficult and lonely one.

The Hummingbird was everything he had heard she was, and far more than that.

She is an ancient spirit reincarnated in a young woman's body. She has knowledge that I have yet to gain.

Her wisdom had surprised him but in many ways, they were the same. He didn't know why, but he felt comfort in her presence – not as one who was defeated, but as young boy in the presence of his teacher.

"You father might have spoken of this. Saul of Tarsus had killed and persecuted many but found redemption on the road to Damascus. Jesus appeared to him and changed his life."

"You are not comparing yourself to Jesus, are you?"

Akira asked, playfully but without a change in his expression.

"No, Akira-san, not at all. I would never dare to be so presumptuous. What I meant was that if a profligate such as Paul can find redemption and change so he attains sainthood, then so can we. It is not too late for you, or me, to find happiness."

"The ancient mystics say there are four types of people - fire, air, earth, and water. Those created in fire are the warriors and destroyers, and those who manifest from air are the artists. The earth people are the farmers and the teachers, and the builders of things, and those who emerge from the oceans are the peacemakers – they are the ones who extinguish the fires of the warriors. I am fire and you, Lienna Quan, are water."

She knew of the five elements known as the mahabhutas: air, ether, fire, water, and earth. These are the five elements that make up the universe and are known as the Tridoshas but she wasn't going to correct him.

She thought about what he had said before answering, "I think that we are all a blend of those four. There is time for war and a time for peace, and my days of war are over."

He didn't respond but after what seemed like an eternity, he made up his mind.

He stood up. "I will do as you have requested. I will return the valise to Wang Jie and avenge your father. I will do it as repayment for a debt I can never fully repay. You will not understand this, and I do not wish to explain, but you have taken a great burden from me."

She replied without pride or ego, "There is no debt and it is I who would be indebted. Does this mean you will take care of the man who orchestrated Kuok-Bai's death?"

"Both. I will deal with him and Fai."

"I will be forever grateful."

Her grace and modesty affected him. "It is better if we keep this pact to ourselves. There are too many eyes and ears and too many who would be angered by our friendship. You may not see me as a friend but I see you as a beacon on this journey to redemption. May I call you friend?"

She smiled and bowed. "I would be honored."

They stood facing each other. The vestiges that fanned the embers of hate and anger had been extinguished, and had been replaced by mutual respect. He felt relief and a childlike exuberance washing over him. The lost young boy had finally found redemption. He wanted to reach out across the infinite chasm of death to his father and tell him how sorry he was for failing him, but it was too late. However, he would visit his mother and together they would visit his father's shrine and offer prayers, and he would make amends.

His emotions that had been bottled up for so long broke free, and he felt the tears welling up. He turned away from her, and try as he might to control them, he couldn't. He cried silently, his body wracked by sobs.

"I will get the briefcase," she said softly to preserve his dignity and pride, and turned towards the stairs.

It was when she was halfway up the staircase that the deafening sound of a gunshot shattered the quiet and changed everything.

CHAPTER 32

YOU GOTTA PAY THE PIPER...

When we arrived at the industrial estate, the driveway was dark but there were lights in every building. Rudd cut the engine and we sat still, peering at the windows hoping to see or hear something that would give us a clue. Nothing! No movement or sound, and except for the chirruping of the ubiquitous crickets, there was no sign of either Lienna or Akira. I had tried Lienna's cell phone several times but each attempt went directly to voice mail. I had this terrible feeling in the pit of my belly. I was concerned, even though I knew just how dangerous and proficient the Hummingbird was. I had witnessed it first-hand when she took out Damir and Paddy. Gordy was lucky to be alive. But this killer, the Ghost Who Kills, was different and the knot in my belly kept twisting and getting bigger.

I couldn't stand the not-knowing so I opened the door, stepped out and said, "Alright, let's get this show on the road."

To speed up the reconnaissance process, we split up into teams. Andros and Ronnie would take the three cottages in front, Rudd and I would search the two smaller sheds and Grigori would handle the remaining two located at the far end of the complex. The second of the five manufacturing buildings was compromised beyond repair. It was barely standing and there was no way anyone could be in there.

Ronnie and I didn't have guns, and I didn't trust Rudd so I opted to accompany him – something about keeping your friends close and your enemies closer. I think it was the Chinese General, Sun Tzu, who came up with it, but what do I know? I'm just a cynical head-knocker with a bad attitude.

"Stay behind me, just in case we run into trouble," Rudd whispered as we entered the building. He seemed pretty comfortable with the Walther PPK which made me even more uncomfortable. *This asshole is full of surprises.*

We were in the second building in what must have been the quality control department when we heard the gunshots; a single crack of a pistol followed by a second. And, then it was quiet. The direction of the gunshots seemed to come from the buildings in the back, the ones Grigori was checking.

"Come on, let's go!" I yelled and made a dash for the door. I was hoping that he didn't shoot Lienna by accident.

"Wait! Caleb, hold on. You have no idea what..." Rudd started, but I was gone.

I saw Andros and Ronnie running in the same direction as I was heading and joined them.

"It come from there," Andros said and pointed at the larger of the two sheds that was towards the rear of the property.

The open door on the side was a dead giveaway. Andros led the way in and what we witnessed was a scene straight out of a Shakespearean tragedy.

Akira Hirai was lying on his back with Lienna seated next to him. Standing behind her was Grigori and he had a pistol in his hand. It was obvious that Akira was mortally wounded. His shirt was soaked crimson and there was a pool of blood around were he lay.

He whispered something to Lienna that none of us could decipher. It was either in Chinese of Japanese and said so softly that she had to lean over him with her ear close to his mouth. I doubt Grigori could hear or make sense of it. After a short exchange, we heard a sigh and it was over. He was gone.

Lienna got up and came to me, hugged me tightly and laid her head against my chest. She was visibly upset.

"He has crossed over. Akira-san has finally found peace," she said. "He wants to be buried as a Christian and not cremated like the Buddhists. I will bury him behind my shrine, near the cross. Will you help me, Caleb? I need to come back to get his body."

"Of course, I will. You don't have to ask. We need

to get…" I was about to suggest renting a van when I was interrupted.

"I do it. It was me who shoot him. I will bring him to your house, Lienna; let me do this for you. Please." Grigori said, then added, "Give me your address; I take care of it personally."

"Thank you, Grigori, that would be nice," Lienna replied. I think the poetic nature of the request was the reason why she agreed.

Peace comes to those who atone for their sins.

I didn't understand the fuss. If it was up to me, I'd fold him up and shove him into the trunk of the MINI Cooper; he was dead, he's not going to feel a thing. But even a Neanderthal like me knew better than to hurt her feelings.

She was in the process of giving the big Russian her address when Rudd walked in. He gave us a cursory nod and without preamble went over to the body. I wondered what took him so long to get here.

"It took you long enough. What happened? Did you get lost or take the scenic route?" My observation was on everyone's mind, so we were all interested in his delay in responding to the gunshots.

"Nature called, my good fellow, or to rephrase it, I had to take a piss and got my jacket snagged in a thorn bush," Rudd explained, showing me his jacket. "It's a bloody jungle out there in the bushes."

I still didn't trust him. A thorn bush, really? His jacket did look ripped but I doubted his story. He could have taken a piss against a wall so why would he venture into the thicket?

"Did he say anything?" Rudd asked.

"Only that he wished to be buried as a Christian. And I will take care of it," Lienna responded.

"Did he mention what he was after and maybe who had sent him?"

"No, nothing else," Lienna answered and turned away from Rudd.

Ronnie wanted to come with us but Lienna intervened, "Please don't misunderstand me, Ronnie, I need to speak with Caleb alone. I will be going back to China for a while and there is much I have to talk to him about. These are personal in nature and can only be discussed in private."

"No problem, Lienna. I understand. I will go with the others. Where are you two going?"

"We're heading for Lienna's cottage first. We'll get the grave dug; I'll see if I can get a makeshift coffin made, and Lienna wants to meditate and pray for his soul. We'll join you once we are done."

He raised his eyebrows in surprise. He was just as confused about her feelings for the dead man.

"Okay, bro, I just want to get back home so hurry it up," Ronnie quipped. It was obvious that he missed his life of pointless fun and wanton profligacy.

"I do too. I never thought I'd say this but I even miss Rico chewing on my foot!"

He laughed, gave me a hug and said to Lienna, "You

keep him safe, girl. I know he's an ugly cuss and can be a pain in the ass but he's my brother."

"You don't worry. I will take good care of him."

Rudd had gone up the stairs and returned with the attaché case. He still had the Walther PPK in his hand. Lienna had collected Akira's katana and the wakizashi when she noticed Rudd.

"That is mine. I will make sure the right people get it," Lienna said, extending her hand.

There was a moment of hesitation on Rudd's part. He seemed to vacillate, weighing the odds when Lienna interjected with a smile, but her eyes were cold glistening knives, "It would be safer for you if give it to me."

He hesitated, then laughed and handed the attaché case over.

"Of course! It's yours. Rachael gave it to you. I brought it down so you wouldn't forget it."

His laughter didn't quite reach his eyes.

"That was thoughtful of you," she replied and added, "You can put the gun away. You are among friends."

He smiled and holstered his weapon. "Oh, yeah! I wasn't thinking."

The mood was somber when we said our goodbyes. We split up again. This time, Rudd left with Andros and Ronnie – they were going to Rachael's place while Grigori stayed back. He had called one of his men and would wait for the van before coming to the cottage. This would give us a jump start to make preparations for the burial.

We drove in silence for a while. I kept glancing at her to make sure she was okay. She was unusually quiet, and I could sense the anguish and pain etched on her face and wondered why she felt so deeply for Akira. I mean, he was planning to kill her! What the fuck was going on? Was this akin to the loyalty shared amongst thieves or some assassin's code I wasn't aware of?

"Peter Rudd was the man who planned it," she said, breaking the silence.

"Planned what?" It took me by surprise.

"He had Kuok-Bai murdered."

"How did you find out?"

"Akira-san... he told me this before he died. Rudd used Fai Wong to kill my father. It was all his doing." She gave me a quick look.

I wasn't really surprised; I had my suspicions about the bastard all along, and though I don't know exactly how he was involved, I knew he wasn't to be trusted. But, this was a double edged sword - I couldn't help but feel badly for Rachael. This whole mess had started with her wanting to save her brother, and as it turned out, her man may have been directly or indirectly responsible for his death. She deserved better. The men in her life seemed to betray her one way or the other, and that included me.

"So now what? Are you going to kill him? And what about Rachael; she loves the guy?"

She didn't answer and I could tell she was struggling with something. Then without warning, she pulled the car onto the shoulder and leaning over the console, gave me a kiss. It was a gentle brushing of her lips against mine but that wasn't going to cut it, not for me. I held her to me and kissed her, really kissed her. I didn't want her to leave and I didn't want her to kill anyone. I loved this woman and even though I had only known her for a short time, I knew that deep down inside she wasn't this coldblooded killer. There was a gentle, loving soul waiting to be set free.

Life is the great puppeteer, and often the strings she pulls can lead you down some strange pathways. It was only a couple of weeks ago that I was a foreman at a machine shop, and here I was in England with a Chinese assassin making plans to live my life with her. Maybe it was just wishful thinking but I wanted us to move past this and to the metaphorical home with a white picket fence.

"I think there has been enough killing, Lienna. Let's forget all this and find a nice little place and start our lives together."

Time seemed to stand still while she looked at me, those beautiful almond eyes staring deep into mine. Her expression though, was inscrutable. Then she smiled and ran her fingers thorough my hair.

"Yes, I think you are right. There has been enough killing. Unless someone hurts you or our friends, the Hummingbird is no more; she will disappear. I will let karma deal with Peter Rudd and Fai Wong."

I kissed her again and cupped her breast, wanting to make love to her. The memory of our lovemaking in the car was still fresh in my mind, but she broke free.

"Not now, my love. Let us take care of Akira-san and then we will have all the time in the world," she murmured. "I know it confuses you, this appreciation I have for a man who wished to kill me but I will explain everything to you, everything! And you will understand. You have to trust me when I tell you that there was a lot more to Akira-san than you know."

She paused, studying me carefully before adding, "You do not have to be jealous, my love; there is no man in my life but you, and I will love no other until my death."

"I trust you and will never doubt you. You do not have to explain anything," I responded almost defensively, but it was what I had wanted to hear.

She smiled and got back on the highway and held my hand. I was happy. Finally, my mountain woman would be with me and we could leave this mess behind us. For some odd reason, the image of Rico trying to chew on Lienna's foot flashed through my mind and I laughed out loud.

"What is so funny?" she asked, squeezing my hand.

"It's nothing, baby doll. I'm just happy."

"I am too. You make me happy inside, Caleb, and I feel complete when I'm with you."

"I want children, many children, and a farm with cows, goats, pigs, chicken and dogs, and a brood of brats to chase around! Would you like that?" I knew I was jumping ahead but I was lost in a state of euphoria.

"Yes. We will have a big family and sit by the fire and

tell our children stories of our lives… at least the nicer parts of our lives - how we met and the wonder of it all."

"Yes! And I'm going to make up stories of the Hummingbird and her husband, the Eagle, and let them think that they are Hercules and Aphrodite reincarnated. I will tell them stories of the beautiful Hummingbird and how she saved the Eagle from the traps of the English barbarians and together, they soared across the sky to the Promised Land, a place called America. It will keep them with eyes wide with wonder, and one day they will know it was us."

It was her turn to laugh, that soft cute, giggle, and that made me feel like a million bucks.

CHAPTER 33

KARMA...

Once we had buried Akira, Grigori, a devout Catholic, said a short prayer at the grave site, and before he and his men took leave, he picked up a small rock and placed by the big headstone. Grigori had no remorse regarding his shooting of Akira. He saw it as retribution for his dog and his men but he sensed just how much it meant to Lienna and wanted to show her the appropriate respect.

Lienna had insisted on a large rock suitable enough for a headstone so she could have it engraved with a short verse as a tribute to Akira. It took us well over an hour searching the twenty acre property to find one that met her approval. It was ungainly and over a cubic foot in size, and must have weighed close to four hundred pounds. Thankfully, Grigori and his men were there and helped get it into place.

Once they left, Lienna continued with her committal prayers for Akira's soul - to her, prayer and meditation were absolutes and non-negotiable. She sat in front of the cross and meditated, head bowed and eyes closed, and after a short while, I decided to leave and get cleaned up. I was sweaty and grimy from digging the grave, and though this may sound sacrilegious, I was looking forward to a romantic evening with Lienna. Who am I kidding? I was downright horny and wanted to fuck her like there was no tomorrow.

I was in the middle of my shower when she surprised me. I'm not sure if it was a case of post-traumatic relief or her eagerness to consummate our future, but she had that look that women get when their hormones are raging. It was a look of unmitigated desire. She took off her robe and stepped into the small cubicle, and without hesitation kissed me. Her usual kisses were gentle and tender, but this was different; it was a deep soulful kiss, filled with passion and need. And while we kissed, the velvety feel of our wet bodies pressing against each other only added fuel to the fires of desire – it was hot and electric.

She took my hand and whispered, "Let's go to the bedroom, my love, I need you…"

"No, this is perfect. You are so beautiful, baby!" It was the first time that I was seeing her fully naked.

She fit my idea of perfection; a vision, tanned and golden, a manifestation of some exotic goddess from a temple in Bali. Attraction is subjective and some guys may not think she was all that but I don't care; my cock was harder than I ever remember it being and that's all that really mattered.

She had lovely pear-shaped breasts, a narrow waist, hourglass hips that flared, and long legs that just wouldn't quit. Some blokes like big breasts, triple D on steroids, but not me, I like them medium sized and firm.

She blushed and came to me, in part to hide her nakedness and more so to pick up where we left off, "There is not much room here. I want to please you, Caleb, I need to…"

"Shhh, just be quiet and let me take care of things."

I cupped her perfect behind and lifted her up so she was straddling me, her arms holding onto my shoulders with her legs wrapped around my waist. She reached between us and guided my cock into her and used her hips to press downwards until I was buried deep inside her.

"Oh…" her moan was a soft enticing cry.

We stayed still, thrilling in the feel of our union; she was looking straight into my eyes, and when her fingers dug into my skin it signaled the beginning of the primordial dance. I closed my eyes, and gave myself up to the sensations shooting through me, feelings that defied description.

I began thrusting into her, slow gentle strokes at first, but urged on by her whimpering and lascivious whispers, I quickened the pace to a piston-like tempo, in and out, in and out, reveling in the silky tightness of her, a mindless slave now driven only by the urgent desire for release.

The bathroom resonated with the sounds of sex; the rhythmic symphony of groans and moans, and the slippery, sensual slapping of our bodies accompanied by the drizzle and spatter of the shower. It didn't take long for us to build towards that familiar tingling crescendo in a space void of any syllogistic thought.

And as I neared the edge, she twitched and gasped, her cunt pulsing around my shaft, sucking me into her, and with cheeks flushed pink, she whispered unintelligible sweet nothings.

"Don't stop, don't stop… oh, yes, yes, fuck me, baby, fuck me, fuck, oh, yes, yes…" she whispered softly, her words interspersed with drunken urgent gasps, fingers clutching me tightly. She buried her head into my neck and let out a long, muted groan. It signaled the end for me.

"I'm cumming, baby, I'm almost there! Oh God, baby…" and with a loud, frantic grunt, I lost all control.

I threw my head back and pumped my juices deep inside her while tumbling into the gray abyss of pleasure. Our bodies jerked and twitched, and writhed uncontrollably; we were lost in that state of physical bliss where no thoughts exist – the small death in pleasure.

We stayed fused together, wallowing in the warmth of our post climatic glow, kissing and caressing each other, whispering things only lovers say. Finally she unlocked her legs and stood pressed against me.

"That was amazing, girl…" I sighed. "You are amazing!"

We washed each other gently before retiring to the bedroom. It didn't take long for us to pick up where we had left off, and it was late, very late, when we fell asleep from sheer exhaustion. I am one who lives in a world of dreams almost every night, but that night, I don't recall a thing except the warmth of her body lying spooned against mine.

The unmistakable smell of bacon and eggs wafting up from the kitchen woke me up. I reached for her but the bed was empty. After a few minutes I tumbled out of bed and drew the curtains, and looked out into the garden. It was a beautiful day. The sun was out for a change, and the melody of birds chirping in the trees was a welcome relief from the incessant drumming of the rain. I took a quick shower, freshened up and brushed the night sleep from my mouth. I could still taste her, a lingering sweet cinnamon spice, and checked my breath – it smelled of her, and I liked that.

She was by the computer when I trudged down and hugged her from behind.

"Hi baby doll, why didn't you wake me?"

"You were so fast asleep, my love, I thought it was better that you rest. I need to tell you some…"

"Shhh, it can wait," I murmured and kissed the nape of her neck nuzzling my face in her silky hair. "I've got a better idea, why don't we pick up where we left off, unh?"

"No Caleb, please listen. I have to go back to China. I got a mail from Kuok-Bai's attorney. I am his sole beneficiary. I need to settle his affairs, and to do that, I have to return to Macao."

The news slammed into me like a thousand-pound sledgehammer. I looked at the screen, a reflex, but it was all hieroglyphics, Chinese script that might as well have been from Mars. Here we go again. Just when I think my life is finally on track, a giant shit-ball comes rolling downhill heading straight for me! It is fucking unreal!

"I'm coming with you and don't argue, Lienna; I'm not letting you go…"

"No!" It was emphatic, "No, Caleb, it is too dangerous. Fai will do everything in his power to stop me. He is living in Kuok-Bai's home. I will need to deal with him and I cannot do that if I have to worry about you. Trust me, my love, I will come back to you. I promise you that."

She got up and hugged me tightly, "Please don't be cross with me, Caleb, I cannot leave knowing that you are unhappy."

"How can I be happy about this? I want us to start our lives together. Let them do what they will with Kuok-Bai's stuff – who cares? Why risk going back there? I don't understand this."

"I owe that old man everything. It was he who freed me from the clutches of the MSS. I…"

"He's dead, Lienna. And if he is watching, he wouldn't want you to risk your life now! He would want you to be happy." I tried my best Atticus Finch impression.

For those of you wondering who Atticus Finch is, no, he isn't the host of an MTV reality show. Get your head out of your ass and Google him – try 'To Kill a Mockingbird'.

She looked up at me and stroked my hair back gently. "We need money for that farm we spoke of and I have money there. I just need to settle matters and fill the right papers so I can transfer it to the US. And I know you think this is unreasonable but I *have* to take the house back. Kuok-Bai's spirit cannot rest knowing that his murderer is living in his home. It is the least I can do for a man who treated me like his daughter. Allow me this and I promise, I will spend the rest of my life by your side making you happy."

Her expression said it all – she was earnest and sincere, and so fucking beautiful. I wanted to stop her, but I realized that this was something she had to do. She needed to settle the old man's estate and get Fai Wong out of his house; even a selfish troglodyte like me could appreciate that.

"You promise you'll come back to me?" I relented. I didn't see any point in dragging this out only to lose in the end. She was going to go, and that was a certainty, and it was an intrinsic part of her that I respected and was attracted to – a strong, self-willed woman.

"I promise, my love, I will get back to you as soon as things are settled," she answered, and kissed me and held on tightly.

"Wait, I have something that you need to return along with the attaché case," I said and held her at arms-length.

"What is it?"

"Give me a second."

I got the gold coin with the lion's head, and the strange writing on it, and gave it to her. "This belongs to them."

"You can keep it, Caleb, I will explain to them…"

"No, give it back to them. It's not important anymore. I want you back and I don't care about anything else."

She put her arms around my neck and gave me one of those mind-blowing, soul shattering kisses and I knew then that as long as I had her, I would be happy even if we were living in a cardboard box.

She said her goodbyes at Rachael's house. She shared a strange bond with Shika, the sisters of Kali, and they spoke for a while before she left. I watched the MINI drive away and felt the hushed fluttering of wings heralding the departure of the metaphorical elusive butterfly. Love in its many shades had formed a dark cloud around me. I heard the ferrets, now back in my head, screaming: *Go after her, you dope, stop her. Don't let her get away!*

Shika came over, and sensing my mood, put a reassuring arm around my waist. "She'll come back, I know she will – she loves you, Caleb. She made me promise that I would look after you until she returns. You know, I feel connected to her in ways I've never felt before."

I kissed the top of Shika's head. "That's sweet but I have this awful feeling that she won't be coming back."

"Do you remember the day I got out of prison and you took me to Bear Mountain? I was distraught and in a very bad place and just when I had given up all hope, you told me that the world was a beautiful place and all it took to bridge the schism of ugliness was a leap of faith. Do you recall that?

"Yeah, I do have my moments."

"I was so touched by that. I never thought there was a sensitive bone in your body but it was so beautiful, so apropos, and you don't know how much it meant to me. I found Andros and now, I will repeat that to you – take that leap of faith, brother, she's worth it."

Two days later, Andros, Shika, Ronnie and I returned to New York. Rachael was going to stay a while and enjoy her place in Chelmsford with Peter Rudd. I was happy for her and relieved that Lienna had decided not to exact her pound of flesh and maybe, just maybe, Rachael could find some happiness too.

Grigori promised to keep an eye on her to make sure she was safe. So except for the fact that the attaché case was now headed for Macao, we returned home none the worse for wear. The past few weeks seemed like an eternity and it might as well have been; the bonds of our friendship were tested and emerged stronger. And through it all, I had found another brother in Andros. Now, if only Lienna…

The Ristorante De La Milano ...

Three months went by and there was no news from Lienna. I had tried calling but got the same preprogrammed message: *the number you dialed is no longer in service. Check the number and try again.* At first I thought she had gotten rid of her phone so no one could trace it back to me but as the days turned into weeks and the weeks into months, I began to have doubts, and a call from Rachael confirmed the worst of my fears.

Rachael was reevaluating her motives and relationships, and was determined to shed the *manipulative, self-righteous assholes* in her life, her words, and replace them with real friends. The warmth and camaraderie that she experienced with us had made an impression on her and she started by ending her relationship with Rudd. That was a big step for Rachael and while she was getting over him, we made sure to include her in our dinners and get-togethers.

Rudd had taken the break-up badly. After several failed attempts to reconcile with Rachael, he flew to Bangkok to meet a potential client and from there had gone to a beautiful resort on Naka Island to enjoy some R and R. A few days later, the maids found him floating in the private pool attached to his room. His BAC

(Blood Alcohol Concentration) was over .30% and since there were no signs of foul play, the local authorities concluded that Rudd had been highly intoxicated and had accidentally fallen into the pool and drowned. He was wearing a beautiful white silk suit at the time of his death.

Now that incident by itself didn't mean anything. It could have been just that – he could have been upset and was drowning his sorrows in a bottle (pardon the pun) but I doubt it; Rudd was in excellent shape and a narcissist, and though he did enjoy his booze, he wasn't an alcoholic by any stretch of the imagination.

It was a few days later, when Fai Wong was found hanging from the rafters of an old warehouse owned by Kuok-Bai, that I knew for certain that this wasn't a coincidence – this was the work of the Hummingbird. She was back and active and Lienna Quan, the woman I loved, was gone.

I wore myself ragged trying to figure out why she would go rogue. I could understand her dealing with Fai but she promised not to kill Rudd, and add to this the silence and it could only mean one thing. She was back to her old shenanigans. There is seldom a congruous alignment of rationale and emotion. I knew I had to move on, but being able to get past her was not that easy. Emotionally I was still deeply invested in her... in us.

So to deal with my new reality, I decided to venture out and explore this great country of ours. I was my father's son and the need for adventure was imprinted all over my DNA. I would pull a Steinbeck and take the historical Route 66 from Chicago all the way to California and visit Dylan, Angie and my mom – boy, were they going to be surprised!

I got the Mustang GT out of the garage and made sure it was ready for the very long trip ahead. I planned to do approximately 2,750 miles in about two and a half weeks. A friend of Ronnie's owned a used car dealership and also worked on muscle cars, at least that was the official take; I was more inclined to think it was a chop shop in drag. But he did do a great job servicing my ride and all that was left now was to get things settled with my landlord. I wasn't sure exactly how long I would be gone, so Rachael offered to take care of the shithole apartment for me until I came back. Though we said it wasn't necessary, she insisted on settling her account with Ronnie and me and paid us for recovering the attaché case. The money came in handy for this little 'get over Lienna' escapade of mine.

Two days before I had planned to leave, Rachael called again. "Hey, big man, we've been discussing having a send-off party for you, what do you think?"

"Who's the 'we'? I'm really not up to it, Rachael," I replied honestly. I missed my woman terribly and the fact that she had lied and was never coming back made me unfit for company, especially the company of people I loved. I didn't want them remembering me as the depressed asshole and thinking: *thank God, he's is gone!*

"Come on, Caleb, don't be a wet blanket. We all want to do this for you. Ronnie and Andros were thrilled when Shika suggested it. They were like little boys singing godawful songs off-key, and dancing like a couple of inebriated monkeys. I swear the two are a pair and haven't grown up. And, *I* want to do this for you, for old time's sake. Please? Please say you'll do it?"

I thought about it and what the heck? Faking it for one evening is not going to kill me and I did want to see them all before I took off. This would make it a lot simpler – one collective 'adios amigos' without the drama and usual fuss and fanfare.

"Sure, why not," I said, trying to sound upbeat.

"Great! Ronnie and Shika wanted to hold it at some small Greek place in Astoria but I thought you might prefer to revisit our old stomping grounds and rub it in the faces of those pompous, reptilian motherfuckers!"

She said the last bit tongue-in-cheek and laughed.

"Ah, *that* fancy stomping ground." The mouthwatering memory of the prime rib at De La Milano came screaming back and any resistance I had was gone.

"How can I say no to that, and I'll get to see Bongo again."

"Who," she sounded bewildered.

"Never mind, it's not important. When and what time?"

"How about 7:30 PM tomorrow night?"

"Let me check my calendar and get back to you," I replied with a bit of playful sarcasm.

"Really?" now she was being sarcastic and rightfully so.

"No not really. It sounds good. I'll be there at 7:30," I said and hung up.

I still had a lot of packing and cleaning up to do and time was running out. My mind was harangued by questions and thoughts: *Why didn't Lienna get back to me? Could it be that she was detained or even worse, murdered? Did she have a change of heart? Maybe being away and back in Macao she realized that I was not the one for her. What in the world could I offer her? And just maybe she met someone more suitable, someone who was more refined and cultured than a rowdy head-knocker from New York.*

It could happen; stranger things have been known to happen.

The first thing I noticed when I turned up at the Ristorante De La Milano was that the snotty bitch was gone. I must admit, I kinda missed her. I would have loved to have seen the expression on her face when she saw me again, but she had been replaced by an older and far more courteous woman.

"Welcome to the De La Milano, sir; do you have a reservation?"

Her neatly coiffed gray hair and the beautiful navy dress with lace accents gave her an air of class and she spoke English, American English, and not that fake British gibberish.

"Hi, the reservation should be under Rachael Swanson. I'm Caleb Montague," I replied.

"Oh yes, Mr. Montague; they are expecting you," she replied, giving me a warm, welcoming smile.

"I'm curious, whatever happened to the lady who was here and Alfredo, the bouncer?"

"Christine was let go. We got too many complaints about her attitude." She lowered her voice, and in a conspiratorial tone added, "She was rude to some of our long-standing patrons and that just wouldn't do. And Fred, well, he quit a few weeks earlier. He wasn't happy here and didn't quite fit in with the rest of our team."

"Damn! I'll miss Bongo but I'm sure he'll be happier in the zoo. And, the pompous bitch just had to go. No ifs or buts."

She ignored the derogatory reference and asked, "Who is Bongo?"

"Doesn't anyone watch Disney anymore? Bongo the Gorilla from 'Who Framed Roger Rabbit'. You must have seen that?"

"No I didn't but I don't watch a lot of movies," she replied almost apologetically. "Follow me, they are waiting for you. After all, you are the guest of honor, Mr. Montague."

She led me past the main dining area, past a banquet hall, to a small, private conference room located in the rear, and held the door open for me. "Here you are, sir."

"Thank you, and you should find time to catch a few Disney flicks, they will warm your heart."

"I'll remember that," she said and gave me a gentle pat on my shoulder and left.

They were all there, Ronnie with a gorgeous redhead I had never seen before, Andros, Shika, and Rachael.

"This is Mikaela. She's with the Norwegian Consulate's office, and this is my brother, Caleb," Ronnie said, introducing us.

Why wasn't I surprised? He just got back and he turns up with a Nordic beauty that would make Ingrid Bergman look like a mouse with a serious skin problem.

Once the hugs, handshakes and hellos were done, I sat next to Rachael with my back to the door, and it wasn't long before we were engaged in a debate over my trip. Everyone had an opinion regarding the reason and the route I was taking. They seemed to know the best B & B joints, the sights I should see, and the most opportune time to hit the highways. If you didn't know better, you would think that they had all driven Route 66 a million times. They certainly seemed to know more about it than I did. That was funny because not one of them would ever think of driving across the country.

And that's exactly why I hate social media and the internet – you have a bunch of people who have done nothing but live vicariously through others and they become instant experts. What a fucking joke.

"Here, eat something; we were hungry so we ordered some appetizers," Rachael said, passing me the plate with battered and deep-fried jumbo shrimp and calamari. It smelled absolutely divine.

I was in the middle of helping myself when the waitress came in and placed a cup of strong tea laced with condensed milk in front of me, and said, "Here's your drink, sir."

That voice and accent! I would have recognized it anywhere, even in the middle of Wembley Stadium during the FA Cup finals. I dropped the plate and got up, spinning around all in one motion, and there she was, Lienna Quan, in the flesh. She was wearing a simple one-piece dress that fell below her knees, the color, an ivory white, contrasting with her tanned skin. Her hair was braided in a loose fishtail and with only a touch of makeup – maybe it was that bit about absence and the heart but she looked freakin' amazing to me. Breathtakingly so!

The room fell quiet and we stood staring at each other, and then before I could make a move, she leaped into my arms and we kissed. I could hear Andros clapping and Ronnie hooting but I didn't care; she was back and that's all that mattered. Plans for my adventure down Route 66 and California went out the window - so much for the DNA; my mountain woman was back and nothing else mattered. We were too busy kissing to notice that the others had politely slipped out from the room.

We kissed and hugged, and touched each other's faces, making sure that it was real, and then kissed again and repeated things at random. After a while, we had to stop to catch our breath. We laughed and hugged and held each other tight.

"When did you get back?" I asked running my fingers along her lips and face. I was finally convinced that this wasn't a dream. "Damn, I've missed you so much."

"Two days ago. I called Shika…"

"Why Shika? Why didn't you call me?" I retorted, interrupting her.

"I thought you would be angry. I was so worried that I may have lost you."

"You could never lose me."

She hugged me tight and kissed me again. She tasted of sugar and spice and all things nice, and yes, I know, that's a cliché but it happened to be true as far as she was concerned.

"Shika and Andros wanted to surprise you so I stayed with them. It wasn't easy, Caleb, I missed you too. I wanted to see you so badly. I almost…"

"Shhh, it doesn't matter anymore," I said, and brushed the hair from her face and stared into those dark, mysterious eyes. "I'm not letting you go, Lienna, and I don't care what else you have to do."

"I made a promise to you - I will never leave your side for as long as I live."

"You made some other promises too. Rudd and Fai Wong were to meet their karmic destiny," I reminded her.

"And they did. I had nothing to do with either of their deaths. I was working with some of Kuok-Bai's contacts within the Ministry to get the house back from Fai when I heard of Peter Rudd's demise. And, I was in Zhuhai cleaning out my apartment and collecting my belongings when I received the news concerning Fai. I would be lying if I told you that I wasn't happy. I know that Kuok-Bai can rest in peace now."

"Then who killed them?" I asked, surprised by her reply.

"I didn't inquire, and as far as I am concerned, it *was* their karma."

I thought about that and yes, it must have been their karma.

"You should have called, Lienna; I was worried sick and I began having all these doubts and thoughts. I tried..."

"I wanted to call but the MSS was monitoring every-thing I did, especially since Kuok-Bai was no longer there and his contacts were being careful. The government does not like money leaving the country. Getting all the paperwork and release forms filed with the bank and the appropriate government agency was a nightmare. Then paying off the right people had to be done with the utmost care – I had never done anything like that before. But it is over; the transactions are done. We have enough money to buy our farm. It was the thought of spending the rest of my life with you and our dreams of raising a family that kept me going when things seemed hopeless." She paused and then added, "I love you, Caleb Montague; I've loved you even before I met you."

"And I love you more and I'm a fool for doubting you."

I held her to me and inhaled the heady scent of her, a potpourri of rose petals and jasmine. I was relieved that she hadn't lied to me and that the Hummingbird was indeed gone, or at the least, in hibernation.

I wanted to clear the table and throw her down on top of it and make love to her like there was no tomorrow, but this was the De La Milano and my friends were waiting. I called Shika and told them to get back in so we could enjoy dinner. I wanted to share our love and joy with the people that mattered most in my life. Lienna sat on my lap for the rest of the evening and no one seemed to mind, least of all me.

CHAPTER 34

THE FARM AND FRIENDS, AND THE PERFECT LIFE, UNTIL...

Lienna and I got married a few weeks after she returned. We didn't see any point in waiting, and decided to have a simple ceremony.

The wedding service was held in a small chapel in the town of Hope, deep in the Adirondacks. It was nestled on a side street off of Route 30 and was replete with stone pillars and an old metal gate. The priest, a whitehaired, ancient soul, was kind and gentle, and spoke to us about the sanctity of marriage and the true meaning of love. He spoke to us as opposed to lecturing us. It moved Lienna to tears, and when I asked her why she was crying, she said the man reminded her of Kuok-Bai. It goes to show that life is viewed through a narrow, subjective prism. Kuok-Bai may have been a cold-hearted killer to many, but to Lienna, he was the kind, old man who had saved her from the MSS.

Ronnie was the best man, and Shika, the maid of honor. It was attended only by our inner circle of friends - Shika and Andros, Ronnie and Mikaela, and Rachael. I was sure Mikaela was the flavor of the week and he would be onto to someone new, but I was wrong; Ronnie seemed to like this gal.

We had invited Ronnie's mother and Jenny, his sister, but they had to be at the restaurant so they promised to celebrate at a later date with a private dinner made especially for us. That was good enough for me – Jenny was a fabulous cook and I couldn't wait for her and Lienna to meet.

We also invited my mother, and on Lienna's insistence, I extended the invitation to include Dylan and Angie. And wouldn't you know it, Dylan said they couldn't make it because his work precluded his leaving on such short notice, and Mom was too old to travel by herself. I wouldn't admit this to Lienna, but deep down inside, I was relieved. Though it would have been nice for Lienna to meet my mom and Angie, I certainly didn't want to have to put up with my brother's anally retentive personality.

Lienna looked gorgeous in a simple white wedding dress. It didn't have Chantilly lace or a ten-foot train, but there couldn't have been a more beautiful bride anywhere in the world. I did my part and wore a tux, and believe me, brother, I felt like the proverbial fish out of water. But when I saw her, I forgot about everything else except how fucking lucky I was.

After the service, we descended on the Mountain West Grill & Restaurant located along the Sacandaga River. The menu may have been limited, but the food was succulent and it offered the perfect ambience for us to celebrate this new phase in our lives. It didn't take long; a few rounds of vodka, a few more rounds of tequila, and the brothers Karamazov were back. Andros and Ronnie got everyone in the place to join in the bawdy toasts and some of the worst singing in all of North America. They even got the waiters and waitresses to dance around our table in some strange and disjointed ritual. And to top it all, Andros did what he called the Hopak, a Cossack dance, and convinced Lienna to join him. It was raucous and hilarious and totally insane, and after a bit of cajoling, we all joined them. It could have been the booze but I laughed so hard I thought I would bust a stitch.

Towards the end of the evening, Ronnie came over to where Lienna and I were sitting, leaned over, put his arms around us and kissed Lienna on the cheek. "I love this man like my brother, and now it's your job to take care of him, Lienna; he's a big man with a child's heart and you need to watch out for him."

WTF? A big man with a child's heart! Really Ronnie? I was about to kick his inebriated ass when we heard a roar. Andros decided it was time for another toast.

"Alright, quiet everybody, quiet. I will make final toast." And when the place hushed up, he said, "To my brother, Caleb, you are good man and in this crazy world you find nice and beautiful woman. Now make babies, many, many beautiful babies or Andros will kick your ass!"

And with that he grabbed Shika, guzzled down what was left of a bottle of Tequila, kissed her on the mouth and said, "We make babies too, my darling, some ugly like me and others beautiful like you. You are best thing in my life!"

Shika looked at me, shrugged, and with a big, radiant smile on her face, said, "I told you, you get used to it!"

How could you not love this guy? Though the evening wasn't the quiet affair we had envisioned, it was more fun than anything we could have imagined, and it was Andros who was the straw that stirred the cup.

The only thing better was the honeymoon; it was simply amazing. We drove to Benson, a nearby town, and stayed in a small, quaint inn and didn't surface until a couple of weeks later. We made love and fucked (the two very different things), strolled down hidden pathways through forests and alongside streams. We talked and cuddled and teased, and got to know each other, and made love on the grass and against trees, and anywhere we thought possible. If I had loved this woman before, I loved her even more now; I knew with certainty that against all odds, I had found my soulmate.

The only reason we returned was because Rachael called with the exciting news that she had found our dream home, our farm. It was located in Woodstock,

Vermont. It had goats and chicken, and a few horses and cows on five hundred acres of endless meadows and rolling green hills.

The house was a contemporary log cabin with six bedrooms and a huge living room sporting large windows with stunning views of the surrounding hills and forests. What I liked best was the bubbling brook that cut through the outer periphery of the property and was teeming with trout. I could see myself with a bunch of kids fishing every chance we got. But it was the kitchen that did it for Lienna. It was spacious with a gigantic, built-in fridge and every modern appliance you could think of. Who would have guessed that the Hummingbird was a wannabe Julia Child? Don't get me wrong, I wasn't complaining; I was ready to trade in the six-pack for a dad-bod.

The price for this gem was over our planned budget but with a bit of help from the bank, we closed the deal. Rachael was the driving force in getting the place ready for us. One of the first things she did was to put up several hummingbird feeders around the house which she and Shika would religiously fill with sugar water. It was fascinating to see the little birds hover around the feeders. Lienna gave every one of them a name – after all, she was the mother Hummingbird. Rachael christened our home the Hummingbird Haven, and we thought that too was apropos, and suited the place perfectly.

Andros and Shika came up to Hummingbird Haven almost every weekend. Lienna and Shika were inseparable and spent most of the time in the kitchen yakking away, giggling, and talking about God knows what. And Andros, he took to the farm like he was born to it. He enjoyed putting the cows and horses out to pasture, and feeding the chicken and goats and making a fuss with our two dogs. They were Anatolian shepherd puppies that were almost six months old and were as big and gawky as him. We named them Jethro and Akira. I had planned to call him Tull, after Jethro Tull, my favorite band, but Lienna insisted and I relented. It had a nice ring to it… Akira! He had an unusual white patch on the side of his black snout. It was the only way to tell the brothers apart.

One day, Ronnie arrived with Rico and left him with us under the guise that his apartment was too small, and he was tired of being dragged all over the neighborhood scooping up poop.

"Let Rico stay here for a while and show the puppies how to be real dogs," he said.

I think he just wanted an excuse to come over whenever it suited his fancy but it wasn't a problem for us. Rico fit right in. The puppies took to the boss from the get-go, and they tag-teamed him in their play fighting and chased him to the point of exhaustion. It was the only time I've seen Rico wiped out.

Ronnie would come over almost every weekend with Andros and Shika. Sometimes he brought Mikaela along but more often than not, he came alone. It was strange because Mikaela enjoyed being at the farm and especially hanging out with Lienna and Shika, and though we wondered what was going on, we didn't interfere. Ronnie was Ronnie and some things are better left alone.

The one thing Ronnie loved, almost as much as he loved food, was dogs, and most afternoons you could find him sleeping in a hammock with Akira lying on top of him. Yes, Akira was his favorite and for reasons beyond me, that pup took a fancy to him.

We were falling into a routine that suited us and most of all, Lienna and I were happy with our new life, I mean, really happy. This was our Shangri La or close to it – the only thing missing was a brood of brats and believe me, I was determined to fix that.

Three months later, we had some great news and Ronnie was the first person I called.

"Lienna's pregnant! Can you believe that? I'm going to be a father!" I yelled into the phone, unable to contain my excitement.

"I'm happy for you, bro; you deserve only good things now," he said but he didn't sound too enthused. "Did you tell Andros and Shika?"

"Are you kidding? Lienna told Shika before she told me!"

"Damn, I swear they are closer than twins! How about Rachael, does she know?"

"No. Lienna said she would call her. What's going on with Mikaela? Is it over or are you still seeing her?" I asked, curious about their relationship and the reason he sounded so damn subdued. This was the longest he had been with any girl and it was possible that it was wearing on him.

"Yes, I am still seeing her. She makes me happy."

"You sure don't sound it," I chimed in, taking a dig.

"Oh, fuck you, Dr. Phil, I'm dealing with some personal shit," came the emphatic reply.

"Okay, fair enough. We are having a cookout this coming weekend to celebrate – bring her along. Lienna likes her and so do I. She's too nice for a jerk like you."

"I know and that's what scares me. I'm beginning to think she's the…" he stopped himself. For him to consider Mikaela as *the one* was a major step in their relationship. He fell quiet before asking, "Hey Cal, do you ever think about the old days?"

"You mean the good old days like last year when we were being chased by that retard, Vincent Giardini? I've never run so fast in my life."

"You were pure lightning, bro, the white Usain Bolt, and the funny thing was the gun was a fake!" He let out a howl, laughing at the memory.

"How was I to know that it was a toy gun? It looked fucking real to me!"

"But that's not what I'm talking about. I mean the old days… do you remember the time you kicked Arlo Stevens in the nuts and saved my ass. You picked me up and dusted me off, and I thought to myself: I wish I had a brother like him." His voice choked up and that was not at all like him. Ronnie wasn't very sentimental.

"What's the matter with you? You do have a brother like me. Me, you idiot! You're the only real brother I have," I assured him, surprised by the emotion in his voice. He had always been more of a brother than Dylan ever was.

And then it occurred to me that this had nothing to do with Arlo Stevens or the good old days. I had Lienna, and with a kid on the way, he was worried that things would change and he would lose this closer-than-brothers friendship that we shared. He would be delegated to the practice team, a second stringer, on the metaphorical Montague football team.

"Hey, listen to me, you moron, you will always be my brother, a part of my family, and with this kid coming along, I will need you to be there more than ever before. He will need an uncle to teach him stuff, take him fishing," I stopped myself. Fishing was not his thing; in fact he was downright dangerous with a rod.

"Okay maybe I'll do that, you might get the hook caught in his eye, but you can show him how to play football and basketball, you know, shit I'm not good at. Ronnie, there would be an empty space in my life if you weren't in it. So before I say something soppy that I will regret, stop with this BS, and come on over. Saturday is the cookout but you can come anytime, you know that, and if you don't want to leave, that's fine with us. That bedroom in the back is yours anyway. Lienna calls it Ronnie's bedroom."

I swear I heard him stifle a few sniffles.

"Thanks, Cal, that means a lot," he said. "We'll be there on Friday early afternoon. Mikaela likes being with you guys and I like seeing her happy. I'll help get things ready for the cookout, you know, arrange the chairs, maybe get the grill fired..."

"You mean, you'll chow down everything in sight, and get on the hammock like a beached whale, right?" I interrupted him.

He said something that would make a Marine blush and hung up. Now, *that* was the Ronnie I knew and loved.

We had the cookout on Saturday evening as planned. Andros decided to be the grill master over some vociferous protests, but nothing could stop him. He had prepared all the meat in advance and wore a ridiculous toque blanche, a chef's hat, while laboring over the large stone grill.

"Andros make steak and burger. It is family recipe from Babushka, so enjoy and say thank you later."

I'm not sure what the heck he put in the burgers but his grandmother sure knew what she was doing - they were fucking delicious. We were seated around the picnic table, enjoying our meal and making bets on whether the child would be a girl or a boy when we saw a van driving up. It looked like a courier van with "ARP Air Cargo" emblazoned on the side.

I was about to get when Ronnie beat me to it.

"You sit, I'll get it," He said between chews.

"Get some beer too, we're almost out," I said as he went inside with the dogs chasing after him like he was the Pied Piper.

My first thought was that Mom or Angie must have couriered a gift, and I was curious but didn't want to mention anything in case it wasn't from them. We saw the van drive off and heard more barking.

"Where the heck is he?" I asked when Ronnie didn't show up.

"He's most probably polishing off that huge crème brûlée that Rachael brought," Mikaela answered and laughed. That made perfect sense so we went back to our conversation.

"If it's a boy I get to name him and if it's a girl, Lienna gets to name her. That's what we agreed on. So I've decided to name him Bubba Montague. It has a ring to it, don't you think?"

"Are you serious?" Rachael asked, quite incredulous.

"Dead serious, sister. If it's a boy, he's Bubba William Montague," I assured them.

"Are you really going to let him name the child Bubba?" Rachael asked Lienna.

"If it makes him happy," Lienna answered with a smile.

It was pretty clear that this wasn't what the ladies wanted to hear. You could tell that Shika and Rachael were both exasperated.

"What about you? Don't you have the right to be happy?" Rachael persisted.

"It makes me happy when Cal is happy," she answered simply, and came over to where I was seated, leaned down and kissed me on the forehead.

"Oh my God!" Rachael exclaimed, "Now I've heard it all."

Shika gave Andros a look and quipped, "Don't go getting ideas, big man!"

He responded without a moment's hesitation, "No! Andros has no ideas. He is happy when Shika is happy because couch is too small for Andros!"

We all laughed and that's when Ronnie came back holding a parcel.

"I swear the driver looked like the Bumblebee – the guy in Heathrow, the one I got the attaché case from," he said, handing the box to Lienna. "It's addressed to you."

"Are you sure it was the same guy?" I asked.

"I tried getting a better look but he took off!"

"Who this package from?" Andros quizzed, throwing scraps of meat at the dogs.

You could hear Rico growl when the puppies got too close. Akira and Jethro weren't stupid, they knew who the boss was and made sure to stay away from Rico when there was food around.

"I don't know," Lienna said, turning the package over a few times before she used a knife to slit it open. She took out a small white-and-gold box with a red ribbon tied around it. It looked like a jewelry gift box.

"Alright, which one of you sent this? I thought I made it clear that there were to be no gifts. Just having you all here to share this occasion with us is gift enough," I said.

"I don't think any of us sent it. Did you, Rachael?" Shika asked.

"Not me. I was going to get something but Caleb said he would ban me from ever coming here if I did that," Rachael answered. She leaned over Lienna's shoulder and added, "Go on, open it. It must be from a secret admirer."

When Lienna undid the ribbon and opened the box, a look of disgust and anger crossed her face. She dropped the box on the table and stepped back. We immediately crowded around. Inside the box, lying on a bed of finely shredded, crinkle-cut paper, was a dead hummingbird with a gold coin in its beak. It was similar to the coin I had returned – a lion's head gold coin. There was a card with a message in Chinese.

"What does it say?"

It was Rachael who picked up the card and read it, then looked up and said, "I can't understand some of the words. You better do it."

She handed the note to Lienna who read it several times. "There is no literal translation but I will do the best I can. It's in the form of a poem."

> "*Lilies wilt in autumn's vale,*
>
> *While the lotus blooms in winter's grail.*
>
> *Lions bend to the Dragon's will,*

*And the Ghost survived the
Hummingbird Kill."*

We were all quiet, trying to figure out the hidden message behind the poem. I was stumped and listened to Lienna recite the poem again, this time more to herself.

"What that mean?" Andros asked.

"Shhh, baby; Lienna knows," Shika said taking his hand.

Rachael took the paper from Lienna and read the passage several times before attempting to interpret the meaning.

"Lilies symbolize humility and devotion. The wilted lilies may indicate pride and betrayal. The lotus represents purity and rebirth. It could mean the rebirth of the Hummingbird as Lienna or maybe Lienna as the Hummingbird. Lions are symbols of royalty and represent the heads of the triad but the Dragon is the most powerful – the Chinese government."

"That's quite amazing, Rachael; it was exactly what I was thinking!" Lienna exclaimed. "The MSS views me as one who betrayed them when Kuok-Bai bought my freedom, and this is a warning that they will use the triads if needed."

"But if Akira Hirai died, then what do they mean by the Ghost survived?" Shika asked.

"He died alright. We buried him and placed a rock the size of the Empire State Building on top as a headstone. No way is he getting out!" I replied.

"They do not refer to Akira Hirai, my love. They are referring to the hundreds of killers like the Ghost Who Kills that work for them, and they are letting me know that they can find me if they wish," Lienna said, her voice soft and barely a whisper.

She placed a hand over her abdomen like she was shielding our baby. I held her to me – I wanted to reassure her that I would protect her. All of us wanted her to feel safe.

"Don't worry, little sister, let them come. Andros will send them back in body bag! You don't worry."

"Hear, hear," Ronnie joined in. "They had better think twice. We can all stay here if that will make you more comfortable, Lienna."

"Andros and I will stay. We're here most of the time anyway," Shika added.

Lienna turned to me and held me tight, "I made a promise to you, to remain by your side, but if they hurt you or the baby, I will give them a war that they will never forget. I will take the fight to them and their families, and they will drown in their own blood."

Oh-oh, I was afraid of this - the Hummingbird was back and she was mad. She stared at the box then grabbed it and flung it as far as she could, gold coin and all.

Rico chased after the box and this is where it got strange. Akira, the most laidback of the three, snarled at Rico and rushed at him with teeth gnashing. The older dog backed off and stood far enough away with a bewildered expression. And when Jethro came near the box, Akira lowered his head, hackles raised, growled and bared his fangs letting his brother know not to get too close. He had never done that before.

A sudden gust of wind swirled around us, whipping through the tree, spooking the dogs and they began to bark; no, it was more like howling. They were baying at the skies like hounds with their heads held high. We looked around but there was nothing, no one, and the only sound apart from their godawful cacophony was the susurrant rustle of fluttering leaves.

"Quiet! Rico, quiet ... hey, Akira, Jethro, calm down boys," Ronnie commanded.

The dogs quietened down, and just when things couldn't get any weirder, Akira trotted over to Lienna, gave her a look, and lay down by her feet.

I felt a shiver run down my spine. Damn, maybe the Ghost wasn't dead after all – and just maybe, this was his way of letting us know that he was there to protect her and to protect us. What the fuck do I know? I'm just a shit-kicker from the south end of Manhattan and if you had told me a few months ago that I'd be married to a beautiful Chinese assassin, I would have told you to stop smoking that funny weed.

Though I love her to death, the one thing I do know is that there is a side to Lienna that is frightening... I have witnessed the Hummingbird Kill.

The End

www.ingramcontent.com/pod-product-compliance
Lightning Source LLC
Chambersburg PA
CBHW061056210726
48294CB00001B/180